STARTLING BLAZE
OF LOVE...

Wherever his mouth touched, she could feel a warmth start, a trembling deep inside her. Without even knowing how it had happened, her own lips were parting, responding. She hadn't dreamed a kiss could be this way, so tender, teasing at her senses, promising ever more pleasure. Not at all the way Charles had ever kissed her or even the brutal way Michael had kissed her so long ago that night in the Kirkland garden.

Then, to her surprise, it was Michael who suddenly pulled away...

FAWCETT CREST BOOKS
by Marcella Thum:

THE WHITE ROSE

BLAZING STAR

Marcella Thum

FAWCETT CREST • NEW YORK

A Fawcett Crest Book
Published by Ballantine Books

Copyright © 1983 by Marcella Thum

Library of Congress Catalog Card Number: 82-90890

ISBN 0-449-20095-7

Manufactured in the United States of America

First Ballantine Books Edition: April 1983

For Sammie

Chapter One

In April 1846, after a long and dreary winter, spring made a sudden, dramatic entrance into St. Louis. Standing at a first-floor window of her father's townhouse on Lucas Place, Star McFarland gazed out at the freshly dug flower beds in the front garden. Patches of grimy snow still lay in the shadowy corners of the privet hedges, but jonquils had thrust their sharp green leaves through the earth; one blazing gold trumpet had already blossomed. A delicate green ran along the branches of lilac bushes, and at the top of the cherry tree, under a damask blue sky, a cardinal was calling lustily to his mate.

Pushing open the shuttered window, the young girl leaned out and took a deep breath of the sun-warmed air. The fragrance of newly turned earth and green thrusting plants, of life stirring, reaching out, provoked an answering longing deep inside of the girl. She could not have put the feeling into words. All she knew was that she was consumed with a vague, restless yearning, as if she sensed that all the eighteen years of her life were only a prelude, a marking time, until this particular year, this particular spring.

When Star turned away from the window, the front parlor, with its massive black mahogany, ivory-clawed furniture, the brown-and-white flocked wallpaper, the maroon Aubusson rug, seemed even darker, more depressing than usual, the air stagnant and chill.

Sighing, Star returned to her chair and picked up her embroidery hoop. The stitches on the linen pillowcase were tiny and feathery, the way she had been carefully taught by the nuns at the Sisters of Loretta Convent School.

1

"Aren't you feeling well, my dear?" Cousin Sophia asked, looking up from her more prosaic job of mending sheets. Although only a very distant relation of the McFarland family, Mrs. Palmer had been called Cousin Sophia by Star ever since, as an impoverished, middle-aged widow, she had been brought into the McFarland home. At first she had been employed as a housekeeper. However, at Mrs. McFarland's untimely death when Star was still a child, Mrs. Palmer had taken on the additional duty of keeping a watchful motherly eye on young Star McFarland.

"I'm fine," Star said hastily. There was no point in mentioning the odd aching sensation she had felt standing at the window a few seconds before. Cousin Sophia would only dose her with castor oil and fret until she felt assured that her charge was not suffering from some dire illness.

Abruptly the girl let her embroidery drop in her lap. "It's just that I'm so, so bored!" she burst out, aggrieved. "Why in the world did papa take me out of school, which heaven knows was dull enough, if he meant to keep me a prisoner here in this house?"

"You're hardly a prisoner," Mrs. Palmer objected mildly, peering over the top of her gold-rimmed spectacles at Star. "You can shop and go for carriage rides whenever you please. And your father is allowing you to attend the Kirkland party next weekend."

Star gave an impatient shrug. "Only after he handpicked my escort, a man I've never even met. He'll probably be as old as papa, and all he'll talk about is banking and whether a war with Mexico will hurt the merchants in St. Louis and their trade with Santa Fe."

A frown line cut between Cousin Sophia's faded blue eyes. "Oh, dear," she murmured. "I do hate all this war talk. Only yesterday I learned that several young men from the finest families in St. Louis were forming their own company of mounted troops, calling themselves the Laclede Rangers. I understand they plan to join Colonel Kearny at Fort Leavenworth and march into Mexico with him just as soon as war is declared."

It wasn't fair, Star thought rebelliously. Why was it that only men could have exciting adventures, could come and go as they pleased, while women were forced to sit at home, stuck away in dark parlors, bored to distraction with their needlework.

Dropping her embroidery on the chair, she sprang to her feet and began to pace back and forth. Her dark gray bombazine skirt, stiffened by innumerable petticoats, made an agitated, swishing sound, matching the excitement shimmering in the wide-spaced, gray eyes as she exclaimed, "Oh, I wish I were a man! I'd be the first to join the Laclede Rangers. Think how exciting it would be, riding off to war, the bands playing and bugles blowing, women throwing bouquets."

Cousin Sophia shook her head bewilderedly. "I'm afraid I've never understood just why in the world the United States wants to fight a war with Mexico."

Star's young, lovely face flushed with exasperation as she gazed at her companion. "Don't you read the newspapers, Cousin Sophia? It's the government of Mexico that's threatening the United States. Why, ever since Texas won her war of independence against Mexico in '36 and was annexed to the United States, Mexico has been threatening war. And you know papa is always complaining how corrupt the Mexican government is, how badly the poor Mexican people are treated. It's like the newspapers say: America has a duty to spread the blessings of liberty and democracy among the less fortunate of the world. It's America's duty ... her destiny ..." Star struggled for a moment trying to remember the exact words that kept appearing in the newspaper articles these days. Then, remembering, rolled off the words triumphantly. "Her manifest destiny!"

Mrs. Palmer, if the truth were to be told, didn't understand those words either. But then war was a man's business, not a woman's, she thought practically, and in any case, it was her young charge that concerned her at the moment. She gazed worriedly at Star's flushed cheeks, the luminous gray eyes sparkling like cut crystal between thick black lashes. She was sure it wasn't good for the girl to upset herself this way. For a moment, studying the girl's delicate features, the glossy auburn hair with its underlying streaks of flame that even the darkness of the room couldn't dim, the surprisingly sensuous mouth above the pointed, rebellious chin, she felt a sudden premonition of disaster, as if an unseen, unknown peril lurked near the girl. Then Cousin Sophia quickly shrugged the thought aside as fanciful.

William McFarland's daughter had a disturbing beauty, to be sure. Did the girl realize how disturbing, Sophia Palmer wondered uneasily? Unfortunately she also had a reckless, impulsive nature. Still, there was nothing innately wicked or deceitful in Star. All she needed was a good husband to settle her down, Sophia told herself firmly.

Star had moved back to the window. The sun's rays limned the elegantly long and slim lines of her body. She was a little too tall, Sophia decided, crooking her head critically as she studied the girl, but fortunately Star moved with such a lithe grace that one hardly noticed her height. Then, observing the girl's figure more closely, Mrs. Palmer sighed to herself. Oh, dear, she'd have to put more ruffles into the neckline of Star's gown again. Despite the tight stays of a corset, and the cascade of white ruffles down the bodice of the gray bombazine gown, the outline of the full young figure was much too obvious. The provocative swell of the ripe young breasts sent a stir of alarm through Mrs. Palmer. Yes, definitely a husband must be found for Star—hopefully, in time. Not wanting to examine that last shocking thought too closely, the housekeeper had returned her gaze to her sewing when, at the window, she heard Star give a soft exclamation.

"What is it?"

When the girl didn't answer, Mrs. Palmer glanced up curiously. Star stood at the window, her body stiffly motionless, as if her whole being was concentrated on whatever had caught her attention outside the window.

Cousin Sophia put down her sewing and crossed to the window. "What is it?" she asked again, then, glancing at the man on horseback who had stopped before the McFarland home, she asked curiously, "Do you know the gentleman?"

Star shook her head. Yet in some inexplicable manner, she felt as if she did know the visitor. Oh, not the man himself; he was a stranger to her. But the fact of him, that he should appear on just this bright spring morning, at just this moment in her life.

Certainly he wasn't the usual visitor to the McFarland home.

Those gentlemen were usually her father's age, paunchy, with heavy jowls, clothed in sober black frock coats, and arriving in sedate black carriages. This man was young and tall, with a lean, muscular body, and the horse he rode was a magnificent sorrel with a California rawhide saddle, the horn of the saddle oddly large as a saucer but not very high.

Watching, bemused, as the young man dismounted from the sorrel with an easy grace, Star was reminded of a romantic poem by Sir Walter Scott she had read at the convent school. "The young Lochinvar is come out of the West, through all the wide Border his steed was the best."

There was no doubting that the visitor was a Westerner. Everything about him bespoke the plainsman, from the western saddle to the broad-brimmed, low-crowned hat he wore to the fawn-colored trousers thrust carelessly within highly polished boots.

Mesmerized, unable to tear her glance away, Star realized belatedly that as closely as she was studying the visitor, he was just as carefully observing her watching him from the window. With a flourish and a wide grin, he whipped off his hat and made a deep, elaborate bow in her direction. Without the hat, she saw that his hair was sun-streaked, his skin so deeply bronzed that his smile flashed white in the sunlight.

Cousin Sophia tugged, shocked, at Star's skirt. "Come away from the window. You know it isn't ladylike to stare." Although the man's bold smile included both women in the window, Mrs. Palmer was well aware that it was upon Star that the man's gaze lingered.

Slowly, Star stepped away from the window. After a few seconds both women heard the knock at the front door, servant's footsteps scurrying down the hall. Then footsteps, heavier this time, passed the parlor. The door to William McFarland's study, next to the parlor, creaked open and slammed shut.

Cousin Sophia returned promptly to her sewing. Star, however, moved quickly to the sliding door that separated the parlor and the study. The sliding door never closed tightly. She could already hear clearly the murmur of voices beyond the wall.

"Star McFarland, you're not eavesdropping!"

The girl made an impatient silencing gesture with her hand and leaned closer to the door.

Cousin Sophia's mouth pursed disapprovingly, her voice stern. "I insist you return to your chair at once, Star. What would your father say if I told him of your behavior?"

The veiled threat drew the girl reluctantly away from the door. Even so, the low murmur of conversation in the next room could be heard by the two women. Mostly it was William McFarland's booming voice, loud enough so that occasional words could be understood. "...No need for this visit to-day...My decision is made..." Then the visitor's voice, lower than Mr. McFarland's, so that Star could not catch the words no matter how she strained her ears. Then her father's voice again. "...foolhardy...conditions on the trail this year...No trader in his right mind...You'll never make Santa Fe, much less Chihuahua..."

Star recognized only too well the obdurate tone in her father's voice; often enough she had heard it addressed to her. William McFarland had his mind made up, and as far as he was concerned, there was no need for further discussion. The visit between her father and the stranger wouldn't last much longer, Star realized. In a few more seconds the man would be gone from her father's home...and from her life? The thought brought a sharp thrust of dismay to Star, and she leapt to her feet, her embroidery tumbling to the floor.

"Where are you going?" Mrs. Palmer asked, startled.

Star was already out the door and hurrying down the hall toward the study. If she knocked on the door, pretended she didn't know her father had a caller, her father would have to introduce her.

There was no need, however, for the subterfuge. As she approached the study door, it suddenly swung open. Her father's guest stepped out into the hall, colliding full force with Star. It was only his hands reaching out and grasping her arms that kept her from falling at the impact. For a few moments she was held so tightly against the man that she could feel the heat from his body, catch the scent of tobacco, bourbon, and an unfamiliar, not unpleasant male odor. His hands bit into the soft flesh of her arms a few seconds longer than necessary before he released her and, stepping back, murmured an apology.

Over the man's shoulder, Star could see her father's craggy-boned face frozen into a mask of stern disapproval. It was obvious that William McFarland had no wish to make introductions, but the man was, after all, a guest in his home. "My daughter, Star," he said, then, stiffly motioning toward his visitor, "Mr. Charles Bradford."

"A great pleasure, Miss McFarland." The smile once more flashed white against the bronze skin, an admiring warmth in the unusual amber-shaded eyes so that they burned like tiny flames where they touched the girl's pale face, the soft expanse of creamy skin visible above the demure bodice. Star felt her own face grow warm beneath that gaze that stroked her skin almost like a caress. She could still feel the touch of the man's hands on her arms, the way they had felt, like steel bands grasping her.

With an effort she regained her composure and managed to return the smile, coolly, she hoped. She suspected by the amused glint in the man's eyes that he was already too well aware of the effect he had had upon her. "Are you a visitor to our city, Mr. Bradford?" she asked politely.

"I'm just passing through," he replied. "I travel a good deal between St. Louis and Santa Fe."

"You're a trader, then?" Star asked, unable to keep the childlike excitement from her voice. She had grown up hearing stories about the already legendary Santa Fe Trail. Before he had settled down to the respectable business of a St. Louis merchant banker, William McFarland had made his fortune taking wagon loads of merchandise down the trail from Missouri, selling his goods in Mexico at Santa Fe, Taos, Pueblo, Chihuahua. Even the names had a magical ring to them, Star had thought as a child, listening wide-eyed to the adventurous tales of her father's life on the trail, fighting off Indians, storms, stampedes, not to mention the venality of Mexican officials who had to be bribed before allowing the wagons to pass. But such story telling had been years ago when her mother was still alive and her father had been a different man, laughing and whistling and smelling of bay rum when he swung Star up in his arms and kissed her—not the cold, remote stranger he had become after her mother's death.

"I'm in St. Louis buying merchandise for my next trip to Santa Fe," Mr. Bradford said. He smiled ruefully. "I had hoped to interest your father in helping finance my caravan."

"I've always wanted to see Santa Fe," Star said, her voice wistful. "And Mexico City. Papa always said it was the most beautiful city in the world." Her gray eyes flashed mischievously. "And the Mexican *señoritas* are the most beautiful, or so I've heard."

Her gaze was fastened on Mr. Bradford's handsome, sunbronzed face, or she would have noticed the irritation gathering in William McFarland's eyes, the same shade of gray as his daughter's except that the father's eyes were hard as steel while the daughter's were as softly gleaming as polished pewter.

Was the girl actually flirting with Charles Bradford, William McFarland thought, annoyed. But that was ridiculous. Star was still a child, hardly out of short skirts. Except—Mr. McFarland stared, shocked, as if seeing his daughter for the first time: the full sensuous curve to her lower lip, the creamy softness to her flesh, the sheen of satin. And most disturbing of all, he couldn't help noticing the rounded breasts pushing against the tightly buttoned bodice of the gray gown.

That gown, he thought, staring nervously at the bombazine dress. Surely Mrs. Palmer could dress the girl more decently. But he vaguely realized that it wouldn't matter if Star were clothed in sackcloth, it wouldn't hide the fact that she was a strikingly beautiful young woman, bound to turn any man's head.

Why hadn't he noticed sooner, he thought, irritated at his own blindness. He supposed he'd have to start thinking about finding a husband for the girl. Someone sound and mature, who would curb Star's feckless nature and headstrong disposition, he thought grimly.

Watching Charles Bradford's gaze linger much too familiarly on his daughter's face, Mr. McFarland bristled. Certainly a man with an unsavory reputation like Charles Bradford's would never do as a husband for Star, he thought, his hands itching to take that insolent young man and throw him bodily out of the house. How dare he look at his daughter in that impudent fashion?

Angrily he cleared his throat, his voice rasping. "I'm sure Mr. Bradford has more important things to do than listen to your foolish chatter, Star." He turned to his visitor and said pointedly, "I wish you good day, sir."

The blunt dismissal in the older man's voice brought a surge of color into Charles Bradford's face. For a second, as he stared at his host, an icy, deadly fury flattened the amber-gold eyes. When he turned his gaze back to Star, though, the rage was carefully hidden behind a charming smile. "It's been delightful talking with you, Miss McFarland."

"I'll see you to the door," Star said quickly.

At the door they paused. When Charles Bradford took her hand, she was aware again of a jolting sensation ripping through her body at his touch. Her glance clung to his face, as if she could not bear to pull her gaze away from that pale gold fire in his eyes, as he said, "I hope we may meet again, Miss McFarland."

Desperation raced through Star. She couldn't let him go, not like this. "I'm sorry your business with my father didn't work out. Will you be giving up your plans for your caravan to Santa Fe?"

"Give up? Hardly! I already have wagons and oxen purchased and waiting for me in Independence. There are other bankers in St. Louis. I have an appointment with Mr. Kirkland of the Merchant's Bank next week. He's invited me to a birthday party for his daughter."

"I'm invited to Mary's party, too!" Star blurted eagerly. Too eagerly, she thought annoyed with herself as she saw the amused glint again in the amber eyes watching her.

Mr. Bradford smiled politely. "Perhaps we'll meet again then, after all, Miss McFarland. Good day."

Charles Bradford was still smiling when he left the Mc-Farland home, but by the time he mounted his horse, the smile had disappeared and anger had pulled his mouth into a cruel, narrow line. Damn the old man! How dare McFarland practically throw him out of his house like some common tradesman!

God, how he hated it, Charles thought bitterly, having to grovel and beg for a loan from these tightfisted bankers. If only he hadn't had to spend every cent he had to buy that special merchandise in New York. Or if he hadn't had that bad run of luck at cards. Thinking of the merchandise, though, that was now safely hidden in his wagons in Independence, the fortune in gold it would bring him in Santa Fe, some of the anger drained from Charles's face.

By the time he reached lower Fourth Street, where the most lavish gambling establishments in the city were located, he was beginning to feel almost cheerful. He didn't stop at any of the gaming houses, however. It wasn't gambling he was in the mood for, he thought, conscious again of that unexpected stiffening of desire that had possessed him when he had held William McFarland's daughter for a moment in his arms. It wasn't only the girl's beauty that had stirred him; there was something about the girl herself, an untapped passion that he sensed lay just beneath those supple, warm curves, a warmth that the right man's touch could bring to that cool, silken skin, the flame of desire that could be lit in those wide gray eyes to match that flaming auburn hair. Fire and smoke, he thought, half smiling at his memory of the girl. That was what she reminded him of. And for all her childish innocent airs he had read clearly the invitation she had handed him, right under her father's long, disapproving nose.

He had reached the back streets of the riverfront area of the city now, riding past the Rocky Mountain House where, despite the early hour, a fandango was in full swing. Through the windows he could see mountain men in blackened, greasy buckskins fringed with Comanche hair, prancing with French belles to the scraping of fiddles. In this section of town, French was heard more often than English, or rather a patois of French, Spanish, and English, from French Canadian voyageurs, dark-faced Mexicans, burly Missouri mule skinners, along with the guttural sounds of beggar-settlement Indians and blacks, all roaming the muddy back alleys of the city.

Before a two-story brick house he stopped and tossed a coin into a group of ragged, half-naked black urchins waiting in the street. One, more enterprising and faster than the others, snatched the coin and the reins of Charles's horse. Inside the house, a midmorning somnolence hung over the front parlor, whose red velvet portieres were so dusty and faded that their original color had long since disappeared. The smell of cheap perfume barely covered other, less agreeable odors in the room, making Charles flinch fastidiously, even as he knew that those same odors added to the unbearable excitement building up to a painful pitch inside of him.

The half dozen women lounging around the parlor, playing cards and listening to a wizened, gray-haired black man pluck listlessly at a banjo, were still in their morning robes. Several roustabouts from the steamboats were playing cards with two of the women, but it was early for customers and the women looked up curiously when Charles entered. Then, as they quickly took in his expensive clothes and the fact that he was lean and handsome, they sprang to attention, clustering around Charles, chattering and cooing like magpies.

An older woman, her gray hair piled untidily on top of her head, her skin with a yellowish tinge, came down the stairs and scattered the girls with a few choice angry words in French. Then she turned and smiled at Charles in an obscene parody of coquettishness, her teeth with the same tinge of yellow as her face. "Monsieur Bradford, what a pleasure to see you again."

Charles glanced around the room. "Is Josie here, Madame Decamier?"

The woman made a disconsolate face. "No, monsieur. That wicked girl Josie ran off." Which wasn't the complete truth. The girl had sickened and lost her looks and had been thrown back into the streets so that she wouldn't die in the house and scare off customers. Madame Decamier gestured to one of the girls, a buxom blonde with a blank face and a soiled pink satin robe barely covering her melonlike breasts. "Annabelle will be happy to serve you." She gave Charles a conspiratorial wink. "Annabelle is very . . . agreeable."

Fleetingly the madam wondered why a gentleman like Charles Bradford patronized her establishment instead of one of the fancier brothels on lower Fourth Street. Until she remembered the welts and bruises on Josie's body after one of Mr. Bradford's visits last spring. The madams who ran the more luxurious establishments did not appreciate having their girls' beauty destroyed by overamorous customers. Madame Decamier shrugged mentally. Well, it made no difference to her how Monsieur Bradford satisfied himself, or why some well-bred gentlemen seemed to find their greatest enjoyment bedding only the most common women. Madame Decamier's girls knew better than to reject any demands made upon them by a customer. They knew full well there were always plenty of other girls on the street more than willing to take their place in Madame's establishment.

Charles's gaze had drifted past Annabelle and fastened upon a young woman seated by herself, playing solitaire at a table in a corner of the room. Unlike the other women, who wore their hair piled in a disheveled fashion on top their head, this girl's hair was parted in the middle and hung long and straight, flowing like a black satin shawl over her shoulders, hiding her face from view. Her robe was sheer enough so that Charles could see that her skin was a dark burnished shade and that her breasts did not sag but were young and proudly upthrust.

He jerked his chin toward the girl. "What about her?"

"Theresa? But surely Monsieur would find one of the other girls more suitable. Theresa is a—what do the Mexicans call them—a *zambo*."

Charles had already seen the girl had Negro blood in her. The fact that she apparently was also part Indian only made her that much more intriguing.

"Theresa is new," the madam said, spreading her hands apologetically. "Not yet well trained, not congenial. I'm sure you would be happier with one of the other girls."

The fact of the matter was that Madame Decamier bitterly regretted ever having accepted the half-black, half-Indian girl as payment of a gambling debt. She had tried everything from beatings to locking the girl in a room without food. Nothing changed Theresa's recalcitrant behavior. Although the girl never refused a customer, she continued to be stubborn and sulky, with a vicious streak that had made more than one of her customers come storming to Madame Decamier and demanding their money back.

"I'll take her," Charles said shortly.

The madam sighed, then rasped out Theresa's name. The girl rose indifferently to her feet. As she walked with a sinuous, barefoot grace past the proprietress and Charles, Madame Decamier spoke sharply to her in an undertone. The girl merely shrugged and continued up the stairs, her hips swinging with a seductive, open defiance.

Charles followed the girl into a small, dark room at the end of the hall. A fetid, stale smell hung in the air, and Charles went to the window and forced it open several inches before turning to face the girl. She had shrugged off her robe, which had fallen around her feet, and stood passively waiting by the tumbled, unmade bed.

He saw that she was thinner than he had thought, for all the deep, conical breasts, and that her legs were long and muscular in the thighs, as if she were used to walking long distances. Her full lips betrayed her Negro blood, but the flaring nostrils and high, flat cheekbones were those of a Comanche or Apache squaw.

Slowly, feeling the tension building up inside him, Charles's gaze roamed over the red-brown body, the curves graceful, lissome, as if carved by a master sculptor from lovingly polished mahogany.

When he walked over to stand before the girl, she stared up at him sullenly. He smiled his disarming smile and said softly, "Just so we understand each other." The back of his hand caught her full across the face with a crack like a pistol shot. She sprawled across the bed, her black hair splaying over the pillow.

Without even looking at the girl, Charles turned and began to remove his clothes. Some sixth sense made him whirl around just as Theresa lunged toward his back, her black eyes glittering, a long, thin-bladed knife clutched in her hand.

Sidestepping adroitly, he reached out and caught her wrist, pulled her hard against him, then jerked her arm behind her, twisting the wrist cruelly until she gave a low hiss of pain. Even after the knife dropped from her hand, his own hand continued its ruthless twisting of her wrist until the muscles in her neck stood out like cords, but she did not cry out again.

When he finally released her, she sank to the floor, rubbing her wrist and staring up at him speculatively with her opaque sloe eyes. He continued undressing, folding his clothes neatly and placing them on the one clean chair in the room. When at last he turned back again, the girl was still crouched on the floor and Charles's leather belt, its Mexican silver buckle gleaming, swung lazily in his hand.

For a moment, looking up at him, her black eyes were charged with fear. Then, staring at the stranger's lean, muscular flanks, the evidence of his desire, his engorged manhood, plain for her to see, a liquid, passionate softness took the place of the fear. A quiver passed through her body as she gazed at the belt then, without a word, as if the ritual were a familiar one, she shrugged and stretched submissively out upon the bed.

Afterwards, Theresa's body still twined around Charles, her legs wrapped around his thighs, her breasts pressing heavy and soft against his chest. The welts that the belt had cut into her gleaming mahogany skin were matched by the scarlet scratch marks her nails had gouged into Charles's back, the teeth marks she had left on his shoulder. Her eyes gleamed as she nibbled teasingly at his ear lobe. "Take me with you," she whispered.

Her last owner had been a trapper. He had bought her from the Comanches who had kidnapped her when they had raided her village. She had trudged after her new owner for miles on foot beside the pack mules, while he rode the horse. She had cooked for him in the wilderness, helped set traps in icy streams, and skinned the beavers they had caught. He had beat her, too, especially after he drank too much, but he was getting old and, what with the liquor and the age, when he bedded her, there was no pleasure in it for her.

She gazed down into the stranger's face. No, she thought contentedly, no longer a stranger. What was it that fat old sow downstairs had called him . . . Monsieur Bradford. Whoever he was, Theresa had never met a man like him before, young and strong and handsome, able to match her savage virility in bed, while other men, she thought contemptuously, exhausted so quickly.

"Take me with you," she murmured again.

Charles's eyes were closed but he wasn't asleep. Always afterwards he had this temporary feeling of self-loathing. Not because of the pain he had inflicted upon the girl—he had no doubt she had endured worse beatings, and long ago he had stopped questioning why lovemaking for him was only satisfactory when he physically forced his partner into submission.

It was the girl herself, smelling as if she hadn't bathed in weeks, who, now that it was over, filled him with revulsion.

All at once he found himself thinking of the McFarland girl, the faint, clean scent of her when he had held her briefly in his arms, her cool patrician features, and yet the promise that had teased him behind the smoky gray eyes. Thinking of the girl, though, reminded him of William McFarland, and a pulse of anger began to beat in his temple. Damn the impudence of the man, treating a Bradford of Kentucky like dirt beneath his feet. And the insulting way he had scowled at Charles when he had so much as looked at his precious daughter.

A faint malicious smile all at once tugged at the corner of Charles's mouth. Of course! He knew the perfect way to repay McFarland, to make the old man squirm. He had only to reach William McFarland through his daughter. And the revenge would be doubly sweet because the girl was not only a beauty but so obviously willing.

Theresa saw the pleased smile play across her lover's face and instinctively knew he was thinking of another woman. Her sharp, white teeth bit down painfully on his earlobe.

"What the—" Charles's eyelids flew open, the amber eyes cold with rage.

Theresa was screaming curses at him in a mixture of Spanish and French and Indian that he could not even begin to understand, but her meaning was clear.

Angrily he flung himself on top of the screaming, squirming Theresa. His hand found the proud peak of a breast and pinched savagely, his mouth effectively and cruelly silencing her outburst until she no longer fought against him but became compliant, eager, her dark body plastered like a shadow against him, touching every part of him, exciting him beyond endurance.

And for a while all thoughts of the McFarland girl were forgotten.

Chapter Two

"*Star, how good to see you again!*"

Mary Kirkland met Star at the door of the Kirkland country home and immediately whisked her away from her escort, taking her guest upstairs to one of the large bedrooms that had been turned into a cloakroom for the women guests. Mary had been a student at the convent school with Star and they gossiped about their days at school as Star removed her cloak and adjusted the skirt of her pale yellow shot-silk gown before the looking glass.

"What a becoming gown, Star," Mary said. "You look lovely."

Star, however, was studying her reflection unhappily. It wasn't that her dress wasn't modish, fitting beautifully snug at the bodice and falling in graceful flounces to her trim ankles. Madame Augustine, the most popular dressmaker in St. Louis, had designed the gown herself. Star tugged at the heart-shaped bodice. If only Madame Augustine hadn't completely filled the neckline with a fichu of white lace.

When Star had protested, Madame Augustine had explained that she had had very strict instructions from Mrs. Palmer. "Madamoiselle's gown was to be most demure, no décolleté, none at all."

Now, frowning at the lace-filled bodice, Star reached suddenly for a pair of scissors lying on the dressing table. Impatiently she began to cut away the stitches that held the fichu in place, pulling at the lace until it fell away, revealing the soft, creamy swell where the yellow silk bodice cut tightly across her breasts.

17

Mary gasped. "You're ruining your gown."

"Oh, I'll sew it back before I go home," Star said, tossing her head. "Cousin Sophia will never know."

Mary giggled. "You haven't changed a bit, Star. Remember those ugly blue serge uniforms we had to wear at school and the day Sister Matilda caught you rustling when you walked and discovered the scarlet taffeta petticoat you were wearing beneath your uniform."

Both girls laughed in memory. Mary's eyes sparkled with curiosity. "You certainly must be anxious to impress Mr. Donley. Is he a special beau?"

"Who?" Star asked absently, pinching her cheeks to bring color to her face.

"Your escort, Mr. Robert Donley."

"Oh, I hardly know him," Star said indifferently.

As Star returned down the wide circular staricase with Mary, holding her gown just high enough to show a discreet amount of ankle, she saw Mr. Donley waiting for her at the foot of the stairs. In his early thirties, with ginger hair, a freckled face, and a stocky build, he watched Star's descent, his soft, shy eyes clinging to her face. Since William McFarland had had to seek out an escort for his daughter, Robert had assumed that Star McFarland would be uncommonly plain. He still had not recovered from his stunned surprise at his good fortune when he had met the ravishing creature that was to be his companion for the evening.

Star knew vaguely that Robert Donley worked in a bank that his father owned. Cousin Sophia had also commented gleefully, as she helped Star dress for the party, that Robert Donley was considered such an excellent catch that half the matrons in St. Louis had set their daughters' caps for him. Star couldn't imagine why. Although she smiled and listened with apparently rapt attention to Mr. Donley's labored attempts at conversation on their carriage ride to the Kirkland country home, she thought her companion excessively dull. And his hands, when they accidentally touched her, were clammy. But in any case, Robert Donley only existed on the outer edge of her consciousness. It was another's face she had sought ever since she had entered the Kirkland home.

Now as they passed the library where their host, Mr. Kirkland, and the unattached male guests were gathered, sharing conversation and syllabub, she paused at the door, her glance searching the room quickly. The confused ebb and swirl of male voices from the room broke around her without her really hearing the words, until one voice, angrier, louder than the others, protested indignantly, "Are you saying, Mr. Kelly, that the Mexican people won't rise up and welcome America's help in overthrowing their corrupt government? Why, Santa Anna, Governor Armijo, and other scoundrels like them have held the peasants in bondage for years."

Star could not see clearly the man to whom the question was addressed. He was standing in front of the fireplace smoking a long black cheroot, and the smoke, drifting upward, hid most of his face from view. She saw that his hair was blue-black as a raven's wing, worn longer in the sideburns than was fashionable, and that he was several inches taller than any other man in the room. His black broadcloth coat fit almost too snugly over wide shoulders and was not the somber black her father wore, but seemed to have a faint silver thread running through the collar so that it gleamed softly in the lamplight.

When the man spoke, his richly timbered voice held a slight foreign accent, a soft slur to the vowels, different from the harsh Missouri drawl to which Star was accustomed. "I'm saying, sir," he replied, his voice more amused than angry, "that even the lowliest peasant will fight to protect his homeland from invasion."

"Fight! Mexicans fight?" The angry voice became jeering. "I've spent five years in the Santa Fe trade and I've yet to meet a greaser that wouldn't turn tail and run when attacked. None of them has the stomach for fighting."

A sudden silence fell over the room, an oddly chilling silence. The cigar smoke drifted away and Star could see the man's face; the chill in the room seemed to enter her own bones. She had watched her father's face grow rigid with anger, but never before had she seen the deadly menace she glimpsed now in the eyes of the man standing before the fireplace. It was a menace that was somehow more frightening because there was a half-moon white scar in one swarthy cheek and because the rest of the man's flat-planed face was expressionless, as if only the eyes were alive.

The man who had made the insulting comment must have felt the danger, too. His face paled, as if he suddenly felt the dank presence of death at his side.

Edward Kirkland stepped quickly between the two men, his voice quiet but with a sharp edge of warning. "Gentlemen, this is a party to celebrate my daughter's birthday. I suggest we lower our voices so as not to upset the ladies present in the next parlor."

Before Star could hear more, Robert had pulled her away from the library door. "That was a close one," he murmured with a gusty sigh of relief.

"I don't understand," Star said, mystified. "Why was Mr. Kelly so upset?"

"Michael Kelly's father, James Kelly, was one of the first traders to open the Santa Fe trail for commerce back in 1820," Robert explained. "Later he married into the Cordoba family, who have large land holdings near Mexico City. So you see, that makes Michael Kelly half Mexican, a breed." He added grimly, "He also happens to be a crack shot. He's already killed one man in a duel on Bloody Island. Dan Redden is fortunate that Mr. Kirkland stepped in when he did. Mr. Kelly doesn't take kindly to slurs on his Mexican heritage."

"Papa says dueling is barbaric and should be banned by law," Star said. A shiver suddenly passed through her body as she recalled that implacable scarred face. There had been something barbaric in the man's total lack of fear, as if death meant nothing to him. How terrifying it would be, she thought, to look into those merciless eyes above a cocked dueling pistol.

They had reached the large double parlor, where the sliding doors had been opened, the carpet removed, and the rooms cleared of furniture for the dancing. The musicians had already begun to play, and couples were crowding the floor. Robert had felt Star's arm tremble under his hand, and eager to put aside a subject that must, of course, be distasteful to a sensitive young woman, he escorted her out onto the floor for the first reel.

His partner seemed to float in his arms, making even his clumsy steps seem graceful. His hands rested on her tiny waist lightly, timidly at first, then, as he saw the envious glances being cast in his direction, more possessively.

The male glances lingered on his companion's thick auburn hair, caught in a cluster of curls held back from the slender, graceful column of Star's throat by a thin black velvet ribbon. Her head was tilted back as she smiled sweetly up at her partner so that the lovely line, from throat to sloping shoulders to the tempting curve of the breasts and expanse of ivory-tinted skin, was artfully displayed by the now revealing décolletage of the gown,

If the glances of the females in the room were not quite as warm, Star neither noticed nor would have cared if she had. This was her very first dance party, and she had never been as outrageously happy before in her young life. When the first set ended she was immediately surrounded by young men, all anxious to claim the next dance. Without a second thought for Robert, who was discovering that being the escort of the prettiest girl at the party was a mixed blessing, Star moved delightedly from one pair of arms to the next as the musicians swung from a Virginia reel to a schottische to a lancer.

She had worried on her way to the dance about what she would say to her dance partners, whether she would be tongue-tied and stupid. Although the good sisters at the convent school had taught her how to enter a room properly, and a visiting French dancemaster instructed the students in dance, the art of flirtation was not a subject taught at the convent. Star soon discovered, though, that conversing with the male sex was not all that difficult. She had only to smile at her partner, hang fascinated onto his every word, laugh at his slightest witticism, and, when paid a compliment, flutter her eyelashes with becoming modesty over her shimmering gray eyes.

The only flaw in the evening was that, no matter how hopefully her glance flew to the door whenever a new gentleman guest entered the parlor, not one of the new arrivals had amber eyes or hair the color of wheat in the sunlight. As she sipped the hot chicken bouillon served the guests between sets to keep up their energy, and carried on a bantering conversation with three young men all vying for the next dance, the depressing thought occurred to her that perhaps Charles Bradford wouldn't show up at the party at all—that perhaps he had forgotten all about her.

"You did promise me this next reel, didn't you, Miss

McFarland?" the young man on her right insisted.

"Not at all," the second young man protested. "I remember distinctly Miss McFarland promising me this next set."

Before the third young man could press his claim, Star heard a familiar voice behind her announce firmly, "I hate to disappoint you, gentlemen, but Miss McFarland has already promised the next dance to me."

Star turned slowly, a flush rising in her face. Charles's smile flashed possessively down at her. Then, before she could answer, the music started again and she felt herself being twirled out onto the floor in Charles's arms.

Despite the fact that she had been on pins and needles all evening watching for his arrival, Star suddenly discovered that she was annoyed at Charles's obvious assurance that she would be waiting patiently for him. Well, really, she simmered indignantly. Did he think that he could suddenly appear after making her wait all evening, and that she would fall at once into his arms?

"How odd, Mr. Bradford," she said coolly. "I don't recall promising you this dance."

His gaze flicked down at her, the amber eyes holding an expression she couldn't fathom and that for a moment made her feel vaguely uneasy, until he smiled, a boyishly disarming smile, and apologized. "I would have been here to claim all your dances, but I had to talk to Mr. Kirkland. I've good news. He's agreed to loan me the money to buy my trade goods for Santa Fe."

"Oh." Star tried to hide the unhappiness that slashed like a knife through her at the news. "All this talk of war with Mexico, though; surely the Mexicans won't welcome trade caravans from the United States if there's a war."

Charles Bradford frowned disdainfully. "The Mexicans will welcome the devil himself if he brings along sufficient money to bribe the custom guards and Governor Armijo, the biggest thief of them all. Anyway, if there's a war, the Americans will certainly blockade the Mexican coast. That will get rid of the French and British merchants and leave the field wide open for the Americans coming down the trail." A touch of boastfulness crept into his voice. "My last trip I brought fifty thousand dollars in gold out of Mexico. This year, if everything goes well, I should double that."

"It will be dangerous, won't it, taking wagons into Mexico now?"

"There's always danger on the trail," Charles said. "But the merchants in the Santa Fe trade aren't a bunch of wet-behind-the-ears emigrants. We're used to taking care of ourselves." He looked down into Star's face, his hand tightening around her waist so she could feel his hand, warm, caressing, against her as if the bit of cloth between his hand and her skin didn't exist at all. He asked softly, teasingly, "Do I dare hope, Miss McFarland, that you are concerned for my welfare?"

Beneath that intense gaze and the tightness of his hand on her waist, Star had the odd feeling that her bones were dissolving, a delicious warmth spreading through her body.

Charles bent his face closer to her, so that she could see where thin lines splayed out around his eyes and mouth, white against the deep tan. "Tell me," he commanded softly. "Will you worry about me when I'm gone?"

It was an effort to push the words past her throat, which felt strangely tight. "Yes...yes, of course...I..."

Then she realized that he was skillfully dancing her toward the French doors that led from the parlor into the candlelit darkness of the boxwood-enclosed garden. "We mustn't," she whispered, shocked, glancing nervously around at the other dancers. "We can't leave, at least not together!"

And then felt her face flame at her words. Laughter leaped into the amber eyes even as Charles nodded gravely. "How discreet you are, as well as beautiful, a devastating combination in a woman. But then I've no doubt I'm not the first gentleman at the party who has noticed your many charms. How many conquests have you made this evening, or have you lost count?" Although his voice was light, she heard the sudden sharp anger behind the question.

Why, he's jealous, Star thought pleased. She lowered her eyelids so that he could just glimpse her silvery gray eyes sparkling flirtatiously through the fluttering lashes. "Why, Mr. Bradford," she murmured. "Surely you don't expect me to kiss and tell?"

Just for a second something moved behind the amber eyes, serpent quick and deadly, so that for a moment her earlier sense of uneasiness returned. But only for a moment. Then Charles grinned engagingly. "Touché, my dear." His arms twirled her expertly into a final spin that left her breathless as the music ended.

His arms continued to hold her a moment longer than necessary, his voice caressing as he gazed deeply into her eyes and whispered, "We both know that lovely mouth of yours was meant only for me, don't we, my sweet?"

Star felt her heart racing, a by-now familiar warmth spreading sweet as honey through her body. He leaned low and said, "Ten minutes. I'll wait in the garden." Then he turned and walked away from her before she could give any answer at all.

She was as aware as he was what her answer would be.

Chapter Three

The night was chillier than she had expected and the moon had slid behind a cover of clouds when Star slipped out of a side door of the Kirkland home. She was glad she had stopped to pick up her Paisley shawl, and she pulled its warmth more tightly around her now as she peered uncertainly through the darkness. The garden was girdled by fragrant shrubs, and despite the late spring chill, a wild plum tree had begun to blossom, a drifting cloud of white above Star. She hesitated beneath the tree, wondering in what part of the garden she would find Charles.

Then she saw a tall, black shadow, darker than the night around him, standing with his back toward her by a fish pond at one side of the garden. Lifting her skirt, she sped soundlessly over the mossy grass, then, mischievously, she stopped behind Charles and placed her hands over his eyes. "Guess or pay a forfeit," she whispered.

At that moment the moon slid out from behind the clouds and she saw, embarrassed, that the man's hair was not blond but dark. The man's voice had the faintest slur of an accent as he murmured mockingly, "I'd prefer to pay the forfeit, *querida.*"

Then his mouth was on hers, hard and ruthlessly seeking, before she could cry out. At first she struggled, outraged, in his arms, her blood pounding in her ears, unable to catch her breath as she felt her breasts crushed against a chest as hard and unyielding as burled oak. Finally it was easier, less painful, not to struggle, to let her body grow limp, as sensations she had never felt before raced through her. The blood was pounding not just in her ears but through all her veins, her whole body. The only way she could take breath into her tortured lungs was to part her lips and let her breath mingle with that of the man kissing her, and she no longer knew whether it was his heart or her own she felt thudding against her rib cage.

When the arms suddenly released her, she stepped back, stumbling over the hem of her gown as she stared, with startled eyes, flaring wide and brilliant in the moonlight, up at the man Robert had called Michael Kelly.

Her shawl had slipped to the grass and, reaching down, he picked it up and handed it to her. "I believe this is yours, Miss McFarland," he said, with a slight, graceful bow.

His voice held no special warmth, only a formal politeness. As if they'd met and shaken hands, Star thought, nothing more, and then instead of slapping his face or telling him in no uncertain terms what a cad he was, she heard herself, annoyed, stammering, "You... you know my name?"

He shrugged indifferently. "I don't suppose there's a gentleman present this evening who hasn't inquired about the mysterious beauty Mr. Donley escorted to the party."

So he had noticed her, Star thought, and felt a thrill of triumph. He wasn't as indifferent to her as he pretended. And that vulgar way he had grabbed and kissed her—well, she would make him pay for that indignity before the evening was over. She fluttered her dark lashes and pouted prettily, "I couldn't have made much of an impression, Mr. Kelly. I can't remember your name on my dance card."

For a moment Mr. Kelly's eyes, that despite the swarthy coloring of his face were dark green rather than black, narrowed as he gazed down at his companion. As if, Star thought uncomfortably, he saw past the fluttering lashes, the coquettish airs, and what he saw displeased him. When he spoke, she detected a fine edge of amused contempt in his voice. "I've never had much interest in adding my scalp to a young lady's collection." He glanced around him thoughtfully. "I apologize if I've interrupted a rendezvous. Which one, I wonder, is the lucky swain, or are they taking turns?"

He saw the gray eyes staring up at him suddenly grow diamond bright with anger, the auburn hair seeming to catch fire in the moonlight. As Star lifted her furious gaze to his, her chin lifting haughtily, Michael Kelly saw that anger had stripped away the artificial, simpering mannerisms, the silly, fluttering eyelashes and shallow coquette's smile from Star McFarland. There was only an incredible blazing loveliness left, a beauty that caught and twisted at a man's insides, so that against all common sense he wanted to cover those sensuously curved lips again with his own until they parted soft as petals beneath his and he found her tongue, hot and seeking.

His hands almost did reach out to pull her to him again, then he saw a man coming swiftly across the garden toward them. Abruptly he stepped back, his voice roughening as he jerked his chin toward the approaching figure. "It seems your devoted, if tardy gallant is arriving, so I'll be on my way. Never let it be said that I stood in the path of young love."

Then he was gone, vanishing into the darkness as silently as a shadow, and Charles stood beside her.

"Wasn't that Mr. Kelly with you?" he asked, and once again she caught the sharp edge of jealousy in his voice.

She nodded, afraid to speak for fear her voice would give her away. Charles looked down into her pale face. "He wasn't annoying you?" he asked indignantly.

She shook her head and took a deep, steadying breath. "No, he wasn't annoying me."

Charles's gaze still fastened suspiciously on her face as he gazed down at her. "Mr. Kelly has quite a reputation with the ladies." He frowned disdainfully. "I suppose there are some women who find half-breeds like Kelly attractive."

Yes, Star thought, all at once shivering. She had no doubt that there were women who found Michael Kelly attractive despite the satanic scar that marred the darkly handsome face. There was a savage, compelling virility about the man. She remembered how she had felt caught in his arms, terrified of the sensations that were sweeping through her, and yet equally terrified that the kiss would stop.

Even now, safe here with Charles, she felt threatened by the memory of that kiss. She said quickly, to change the subject from Mr. Kelly, "You haven't told me yet: how soon will you be leaving for Independence?"

"Oh, not for several weeks," Charles assured her. "It'll take that long to buy the goods and arrange to have them shipped to Independence."

"How long will you be away on your trip to Mexico?"

"It depends upon whether I can sell all my goods in Santa Fe or have to travel farther south to the markets in Chihuahua. It could take a year."

"A year!" A lifetime, Star thought.

Charles heard the disconsolate note in her voice, and he pulled her into the shadows under the trees. "Will you miss me?" he asked softly.

"You know I will," she replied, all attempts at flirtatious, teasing behavior forgotten now. "Oh, how I wish I could go with you," she blurted impulsively.

Charles's arms pulled her close, his mouth brushing hers lightly. "Sweet," he murmured hoarsely. "So sweet."

Once again Star was aware of new surprising sensations flooding her body, as she had felt only a few minutes before when Michael Kelly had kissed her. But Charles's mouth was feather-light on hers, not ruthlessly searching as Mr. Kelly's had been, and his arms held her tenderly, not crushing her in his embrace so that she couldn't breathe. And the sensations she felt were not frightening, as if forces over which she had no control had taken possession of her, but pleasant, almost comforting.

She relaxed in Charles's embrace, as if she were a child again with loving arms holding her close. How strong and yet gentle Charles was, she thought blissfully, as his lips caressed her eyelids, the soft outer corners of her mouth. She wished she could stay here always, safe within the circle of his arms.

It was Charles who ended the kiss, who stepped away from the girl so suddenly that her softly curved mouth was still half-parted from his kiss, her shimmering silver-gray eyes lifted to his, still dazed.

For a second a look, slyly triumphant, slipped into the amber eyes watching Star, then it was quickly gone, a trick of the moonlight, she decided, and there was only the reassuring warmth of Charles's smile, boyishly sheepish as he murmured, "Forgive me, but a man would have to be made of iron to resist your charms, Miss McFarland." He grinned suddenly. "I can't call you that, not any longer. What was it your father called you: Star?"

"Margaret, when he's angry with me," Star laughed. "Star is a pet name. There's a wild flower that blooms along the Santa Fe trail called the blazing star. Papa started calling me Star after the flower when I was first born."

She remembered the story her mother had often told her about the first time her father had seen her in her mother's arms. Even as a baby her hair had been auburn tinted, her skin the creamy texture of flower petals, not the usual red color of the newborn. "You were such a beautiful baby," her mother had told her, giving her daughter a loving squeeze. "He called you his star, his blazing star. And you clung to his fingers as if you would never let go."

Charles's hands were stroking the flaming auburn hair, tracing the soft curve of her cheek. "How beautiful you are, how very beautiful."

His arms started to tighten around her again, but she pulled free, belatedly remembering Robert. What if he should come looking for her? "We should go back inside. We'll be missed," she said, worried.

For a moment, Charles's face held a small boy's petulance at being denied, then he shrugged impatiently. "You're right. This isn't the time or place. But I must see you again, soon. Promise?"

"Yes," Star breathed happily. "Oh, yes."

When they returned to the house, a warm glow lingered on Star's face, her gray eyes luminous as if lit from within by candles, her mouth caught in a dreamy half smile.

The soft dreamy look was still there on her face the next morning at breakfast, and Cousin Sophia studied the girl's expression uneasily from across the breakfast table.

"Did you have a good time at the Kirkland party?"

Star nodded, smiling vaguely at her companion. Mrs. Palmer noticed, even more uneasily, that the girl had hardly touched her breakfast. Star, who usually had to be scolded for eating her meals in a much too hearty, unladylike fashion!

"You enjoyed Mr. Donley's company?"

Star looked up, her face pinkening. "Mr. Donley? Oh, yes. He's very nice. He's asked to take me to the Chouteau party next week, if it's all right with papa."

Cousin Sophia nodded, pleased. "I'm sure it will be. Your father thinks very highly of Mr. Donley."

So it had been Robert Donley who had put that smitten look on Star's face, she thought, gratified and, she had to confess, a little surprised. She gave a silent sigh of relief, deciding that she had been foolish to worry about the girl. Robert Donley would make an ideal husband for Star, not only wealthy but kind and dependable. And there was no doubt the young man was equally smitten with Star.

The next few weeks Mrs. Palmer's matchmaking hopes continued to rise happily as Mr. Donley became Star's constant companion at musicales, theater parties, and balls. If Mrs. Palmer had been aware that Charles Bradford always managed to show up at the same social functions as Star, that somehow they arranged it so they could slip away for a few minutes alone, she might not have been so blissfully confident.

Then, on May 11, news arrived in St. Louis by steamboat from New Orleans that made Mrs. Palmer forget for a while her matchmaking plans. Mexican cavalry under General Arista had crossed the Rio Grande and had been repulsed by the artillery of General Zachary Taylor at Palo Alto. On May 13 the United States declared war on Mexico.

When the announcement of hostilities reached St. Louis, a war fever swept the city. Torchlight patriotic rallies were held at the courthouse, and the most infamous Mexican of them all, ex-President Santa Anna, the butcher of the Alamo and Goliad, was hanged in effigy. Newspaper headlines called "To Arms! To Arms!" and urged young men to fly to the rescue of their country.

The 64th Regiment of Missouri militia was ordered to report for duty at Camp Lucas, which was hastily constructed just outside the city limits. Now, in the afternoons, Star, along with other young girls and matrons, colorful parasols shielding their faces from the sun, rode out in their carriages to watch the volunteer soldiers, farmers, clerks, frontiersmen, and rousta-bouts, drilling on the parade ground. Even to Star's untutored eye, the marching lines of soldiers were ragged, the men handling their arms with more exuberance than skill.

Nevertheless, the crisp, blue uniforms of the dragoons were dashing, with the bright yellow stripe down the trouser leg and colorful kerchiefs tied around their necks. Sunlight flashed on saber hilts and carbines as they rode by to the rousing music of a marching band playing loudly, if not well, "The Girl I Left Behind Me." Watching the passing troops, the flags snapping in the wind, Star felt goose bumps of pride. Even Robert, who had joined the Laclede Rangers the day after hostilities with Mexico were declared, looked sternly handsome with a shako covering his ginger hair, a saber swinging at his hip, as he rode by Star's carriage, giving her a self-conscious salute.

"A stirring sight, isn't it?"

Star turned and glanced up into the sardonic smile of Michael Kelly. She hadn't seen him since the evening of the Kirkland party and the embarrassing episode in the garden. Now her face grew warm at the memory of those moments. She debated whether or not to cut the man dead, which was certainly what he deserved after his boorish behavior. But Mr. Kelly had already turned his gaze away from her, back to the drill field and the passing troops. "I wonder how long those fancy uniforms will last when they march through the Jornada del Muerte," he said, thoughtfully.

"Jornada del Muerte," Star echoed, curious in spite of herself.

"'The journey of death,'" he translated. "It's a stretch of desert between El Paso and Chihuahua." His mouth thinned in a grim smile. "Though I doubt if half of these men will ever live to get that far."

"I gather, then, that you're not planning to enlist, Mr. Kelly?" Star asked, not attempting to hide the scorn in her voice.

If she had expected to disconcert her companion, she was disappointed. He turned to her, laughter in the dark green, almost black, eyes. "Enlist? I'm a businessman, Miss McFarland, not a soldier."

She glanced toward Robert, who had left the line and was cantering toward the carriage. "There are some men," she said coldly, "who are patriotic enough to be both."

Robert Donley glanced curiously at Michael Kelly, but it was upon Star his gaze swiftly fastened, as if he could not bear to keep his eyes away from her for long. How beautiful she was, he thought, a raw ache in his throat as he watched how the sunlight filtered through the yellow ruffled silk umbrella cast a golden glow over the girl's lovely features, the softly curved mouth and delicately arched brows. He still could not believe his good fortune, that of all the men in St. Louis this desirable creature should have chosen him. Not that he had yet formally asked for her hand, but surely Star would not be spending so much time with him if she didn't care for him, too. Of course, the war made a difference in his marriage plans. Mr. McFarland might think they should wait. If only, he thought a little fearfully, he could be sure that Star would wait, too.

He was only vaguely aware that Michael Kelly was watching him, a wryly compassionate look in his eyes as he saw the moonstruck look on Robert's face when he gazed at the woman in the carriage. Then a confusion on the parade ground drew Robert's gaze back to the drill field, where a group of dragoons had flung themselves on the grass and were laughing and hooting good-naturedly at the drill sergeant who was trying, in vain, to get them to their feet. Several of the men had thrown off their jackets against the hot sun, and when the sergeant protested, one guffawed loudly, then protested, "Hell, Joe, we came to fight for our country, not dress for it!"

"I admire your optimism, Mr. Donley," Mr. Kelly said, smiling broadly at the defiant men, "thinking you can turn those farmers and backwoodsmen into soldiers."

A flush of anger turned Robert's already ruddy face a brick red, even though he had to admit that the young men rushing to the colors were an unruly, undisciplined lot, stumbling over their own feet on the parade ground, taking orders only when they made sense and going their own merry way otherwise.

Feeling the need to defend the ragtag army, he said stiffly, "Once we reach Fort Leavenworth and are under the command of regular army officers, West Point graduates, the men will turn into good soldiers. They'll certainly make a better show than the Mexican dragoons who broke ranks and fled at Palo Alto."

Star saw Michael Kelly stiffen, his eyes darkening to a dangerous opaque green-black beneath black slashing brows. "I've met few men who have the stomach to face a direct artillery barrage," he drawled, then added, smiling coldly, "Or a pistol at thirty paces."

Star found herself remembering those moments in the study of the Kirkland home a few weeks before when Mr. Redden had denigrated the courage of the Mexican people and Michael Kelly's face had worn that same imperturbable mask, with only his eyes savagely alive. She cast a worried glance at Robert. Although his shy, fumbling caresses aroused no response in her, nonetheless, she had grown fond of Robert these last weeks. She had even felt an occasional pang of guilt when she thought of how she and Charles were using him for their own ends. She certainly had no wish to see him drawn into a duel that could end in the young man's death.

Unlike Mr. Redden, however, Robert Donley, remembering Mr. Kelly's ancestry, had the grace to feel ashamed of his remark. Anyway, he recalled that from all accounts, except for their breaking under the American army's mercilessly accurate artillery barrage, the Mexican soldiers had fought bravely at Palo Alto, as well as at the battle of Resaca, the next day. He would have apologized except for Star's sitting there, watching. He could hardly back down in front of her, he thought, despite his quivering stomach. It would be too humiliating. Let Mr. Kelly call him out if he wanted to.

Then he heard Star give a gentle sigh and slump gracefully forward. Robert leaped from his horse and caught her just before she fell from the carriage seat.

"What is it?" he asked anxiously, studying her pale face.

She struggled bravely to sit up, pushing Robert's arms away as she murmured, "It's the sun, I'm afraid. I suddenly grew faint."

Amusement pulled at the corners of Michael Kelly's mouth as he watched Star's performance, even as he felt a flicker of relief at the girl's resourcefulness. In another moment he might have been fool enough to challenge young Donley, and he had no desire to leave any more bodies sprawled on Bloody Island.

"I'll take you home," Robert said immediately.

Star shook her head quickly, too quickly, it seemed to the watching Michael. "That's not necessary. My coachman can drive me. You mustn't neglect your military duties."

"I'll be happy to see Miss McFarland safely home," Michael offered gravely.

Robert gave the man an uncertain glance. Mr. Kelly was hardly the sort of escort he had in mind. Evidently Star felt the same way for she drew herself up and said coldly, "I wouldn't dream of inconveniencing you, Mr. Kelly."

For a moment, looking into those amused eyes beneath the slanting black brows, she had the disconcerting feeling that the man knew exactly what she was thinking and planning. But before either man could insist further, she spoke sharply to her coachman, and the carriage pulled away.

Almost the moment the carriage was out of sight of the parade ground, Star gave new instructions to the coachman. Instead of driving toward the McFarland home, the carriage turned into Lucas Grove, a stretch of woods on the edge of the city, wound through with curving footpaths and carriage trails.

His curiosity piqued by Star's behavior, Michael Kelly trailed behind the carriage, far enough back to stay out of sight. He saw the carriage turn into the grove, pull off into a side road, then stop. As he waited, hidden in the shadow of the trees, he wasn't too surprised to see Charles Bradford step out of the woods and Star McFarland descend from the carriage and rush into her waiting lover's arms.

Watching, Michael frowned, then mentally shrugged. After all, it was no concern of his if Miss McFarland had one or a dozen lovers. Or that she was playing poor Robert Donley for a fool. Nevertheless, Michael was startled at the brief, sharp thrust of anger he felt at the girl's duplicity as he turned his horse and rode back toward town.

Almost as soon as Star ran into Charles's waiting arms, he was pulling her back into the shelter of the trees. His arms tightened with a by now familiar hardness around her, his mouth moved warmly, possessively over her face and down the soft, long line of her throat until her heart thudded in her chest and her knees felt as if they had turned to water.

When he finally released her, her face was flushed and her

bonnet pushed back off her head. Her auburn hair fell, disheveled, around her shoulders.

She cast an anxious eye at the road. Had she heard a carriage drive by while she was lost in Charles's embrace? She murmured, concerned, "Your note said it was urgent that we meet. Is something wrong?"

"I've had word from my wagon master in Independence. The army is threatening to stop all trade caravans from going into Mexico. The merchants are gathering their wagons, planning to leave for Santa Fe at once before the army can interfere."

"Then you'll be leaving, too?"

He nodded. "I should have left days ago. I've finished my business here. I would have left, too, except..." His arms pulled her close again, his breath warm against her cheek as he murmured huskily, "I couldn't bear the thought of leaving you."

"When?" she asked, her voice trembling. "When will you go?"

"I've booked passage on the *Pride of St. Louis*. She's leaving for Independence in the morning."

"So soon?" she wailed, burrowing deeper into his arms. Then, as a carriage passed on the road, she pulled away hastily.

Charles scowled, annoyed at the interruption. "We can't talk here. I have to see you, someplace where we can be alone. If I bring a carriage by your house tonight, can you slip out and meet me?"

"I might be able to leave the house after Cousin Sophia goes to bed," she said slowly. "I don't know."

His arms tightened around her, his voice softly coaxing. "Please say yes, darling. I love you so much." His mouth traced a path to the warm hollow in her throat, his hands holding her close until he felt her grow soft and yielding in his embrace. "Tonight will be our last chance to be together. We have to talk, make plans."

Star clung to Charles, a helpless, breathless feeling sweeping over her. "Yes," she whispered. "I'll try."

In all the times they had been together these last weeks, there had been only a few scattered moments when they had managed to meet alone. How could she bear to have him leave her now without at least saying good-bye, she thought, despair tugging at her heart.

"I'll wait in a closed carriage at the corner near your house," Charles said. He buried his face in the fragrant softness of her hair. "If you don't come . . ." His voice trailed off with just the proper dramatic sadness and brave acceptance of his fate.

But of course she'd be there, he thought smugly. He'd lay any odds that she would. How that pompous old fool of a father would squirm when he learned of his daughter's deflowering at the hands of a man he had thrown out of his house. And Charles planned to make sure he did learn—afterwards. Of course there would be nothing William McFarland could do about his daughter's disgrace then, not with his precious McFarland name and the girl's reputation at stake.

If, gazing down into Star's lovely, pale face lifted trustingly and adoringly to his, Charles felt a slight pang of guilt, he did not allow that emotion to swerve him. Conscience was a luxury Charles Bradford had long ago discarded. Anyway, he thought, it wasn't as if the girl weren't as eager as he was. He hadn't been wrong in his first appraisal of Star McFarland, he decided. He seldom was about women. Despite her virginal kisses, her maidenly flutters of protest, he sensed a depth of passion within the girl, an unconscious sensuality only waiting to be aroused. And with her beauty attracting men like moths to a flame, if it wasn't his bed she shared, it would be another man's before very long.

As a matter of fact, feeling the soft warmth of her breasts, the tempting curve of hip and thigh pressing against his body, he had a difficult time restraining himself from taking her right now, here in the woods, by force if necessary. An almost unbearable excitement burned within him. Thinking of the special pleasure that provocative body, unknowing, untouched, could bring him, it seemed an unendurably long time till that evening.

It seemed a long time till evening for Star, too, but for other reasons, however, as a half hour later she hurried into the front hall of the McFarland house. A dreamy smile of anticipation curved her lips. Charles's wanting to see her that evening, his mentioning their making plans, could mean only one thing, of course: a proposal of marriage.

She was sure the subject would have come up sooner between them but that they had had so little time together. Now there was no more time. Naturally Charles wouldn't want to leave her without some sort of understanding between them. If only, she thought wistfully, she could convince Charles to take her with him to Santa Fe. Not that it was usual for the traders to bring wives along with a caravan. The trip to Santa Fe was not an easy one under the best of conditions, even for the men. Star was sure, though, she could endure any hardship just as long as she could be with Charles.

As she changed for dinner that evening, however, it wasn't Charles she found herself thinking about, but her father. Obviously Charles would have to ask her father for her hand in marriage, and remembering the unreasoning dislike her father had taken to the young trader, she felt a momentary uneasiness. Still, she reminded herself that Charles came from an old, respected Kentucky family and had excellent financial prospects. After all, her own father had built his fortune from money he made in the Santa Fe trade, so how could he object to Charles's business? And once her father saw how desperately she and Charles loved each other, surely he would give permission for the marriage.

She was still feeling buoyantly optimistic when Cousin Sophia knocked at the bedroom door. So much so that at first Star didn't notice the strained look on the woman's face when she announced, "Your father wants to see you in his study."

"Before dinner?" Star asked, surprised. Mealtimes were always punctiliously observed in the McFarland household.

"Yes, dear, right away." Mrs. Palmer's face was a sickly pale color, and her worried glance didn't meet Star's directly.

Star felt a coldness gather in her stomach. "Is something wrong?"

Her companion bit her lower lip nervously, then dabbed helplessly at eyes all at once brimming with tears. "Oh, my dear," she said pathetically. "How could you be so foolish?"

Then the woman turned and fled. The coldness in Star's stomach turned to a lump of ice when she walked into the study and saw her father's face. He knows, she thought, bracing herself even before her father's wrath exploded over her head. His words flung deliberately at her stung like stone pellets,

matching the violent anger in his glistening, flat gray eyes. "To
be caught in the woods, my own daughter, like some cheap
whore, no more sense of decency than the lowest animal, rutting in the bushes. If Mr. Cardwell hadn't been passing through
Lucas Grove, caught a glimpse of you with that scoundrel
Bradford... Thank God Cardwell's a friend of mine and can
be trusted to keep his mouth shut."

So she and Charles had been seen, Star thought, remembering the passing carriage. Well, she supposed it was remarkable that their secret meetings hadn't been discovered
sooner, no matter how discreet she and Charles had tried to
be.

"How long?" her father demanded. "How long have you
been carrying on with Bradford?"

"It wasn't the way you make it sound," Star protested, her
face flaming. "You don't understand. Charles and I love each
other. We want to be married."

"Married!" The shock in William McFarland's voice drove
the anger from his face. A fleeting look of pity softened the
gray eyes for a moment as he gazed at his daughter. He shook
his head wearily. "There'll be no marriage. You don't know
Charles Bradford."

"I know everything I need to know about him," she insisted
stubbornly. "I know we love each other. We belong together."

"The man's an unprincipled scoundrel," her father said
sharply. He remembered the stories he'd heard about Charles
Bradford, tales of loose women and the gambling that had
wiped out all the profits the man had made from his last trading
trip to Santa Fe. And there were other, even more repugnant
rumors, certainly not the sort of information he could pass
along to a young girl like Star. He half suspected that the man's
pursuing of his daughter had been a way of getting even with
him for turning down his request for a loan. He wouldn't put
it past the man.

William McFarland's mouth twisted painfully. Thank God
he had been stopped in time. William McFarland studied his
daughter speculatively, a cold fear racing through him. Or was
he in time? Was the girl still a virgin? It was not a subject that
McFarland could bring himself to discuss with his daughter.
If only her mother were here to talk to the girl. But memory

of his lost, beloved wife only brought back his grief and anger full force, so that McFarland's voice trembled with rage. All warmth drained from his face as he said, "I can see I made a mistake, removing you from the convent school. As soon as arrangements can be made, you will be returned to the care of the good sisters."

Star thrust out her chin rebelliously, her eyes turning almost the same stone gray as her father's, so that for a moment the resemblance between father and daughter was uncanny. "It doesn't matter if you lock me away forever, papa," she said. "It won't change anything."

She saw her father's hand half raise, as if he meant to strike her, although he had never struck her before in her life. Then his hand clenched into a fist and fell to his side.

"Go to your room," he said, his face remote, closed, as if he had slammed a door in her face. "You will stay there until I send for you."

Star walked to the door, moving with a cool, defiant grace. At the door, she stopped and turned, her eyes bright with unshed tears but her voice composed. "It won't work, you know, papa," she said quietly. "I won't forget Charles, and I'll never stop loving him."

Chapter Four

*O*nly a few seconds after she entered her bedroom, Star was startled to hear the door being locked behind her. She rushed to the door, lifted her hand angrily to pound on it, then stopped and let her hand fall to her side. What was the use? she thought bitterly. No one would come. Mrs. Palmer and the servants wouldn't dare cross her father.

Turning her back, she walked to the window. It had already grown dark enough so that the street lamps had been lit, casting yellowish puddles of light onto the ground. She could not see the street corner from her window, but she could imagine Charles waiting in the closed carriage. How long, she wondered? How long would he wait until he decided that she had changed her mind, that she was not coming after all? If he knew that she was being held here in the house against her will, she was sure he would devise some plan to free her, even if it meant breaking down the door to get to her.

But there was no way she could send him word, she thought unhappily. He would leave for Independence in the morning, and she would never see him again. The thought sent a spasm of pain through her body, and she began to pace back and forth, her arms crossed, hugged against her body, against the pain.

For two days the door to her bedroom was kept locked. Cousin Sophia brought her meals, but though the housekeeper's eyes were filled with sympathy, she did not speak. Star guessed that Cousin Sophia was under strict orders from her father and that silence was to be part of the punishment for her crime. Since Mrs. Palmer's livelihood depended on William Mc-Farland, Star knew the woman could not afford to defy him.

And except for the unhappiness the silence was causing Mrs. Palmer, Star had no wish to talk to anyone. The trays of food returned to the kitchen, hardly touched.

The third day, however, when Cousin Sophia brought Star her breakfast, she handed her charge a folded newspaper. On the back page was a brief mention of prominent merchants who had recently left St. Louis for Independence with trade goods for Santa Fe. Charles Bradford was among the merchants named.

So he was gone, Star thought dully.

Mrs. Palmer saw the blood drain from the girl's face, and her good-natured face was wracked in sympathy. "Oh, my dear child," she blurted, unable to keep her silence any longer. "I'm so sorry, but believe me, it's for the best. In time you'll see—"

She was startled when the girl lifted her face to her. The wide-set gray eyes were not blurred with tears as she had expected but hard as slate, reminding her uneasily of William McFarland when he had set his mind stubbornly to do something.

"When am I to be returned to the convent school?" Star asked coldly.

"That may not be necessary," Mrs. Palmer said eagerly. "Mr. Donley visited your father just this afternoon. He's asked your father for permission to call upon you formally. No doubt he means to propose to you. And your father is fond of Mr. Donley. I'm sure he would forget about the convent school, if you agreed to—"

"To marry Robert," Star finished bitterly.

"Mr. Donley is a fine man. And he loves you, I'm sure."

"But I don't love him," Star replied, her mouth drooping tragically. "I love Charles. I'll never marry another man."

Mrs. Palmer sighed. She had almost forgotten how it was to be young as Star and have your whole life teeter in the balance of one man's smile. And she couldn't help wondering ruefully how many marriage pillows had been dampened by the tears of young women who had married men they had believed they couldn't live without. "At least agree to see Mr. Donley," she coaxed.

Star, only half listening, had already turned away, afraid that the sudden excitement she was feeling might betray itself in her face. For she had noticed something else in the newspaper Cousin Sophia had given her, a listing of steamboat departures from St. Louis, one steamboat in particular, the *Western Star*, leaving that Friday for Independence, Missouri.

Making her voice carefully indifferent, she said, after a moment, "If it's all right with papa, I suppose it can't hurt, my seeing Mr. Donley."

It was a wet spring in Independence that year. The town, sitting like a port at the edge of a prairie sea, was mired deep in red Missouri mud. Not that it was much of a town: a court-house square, a hotel, several stores, surrounded by numerous smithies and wagon shops, a few scattered homes and clusters of tents reaching out into the prairie. Since the town of Franklin had slid into the Missouri River the year before, Independence had become the jumping-off place for traders taking their car-avans over the Santa Fe Trail, as well as eastern emigrants who poured into the town to join the wagon trains heading west to Oregon.

The newly arrived emigrants in their homespuns roamed through the bustling, overcrowded town, gaping at the Shawnee and Kansa Indians from the Territory, the mountain men in buckskins, Mexicans in colorful pantaloons, and the shouting bullwhackers, cracking their whips over freight wagons that struggled in from the steamboat landing, their wheels stuck hub deep in the mud. The sound of the whistle and then the explosive crack of the whips, snapping over teams of mules and oxen, blotted out temporarily the deafening noise from the wagon shops, the blows of hammers beating out hot iron.

Charles Bradford hardly noticed the noise and confusion, the babble of several tongues, in the street around him. Ignoring the rain, he left the wheelwright's and waded across the street to Smallwood Noland's inn, which proudly advertised itself as the last American hostel this side of the Sandwich Islands.

Despite the mud creeping over his boot tops and the in-clement weather, the trader was feeling pleased with himself. The army sergeant from Fort Leavenworth who had orders to inspect all Santa Fe—bound wagons for contraband arms and ammunition that might end up in enemy hands in Mexico, had given the Bradford wagons only a cursory search. After glancing through the bales of cotton goods, boxes of cutlery and hardware, he hadn't even come close to noticing the special cargo in its hidden compartment beneath the wagon beds. He had left, whistling happily, a bottle of good Kentucky whiskey, donated by Charles, stuck within his coat jacket.

Charles was still congratulating himself at how easily the sergeant had been hoodwinked when he stepped into the lobby of the Noland Hotel. To his surprise, he was immediately buttonholed by the innkeeper, Mr. Charles Noland, himself. The innkeeper's plump face was flustered and he spoke in a whispered rush. "There's a young lady waiting to see you, Mr. Bradford. It didn't seem right she should wait in the lobby by the taproom. I told her she could wait in your room."

"Did she give her name?" Charles asked, puzzled.

"No, that she didn't. But she's a lady, no doubt of that."

But Charles had already broken away from the man's grip and was striding up the stairs to his parlor suite. Pulling open the door, he stared, startled, into the face of Star McFarland. She had been seated when he entered, and now she rose quickly to her feet. Fear, uncertainty, embarrassment flickered across a face pale with fatigue beneath her gray bonnet. When Charles made no move toward her, simply stared at her in shock, she swallowed hard and, straightening her shoulders, lifted her chin proudly. "I'm sorry," she said. "I shouldn't have come."

She started toward the door. Charles reached out a hand to catch her arm, his voice bewildered. "Wait. I don't understand. When did you . . . how did you get here?"

"The *Western Star*. I left St. Louis four days after you did." Her voice broke for a moment, betraying her fear, then steadied. "I was afraid that I'd be too late, that you'd already left for Santa Fe."

Charles shook his head absently. "The army's been holding us up. We finally got permission today; we can leave tomorrow with our wagons." His hand tightened on her arm, his voice incredulous. "You came all this way alone? What did your father have to say about that?"

A flush crept into the pale cheeks. "He didn't know. I . . . I left him a note."

It had been difficult writing that note, trying to explain to her father why she had to go to Independence, why she could not possibly marry Robert Donley when she loved Charles Bradford. It had been even more difficult leaving the house with only a carpetbag early in the morning before anyone in the house was awake. Fortunately her father had always been generous with pocket money, more than she had ever managed to spend, and there was the pearl ring that had belonged to her mother. Between the gold coins in her reticule and the ring and using a fictitious name, she had talked the captain of the *Western Star* into finding her a cabin only an hour before the boat had pulled away from the St. Louis riverfront.

Charles spoke slowly. "When you didn't come that last night, I thought you had changed your mind."

He could speak about it calmly now, but that night he had been enraged at the girl's disappointing him. When finally convinced that she wasn't coming, that all his careful planning to revenge himself upon the father by seducing the daughter was for nothing, he had stormed into Madame Decamier's. Savagely he had inflicted upon the Indian girl Theresa all the anger and frustration he had felt at being thwarted from possessing Star McFarland's slim, white loveliness.

Gazing down at the girl, he saw now that despite the travel weariness that shadowed her features, she was as beautiful as he remembered, the hair with the ripples of flame running through it, the wide, soft gray eyes framed in smudged black lashes, the creamy skin shadowed now with exhaustion. Studying her face, the gentle slope of her shoulders, the rounded breasts, just the right size to fit a man's hand, he felt a familiar stirring of desire in his loins.

Star saw the fire leap into the amber eyes, and the hard knot of fear in her stomach relaxed. "You don't mind, Charles, that I came?" she asked softly.

"Mind!" For answer, he pulled her into his arms, his hand quickly untying the ribbons of her bonnet and tossing it on the bed so that he could bury his lips in the glorious hair. "How can you ask?" he murmured huskily.

Flustered, she pulled free, as if suddenly aware she was embracing a man while alone in his hotel bedroom. She glanced around uncertainly, her face pinkening. "I think, perhaps, darling, if you could ask the innkeeper to find me a room. I'd love a nice hot bath and a chance to change my clothes."

Charles gave her a surpised glance, then threw back his head and laughed. "My dear little innocent. There's not a room to be had in this hotel, or anywhere else in Independence, for that matter. The town's jammed full." He glanced around him, frowning. "You'll have to stay here. It's not exactly the Planter's House, I'm afraid." Then, as he saw the color deepen in her face, he smiled teasingly. "We'll be married, of course, my sweet. You surely didn't think otherwise?"

Although the idea of marriage had arrived newly born in his mind, still he thought, why not? When he returned to St. Louis with the fortune he'd make in Mexico, he had planned to retire from the trade, buy a home and business, pick up the social position that should by rights be his. A wife, especially one with the McFarland name and wealth behind her, would be a great help in establishing himself. And it didn't hurt matters that she was beautiful and desirable in the bargain. Charles shrugged mentally. And in case he should in time become bored with married life, well, there was a way he could hedge his bet on that, too.

When Star didn't answer at once, he said a little impatiently, "It's what you want, too, isn't it? You always said you wanted to see Mexico. Well, we shall, together, on our honeymoon."

An odd reluctance that had suddenly gripped Star at Charles's sudden proposal, like a cold hand of reason clutching her shoulder, fell away at his words. "You mean it?" she asked happily. "You'd take me with you to Santa Fe?"

"There's no way I'd leave you behind," Charles said firmly, and then, in a warning afterthought, "It won't be the most luxurious of honeymoons, you know. There'll be eight hundred rough miles of hot, dusty trail before we reach Santa Fe, even if we take the Raton Pass and not the desert route. It could be months before you'll see another white woman, and there are few comforts on a caravan."

"But we'd be together," Star said, her eyes glowing with excitement, a sense of drama possessing her as she thought about the trip. Why, she'd be a pioneer woman, as brave as her grandmother Cora, who had traveled with her husband to Harrodsburg with Daniel Boone's party, she thought proudly.

Even papa would have to respect her courage, and realize she was no longer a child.

Thinking of her father, though, brought a look of sadness to her face, and Charles asked, a hardness entering his voice, "What is it? Don't you want to come with me?"

"Oh, yes. It's just . . . I was thinking of papa, how furious he'll be." She sighed. "Do you suppose he'll ever forgive me?"

"Of course he will," Charles assured her, grinning wickedly. "Especially when the first grandson comes along."

Children. Star felt a jolt. Strange she hadn't thought about that. But then having children was something else the good sisters at the convent school had never discussed with their students. She wasn't even sure how long it took for a woman to have a child. Surely it must be months, she thought uneasily, suddenly remembering how one of the girls at school had bragged that she had been in the next room when her sister had had a baby. "She screamed the whole time," the girl had said in a horrified but self-important voice.

Charles turned toward the door. "I'll fetch a maid to bring water for your bath, and while you're freshening up, I'll see what I can do about rounding up a minister."

Star blurted, startled, "You mean—now? We'll be married today?"

"It has to be today," Charles said. "I told you we were leaving Independence tomorrow to join the others at the wagon camp."

"But I, I haven't any wedding dress," Star stammered. "And where will you find anyone to marry us so quickly?"

"There are at least two ministers in town. I admit it's unconventional, but I'm sure one of them will marry us when I explain the situation to him." He reached down and brushed her lips with a kiss. "And you'll make a beautiful bride, sweetheart, in whatever you wear."

Then he was gone, and a half hour later a young, dark woman appeared at the door with buckets of water and soap and towels. For all the unusual mixture of Negro and Indian features in her face, Star decided the girl could have been quite attractive if only she weren't so sullen looking. She didn't speak two words the whole time she poured the water into the porcelain hip bath behind a screen and helped Star undress. Afterwards, she simply stood, staring impassively at the white girl until Star said nervously, "That's all, please. Thank you."

Surely the maid didn't intend to stay and watch her bathe, she thought uncomfortably. The young woman's glance roamed almost insolently over Star's small waist and slender hips. For a moment Star could have sworn it was hatred, not mere insolence, she glimpsed in the black opaque eyes studying her. Then the woman lowered her eyelids swiftly and there was only a sullen indifference on her face. She turned and walked from the room, her hips swinging with a lithe, feline grace.

Then Star forgot all about the girl as she slid, sighing happily, into the cool, soapy water, soaking away at least some of her weariness and the ugly red marks that the stays from her corset had dug into the flesh beneath her breasts. She would liked to have washed her hair, too, but she had to content herself with a brisk brushing until her scalp stung and her red-streaked hair shone as if burnished.

She was struggling into the one other good dress she had brought with her, a gray poplin with a demure white lace collar and cuffs that would have to do for her wedding dress, wishing as she struggled with the tiny buttons that she hadn't been so quick to send the maid away, when Charles pounded at the door. "Hurry up, Star. The minister's waiting."

There was barely time to replace her bonnet, slip on her gloves, and snatch up her shawl before he was hustling her from the hotel and into the buggy he had waiting at the inn door. She had a confused sensation of time both standing still and rushing by, of each moment crystal clear in her mind, and yet all her emotions jumbled, as if she were caught up, helplessly swept along by events, like a whirlwind over which she vaguely sensed she had no understanding or control.

When she clutched at Charles's arm in the parlor of the minister's home a few minutes later, her heart was jumping so that she felt giddy, and she gazed around her as if bewildered. What was she doing here? Suddenly everything and everybody in the room seemed strange, almost frightening. She had always expected to be married in a fashionable church with a white lace gown and veil, not in a shoddy little parlor by a minister who stumbled over the marriage lines and a minister's wife, standing by, in a calico dress that was not quite clean. The other witness was Dutch Johnson, Charles's wagon boss, who had the same sun-bleached hair and tall build as Charles but his mouth had a looseness to it and his pale brown eyes made Star feel uncomfortable as they furtively touched her breasts and face. Even Charles all at once was a stranger. The glittering amber eyes, the handsome, boyish features were those of a man she didn't know at all.

She couldn't remember making the proper responses to the minister's questions but she must have, because the ceremony was over and Charles's mouth touched hers lightly. For a moment, horrified, she thought the wagon boss meant to kiss her, too, but thankfully Charles was ushering her quickly to the door and back into the buggy.

She gazed down at the new golden circle on the third finger of her left hand. How small it was, and yet how oddly heavy it felt. "Where did you get it, Charles?" she asked, relieved to hear again the reassuring sound of her own voice. She lifted her hand. "The wedding ring? Where did you find the ring on such short notice?"

"You forget you married a trader, darling. I've got a box of such trinkets in my wagon. Of course once we return to St. Louis, I'll replace that one with a ring more suitable to your position as Mrs. Charles Bradford."

Mrs. Charles Bradford. Star repeated the name to herself, rolling the sound of it silently on her tongue, where it felt oddly alien. They came to the inn again, and as they walked into the lobby, Mr. Noland came hurrying to them, a fatuous smile on his face, a bottle in his hand. "For the newlyweds," he said, thrusting the bottle into Charles's hand and beaming at Star.

Behind the innkeeper, in the taproom, she could hear sounds of raucous merriment, glasses clattering, men's voices raised in shouts and laughter. One man declared loudly, "You mark my words, old Zack Taylor will take care of those greasers in short order. The word is he's already crossed into Mexico and that recruits are swarming into Fort Leavenworth to join Kearny. The war won't last a month."

Mr. Noland cocked his head toward the noise, frowning disapprovingly. "You would prefer, I'm sure, to have your meal served in your room."

For the first time in her young life, Star discovered that the thought of food made a nervous knot in her stomach. "I'm not hungry," she murmured.

Charles turned toward her, speaking quickly, "Why don't you run along upstairs, Star? I'll just have a bite to eat down here, catch up on the latest news, and join you in a short while."

Star stared at him, wide-eyed with disbelief. How could he be so insensitive as to leave her alone, she thought furiously. After all, it was their wedding night. But her husband had already turned and was walking toward the swinging doors that led into the taproom. She was still fuming when she reached their room and saw that someone had unpacked her carpetbag. Her nightdress and wrapper lay across the coverlet.

But as she undressed for bed, slipping into the white cambric nightgown with its high lacy collar and long sleeves, weariness overcame her anger. Weariness and a guilty sense of relief, as if some unknown event, mysterious and slightly frightening, had been for a while postponed. No doubt Charles had sensed her feelings, she thought drowsily, and had given her this time to be alone. Then her head touched the pillow and she was almost immediately asleep.

It was almost eleven o'clock when Charles left the taproom and the noisy sound of revelry that he knew would continue far into the night as the traders and their trail hands made the most of their last night in town before the long, grinding months on the trail. He had planned to leave earlier, but his friends had insisted upon buying him drinks to celebrate his new matrimonial state; there had even been talk of giving the newlyweds a shivaree, which calmer heads fortunately had prevailed against.

Now, only a little the worse for having too much to drink, he stumbled through the darkness of the bedroom to light the lamp beside the bed. Damn it, he thought irritably, as his knee banged into the brass bedstead, why hadn't Star left a light for him? His irritation was compounded when he discovered that his new bride was sound asleep and that even his stumbling noises hadn't awakened her.

He lifted the lamp so that the light cast golden shadows across the bed, and he drew in his breath sharply. Star was as lovely asleep as she was awake—even lovelier, with her auburn hair unbound and tumbling across the pillow, her eyelashes like black silk fans resting on a petal-soft, creamy skin. It was a warm night, and in her sleep she had tossed off the coverlet. Her gown had ridden up her hips and she was curled up childishly in a ball, her skin softly gleaming in the lamplight.

Coming up the stairs a few minutes earlier, tired himself from a long busy day, Charles had decided to forego the pleasures of the marriage bed for one night. Now, gazing down at the loveliness of his sleeping bride, a tightness gathered in his loins and all thought of postponing taking possession of that softly tempting body was forgotten.

Putting the lamp on the table, he undressed quickly, letting his clothes fall in an untidy jumble on the floor before sliding into bed beside the sleeping girl. Quickly, skillfully, he undid the buttons that confined the bodice of the prim nightgown and slipped his hand inside the gown. The moment his hand grasped a soft, warm breast, Star jerked awake. Her eyelids flew open. Misty gray eyes blurred with sleep stared up at him, at first uncomprehending, then widening with bewilderment and disbelief as she felt the unfamiliar touch of a man's hand on her body, and the even more shocking sight of Charles, without a stitch of clothes on, in bed with her.

Instinctively, she tried to pull away. Charles laughed and flung one leg heavily across hers, effectively pinning her to the bed while his hand continued its casual kneading of her breast. "I apologize for being so late in coming to bed, my sweet, but you must admit, it isn't flattering to find my new bride sound asleep." Then without changing the lightly teasing note in his voice, he added, "Take off that ridiculous nightgown, Star. A bride's nightgown belongs across the foot of the bed."

When she didn't move but continued to stare up at him as if frozen with shock, his free hand clutched the soft material of the bodice of the gown. A coldness crept into the amused voice. "Or would you prefer that I tear the gown off, my sweet?"

When she felt his hand jerk at the cambric material, heard a soft tearing sound as it began to rip, she cried out, "No, wait!" It was the only nightgown she had brought with her, she thought vaguely, startled to discover that she could still think of such practical matters while her mind raced frantically, unable to accept the enormity of what was happening, like a nightmare in which she was trapped, unable to wake herself.

She lifted the gown over her head, then reached quickly for the sheet to cover herself. But Charles jerked the sheet away from her hands and tossed it to the floor. She could not see his face clearly in the lamplight but she could see his eyes, glittering, yellow-bright—like a wolf's eyes, she thought, terror-stricken. How odd she had never noticed earlier how predatory Charles's eyes were as they moved greedily over her naked limbs, the curve of her hips, the indented waist, the pertness of the uptilted breasts. A trembling started deep inside her at the feel of that rapacious gaze and set her whole body to shaking violently.

She could hear Charles's breath coming more quickly in the darkness above her, the thickness in his voice as he warned, "Don't ever hide yourself from me, my sweet. I have the right to see and enjoy what's mine."

Then, before she could turn away, his mouth covered hers, not lightly, gently as he had always kissed her before, but brutally, forcing her soft lips apart while his tongue probed inside her mouth's softness. Shock and fear changed to a blinding, furious anger, as she felt his hand roughly, humiliatingly, explore her body. Anger lent her a strength she didn't know she possessed and she fought violently against him, beating at him with her fists, scratching at him with her nails, and finally biting down hard upon the tongue in her mouth so that Charles drew back with an angry, painful curse.

Swiftly, she managed to wiggle free of his imprisoning leg and slide from the bed. Snatching at the gown and holding it before her, she faced Charles furiously from across the room. "Don't come near me," she hissed, "or I'll scream!"

Charles sat on the side of the bed, glaring at her, his face flushed, his tongue throbbing where her teeth had bit him. He had planned not to hurt her. After all, she was his wife and a lady, not some trollop from Madame Decamier's. But he should have known better, he thought, sudden raw anger pounding at his temples. They were all the same beneath those softly enticing bodies, cheap trollops or your gently bred ladies. It was only the fist, the whip, they understood.

He got slowly to his feet and walked across the room toward her. As he approached, Star backed away hastily, ending up hard against a wall, her gray eyes wide but angrily defiant.

He smiled lazily down at her. "You won't scream, my sweet. And if you do, do you really think it will matter? You're my wife. No one is going to break into a bedroom to interfere between a man and his wife in bed."

His one hand suddenly descended over her mouth, pushing her head hard against the wall so that for a moment the room spun dizzily around her, while his other hand found and gripped beneath his finger and thumb the velvet soft peak of her breast.

"What you are going to do," he said coldly, "is exactly what I tell you to do, everything exactly as I say." He could not see her face in the darkness, but exultantly, he could imagine the pain leaping into her eyes, could feel her body stiffen as his fingers tightened their agonizing grip on the velvet softness, heard the soft whimpering sounds that came finally from behind the hand held hard against her lips.

It was only when he felt her body go limp that he released her, catching her in his arms and carrying her to the bed. Gently he laid her on the bed, then waited till she opened her eyes, the gray eyes filled with a glazed fear as she stared at him.

Lovingly, he stroked the pale cheek, the tangled hair, dropping a kiss into the warm hollow of her throat, his voice caressing. "You'll make a very apt pupil, Star, my sweet. It will be a pleasure to teach you what a good wife should know."

She lay quietly, her face blank, only her eyes alive with fear as he lowered his body over hers. Only once did she cry out, and then he quickly covered her mouth with his, shutting off her scream as her body arched upward, helplessly, feeling if it were being torn in two.

Then the crushing weight of his body on hers was gone. She could hear his breathing, more quietly now. For an eternity it seemed she lay there, perfectly still, afraid to move, feeling the warm tears stream down her face. Finally, carefully, hardly daring to breathe, she inched away from him to the very edge of the bed.

Then, to her horror, she felt his arm fling out heavily across her body, his other hand reaching out to grip painfully the softness of her thigh.

"Please, Charles," she whispered, hating herself for cravenly pleading, but hating more what she knew was about to happen. The thought turned her flesh to ice while her heart felt it would break, crashing against the wall of her chest. "It's late, I'm tired."

He pulled her back beneath him, raising himself on one elbow to smile smugly down at her, her face suddenly still. "It's early, darling. You should be pleased that you didn't marry some tired old man. We can take our pleasure all night long, if I wish," he bragged. His hand caressed roughly, bruisingly the length of her body. His eyes gleamed in anticipation, his voice rasping as he whispered, "And you have many more lessons to learn, my sweet."

Chapter Five

When Star awoke the next morning, for a moment she thought she was back in her bedroom in St. Louis. She stretched lazily, her eyes shut against the sunlight that she could feel heavy against her eyelids. Why had Cousin Sophia opened the blinds so early, she thought drowsily, and why did her body ache so? Then she remembered. Her eyelids flew open as memory of the events of the night before rushed back, the shock like being plunged suddenly into icy water.

Cautiously she turned her head on the pillow and saw, relieved, that she was alone in bed. For a few desperate seconds she tried to convince herself that none of it had happened, couldn't possibly have happened. But there was still the hollow in the pillow beside hers where Charles's head had lain and the flecks of blood on the sheet under her that she couldn't help seeing as, biting her lip against the pain, she pulled herself slowly from the bed.

Gazing at the undisputable evidence of the torment her body had suffered at Charles's hands, she was unable to stop the flood of memories from shaking her, the humiliation and indignities those hands had cruelly and knowingly inflicted until the final humiliation when she had become mindlessly, almost eagerly, submissive, agreeing to do anything, say anything, to end the nightmarish terror.

As she relived, helplessly, the terrifying memories, a sour taste rose in her mouth, and for a few moments she was wrenchingly sick in the chamber pot. At last she walked slowly to the wash basin, every muscle in her body seeming to scream in protest at her slightest movement. She washed herself thor-

oughly, as if trying to rid herself of some invisible stain that
clung to her body.

In the wall mirror above the basin, she saw the ugly, blue-
black bruises on her body, and a shudder shook her so that she
felt faint and had to sit down quickly on the edge of the bed.
A picture flashed all at once into her mind: Charles and herself
coupled violently together on the bed. A bewildered anger filled
Star. So this was what happened between husbands and wives,
she thought, appalled. This was the reality. All the rest was a
lure by men, the tender kisses, the flattering words, all to seduce
a woman into his bed and the terrible indignities that awaited
her there. Why in God's name did a woman ever marry, willingly become the legal chattel of a man so that her body could
be used and abused as he pleased? Mystified, Star couldn't
understand why any woman ever stayed married.

She heard the key at the bedroom door, the door opening
almost before she could snatch up her wrapper and pull it around
her. Charles walked into the room, followed by the maid Star
had met the day before. The maid hung back by the door, the
sullen look still on her face as Charles crossed the room swiftly
to Star's side. "Good. You're awake, darling," he said, pleased.
"We have to make an early start if we want to reach the wagon
camp by this evening."

When he reached down to drop a kiss on her forehead, she
flinched and pulled away. If Charles saw, he gave no sign,
only the amber eyes seemed to sparkle more brightly, his voice
filled with a hearty cheerfulness as he turned to the black
woman. "This is Theresa, Star. She'll be your maid on our trip
to Santa Fe."

"Maid!" Star blurted, surprised.

Charles laughed as if delighted by her amazement. "Of
course, darling. Did you think I'd let you make that long, hard
trip without a woman to look after your needs?" He frowned.
"I'm afraid Theresa hasn't had much experience as a ladies'
maid, but I'm sure you can see to her training." He turned to
the door, then stopped, snapping his fingers. "I almost forgot.
I noticed that you hadn't brought many gowns with you, so I
persuaded Mr. Carson to open his dry-goods store this morning
while you were still sleeping. His selection of dresses was rather
limited, but I picked out some I thought you might like." He

grinned boyishly. "Along with some other necessities to go with the gowns. But no corsets or whalebones." He gave Star a husbandly frown of admonishment. "It may not be conventional, but you'll find you'll be much more comfortable without them on the trail. Now hurry and dress, dear. Theresa will help you while I see about getting breakfast."

"Charles, wait!" He had half turned to the door, and he swung back at once. She stared at him, a cloud of confusion filling her mind. Charles had washed and shaved. She could smell the scent of his soap, and the crisp white starched shirt he wore only accented the sun-brown skin. How could it be, she wondered bewildered. How could this smiling, considerate Charles, so thoughtful of her every comfort, be the same monster who had shared her bed last night? "We have to talk," she said desperately.

He lifted an inquiring eyebrow. "Can't it wait till later?"

. "No." She could feel the beginning of fear, thick and cloying in her throat. "No . . . no, it, it can't wait," she stammered.

He shrugged and glanced at Theresa, who slipped quietly out of the room. Then he turned his attention back to Star. "What is it, then? There isn't much time."

"I want to go home." She spoke in a rush.

"Home?" He frowned, perplexed. "Your home is with me now, with your husband."

"No, I can't." She flung out her hands helplessly. "I can't stay with you, Charles. I made a terrible mistake, coming here. I want to go back to St. Louis."

She didn't know how she expected him to react; she cringed inwardly at the thought of his anger, remembering only too well the icy rage that had consumed him last night when she had defied him. But there was no anger in the cool amber eyes assessing her, only a contemptuous amusement as he said with a shrug, "Don't be ridiculous, my sweet. You don't actually suppose your father would take you back? How would you live?"

She felt a wrench of dismay, knowing that he was only speaking the truth. "I'll . . . I'll find a job."

He laughed lightly. "And what sort of work are you trained to do? Without any money and no job, you'd be walking the streets in a week." He reached out a hand and playfully caught a coil of auburn hair falling across her shoulder. This time when she tried to pull away, the fingers tightened on the hair, jerking her face painfully toward him. His voice was maliciously teasing. "Not that you don't have sufficient beauty for that particular profession, my sweet, but I'm afraid you haven't the necessary skills . . . not yet, anyway."

The amber eyes were so close to her now, she could see the flickering predatory gleam that lurked in their yellowish depths. It took all the courage she possessed to lift her chin defiantly, to force the words from her suddenly dry mouth. "You can't make me stay with you, Charles."

For answer, his hand dropped suddenly from her hair to circle her waist, pulling her hard against him while his free hand slipped inside her wrapper. She winced as he touched her bruised flesh, biting back a cry of pain. His smile thinned as he gazed down at her, at her futile efforts to pull free of his tightening grasp, while his hand continued to fondle her body, the still-raw welts and bruises, with a rough, almost casual familiarity, until her struggling ceased and the defiance faded from her face, leaving the gray eyes dull with fear.

Satisfied then, he released her abruptly. "You're my wife, Star," he said coldly. "Your place is with me. I hope you won't make it necessary for me to remind you of that fact again."

Then, with one of his lightning changes of mood, he dropped a playful kiss on her mouth, his voice gently chiding. "You'll feel better once we're under way, my sweet. You're just having a case of nerves. I understand it's not uncommon among new brides. Now hurry and get dressed. It's ten miles to the wagon camp, and I want to reach there before dark."

She stood frozen after he left the room, a mixture of fear and black despair slowly taking hold of her. For the first time she faced the fact that she had stupidly and of her own volition stepped into a deadly quagmire; she now knew finally, hopelessly, that no matter how she struggled, she would never be able to free herself.

When the door opened and Theresa entered the room, she stared at the girl blankly for a moment before some remnant of self-possession stirred within her and she said sharply, "Please knock before entering a room, Theresa."

"Yes'um," the girl said, then, not trying to hide the impudence in her dark eyes, she remarked, "Reckon there won't be many doors, though, on the trail."

Gazing at her new maid, at the sultry beauty that the plain gown and sullen looks couldn't disguise, it occurred to Star that Theresa would need a good deal of training to be turned into a proper ladies' maid. And despite Charles's optimistic assurance, Star had had little experience with training household help. That had always been Cousin Sophia's department. Thinking of Cousin Sophia, though, was too painful, bringing back memories as it did of the safe, innocent world of the house on Lucas Place that was lost to Star forever. Quickly she thrust the thought aside. In any case, she decided, she would be foolish to start out making an enemy of Theresa. She suspected she would need all the friends she could get in the journey ahead, even the friendship of a woman as apparently hostile as Theresa.

As Theresa brought her clothes, Star wondered, embarrassed, what the woman thought about the black and blue marks on her mistress's body. But Theresa's face showed no emotion or interest as she helped Star dress. Trying to mollify and perhaps draw some warmth from the woman, Star asked, "Have you worked here at the hotel for long, Theresa?"

"Never worked here at all."

"But I thought . . . Didn't Mr. Bradford hire you from Mr. Noland?"

"He didn't hire me. He bought me from Madame Decamier in St. Louis," the young woman said flatly.

So Theresa was a slave, Star thought, surprised. William McFarland had never allowed slaves in his home, but St. Louis was a Southern town and Star, of course, knew of the existence of slavery. It was just that it had not occurred to her that her husband might be a slaveholder. But then . . . A shiver shook her body; there was so much about her husband she was discovering she didn't know. Then another, more bewildering, thought occurred to her. If Charles had bought Theresa in St. Louis, that meant he must have brought the girl with him to Independence, had meant to take her with him on the caravan even before Star had arrived on the scene.

She had no time to pursue the thought further. Theresa had packed her clothes and was hurrying her out the door, handing

her her shawl and gloves. Charles stood at the door of the hotel
and beamed proudly as he handed Star into the sleek little
Rockaway buggy waiting outside the hotel, while Theresa
climbed up beside the driver.

"How do you like your wedding present?" he asked Star as
he climbed into the buggy beside her and motioned the driver
to start.

"The buggy? You mean it's mine," Star said, surprised.

"Of course. I could hardly expect you to ride on horseback
or in the Dearborn wagon with Theresa all the way to Santa
Fe," he said. "At least riding in the buggy should make the
trip a little easier for you."

Once again a feeling of bewilderment swept over Star as
she gazed at her husband. How could he be so changeable, she
thought, perplexed, so thoughtful and protective one minute,
as if she were a precious piece of porcelain, and then behave
as he had toward her last night, as if he took pleasure in abusing
her.

The confusion remained with her as the carriage traveled
through deep woods and passed stretches of peaceful farmland.
But by the time they reached the wagon camp in late afternoon,
the churning fear in Star's stomach had eased a little. If it were
not for the twinges of pain she felt when she moved too suddenly, she could almost think last night had never happened.

Star's eyes widened disbelievingly when she saw the wagon
camp. There were literally hundreds of wagons gathered in a
clearing: bright blue-and-red-painted Conestogas, Pittsburghs,
freighters, their white canvases like balloons rising amidst the
treetops.

"But they're so huge!" Star gasped, gazing at wheels almost
twice again as tall as she was, at enormous iron-shod wagon
tongues and wagon beds that rose high at prow and stern and
towered above the suddenly toy-sized Rockaway buggy. "Will
they all be going to Santa Fe with us?"

"Not all, perhaps a hundred of them. We'll pick up the
remainder of the caravan at Council Grove, about eight days'
travel from here. More wagons would have been going, but
some traders were scared off by the war and Kearny's threatening to stop all wagons at the Arkansas." Charles smiled

complacently. "The fewer wagons that make the trip, the more profit for the rest of us."

"What sort of trade goods do you carry?" Star asked, and was startled when Charles's face suddenly froze, his eyes darting coldly toward her.

"Why do you ask?"

"I . . . I was just curious," she stammered.

The icy look faded from his eyes and the sunny smile returned as he replied casually. "The usual cotton and woolen goods, silks and velvets, shirting, hardware, watches, traps, even eyeglasses, all sorts of trinkets that we Americans can make and sell cheaper than Mexican merchants. And what we can't sell in Santa Fe, they'll be eager to buy in Chihuahua. A clever trader can make his fortune in Chihuahua." He placed an arm around Star and gave her a husbandly squeeze. "But you're much too beautiful, my sweet, to bother your pretty head with business matters."

It was the first time he had touched her since that morning, and she felt her body stiffen within his embrace. She was sure that Charles noticed her instinctive reaction, but he made no move to release her. His arm was tightening around her, deliberately pulling her closer, when a whistling sound split the air, ending in an explosion like a rifle shot.

"What was that?" she asked, peering alarmed out of the carriage at a brawny man standing beside six yoke of oxen, a vicious black snakelike whip trailing in the dust at his feet.

"Just a wagoner breaking in his oxen to the trail. They're stupid animals, oxen. They have to be taught to pull together and obey the sound of the bullwhip. It's easier to break mules to harness. You snub them to a wagon wheel with two inches of rope, just enough so they can breathe, then leave them to starve for a day and night. After that, they're usually willing to endure the harness," Charles said, grinning.

"It seems cruel," Star said, the terrifying crack of the bullwhip still echoing in her ears.

Gazing down into the girl's pale face, feeling the shiver of fear slip down her spine beneath his hand, an excitement stirred in Charles. His hand slipped beneath her shawl to cup her breast, smiling as if in secret amusement as he drawled, "Sometimes cruelty is necessary, my sweet. You'll grow used to it in time."

Star felt her face grow warm with embarrassment as she saw the bullwhacker stop and stare after the buggy. She had already become aware of the glances directed toward her as the carriage drove past grizzled, plaid-shirted mule skinners, thick-necked drovers, and Mexican muleteers. The fascinated glances weren't for Star alone. They also lingered on Theresa. The warmth of the men's stares didn't seem to bother the maid. Theresa gazed openly back at the men, her skirt hitched up so that a length of brown leg could be seen.

"Please, Charles," Star whispered. "That man is staring at us."

"And why shouldn't he?" Charles asked indifferently. "He knows it's not every man who has a beauty like you to comfort him on the lonely nights on the trail." Nevertheless, his arm fell away as he gave instructions to the Mexican driver so that he could find the Bradford encampment in the maze of wagons.

At the wagon site Charles helped Star from the buggy, then led her a short distance to where a small canvas tent rose incongruously from the prairie. Waving his hand grandly toward the tent, he asked, "How do you like your new home, Mrs. Bradford?" Then laughed, pleased at the surprise flooding her face. "I got tired sleeping on the hard ground and sheltering under the wagons when it rained, so I had the tent specially made to my specifications at an army supply house. You'll find there's everything you need inside."

When she lifted the tent curtain and stepped inside, she saw there was indeed everything, from a double-sized bed complete with quilted counterpane to a collapsible vanity table that held a china wash basin.

Theresa slipped into the tent behind them and was already pouring water into the china basin. "You'll want to freshen up," Charles said. "And I have some business to attend to. I'll be back in time for supper."

The cold water did feel good, Star discovered, as she gratefully splashed water on her face and arms, then watched as Theresa placed Charles's silver-backed hairbrush and comb next to hers on the vanity shelf. Gazing thoughtfully around the luxuriously appointed tent and remembering the expensive tailoring of Charles's suits, it occurred to Star that her husband had a taste for living well.

Then Theresa was unpacking her carpetbag, placing Star's nightgown and wrapper neatly across the foot of the bed before she turned to leave. Star averted her eyes quickly from the gown, from the painful memories it invoked. Fear suddenly dug with icy fingers at her insides, and she could not bear the thought of being left alone here in this camp of strangers, alone with a husband who terrified her and would undoubtedly be returning any minute.

"Wait, Theresa," she blurted. The woman turned, her face blank, offering no sign of warmth or friendship. Star searched desperately for some subject of conversation that would hold the woman. "Are you comfortable in the Dearborn?"

The young woman shrugged. "It's good enough."

Remembering the eyes of the men following the carriage and the slim figure of the maid sitting beside the driver, Star asked, all at once worried, "You'll be . . . safe?"

The girl shrugged again, her mouth splitting into a spiteful grin that disappeared as quickly as it touched the full lips. "I got my knife. No one touches me less'n I want them to."

"Oh." Star fell silent, aware that the maid was watching her, and was all at once sure that the girl was well aware of Star's fear. It was the look of scarcely veiled contempt in the woman's eyes that stung Star, made her straighten her back stiffly, her voice, sharp. "That will be all, then, Theresa. I'll see you in the morning."

"You want me to come back later, help you get ready for bed?" Theresa's voice was obsequious, but there was nothing submissive about the sly look of amusement in the sloe-shaped dark eyes.

"That won't be necessary," Star said coldly. She turned away and, picking up her hairbrush, became very busy brushing her hair.

It was only as she undressed later for bed that she discovered, exasperated, how difficult it was to undo the row of buttons up the back of her gown without the help of a maid. Finally she managed to extricate herself and slip into her nightgown.

Earlier, after a delicious dinner of prairie chicken and hot biscuits, cooked over a campfire, Charles had excused himself, saying he had guard duty that night and that she shouldn't wait up for him. Star slid, relieved, into the empty bed, although gradually she began to realize how very alone she was, the lamp light casting grotesque shadows on the canvas walls of the tent.

The screech of an owl brought her upright in the bed, clutching, terrified at the coverlet. She thought she saw something move in a corner of the tent, a rustling sound . . . mice . . . a snake! Her flesh grew cold at the thought.

All at once she began to cry. All the fear, misery, and loneliness she had pushed inside of her overwhelmed her. The sobs shook her body like a fever until finally there were no more tears left to shed, only the rather startling conclusion forced upon her that no matter how much she cried, it would make no difference. There was no Cousin Sophia to come running and cuddle her in her ample, motherly arms, nor even her father's presence like a rock, at times to be sure an uncomfortable rock, but a rock nevertheless upon which she could always lean. There was only herself she could turn to now, no one else.

Wearily she rose to her feet and splashed water from the basin onto her tear-swollen face. Then a noise outside the tent, the stealthy sound of a booted foot breaking a twig nearby, made her snatch up her robe and wrap it closely around her. It took the greatest effort of will to force herself to lift the flap of the tent, to peer out into the darkness. "Who's there?" she demanded with a courage she was far from feeling.

A figure loomed silently up before her in the darkness, the largest man she had ever seen. He was dressed in a plaid woolen shirt and his trousers were shoved down into worn boots, but it was the breadth of his arms and neck that amazed Star, before she lifted her eyes to a face burned red by sun and wind. His beard was sun-bleached blond, as were his eyebrows and eyelashes, but his eyes were a bright blue, splayed with wrinkles as if from squinting for years against the sun.

"Didn't mean to scare you, Mrs. Bradford." The voice, with a slight gaelic accent, was surprisingly soft and gentle for such an enormous man.

Star recognized him then. He was a wagoner, one of Charles's employees in the caravan that she had met briefly.

"The name's Ben Malone, Mrs. Bradford." Then, as if sensing the girl's fear, he added quietly, "No need to fret. There's none that'd harm you here in camp."

Star laughed a little shakily. "I'm afraid I'm not very brave. It's all so strange." It had seemed so exciting back in St. Louis, imagining herself traveling with a caravan to Mexico, that beautiful, fabled land. Now the dread of the unknown had taken the place of the excitement.

"You've been down the trail often?" she asked. She knew it wasn't proper, standing in her robe talking to this man, but she couldn't bear for the man to leave, to be alone again.

"That I have," he said cheerfully. "I know every mudhole, stream, river, and buffalo wallow between here and Santa Fe."

She shivered. "It's dangerous, isn't it, the trail?"

He nodded gravely. "I'd be lying if I said otherwise." Almost, he added grimly, "And no fit place for a man to bring his wife," but shut his teeth against the words.

"But you keep returning?" Star said slowly.

The man laughed, a huge bellowing laugh. "It's a stupid gossoon I am no doubt, but it gets in the blood, the prairie as far as a man's eyes can see, like the great ocean itself. Even outwitting the wily Comanches at their own game."

Then, seeing the girl stiffen, he added hastily, "Not that there's any cause for concern with Indians, not in a train of this size." Then, awkwardly, "Maybe it's some sleep you should be seeking, Mrs. Bradford. We'll be breaking camp at sunup."

"Yes." Suddenly Star felt as if she could sleep. The fear was still there, she knew, curled up inside of her, but it was not as bad as before, as if she had taken a timid step across an invisible threshold. And perhaps the next step would be even easier.

She did not try to explain it. She only knew that when she returned to bed and extinguished the lamp, that she fell at once into a deep, dreamless sleep.

Chapter Six

"*Turn out!*"

The loud cry roused the sleeping camp, penetrating the tent where Star groaned and, burying her face in her pillow, tried to snatch a few more moments of sleep.

But it was impossible to ignore the second bellowed command: "Catch up! Catch up!" or the pounding of heavy booted feet as wagoners chased after their animals, harness was thrown on mules, oxen coaxed into yokes. The oxen bawled loudly in protest, mules turned stubborn, and the wagoners swore lustily in French, Spanish, and English.

They had been on the trail for five days now, and although at first Star had covered her ears, shocked, against the early-morning profanity of the teamsters, now she simply ignored it.

"Catch up. Ca-atch up!" The men repeated the call up and down the line, some yiping in Indian fashion, adding to the confusion.

Star was out of bed now, pushing aside the mosquito netting. Although there had been a violent thunderstorm during the night, it had done little to discourage the assault of the ferocious mosquitoes, or nighthawks, as Ben called them. Her arms were covered with tiny red bites that itched like fury.

Charles was already gone and Star dressed quickly, pulling on the fresh undergarments that Theresa had laid out for her the night before, and a brown and yellow print calico gown, one of the gowns Charles had bought for her in Independence. Although Star would have scorned wearing the simple cotton gown in St. Louis, it was practical here on the trail and she could at least manage the buttons up the front of the gown herself. Then she drank the coffee Theresa had left earlier, and forced down some of the salt pork that had grown cold with sitting.

By the time she had finished and stepped outside the tent, the cry of "All set!" was being bellowed throughout the camp, the cry repeated up and down the line, "All set! All set!" as oxen and wagons took their place in line.

The caravan had reached the long-grass country the day before, and Star paused a moment now, gazing delighted at the grassland stretching in front of her, stirrup high, its surface rippling like a billowing, restless sea. Horses and riders wandering off into the tall grass seemed to be swallowed up by its vastness, and the canvas tops of the wagons moved over it like the white sails of ships.

"Ain't that lazy Mario got your tent pulled down yet?"

Star turned, trying to hide the distaste she felt when she looked at her husband's second in command. The rest of Charles's wagoners, the drivers and herders, she had grown to know and respect. It was only Dutch, the wagon boss, who made her feel uncomfortable, with his habit of somehow always appearing whenever Charles wasn't around.

"Mario is packing the carriage," she said coldly. Dutch knew as well as she that pulling down the tent was Mario's last task, that readying the wagons for the trail was the most important chore of all the hands. "Do you know where Mr. Bradford is?" she asked, more to remind the man of the fact of her marriage than with an interest in Charles's whereabouts.

"He's out chasing a half-dozen mules that ran off last night. He said he'd catch up with the caravan as soon as he could." Dutch grinned wickedly. "He almost took the hide off the herder that let the mules run off."

So Charles would be in a foul mood when he returned, Star thought uneasily. She was already learning to be watchful of her husband's moods, the genial charm as well as the black wrath.

Dutch's grin dropped from Star's face, moved greedily downward. "Myself," he said huskily, "if I had a pretty little wife, I wouldn't go off and leave her, no sir, not for a minute."

The heavy-handed compliment, which he apparently thought

would flatter her, brought a flush of anger to Star's face. Before she could retort, though, she saw the grin fade from the man's face, a surly irritation taking its place. Turning, she saw that Ben Malone was coming toward them. "The captain's waiting, wanting to know if our wagons are ready to pull out," he said pointedly to the wagon boss.

Dutch glared resentfully at the blond giant. Was the man trying to tell him his job? His resentment went no further than the glare, though, before he turned and marched away. As gentle and soft-spoken as Ben Malone was, there were few men in the camp who would care to tangle with the Irish bullwhacker.

Mario had appeared and was swiftly dismantling the tent. "I'll walk you to your carriage," Ben said. "The captain moved it to the front of the train so you'd be out of the dust."

Star gazed out at the swells of the prairie, like a mysterious, trackless sea. "How does the captain do it?" she marveled. "How does he know how to find the trail?"

"There's always been a trail," Ben said. "First the Indians made one, then the trappers. Even the army's surveyed it. But the real trail is made from the wagon tracks left by the wheels of other wagons. You can't see them for the tall grass, but you can't miss the ruts. They're dug deep in the mud, then frozen in the winter, solid as rock."

"It would be easy to get lost, though, wouldn't it?"

"It's happened," Ben nodded soberly. "To greenhorns, mostly, who roam too far away from camp. They lose all sense of direction, usually wander in circles until someone sent out from the caravan finds the poor sods or—" He broke off, frowning at Star, not wanting to upset her, then said firmly, "You'd do well not to roam too far from the wagons, Mrs. Bradford."

"Yes," she agreed meekly.

"You needn't be worrying your head about your husband," Ben assured her. "He knows the trail too well to get lost."

Star averted her face guiltily. She wasn't concerned about Charles. In fact it hadn't even occurred to her to wonder if he could find his way back to the train. Suppose he didn't come back, she thought, and was appalled at the rush of happiness the thought brought her, followed by a pang of guilt. After all, hadn't the sisters at the convent school warned often enough that wishing evil in your heart was as sinful as the evil act itself.

Then she hurriedly thrust the thought aside as Ben handed her up into the carriage. Mario, her driver, was waiting, a spray of wild pinks festooning the harness of the mules, another bouquet of pinks in his grubby hand, which he handed to Star, ducking his head shyly.

"*Gracias*, Mario," she said, smiling at the boy and the flowers. "*Muy bonita.*"

A glow of pleasure rose over the boy's dark face, and he silently blessed the good fortune that he should have been chosen to drive the beautiful *señora* with the flaming hair and the smile of an angel.

"You speak Mex lingo pretty good," Ben said, surprised.

"Mario's teaching me," Star said. She was proud herself at how quickly she was picking up the Mexican phrases. Fortunately she had a good head for languages, and the French she had learned at the convent helped.

Now at last the teams were all hooked up and the captain rose in his stirrups and bellowed, "Stretch out. Stre-etch out!"

Ben left to rejoin his wagon while Star settled back in her buggy, the great white-canvased lumbering wagons stretching out behind her in a double file, a rumble like thunder making the ground shake as the wagons swayed dizzily and moved slowly forward.

Star adjusted her bonnet with its thick silken veil covering her face. The veil was useful not only against the dust but also the wretched gnats that swarmed mercilessly around animals and humans alike as the morning grew warmer and the breeze died down and disappeared.

It was midday and the train had stopped for nooning when Charles returned with the runaway mules. The men had finished eating and crawled under the wagons or wherever they could find any shade on the treeless prairie, to take a few moments' rest. Star brought Charles a plate of food and coffee and he glowered at her, without speaking, furious at the wasted morning, chasing the headstrong mules in the heat and dust until finally catching up with the lead mare.

After he finished eating, he spread his blanket under the

carriage and at once fell asleep. Restlessly, Star wandered a short distance from the somnolent wagons. Everyone seemed to be taking—what was it Mario had called it—a *siesta*. Theresa was sound asleep in the Dearborn, the Mexican boys curled up like puppies together in the shade cast by a wagon. She had the odd sensation, looking out into the vast, still emptiness around her, that she was the only person awake on the face of the earth.

A short, twisted tree stood on a knoll not far from her, like a buoy in a sea, spreading a tiny circle of shade. She walked to it, and even that short walk made her face grow flushed in the heat that rose in waves from the ground. It was hard to remember how fresh and cool the air had felt that morning, the rain the night before that had turned the tent chill so that she had snuggled unwillingly closer to Charles.

Charles. She did not want to think about him or about their marriage, but it was impossible not to. She had loved him once, she reminded herself—or thought she had. But now she could not even remember how it had felt. It was like trying to remember a dream that had long since been destroyed in the light of day. Now her marriage was like a charade she played, pretending a wifely affection and devotion when she and Charles were in the presence of others. And at least now in bed when he took her callously, brutally, the shock was not as great as the first time. She responded obediently, cravenly, to his hoarsely whispered commands, but a part of herself had craftily learned to elude him, to retreat to the safety of a dark, inviolate corner of her mind where even Charles could not reach.

Surely it couldn't be like this with all marriages, she thought. Or was it? Were all husbands and wives strangers to each other, playing a role of marital devotion in public, remote and separate when they were alone? Star sighed. They hadn't dwelled much upon marriage in the convent school, except to stress that the wife must be obedient to her husband as the man must be obedient to God. Perhaps, Star thought, in time it became easier, perhaps her skin would no longer crawl with revulsion when Charles touched her, or looked at her in that certain way so that she knew at once, shivering with fear and disgust, what would follow.

At least here, alone like this, she was, for the moment,

content. The stillness of the open, empty prairie lulled her with its silence, its undemanding beauty. A prairie lark whistled, a grasshopper suddenly whirred up before her, but not a breeze stirred the grass.

She strayed a few feet farther from the knoll, but remembering Ben's warning, she turned every few feet to make sure she could still see the white canvases of the wagon train. She was humming a few Spanish phrases from a song that Mario liked to sing as he drove the carriage, when she turned again to look toward the caravan. And discovered she was no longer alone.

Where had he come from? she wondered, more startled than frightened. It was as if the Indian had sprung from the earth at her feet. If it were not for the broad, brown face, the black hair worn in long braids, plaited with calico cloth, he might have been a white man in his dirty trousers and faded blue shirt. Then he spoke a few phrases in some guttural tongue that Star couldn't understand and stepped toward her, his hand rising to his waist. She saw that he had a knife stuck into the rope holding up his trousers.

A scream rose in her throat. Then she saw Charles, carrying a rifle, striding toward her from the wagon train. The Indian must have seen the relief on her face for he turned quickly, but he did not retreat at sight of Charles.

He waited almost placidly for Charles to reach them, then he spoke in that same guttural tongue to Charles. Although Charles's face did not change expression, Star had the impression that he knew the Indian. Then Charles spoke to the Indian in the Indian's tongue. Star caught only a few words: "Fort Bent . . . dragoons . . ."

When Charles finished speaking, the Indian held out his hand. Contemptuously, Charles dropped a coin into it. The Indian didn't move, held out his hand obviously for more, a dull anger filling the dark brown face. Charles raised his rifle threateningly. The Indian hesitated, then shrugged and turned and started walking toward the caravan.

What happened then occurred so quickly that Star didn't even see Charles aim the gun. At the explosion of the rifle, the Indian's body seemed to jerk into the air, then fling forward, disappearing into the tall grass as if he had never been.

The rifle shot had been heard at the caravan. Men were tumbling out from under the wagons, carrying guns, heading toward the knoll. Charles stepped forward, swung his rifle above his head, and shouted, "No need for alarm. Just doing some target shooting."

The men hesitated, then stopped, turned slowly back to the camp. For the first time Charles glanced at Star. Her face, even her lips, were bleached white, so that the gray eyes, wide with shock, were the only color in her face. Taking her arm, he pulled her away from the knoll, through the tall grass pulling at her skirt. "Target shooting's not a bad idea," he commented thoughtfully. "Have you ever handled a gun?"

She shook her head numbly.

"Of course you weren't in any real danger from him." Charles gestured almost indifferently back to the spot where the Indian had fallen. "He was a 'Kaw, a tame settlement Indian, living on handouts."

"Then why did you kill him?" Star could hear the words screaming in her head, was surprised that her voice sounded instead like a tremulous, accusing whisper.

Charles stopped and faced her, his eyes cold. "Because he threatened me. I don't like being threatened."

"But to kill him . . . like that." Horror clutched at Star's throat at the memory. One minute the man had been alive, and the next . . . She could still see his body, the way it had jerked into the air then fallen, like a puppet whose strings had been suddenly cut. "If he wasn't any danger . . . If he was a tame Indian . . ."

Charles shrugged. "Even tame Indians can't be trusted. They're no better than animals, any of them. The sooner all the plains Indians are exterminated, the better, braves, squaws, and their brats."

"They're people, human beings," Star protested.

Charles's mouth twisted into a wolfish grin. "If you'd ever seen white women and children after the Comanches have finished with them, you'd know how far removed they are from human beings. The babies, the ones they don't raise as slaves, they amuse themselves with by tossing into the air and catching, still alive, on their lances. As for the women . . . Shall I tell you how they treat women captives?"

"No." Star shuddered. She cringed inwardly.

When he thrust a revolver into her hand and showed her how to load it, cock it, then shoot it, using the tree on the knoll as a target, she made no protest. Finally, after a dozen tries, she managed to hit the trunk of the tree. Charles nodded approvingly as he took back the gun and returned it to the holster at his waist. "That's not bad shooting for your first time," he said. "You've got a good eye for a woman."

The sun was no longer high in the sky, and glancing back toward the caravan, they could see signs of movement. "We'd better be getting back," Charles said. "The captain wants to make the narrows by nightfall."

They started toward the caravan, the tall grass opening and closing around them. Star asked hesitantly, "What did that Indian say to you—something about dragoons? Will the army be joining us soon?"

"No doubt," Charles said, his voice annoyed. "They'll probably try to stop us from crossing the Arkansas, although they have no right to poke their nose into caravan business. They seem to forget we're American citizens. They should be fighting the Mexicans, not harassing the traders."

"Charles," Star blurted, "did you know that Indian?"

She felt his grip on her arm tighten, as he whirled her around to face him. "What a ridiculous question," he said. "Of course I didn't know him." He gave her a short, impatient shake. "Forget about that damn Indian. No one will ever miss him. As a matter of fact, it'd be best if you didn't say anything to anyone in the caravan about the shooting." His voice took on a studied casualness. "No point in alarming the train."

When she didn't answer him at once, her eyes studying his face with a disconcerting directness, he glared irritably down at her. It was bad enough, the news that Red Shirt had brought him, that the army was still on the trail of the wagons carrying contraband to the enemy. It was even more awkward that Star should have been present at their meeting, especially when Red Shirt had had the gall to threaten to tell the train what was being carried in the Bradford wagons if he didn't get more money for his silence. Charles cursed his own stupidity in using Red Shirt as a necessary messenger between himself and Governor Armijo in setting up the arrangements for the transfer of the guns and ammunition to the Mexican army. It wasn't that the wagoners would be too upset by the killing of an Indian, but there were sure to be questions, and one of the men in the caravan might recognize Red Shirt as a sometimes scout for the Mexican army.

They had stopped by the stunted tree, and now he leaned his rifle against the trunk and gave his full attention to Star.

"Why so quiet, my sweet?" he asked lightly, but the amber-shaded eyes hardened as he looked down at her, even as he felt an unexpected stab of desire. The hardships of the trail had not dimmed her beauty, he decided. Her creamy skin had picked up a warm apricot undertone from the sun, and the simple calico gown she wore, without the confining stays beneath, only displayed more enticingly the temptingly unbound curves.

Charles frowned. It was the gray velvet eyes behind the dark lashes that annoyed him, their direct questioning stare, the unconscious defiance in the tilt of the pointed chin. He had thought that by now she had learned the futility of opposing him. He had, in fact, become a little bored with her, as he often became uninterested when his bedmates became too compliant, too submissive. It was the struggle, the forcing of his will upon another, that excited him, not the final surrender. Now he wondered suddenly if he could have been mistaken; that she had been only pretending to submit to him, that from somewhere she had drawn the strength to continue to resist him, not openly, of course, but secretly. The thought angered him, even as it made him more eager to possess her, and he demanded harshly, "Well, Star?"

Her voice, for all that it was little more than a whisper, was firm. "You . . . you murdered that Indian, Charles."

Furious, without thinking, his hand swept out and caught her full across the cheek, sending her bonnet flying off. She staggered and fell to the ground. Immediately he regretted his action. Not that she didn't deserve to be taught a lesson in obedience, but this wasn't the time or place. He could hardly return her to the camp with her face bruised. There were sure to be suspicions, gossip, and if he didn't manage to convince her to keep her mouth shut about Red Shirt, the questions could become even more pointed. He didn't dare take the risk. There was too much money at stake. Governor Armijo was prepared to pay a fortune in gold for the guns Charles had hidden beneath the floorboards of his wagons.

Reaching down, he helped Star to her feet, a boyishly apologetic smile quirking the corners of his mouth. "Forgive me, my sweet," he murmured repentantly. "It's just that, at times, you provoke me beyond endurance."

His lips caressed the red mark his blow had made on the pale skin by her mouth, while his hands moved with deliberate pressure over her breasts, reminding her of the pain those hands could inflict if he chose. She held herself stiffly within his grasp, not moving, hardly breathing, as he continued coaxingly, "It isn't as if I'm asking you to lie. Just don't volunteer any information about the shooting." His voice took on a veneer of tenderness. "I realize it hasn't been easy for you, a gently reared young woman, becoming accustomed to the hardships of trail life and to marriage at the same time. Perhaps I've been...overzealous in showing my desire for you. Suppose for a while I forego my, my conjugal rights, give you a chance to forget about Red Shirt."

For a moment Star wasn't sure she understood his meaning, and then she grasped eagerly at the bait he dangled before her, as understanding, like a subtle unspoken blackmail, passed between them.

"It's agreed, then," Charles said, watching the relief flooding her face. He would make her pay for that look, he decided coldly, for pushing him into a corner so that he was forced to bargain with her. But his smile, as always, was charming as he picked up her bonnet and handed it to her. "Put your veil down, sweetheart. You don't want your face to get sunburned."

Quickly she tied the ribbons of the bonnet under her chin, pulled the silken veil over her face. She was not any more eager than Charles for the men in camp to see the telltale bruise she was sure was already discoloring her face.

When they reached the camp, the captain was calling, "St-tretch out. Stretch out!" The lines of wagons, double file, had already formed.

Charles went off to make sure the Bradford wagons were ready while Star climbed into the Rockaway. Mario watched her anxiously. "The *señora*, she is all right?" he asked. "I was beginning to worry. It is not safe to roam too far from the train."

Star glanced back to the knoll where the grass waved gently over the body of the dead Indian. With an almost physical effort she forced herself to speak over the guilt, like a stone, in her throat. "I'm fine, Mario. I'm sorry if I worried you."

But the stone was still there in her throat later that evening as she lay in bed in the tent, waiting for Charles. Suppose he hadn't meant what he said? Suppose he would still insist upon—what had he called them—his "conjugal rights"? The words tasted bitter in her mouth, as bitter as the guilty knowledge she tried to push to the back of her mind. She had witnessed a murder and had not spoken out. Because of her, the Indian's body would lie unburied, rotting away till it became like the bleached and brittle bones of the dead oxen that littered the ground alongside the trail. Surely even a savage like Red Shirt deserved a proper burial, she thought, and then, startled, sat upright in bed.

Red Shirt. That was what Charles had called the Indian, she realized belatedly. So Charles had lied. He did know the Indian he had murdered. Why? What was Charles involved in that he would resort to murder, even go so far as to bribe her to keep her silent? She was sure doing so had infuriated Charles, for in a small way she had bested him. Yet whatever lay between him and Red Shirt had been important enough for him to temporarily need her silence. For how long? she wondered. How long before he no longer needed her cooperation? She lay back, pulling the coverlet over her, feeling suddenly chill even though it was a still, warm night.

The next few days, though, as the train lurched forward, plodding its way across the prairie, Charles made no move toward her when they were alone in the tent, and, in fact, seemed to spend most of his evenings away from the tent. She relaxed and grew less fearful.

The stream before Council Grove was flooded, and it took most of the day before the overloaded wagons were able to make the crossing, the bullwhackers using their goads and whips as the frightened, straining oxen struggled to reach the far bank. It was late afternoon before the last wagon reached the camp in a small forest of trees stretching on either side of Council Grove Creek. Other freight companies had arrived earlier and men were already hard at work, repairing wagons and cutting the ash and walnut and oak trees, the trees toppling with a crash that made Star cover her ears.

Ben, stopping by after supper at the Bradford tent, explained to Star that the cut timber would be tied beneath the wagons, to be used during the rest of the journey when lumber to repair broken wagons would be scarce as hen's teeth. Star was sitting alone by the fire, and at Ben's unspoken question, she said, "Mr. Bradford heard that Mr. Bent has joined the train briefly before going on to the fort. He wanted to find out if he had any news of the war."

She wondered, a little embarrassed, if Ben had noticed how often Charles Bradford left his bride alone. But if so, Ben gave no hint as he hunkered down companionably beside the fire. "Damn fool thing, this war," he said thoughtfully. "Now that we're in it, though, we'll have to win. The French and the Limeys are hoping Jimmy Polk will take a good licking and then they'll move into California and Texas, and we can't have that." He grunted contemptuously. "Was thinking of joining up myself back in Missouri, but the soldier boys I saw were a pitiful lot. They think it's going to be a picnic, just waltz into Mexico. Be lucky if the wolves and vultures don't make a feast on their bones before half of them ever reach Santa Fe."

Star frowned, trying to remember. Hadn't someone else said much the same thing to her? Michael Kelly's face suddenly flashed into her mind, that afternoon she had last seen him watching the volunteers parade in St. Louis. Strange, she hadn't thought of the man in weeks and yet his face was suddenly as clear before her as if it had happened only yesterday, the dark, almost reddish-tanned skin that made the white scar stand out in bold relief, the unusual greenish-black eyes, undoubtedly an inheritance from his American father while the flat-planed cheek bones, the long, sensuous mouth, and aquiline nose, from what Mexican or Indian ancestor had they come?

But thinking of Mr. Kelly reminded her of that night in the Kirkland garden, the memory of that mouth covering hers and the excitement she had felt drumming in her veins, the abandoned way she had responded to that kiss. Well, she wasn't that silly young girl in a ball gown any longer, Star thought coldly. She had learned only too well to what pain and humiliation that delicious excitement led, the cruel trick that nature played upon women, snaring them with a man's caresses.

Deliberately she thrust all memory of Michael Kelly from her mind and turned to look at a large mound not far from the hill where the Bradford tent was pitched. "There must be a beautiful view from up there," she said wistfully. "Would it be safe for me to climb, do you think, Ben?"

"Don't see why not. No fear of Indians here at the Grove."

Making her way cautiously, Star found the climb was not as easy as she had thought, but once she reached the top, the view was well worth the effort. With the wind whipping at her hair and skirt, she felt as if she were standing braced on the brow of a ship. The sun was beginning to set and the horizon was streaked with pink and mauve and gold, while to the west, as far as her eye could see, the tall grass stretched like a billowing sea. For the first time, though, as the last rays of the sun filled the land with an iridescent glow, Star felt a sadness tug at her heart, the feeling that such beauty should be shared, not enjoyed alone.

As she returned down the hill, it had already grown dark. She could see the tiny flames from the camp fires scattered throughout the camp, leaving the outer edges in darkness. She hesitated a moment, feeling foolish as she tried to recall: was the Bradford tent to the left or the right? In the shadows all the wagons looked the same, looming ghostly white in the darkness. Then she saw the shadowy figure of a man standing alone, outlined by firelight, not far from where she stood. Rather than wander aimlessly, she decided to ask directions. As she approached the man, she saw he had his back toward her and was gazing out across the landscape, as if he were savoring the tranquil beauty of the evening as she had been.

She had almost reached the man when to her shock, and before she could utter a sound, he had swung around with a pantherlike swiftness. And she saw the knife, stiletto thin, flashing silver in the night, stabbing downward at her.

Chapter Seven

For a heart-stopping moment, Star imagined she felt the knife tearing into the softness of her flesh, so close its deadly point came to her body, before an explosion of angry sound battered at her ears.

"Damn it! Haven't you more sense than to come up behind a man that way?"

She looked up, stunned, into the scarred face and furious dark green eyes of Michael Kelly. At first, she felt a sense of incredulity: how could he be here, suddenly materialized, in the middle of the prairie? Following closely was an even more shocking thought. He meant to kill her. And as the knowledge swept over her, the realization that that was exactly what had almost happened, she felt her knees grow weak and the ground dip beneath her feet.

She heard his voice, as if from a distance, less angry now but still crackling with annoyance. "Here—you're not going to faint, are you?"

"I never faint," she protested, and although she felt oddly light-headed, she did not lose consciousness. She was well aware of arms lifting her as effortlessly as if she were a sack of feathers, of being carried, held close against a jacket of some buttery-soft leathery material. The feel of the hard muscles beneath the jacket reminded her of that other time in the Kirkland garden when she had been pinioned helplessly in this man's arms. Only this time, the arms were gentle and oddly comforting.

Then she was being sat down on a log beside the fire and her hands were being rubbed so roughly that the skin burned.

Irritably she pulled her hands away and, taking a deep, ragged breath, glared up at the man.

"That's better," he said cheerfully. "The color's back in your face." The dark green eyes that looked black in the firelight held a glint of amusement as he said, "You really should break that dangerous habit of yours of sneaking up behind a man."

"I wasn't sneaking!" she sputtered indignantly. "Why, you might have killed me!"

"I might have," he agreed equably. "Except at the last moment I caught your scent."

Scent? Star frowned. "I'm not wearing perfume," she protested.

A mocking smile suddenly twisted the man's mouth. "Oh, but you do have a scent. I remember yours very well." One black eyebrow slanted amused. "Shall I describe yours to you?"

Star felt her face grow warm. "No," she said quickly. She was sure this wasn't a proper conversation between a gentleman and a lady. Then, crossly, "You could at least apologize. You scared me half to death."

"I do apologize for frightening you, Mrs. Bradford." He put one foot on the log and stared down at her, his voice all at once flat, his face impassive. "My only defense is that, in this country, a man has to develop a fine instinct for survival. When someone comes at you from behind, the way you did, you learn to attack first and ask questions later. Or you don't survive."

Yes, Star thought, feeling a shiver like ice water trickling down her spine as she gazed up into that impassive face. She could imagine only too vividly this man thrusting that wicked knife into another man without a second thought, with an animal's instinctive reflex.

She laughed a little nervously. "Now you are frightening me, Mr. Kelly."

"You should be frightened, Mrs. Bradford," he said. "Your husband is *loco*, bringing a woman down the trail at any time. In the middle of a war, it's sheer insanity." His gaze roamed over the pale, delicate beauty of the face lifted to him, and that fleeting mocking look once again touched the dark jade eyes as he drawled, "Not that I don't understand his reluctance to leave you behind. Nights can grow chill on the trail."

Star jerked to her feet, her chin lifting haughtily, as she said coldly, "It's none of your business, Mr. Kelly, whether or not I choose to accompany my husband."

She was right, of course, Michael thought. It wasn't his concern if Charles Bradford was fool enough to place his wife's life in danger. And remembering Mrs. Bradford's flirtatious nature before her marriage, perhaps her husband was wise in not leaving his new bride alone for a year in St. Louis, Michael decided cynically. No doubt a beautiful woman like Star Bradford wouldn't be alone for long. Once more the dark gaze traveled with a lazy insolence over the slender woman standing before him, the red hair catching the firelight, the eyes shimmering, silver-gray with anger. If anything Star Bradford was more lovely than he remembered, with an innate elegance and grace that not even the simple cotton gown could hide. There was something different about her, though, Michael sensed, a stiffness, a wariness that had not been there before. And that almost childlike, naive look was gone from the gray eyes. But Michael had always considered innocence in a woman vastly overrated. His eyes narrowed contemplatively as he studied the sweet, long curve of Star's mouth, remembering how those lips had felt beneath his, the passionate warmth responding to him with a joyous, reckless abandon.

He hadn't much wanted to take the Cordoba wagons to Santa Fe this trip, hoping to turn the job over to his half brother, Esteban. But with the unsettled conditions in Mexico, his grandmother had wanted to keep Esteban close to the rancho. Now Michael grinned wickedly and decided the trip might turn out to be interesting after all.

Feeling vaguely uneasy beneath that speculative, too searching, gaze, Star swung away. "If you'll excuse me, Mr. Kelly," she murmured.

He caught her arm before she could step outside the ring of firelight. "I'll escort you back to your camp, Mrs. Bradford," he said smoothly, falling into step beside her. "I haven't had the opportunity yet to wish you happiness in your new marriage. A whirlwind romance, wasn't it?" The mocking note was there again beneath the surface politeness. "I must admit I was surprised to hear the news when I passed through Independence. I saw your father the morning I left St. Louis, and he never said a word about the happy nuptials."

He felt his companion stumble, and his hand tightened on her arm. "You know papa?" she asked.

"A business acquaintanceship," he said. He found himself remembering the bleak desolation he had seen in William McFarland's face the morning he had run into him on the levee in St. Louis. Michael had thought the man was ill, he seemed so gray and drained. Now he wondered if McFarland had been checking the steamboat offices and had learned that he was too late to stop his daughter, that she was already on a boat bound for Independence and her lover. Michael glanced at the girl beside him curiously. Did she care at all, he wondered, what a devastating blow her impulsive elopement had been to her father?

"The news of your marriage must have been quite a shock to Mr. Donley," he added deliberately.

Star felt a quick, painful stab of guilt, realizing she hadn't even thought once in the past weeks about Robert or how he must have felt when he heard of her marriage. Still, she wasn't about to give Michael Kelly the satisfaction of knowing how accurately his words had hit home. If nothing else, she thought wryly, her marriage to Charles had taught her how to hide her feelings. "No doubt Mr. Donley will recover," she replied shortly.

"No doubt," Michael agreed. What a cool little baggage she was, he thought, recalling the devotion he had glimpsed in Robert Donley's hopelessly open face when he had looked at Star. There probably wasn't an honest feeling in her whole soft, seductive body, he thought grimly.

They had reached the Bradford camp, and Star saw that Charles had returned and was standing by the fire, along with another gentleman. When Charles saw Star with Michael Kelly, he scowled. "Where have you been, Star? I brought Colonel Owens back to our camp to see you."

Star's quiver of alarm at the anger in Charles's face was forgotten in her delight in meeting Colonel Samuel Owens again. The trader was a friend of her father's from his early Santa Fe trail days and had visited their home in St. Louis. "I didn't know your wagons would be joining our caravan, Colonel," she said eagerly. "It's so good to see you again."

The colonel, gray haired and courtly, unobtrusively studied Star's face as he pressed her hand. How had it happened, he wondered, surprisedly, that William McFarland had permitted his daughter to marry Charles Bradford, much less allowed her to take a hazardous trip like this one to Santa Fe? But the colonel was too discreet to ask embarrassing questions. He smiled at the girl. "It's my pleasure. A caravan isn't often graced with a woman's presence."

Then over Star's shoulder he saw the man standing quietly beside her, and his smile widened. "Don Miguel, it's good to see you. I'd heard the Cordoba wagons were joining our caravan, but I expected Esteban."

Michael shrugged ruefully. "Doña Isobel decided to keep my brother close to the *rancho*. I think she's afraid he'll join the Lancers if she lets him out of her sight." He spread his hands with a grin. "And you know my grandmother when she makes up her mind about anything."

Colonel Owens chuckled. "A most charming woman, Doña Isobel, but formidable," he agreed. And then somberly, "She's right to keep an eye on Esteban. This war, I'm afraid, will bring sadness to many families, Mexican and American, before it's finished."

"Is there any news?" Michael asked of the older man.

Colonel Owens shook his head. "Only what you probably already know. General Taylor and his men have crossed the river into Matamoras and are awaiting supplies and reinforcements before proceeding south, while Kearny and Doniphan have already left Fort Leavenworth with their dragoons for Fort Bent. No doubt we will be running into their advance patrols before too long."

Charles had crossed over to Star and, before she could move, slipped an arm around her waist, drawing her hard against his side so that the gun he always wore beneath his broadcloth coat jabbed cruelly into her flesh. His hand rested against the soft cotton material of her gown, and the fingers splayed, moving slowly, caressingly. Star felt a warmth rise in her cheeks. She did not have to see the triumphant spite glittering in Charles's eyes as he stared at Michael Kelly to know that his behavior was deliberate, to embarrass her and flaunt his possession over her at the same time. Yet without making a scene which would only humiliate her more, there was nothing she could do but endure the caress and pretend to listen with suitable wifely devotion, as Charles snapped irritably, "I don't see why the army should bother us. The war will be over long before we reach Santa Fe."

"If the caravan reaches Santa Fe," Michael said.

"What do you mean?" Star asked, startled, forgetting that it wasn't her place to thrust herself into a men's conversation, into matters that did not concern her.

She felt Charles's arm tighten around her annoyed, but Michael answered thoughtfully. "Kearny's dragoons will be stretched out along the Arkansas with orders to stop the wagons from crossing. And even if we're allowed to cross, there's the mountain passes between Bent's Fort and Santa Fe. A company of General Armijo's lancers could hold Raton Pass or Apache Canyon against Kearny's whole army."

Charles laughed jeeringly. "Armijo? That fat coward will never fight. The greasers will turn and run before a shot is fired."

Star felt her breath catch in her throat as she watched Michael's face go dangerously still, the eyes narrowing to icy slits. She remembered how rapidly that lean, long-muscled body could move, and she was sure Michael Kelly wore a gun strapped at his hip the same as her husband did. Then, for a split second, that narrowed gaze moved to Star, pulled so close to her husband that she could not help but be directly in any line of fire. And although the dark green eyes did not lose their deadly coldness, she sensed the tension in Michael letting go, a smile twisting the long, sensuous mouth as he shrugged and said, "General Armijo is a corrupt buffoon, but his second in command, Diego Archuleto, is not a man to turn away from a fight."

"If you think so highly of your Mexican compatriots, Mr. Kelly," Charles said disdainfully, "I'm surprised you haven't joined their army."

Michael flashed a smile toward Star, a smile that did not touch the icy fury in his eyes. "As I explained to your charming wife, Mr. Bradford, I'm a businessman, like yourself, not a soldier." Then, his smile thinning, "I assume, Mr. Bradford, that that is why you haven't joined the army."

Colonel Owens had been frowning uneasily during the interchange between the two men. Now he stepped forward quickly. "I'm sure Mr. Bradford meant to cast no disrespect on your patriotism, Don Miguel. As you know, my own wife is of Spanish descent but my first loyalty, like yours, is to the United States." He glanced toward Star. "And all this talk of war and fighting must be distressing to Mrs. Bradford."

Star picked up her cue eagerly, managing to pull free of Charles's grasp as she murmured, "Yes, if you will excuse me. It's late, and I am tired." She gave the colonel a grateful smile. "I saw some gooseberries growing along the creekbed, Colonel Owens. If you'll join us for dinner tomorrow evening, perhaps I can arrange somehow to bake a pie for you."

"It will be my pleasure," he said, bowing gallantly.

Once within the tent, Star stood still for several seconds, her heart racing, trying to push from her mind those disquieting seconds when she suspected Charles and herself had been just a hairsbreadth from death. Except, she thought wryly as she undressed for bed, hadn't Charles been counting on the fact that Michael Kelly wouldn't draw on him, not with a woman standing so close?

As she slipped beneath the mosquito netting and into bed, she had a harder time forcing herself not to think about the fact of Michael Kelly's joining the caravan. It was difficult enough, Star thought, being a woman in a man's world, of pretending oblivion to the constant, shocking obscenities the wagoners yelled at the oxen and mules, of ignoring the furtive, lustful glances cast her way when she walked by. It would be twice as difficult knowing that Michael Kelly was in the company, that amused, too probing glance following her, and remembering those moments when his mouth and arms had held her captive.

She was asleep when Charles returned to the tent, but his thrashing around in the dark before he found and lit the lamp, his mumbled curses as he stumbled over a stool, awoke her immediately, although she kept her eyes tightly shut, feigning sleep.

Then she felt the lamplight warm on her face as Charles

jerked the mosquito netting aside, his hand on her shoulder pulling her erect in the bed. Her hair tumbled around her shoulders as he shook her violently, his face flushed, his voice slurred and ugly with drink. "Don't pretend you were sleeping," he snarled. "I know better. Did you think you could come strolling into camp with that half-breed and I wouldn't suspect anything? I saw the way he looked at you. What were you and that breed doing out there in the dark?"

"Nothing!" Star gasped, trying to break free of the hand shaking her so that she felt as if her neck would snap. "Nothing, Charles, I swear."

"You're lying." Charles's voice was suddenly softly menacing.

"No. No, I'm not." Star could feel the terror like a nausea spreading in the pit of her stomach, making her voice quaver. She despised the weakness in herself that turned her into a coward when Charles looked at her with that predatory gleam in his amber eyes.

The hand released her so abruptly that she fell back limply against the pillows. Charles peered down at her, lifting the lamp so that the light fell full upon her face. "Are you sure? He's never touched you?"

Unbidden, those moments in the Kirkland garden with Michael Kelly slipped into Star's consciousness, and a heat leaped into her face before she could avert her eyes from her husband.

Charles's smile stretched tightly over straight white teeth; his eyes glittered like bits of glass in the lamplight. "Shall I make you tell me the truth?" he asked, his breath coming more quickly. His gaze roved slowly, deliberately over her body. "You know I can, don't you?"

She felt a faint flicker of rage deep inside of her, but the anger was too faint, too hidden beneath the craven fear. He was right, she knew. She couldn't hold out against him, and she cried, despairingly, "Once. It was only once he kissed me."

Charles stiffened, his voice curiously toneless. "I'll kill the bastard."

"You can't," she said, shocked. "You mustn't try. You know his reputation with a gun!"

Charles shrugged, a blond lock of hair falling across his forehead adding to the look of boyish charm, the charm that she had fallen in love with and that, at odd moments, before she remembered, could still catch her unawares. "You needn't worry, my pet. You didn't really think I'd lower myself to fighting a duel with a half-breed. Oh, I'll kill the dirty greaser all right, but I'll pick the time and place."

He smiled tauntingly. "Or is it me you're worried about, not your lover?"

"He's not my lover."

The amber eyes flicked across her body, saw the trembling begin beneath that pale luminous white skin, and knew, suddenly furious, that it was not an answering quiver of passion he had aroused. If he took her now, the silvery gray eyes would gaze up at him like twin ice-glazed pools, with no warmth in them at all. Just as her body, so trembling and alive to the touch, would hold no warmth for him. All her movements beneath him would be wooden, her face still and closed to him, as if in some maddening way he didn't exist for her at all.

Damn her, he thought aggrieved. How dare she look the way she did, with her hair like flame, those pale, perfectly formed breasts, the temptress incarnate. He remembered the way she had chased after him from the moment they had met, as if she couldn't wait to get him into bed. And then to cheat him this way, behave like some sort of frozen goddess, barely enduring his touch.

Anger pounded in his temples and he wanted to hurt her, not physically, but in another, more special way. "You might as well forget about Kelly," he said, his voice malicious. "Everybody knows about his mistress in Santa Fe. They call her Señora de las Flores. She made her fortune with her monte games and runs the fanciest gambling establishment in the town. She'll put a knife into any woman who looks at Kelly the wrong way." His smile traveled coldly, insultingly over Star. "Not that the *señora* has to worry about you, my pet. From what I hear, the Señora de las Flores is a real woman, who knows how to warm a man's bed. She's not a half woman like you, cold and empty inside with nothing to give."

"That's not true," she whispered, but he saw her wince, the gray eyes darkening, and knew triumphantly he had hit a vulnerable spot, leaving another bruise, an invisible one this time, but just as painful and much more long-lasting.

"Isn't it?" he asked coldly, putting down the lantern and moving away from the bed.

"Where . . . where are you going?"

He didn't bother answering, the tent flap closing behind him. It was a warm, muggy evening, promising rain. But lying in the bed, Star pulled the coverlet over her, feeling all at once chilled to the bone.

The third morning after their arrival at Council Grove, the caravan rolled out of camp. There were over sixty wagons now, and the wagons traveled four abreast, with outriders ranging on either side and ahead watching carefully for Indian signs.

Star's carriage had been placed in the forefront of the company to avoid the dust the caravan raised. As the cry of "Stretch out" echoed up and down the line, she recognized the man riding ahead of the carriage. Mr. Kelly was riding a rangy mustang with oddly split ears, and his carbine rested across a plain leather working saddle.

Mario held the carriage door open for her. Following Star's gaze, his voice dropped to a hushed, respectful whisper. "The scar on Don Miguel's face, señora, did you notice? The Comanches put it there. He was kidnapped as a niño from his family's rancho. It is said that when his family ransomed him, he was more Comanche than white and had to be tied to his horse and dragged home."

Remembering the snakelike quickness with which the knife had appeared in Mr. Kelly's hand when he attacked her, the unnerving blankness in the man's face across the fire from Charles's last night, Star could readily believe that Mr. Kelly was part savage. Then she remembered what Charles had told her about Mr. Kelly's woman in Santa Fe, la Señora de las Flores, and she scowled irritably at Mario and snapped, "I'm not interested in hearing about Mr. Kelly's childhood, Mario."

Then she climbed into the carriage, and tried to adjust her body to the most comfortable position. But no matter how carefully Mario drove, the carriage wheels seemed to find every rock and rut in what passed for a road.

The next week the caravan crawled at a snail's pace from Diamond Spring to Lost Spring, Cottonwood Creek to Turkey Creek, for the day after the caravan left Council Grove, it began to rain and never ceased. Star went to sleep each night with the sound of rain beating at the canvas tent and awoke each morning with the tent floor a quagmire of mud as she struggled to dress in the chill damp. The oxen inched laboriously forward under threat of whip and prod, dragging the wagons through mud that was often hub deep.

When the rain finally stopped, it was replaced by a yellow-bright sun laying a stifling blanket of heat over the wagons. Streams dried up almost overnight, making crossings easier, but water scarce, for man and beast. At last the caravan reached the big bend of the Arkansas River, and the landscape changed. Now the tall grass and the prairie was behind them. This was the start of the great plains, with the short, greenish-gray grass matted like vines beneath Star's feet. And everywhere the ground was scooped into shallow saucers, filled with water and edged with golden coreopsis and scarlet mallow.

"Buffalo wallows, ma'am," Ben said, when the caravan nooned it one day near Pawnee Fork and she asked him about the curious depressions. "Did you hear the wolves last night?" he asked. "We're in buffalo country now." He nodded at a group of men who, as soon as the wagons had formed into a corral, had gathered up their horses, reloaded their weapons, and, like a bunch of schoolboys, were shouting and laughing as they rode out of camp. "Hope they get us some buffalo meat," Ben said, grinning. "No better eating than buffalo tongue."

Star saw that Michael Kelly was one of the buffalo hunters. He was riding his wiry mustang without a saddle and bridle, using only a halter knotted about the lower jaw of the horse. A lariat was tied about the horse's neck and looped about the man's waist, the slack coiled and tucked up under his belt. With a handkerchief tied around his head, his dark brown face, and the effortless way he rode, using only his knees to control the horse, Star suddenly saw in the man the boy who had lived and hunted with the Comanches.

Although he must have seen Star as he rode by, he gave no sign of noticing her, any more than he had in camp after their first encounter at Council Grove. He seemed in fact to go out of his way to avoid her. When their paths did cross accidentally, the mocking look was there in his eyes, making her feel vaguely uncomfortable although he was always punctiliously polite. Not that she cared whether he liked her or not, Star decided irritably.

She saw that Ben was watching her curiously, and realized she had been staring at Mr. Kelly. She quickly removed her gaze from the buffalo hunters but couldn't resist asking, "Is it true what Mario told me, that Mr. Kelly lived with the Comanches?"

"Yes, ma'am, it's true enough. He was one of the lucky ones. Most of the children captives don't live to be ransomed but some, like Don Miguel, who get adopted into the tribe, take a real liking to the life. Not that it's such a bad life," he said thoughtfully.

"How terrible for Don Miguel's family."

Ben nodded. "It took his grandmother two years to find the boy and get him back. Stubborn old lady, from all accounts, and proud, too, like most of the *criollos.*"

"*Criollos?*"

"Someone of Spanish descent but born in Mexico," Ben explained. "They can be very wealthy like the Cordoba family, but they don't set as high in the government and society as a *gachupin,* who has pure Spanish blood and was actually born in Spain. Don Miguel is a *criollo,* too, through his mother. Rightly his name is Michael Roberto Kelly y Cordoba." He smiled faintly at Star's bewilderment. "It's a funny habit they have in Mexico, tagging a mother's maiden name after the father's name."

Star glanced at her young driver. "And Mario? Is he a *criollo,* too?"

Ben shook his head. "Mario's a *mestizo,* a mixture of Mexican and Indian blood, a much lower step on the ladder. And at the bottom of the heap are the Indians. Those the Conquistadores didn't kill, they put to working in their fields or down their silver mines. Most of them are still peons today, in debt to their masters from their father and father before them, so that they can never get free." He added wryly, "Of course, the church is still the greatest power in Mexico. She owns half of the land and wealth, and the top church officials live like kings, in their own palaces."

"When we win the war, such injustices will surely end," Star said, appalled.

"Perhaps," Ben said, frowning, his voice dubious. It was his experience that change came slowly, if ever, to Mexico, where life was lived in the same way it had been for centuries.

He saw that Mrs. Bradford's gaze had turned back to the horsemen, now almost out of sight, disappearing into a swell of the plains. Ben's frown deepened. He hadn't been standing too far from the Bradford campfire when Mrs. Bradford had returned to her tent on Michael Kelly's arm. He had watched the two men square off, Don Miguel's hand hovering too close to his gun for Ben's peace of mind. He had seen the looks on the faces of the two men, like two rams butting horns in the rutting season, and knew it wasn't any insult that Bradford was throwing that had gotten under Don Miguel's skin. It was the woman who stood beside him now, with those wide, artless gray eyes and flaming red hair.

Ben's gaze fastened uneasily on Star's face, and his voice roughened, unusual for him, as he said, "Kiowa and Comanche like to camp around here. Saw some signs yesterday. Best stay close to your tent."

"Yes." Star's gaze was still on the horizon, so she did not see the worried look in Ben's eyes and would not have understood it if she had, or the hidden warning in his words.

A bleached heavy white skull lay near a buffalo wallow, and she studied it as her gaze drifted back to the camp. These weren't the first bones Star had seen littered along the trail— buffalo, no doubt, or some unfortunate ox that had wandered off from a caravan, sickened, and died. But it could as easily have been the bones of an Indian or white man. She shivered, hugging her arms to her. It was so beautiful, so peaceful, the plains stretching to the horizon, the splash of colorful wild flowers against the short grass like a patchwork. And yet underneath the beauty, she could sense . . . a danger, a loneliness.

"It makes me feel as if we're the only people on the face of the earth," she murmured.

"Not for long, ma'am," Ben said, pointing to a dust cloud hanging just above the earth, in the distance.

"Indians?" Star asked, frightened.

Ben spat into the earth, his voice disgusted. "Soldier boys, more likely. The army's catching up with us, heading for Fort Bent."

By the time the caravan reached Pawnee Rock, a huge mound towering suddenly out of the plains around it, Stephen Watts Kearny's Army of the West was already sprawled around the base of the rock. The tents were arranged in no apparent order, and the soldiers, unshaven, unwashed, their faces drawn with exhaustion, groaned loudly at blistered feet worn raw, at legs swollen from the long march from Fort Leavenworth. They complained about packs that were too heavy to be useful, clothes too warm for the climate, officers who knew even less about soldiering than they did. The noisy sounds from the army encampment, the hollering and roughhousing, reached even Star's tent as she prepared for bed.

It was a warm night and she was still in her chemise, wishing regretfully that she didn't have to put on a nightgown, when Theresa came into the tent. The maid had brought a pitcher of cool water for bathing, a luxury on the trail. As Theresa made up the bed for the night, Star studied the young woman covertly. She had given up trying to make friends with the maid. It was impossible to break through Theresa's sullen reserve.

Star slipped the chemise off her shoulders and began to bathe her neck and breasts with the cool water. She noticed that Theresa, too, was wearing less than usual, a gown scooped disgracefully low in the front and back, a scarf over her shoulders not completely covering the burnished mahogany skin of back and breasts.

Star wondered if she should scold the girl for displaying herself so scandalously, especially with the soldiers' camp nearby. Then the maid leaned forward to spread the counterpane over the bed, and the scarf fell away from her back.

Speechless with shock, Star stared at the ugly scars crisscrossing the girl's otherwise unblemished skin, finally gasping indignantly. "Theresa! Your back! Who did that to you?"

The girl straightened, gave her mistress a long, amused glance, shrugged, and returned to making the bed.

"Theresa, I demand to know—" Star fell abruptly silent. For a moment she was assaulted by the same sensation of painful shock she had felt when she had stepped out among a cloud of buffalo gnats. Charles, she thought dully. Of course: Charles. Those nights when he had left her bed, and she had been too happy to have him leave to care or wonder where he had gone. And Theresa's Dearborn wagon where she slept, always placed conveniently near the Bradford tent but out of earshot, removed from the other wagons so Charles could come and go with impunity to his mistress, with no one knowing, no one guessing.

Anger was a hard knot in Star's stomach, the acrid taste of fury in her mouth as she gazed at that tortured flesh. It was bad enough, what passed between Charles and her. But she was his wife. She had freely, if stupidly, gone into marriage. How dare he inflict his cruelties upon a slave girl, unable to protect herself?

"I'll speak to . . . to Mr. Bradford, Theresa," she said stiffly. "I'll make him stop."

The amusement slipped away from the black eyes. The look Theresa gave her mistress was part scorn, part anger, her voice fairly spitting contempt. "You think you can stop him from coming to my bed? You! He told me how you are with him, like a lump of ice. I give him what he wants, what I want." The dark face became venomous, reminding Star all at once of the head of a rattlesnake, lifting its head to strike. "You try and keep him from my bed and you'll be sorry."

"That's enough, Theresa. *Vamos!*"

Unnoticed, Charles had come into the tent. His face was mottled with anger and he jerked his finger toward the tent flap. Theresa shrugged imperceptibly but left immediately, giving Star a smug half-smile as she glided past her.

Charles turned to Star. The anger was replaced by a look of boyish confusion as he grinned, abashed. "Sorry about that, Star. But then you were bound to find out sooner or later, weren't you?"

"What . . . what are you going to do?"

"Do?" The grin wavered and an impatient look crept into the golden eyes. "Nothing, of course. What should I do?"

"Get rid of her! I won't have her here in camp."

Charles scowled. "You're being ridiculous, Star. I can hardly turn the girl out in the middle of the trail."

"There are laundresses with the army camp," Star said. "She can find a job there."

"Perhaps," Charles said indifferently, unstrapping his gun-belt and throwing it on the bed. "But I don't choose for Theresa to leave the caravan." His eyes glinted coldly. "You need a maid, and let's just say I enjoy her company."

"No!" Star blurted. "I won't allow it."

"You won't allow," Charles said tauntingly, his gaze following the gentle slope of her shoulders, the soft outlines of her body clearly revealed beneath the thin chemise. He smiled as he began to walk slowly toward her, his amber eyes softly gleaming in anticipation. "It's time you learned, once and for all, who gives the orders around here, my pet."

Star gazed as if hypnotized at that charming, smiling face, and then suddenly, like a dam breaking inside of her, all the anger she had felt earlier, looking at Theresa's scarred flesh, swept back over her. She was filled with a blinding rage so that there was no room left for the fear, the abject terror that usually gripped her under Charles's threats.

No! The word screamed, an explosion in her head. Not again. Never again.

Almost without realizing she was doing it, she took a quick step toward the bed and picked up Charles's revolver. She was surprised at how steady her hand was as she lifted the gun and pointed it at her husband, how calm, almost dispassionate, her voice. "Stay where you are, Charles. Don't come any closer."

He stopped abruptly, his face a mixture of anger and, as he gazed at the gun, disbelief. Almost hesitantly, he took another step toward her.

She cocked the gun. Its click sounded like a thunderclap in the stillness of the tent. "You taught me how to use the gun," she said quietly. "Even I can't miss at this range."

For a second longer, Charles hesitated. Then a scratching at the tent flap, announcing a visitor, jerked both their heads toward the opening. Charles moved to the flap and lifted it. Dutch stood at the entrance, his small eyes shifting curiously from Star with the gun, back to Charles. Then he spoke swiftly to Charles in an undertone. Charles nodded. "I'll be right with you."

He turned back to Star, and she saw that his face held a mixture of fury and fear. "Stay in the tent," he snapped. "Colonel Moore and his soldiers are in camp. We'll settle this later."

For a long moment after Charles left, Star stood quite still, the gun in her outstretched hand. Now that it was over, she began to shake. Not in fear. Never in fear of Charles again, she thought, vaguely startled. It was as if she had crossed another invisible line, taken a last, necessary step on a journey that had started in the tent outside of Independence. Almost gingerly, as if testing her newly discovered courage, she realized that if she felt anything toward Charles, it was hatred and outrage at his having discussed her, his wife, while in bed with his mistress. How dare he? Her hand tightened furiously on the gun. I wish I had killed him, she thought, and then was shocked at her own wickedness.

She changed into her nightclothes and robe, curling up at the far side of the bed. What would happen when Charles returned, she wondered. Well, she would cross that bridge when she came to it, she decided wearily. What mattered was that she knew she would never allow him to touch her again, Charles or any other man. She would leave him, she thought, before she would let him hurt her again, in any way. Perhaps Colonel Owens would help her, she thought, except he would no doubt insist upon her returning to St. Louis, to her father. And her pride could not bear that, even if her father would take her back.

She was so wrapped up in her own problems, at first she hardly heard the commotion in the camp, men shouting, the sound of horses pounding through the camp. Had some of the oxen broken free? she wondered. Was that why Dutch had fetched Charles? Then she forgot the noise, as she returned again to her own dilemma, worrying at her problems, trying to find some solution, until, exhausted, she fell asleep.

She awoke early the next morning. She knew the camp was staying on at Pawnee Rock for several days, awaiting word from the army as to whether or not they could proceed on to Santa Fe, so there was no need for her to stir before the crack of dawn as she usually did on the trail.

Theresa hadn't brought her any water or laid out her clothes, she noticed as she dressed quickly. She twisted her hair in a coil, its weight warm against the nape of her neck, her dress already sticking to her. It was going to be another blistering hot day, she thought.

She noticed that Charles's side of the bed had not been slept in. Had he spent the night in the Dearborn with Theresa, she wondered indifferently, no longer caring, wondering why she had ever cared.

"Mrs. Bradford."

It was Colonel Owens's voice outside the tent. "Are you awake? I have to speak to you, please." His voice sounded strained.

Curious, she lifted the tent flap, stepped outside, and discovered that the colonel was not alone. Ben Malone stood to one side of him, and an army officer she didn't recognize. At the end of the circle stood Michael Kelly. For a change, his gaze, resting on her, held not a hint of mockery. She wondered about that briefly before she turned her attention upon Colonel Owens. "There's something wrong." It was not a question but a statement of fact. And then, without knowing how she knew: "It's Charles, isn't it?"

The colonel took both her hands in his and pressed hard. "You must be brave, my child. I'm sorry to be the one to tell you, but last night, Colonel Moore"—he nodded toward the officer—"came to the camp with instructions to check the wagons for contraband, military supplies being shipped illegally to General Armijo in Mexico. When your husband was seen riding out of camp last night with his wagon boss and—" He stopped, embarrassed.

"Theresa," Star said slowly. "Theresa was with them, wasn't she?"

"Yes, she was. Anyway, the colonel became suspicious and had the Bradford wagons thoroughly searched. There were rifles and ammunition hidden beneath the regular trade goods."

So that was why Charles had always been so nervous about the caravan crossing the trail of the army, she thought almost absently. And the Indian, Red Shirt, he had killed, she thought. He had known about the contraband, too, and threatened to expose Charles. And Charles had killed him.

The colonel cleared his throat, looked uncomfortably down at his feet, then back at the woman standing rigidly before him. The slate-gray eyes were almost frighteningly expressionless behind the thick black lashes. "I'm sorry, my dear, but there's more. As soon as the wagons were searched, the soldiers set out after your husband. They found him early this morning, about ten miles south of the camp. Unhappily, the Indians had found him first. Comanches, the colonel thinks, from the . . . the mutilation of the body."

Star's throat felt suddenly dry as sandpaper. "Dead? He's dead?" she whispered.

The colonel shrugged helplessly. "The soldiers brought his body back so he could be given a proper burial. I . . . we thought you'd want that."

"Mr. Johnson, Theresa? What of them?"

"No sign of them. Either the Indians carried them off or they managed to get away."

"May I see him, Charles?"

The colonel frowned, his voice uneasy. "I wouldn't advise it, child. Better not to."

"Mrs. Bradford has the right to see her husband's body, Colonel Owens." Michael Kelly stepped forward, his voice flat, his eyes never leaving Star's face.

Star saw then the canvas bundle, long, wrapped like a mummy, that had been placed on the ground next to a wagon.

"Mrs. Bradford, I don't think you should," the colonel protested shocked, but it was too late.

Michael had drawn aside the canvas, and Star saw Charles's body. Or what was left of it. The familiar clothes were blood-soaked. Charles's face had been savagely slashed again and again. The wheat-colored hair was black, stiff with blood. One hand lay across his chest, the other hand was lopped off at the wrist. Michael removed a heavy gold ring from the index finger of Charles's remaining hand and dropped it in Star's hand. "You'll want to keep this."

Star had taken one look at the body then turned away, her face a greenish-white, the sour taste of nausea in her mouth. She stared blankly at the ring in her hand. And all she could think of was how icy cold the ring had always felt against her body when Charles had made love to her, how heavy and cold it still felt now in her hand.

She looked up and saw that Michael Kelly was watching her curiously. What did he expect, she thought bitterly. That she would scream or faint? Is that why he had insisted she see the butchered remains of her husband? Well, she wouldn't give him the satisfaction, she thought. Pushing down the nausea that threatened to gag her, she lifted her chin, looking full into those probing dark green eyes, and said coldly, "Thank you, Mr. Kelly."

Then Colonel Owens's hand was under her arm, his voice solicitous. "There are some women with the army, not, I'm afraid, ladies, but I can have one come and stay with you."

"No," Star said. "I'll be all right. I'd like to be alone, please."

She made it to the tent and got safely inside in time to reach the washbasin before she became violently sick to her stomach.

Chapter Eight

She *was wandering alone across an empty prairie,*
the high grass pulling at her skirt so that it was like walking
through water, a cold, gray mist drifting around her. Suddenly,
shockingly, the mist parted before her and she saw Charles.
As she had seen him last, his naked body bloody, mutilated.
Only this time those amber eyes were not shut but wide open,
staring at her from the gouged and bloody face with such a
furious, accusing look that she felt a scream of horror rise in
her throat.

"No!" Star sobbed and jerked upright in bed. Her nightgown
was soaked with perspiration, and remnants of the nightmare
still clung to her as she stumbled out of bed. For a moment
she stood uncertainly in the middle of the room, staring around
her, bewildered. For one thing, the earth floor beneath her feet
was blessedly still, not moving in the constant up-and-down
motion of the trail. For another, there were walls around her,
solid whitewashed walls, not tent fabric, and a hewn wood
ceiling overhead.

Gazing at the low-beamed ceiling, at the deep-embrasured
window that showed the walls of the room to be at least four
feet thick, she remembered where she was. Bent's Fort. She
had arrived here with the wagon train over a week ago now
from Pawnee Fork.

Pawnee Fork. Her throat tightened and, against her will,
memory rushed back. The soldiers with Charles's desecrated
body, the hasty burial beside the trail as she stood, dry eyed,
while rocks were piled on the body and the wagons rolled
back and forth over the site to obliterate any sign of the grave

site and prevent coyotes—or Indians—from digging the body up and inflicting still further indignities on Charles.

Then the four-week journey from Pawnee Fork to the fort, following the Arkansas River through land that became more and more arid, ghostly white sandhills and prickly cactus along the trail, and the sun-cracked wagon wheels giving agonizing shrieks as they rolled over the parched grass and sandy soil. Then the fort, with its adobe, bastioned walls, looming suddenly above the treeless plain.

The owner, William Bent, and his Cheyenne wife had shown Star every courtesy. Despite the fact that the fort was jammed to overflowing with Mexican, French, German, and American traders, along with teamsters, buffalo hunters, Indians, and the latest arrivals, dragoons from Kearny's Army of the West, a room had nevertheless been cleared out for Mrs. Bradford. And when it was apparent the bereaved widow didn't want company, she was tactfully left alone with her sorrow.

Star stared absently out of the window that looked out over the patio of the fort. What time was it, she wondered? Well past sunrise, from the already oppressive heat she could feel even through the cool, thick walls. She had overslept again. She pressed her hands against her aching temples. She hadn't had a good night's sleep since coming to the fort, what with the continuous noises, night and day, from outside her room, a blacksmith pounding incessantly on an anvil and the rasp of a carpenter's saw from a rear building where wagons were being repaired and horses shod, mules braying and cocks crowing, the shrieking of magpies that for some unknown reason were hung in cages around the patio yard. And always there were men's voices shouting, brawling, boots grating on the graveled yard of the fort, the occasional bugle from the army encampment outside the walls.

Even sleep, when it finally came, brought no rest. Only the same nightmare, over and over again, driving her to wakefulness. Charles dead and yet not dead, his eyes terribly alive, mutely reproachful. "You wanted me dead," they seemed to say accusingly. "See, here I am, just as you wanted me."

And although the nightmare disappeared with wakefulness, the guilt remained. It was true. She had wanted Charles dead, had come close to killing him herself. Was she any less guilty than the Indians who had murdered Charles? What sort of unnatural, unfeeling woman was she? She had closeted herself in this room, refused to see anyone, as if fearful that her shameful lack of grief and sorrow would show in her face.

There was a soft knock at the door, and a young Indian woman, who had been introduced to her as some distant kin to Mr. Bent's wife, brought in a pitcher of water and a tray of food, biscuits, still hot, freshly made coffee, covered with a neat white cloth.

She placed the food before Star, mumbling shyly, "You eat."

For a moment Star almost did feel hungry, until she came closer to the girl and caught an unpleasant odor. Her hair, she thought, startled. The girl's hair, snaking black and shining across her back, was coated with grease. Star felt her stomach flipflop; the thought of food was suddenly nauseating.

"I'm not hungry," she murmured hastily. "Just coffee will be fine."

At the door the girl turned. "Don Miguel, he say, tell you, he visits you today."

"No," Star said sharply. She knew that Mr. Kelly's wagons, along with those of the others in the caravan, had been stopped at the Arkansas by the army, forbidden to cross over into Mexico until Colonel Kearny gave his permission. On the trip from Pawnee Fork she had stayed as much as possible in her carriage or tent, away from Mr. Kelly's too searching, knowing gaze. She had the uneasy feeling that if anyone suspected her lack of feelings about Charles's death, it would be Mr. Kelly. "Tell Don Miguel I'm not . . . not feeling well enough to receive callers."

The girl gave Star a curious glance, then smiled knowingly. "It will be a son, I think," she murmured as she slipped out the door.

Star stared, dismayed, at the closed door. The possibility that she had steadfastly ignored ever since her arrival at the fort now surfaced again in her mind. Panic stricken, she tried to remember what little she knew about pregnant women. The sickness she had suffered lately, her sudden attacks of nausea, her dizziness when she arose too suddenly, even the lack of her usual monthly period, she had put to the strain of these last weeks. She couldn't have a baby, she thought now, her throat tightening. Why, she didn't see how she was going to support herself, much less take care of a child.

She stared out of the deep-embrasured window, her headache worse now. Over the promenade that edged the wall of the fort, she could see in the distance an Indian encampment on a rise of land. Supposedly they had come to the fort to trade, but Star knew the traders suspected they were spying to discover the strength of the "white-faced warriors."

Star saw an Indian girl from the camp riding bareback on an Indian pony, her black hair streaming out behind her. There was a freedom about the girl riding heedlessly as the wind that made Star even more aware of her own predicament. After all, she couldn't impose on the Bents' hospitality at the fort indefinitely. No doubt Colonel Owens and Colonel Bent assumed she would be returning to St. Louis, to her father's house. But to Star's mind that would only be exchanging the prison of her marriage to Charles for another prison in the townhouse in St. Louis, assuming, she thought wryly, that her father would take her back.

Yet what else could she do, especially if she were carrying Charles's baby? She began to pace the tiny room. If only she were a man, she thought bitterly, how different it would be. She could come and go as she pleased, work and live as she choose. But a woman had so few choices: to stay home with her family; to marry; or to be like Cousin Sophia, an overworked, underpaid servant in someone else's home.

It wasn't fair! Star's gray eyes grew stormy, her soft mouth tightening angrily. Of course if she had money, if she were a wealthy widow, she could be independent. No one would then dare tell her how to live. But she had no illusions that Charles had left her well off. The army had confiscated the guns and ammunition he had planned to smuggle into Mexico. Star's thoughts skirted quickly the memory of Charles's traitorous act. As for the trade goods and the wagons themselves, she knew that Charles had borrowed the money to buy the goods. It was the profit that Charles had expected to make from selling the trade goods in Santa Fe and Chihuahua that would have brought him a small fortune. Only with Charles dead, the wagons would never reach Santa Fe.

Star stopped short, a pulse suddenly beating with excitement in her throat. Why? Why shouldn't the Bradford wagons continue on to Santa Fe? Why shouldn't she herself take them? Once the trade goods were sold, she could repay Charles's loan and still return to St. Louis a wealthy woman, beholden to no one. She was sure that Colonel Owens would be shocked at the idea, but he couldn't stop her, could he? The trade goods and wagons were hers now. And there was Ben, she thought, her spirits leaping upward. Ben would help her. She would talk to him right away. Her headache forgotten, she slipped out of her nightgown and put on her chemise, and several ruffled petticoats, was twisting her hair into a coil that would fit beneath a bonnet when the knock came at the door.

Thinking it was the servant returning for the tray, she called, "Come in," jabbing another hair pin impatiently into her hair, trying to skewer the heavy coil into place.

Michael Kelly stepped into the room. Star whirled around, then snatched up a shawl to cover her bare shoulders, her voice indignant. "What are you doing here?"

"You did say to come in," he said coolly.

His eyes amused, he watched as she gathered the shawl more closely around her. When his gaze lifted to her face, though, he was startled at the pallor he saw there, the shadows like bluish smudges beneath the wide gray eyes. Somehow, cynically, he hadn't expected the Widow Bradford to be so grieved at her husband's death.

His voice hardened. "You've been closeted in this room for more than a week. You need to get out in the sunshine. And we have to talk. Get dressed and we'll go for a walk."

"I am planning to take a walk to the Bradford wagon camp, alone," she said coldly. "Now if you'll excuse me, Mr. Kelly—"

"You're going to parade through the Army of the West by yourself?" he asked, lifting an amused eyebrow. "The army's tents are all around the wagon train. I'm sure you'll cause a sensation among the soldier boys."

Star frowned, uncertain. She supposed it wouldn't be wise, a woman alone, to walk through the army camp. Grudgingly, she said, "Very well, if you'll wait a moment outside, Mr. Kelly, I'll finish dressing and join you."

She was only a few moments. When she stepped outside the door, she was clothed demurely in a dark green bombazine gown that covered every inch of flesh, buttoned high to her neck, and a frilled matching bonnet under which only a glimpse of the burnished red hair could be seen. Since she had no black gown with her, it was the closest she could come to mourning clothes.

Even modestly clothed as she was, through, she saw heads turning as she walked beside Mr. Kelly through the fort patio and out the iron gate, the wind whipping at her skirt, outlining the trim lines of her figure. Once outside the gate, she was surprised at the expanse of tents placed haphazardly in the river bottom below the fort. Some of the outfits Star recognized—the First Regiment of Dragoons and Doniphan's First Missouri Mounted Volunteers—but there were many others she didn't know. And they were not only Missourians. She recognized a Carolina drawl, a Kentucky twang, and the clipped voices of New Englanders attached to the Army of the West. The soldiers were so young, she thought, catching glimpses of the men lounging before their tents, playing cards or washing clothes or laughing and tussling with each like young puppies. The mounted dragoons swaggered by on horseback with the broad yellow stripe down their shoulder leg, carbines in white slings, and scabbarded sabres.

One young man, not much older than Star herself, plucking at a guitar, grinned as she passed by his tent, struck a chord, and sang softly:

"Listen to me! Listen to me!
What do you want to see, to see?
A woman under a bonnet,
A woman under a bonnet,
That's what we want to see, to see."

"I didn't dream there were so many," Star said, gazing around the encampment.

"They won't seem so many once they cross the Arkansas," Michael said. "Mexico will swallow them up."

"You didn't think they'd get this far," Star reminded him.

Her companion nodded. "That's right. I didn't." Admiration

crept, almost unwillingly, into his voice. "The regulars complain that the volunteers don't know the meaning of discipline, straggle off as they please, ignore their officers, and care nothing about soldiering. Yet they've somehow managed to march this far. Now they're leaving tomorrow for Santa Fe. The engineers have already gone ahead, making a road for the army across the Raton."

"What of the traders? Will they stay behind at the fort?"

"No, we'll be leaving, too. Colonel Kearny has given his permission." Michael Kelly grinned. "I guess he knew there was no way he could stop us from crossing the Arkansas once the army was gone. The traders have too much cash tied up in their goods. Every day they sit idle is money wasted."

They had passed the army camp now and she could see ahead the towering Bradford Conestogas, Colonel Owen's Pittsburgh schooners, canvas tops billowing white against the greenery that edged the river. They stopped in a grove of cottonwoods, the wind making the leaves rustle like paper overhead. She felt Mr. Kelly's hand on her arm, turning her to face him. Once again she was aware of the striking contradictions in the man, the brilliant green eyes in the darkly bronzed face, the sensuous mouth so oddly at variance with the always guarded expression. Even his voice, which at times held a rich, almost musical softness, was now sharp as he said abruptly, "That's what I wanted to talk to you about, Mrs. Bradford. There's a troop of army men heading back to Fort Leavenworth to check on some commissary wagons that haven't arrived. Colonel Owens and I have made arrangements for you to travel back to Fort Leavenworth with the army troop. You can catch a stage for St. Louis from the fort."

So that was it, Star thought, feeling a wave of helpless fury break over her. No doubt Colonel Owens and Mr. Kelly had talked it over between them, and her future had been decided. She was to be packed up and sent home, with neither man even bothering to ask her what she wanted to do, how she felt—as if, being a woman, she was a child with no mind or opinion of her own worth listening to.

She jerked her arm free; anger chased the pallor from her face, a flush ran along her cheekbones. "Thank you for the offer, Mr. Kelly," she said coldly. "But I have no intention of returning to St. Louis. I plan to continue on to Santa Fe with the Bradford wagons."

And was pleased to see, by the startled look that flickered for a moment through the green eyes, that she had succeeded in penetrating, for once, that impassive bronze mask.

"You're not serious? You don't actually think you can lead a caravan of freighters to Santa Fe?"

"Why not? They're my wagons, aren't they? And Ben and the other drovers will help me."

To her surprise, he threw back his head and laughed, loud roars of laughter that brought tears to his eyes. "Drovers— work for a woman?" he finally gasped, the laughter diminishing to a hard, cold amusement in the narrowed eyes studying her. "And a greenhorn at that, who's never been down the trail before. The men would be the laughingstock of the trail. And even if, by some miracle, you did reach Santa Fe, you don't speak Spanish. You'd be robbed blind."

Star bit unhappily at her lower lip. She suspected he was only speaking the truth. For all Ben's kindness, would he be willing to accept her as his employer, take orders from a woman? And what did she know of hawking merchandise, or what her goods were worth on the market?

"As for your drover, Ben," Michael continued, "I thought you knew. He must have decided you wouldn't be needing drovers any longer, and he's joined Doniphan's volunteers." At the crushed look in the gray eyes, he said quickly, "I'm sure he would have come and told you himself but you've been locked in that room, refusing to see anyone, ever since we reached the fort."

"Oh." It was not so much a word as a quick, indrawn despairing breath. She turned her head away, her face half hidden by the bonnet, but there was a look of defeat in the droop of the shoulders, the lowering of that usually proud chin, that made Michael frown.

"Forgive my prying into your affairs, Mrs. Bradford." He hesitated, then said with a shrug. "But if it's money you need, I'll buy your wagons and goods. Colonel Owens can set a fair price. It should be more than enough to meet your needs."

"I don't own the wagons and goods," Star said. "The Merchant's Bank in St. Louis does. And I can manage very well without your charity, Mr. Kelly. Good day."

Her haughty exit was marred by a sudden gust of wind that tore the bonnet back from her head and sent her skirt ballooning around her like an ungainly sail. If Michael Kelly's hands hadn't reached out, fastened on either side of her waist, holding her steady, she would have toppled off balance. The acrid dust stung her face, snatching the breath from her as she clung to him, the wind tossing her skirt around his legs. A coil of auburn hair, whipped free of its pins, flew in lovely disorder around her face. Her companion caught its faint, freshly washed scent in his nostrils, felt its silken softness brush his cheek like a caress.

For a moment he found himself wondering how it would be to remove all the restraining pins and watch that hair tumble gloriously over Star Bradford's shoulders down to that tiny waist that his two hands practically spanned, how it would feel to bury his face in its silken glory while his hands stroked the softness that swelled so invitingly above the narrow rib cage. Instinctively his hands tightened to pull the slender body closer, to fits its soft curves against the tightness growing in his loins.

"You're too beautiful, *querida*, to worry your head about money," he murmured huskily. "I can think of much more pleasant ways to occupy your time."

His head bent over her, his mouth lowering to possess the sweet curve of her lips when, belatedly, he realized that the quick-silver brilliance in the wide gray eyes staring up at him was not passion, but something else, something oddly akin to terror. Startled, he hesitated a second, long enough for Star to pull free of his embrace.

Her voice was icily contemptuous. "A gentleman, Mr. Kelly, would wait a decent interval before proposing marriage to a woman who has so recently lost her husband."

He made her a deep, mocking bow. "My apologies, Mrs. Bradford. Only I'm afraid it wasn't marriage I was proposing. I have no need or desire for a wife."

She glared at him, her eyes flashing diamond bright behind the dark-fringed lashes. Almost, her hand lifted as if to strike him, but looking into the stony mask of his face, she thought better of it. Instead she contented herself by lifting her chin haughtily, her voice contemptuous. "Hell will freeze over before I'd become your mistress, Mr. Kelly."

And this time she did manage to stalk away from him. Michael Kelly stared after her retreating figure, half annoyed, half amused, as she clutched the ridiculous bonnet she had jammed back on her head and with her other hand tried vainly to keep her wind-whipped skirt from revealing an expanse of trim ankle and a flurry of white petticoats.

Damn the woman, he thought. Let her go. Yet even as he was thinking this, he was remembering the feel of her body beneath his hands, imagining those diamond-glittering eyes softening, filling with passion, wanting him as much as he wanted her, more than he'd ever wanted a woman. Or perhaps, he thought, more than the desire to have her in his bed urging him on, it was his own damned pride challenging him. He couldn't ever remember a woman refusing him before, especially with the contempt he had heard in Star's voice. Was it his half-Mexican heritage that placed him outside the pale? Did she perhaps think she was too good to share the bed of a breed? Michael Kelly's eyes narrowed coldly. It might be interesting to show the Señora Bradford just how wrong she was, how easy it would be to tumble her off her high horse.

Whatever his motives—and he was not a man to question his behavior for long—Michael Kelly decided that he could not let Star Bradford walk out of his life, not this way. In three strides he had overtaken her.

"Mrs. Bradford."

She paused, turned warily to face him.

"I have a proposition to make to you."

At her instant indignant recoil, he held up his hands, laughing. "A business proposition, I assure you, at least partly. Suppose you join the Bradford wagons with mine. I'll take you and your merchandise to Santa Fe and see to the sale of your goods, along with mine."

He saw the flicker of hope burn like a flame in her eyes, and then, cautiously, her voice still suspicious, she asked, "Wouldn't that rather be like stepping from the frying pan into the fire, Mr. Bradford? I don't fancy sleeping with a pistol beside my pillow for protection all the way to Santa Fe."

"If you're worried about protection against me or any of my men," Michael said coldly, "I give you my word that you'll be perfectly safe."

Almost against her will, Star found that she believed him. And it would be a solution to all her problems, she thought eagerly. Certainly her drovers wouldn't object to working for Michael Kelly. "There'd have to be some sort of arrangement made about your payment," she said slowly. "Perhaps you could take a percentage of whatever profits I make from the sale of my goods."

"I wasn't thinking of payment in gold, Mrs. Bradford," Michael replied. "I had another sort of payment in mind, once we reach Santa Fe. A chance to continue the discussion we began earlier about that unlikely possibility of hell freezing over. My taking your wagons would include your promise to spend one evening with me when we reach Santa Fe." Before she could protest, he continued, smiling thinly. "I've never found any particular pleasure in forcing myself upon a woman. The evening need only include dinner and conversation. Anything more than that..." he shrugged. "The choice will be yours."

She stared at him uncertainly, trying to fathom what lay behind that chill, green gaze, that mocking smile. "You mean..." she hesitated, embarrassed. "We'd spend one evening together and at the end of the evening, I could still refuse—" She broke off, feeling her face growing warm.

"That's exactly what I mean," he nodded. "The decision will be entirely yours. And whichever way the evening ends, all the profits made from the sale of your merchandise will be yours alone."

It was, Star sensed uneasily, an outlandish proposition, one she should, as a well-bred young woman, turn down immediately. It would mean trusting Michael Kelly to keep his word. Yet as much as she found the man's proposition insulting, certainly outrageous—his insufferable male sureness that he could no doubt persuade her so easily to his bed—oddly enough she did trust him to keep his word. Anyway, she thought practically, what other way was there for her? Refusing Mr. Kelly would only mean accepting the army's companionship to St. Louis, to the uncertain welcome in her father's home, to his grim disapproval, and to a life as dull and restrictive as the first eighteen years of her life had been.

Michael saw the indecision wavering in her face and pushed his advantage. "Is it a deal, Mrs. Bradford? Of course," he added, his voice lightly taunting, "if you're afraid once we get to Santa Fe, you won't be able to resist my charms..."

The impossible arrogance of the man, Star thought, her eyes blazing. Did he really think no woman alive could resist falling into bed with him?

She thrust out her hand to him, her chin lifting defiantly. "It's a deal, Mr. Kelly," she said coldly.

Chapter Nine

"*See, señora, see, the Spanish Peaks. Muy bonito!*"

Star shifted wearily in her saddle, wincing as her muscles cried out in protest, and glanced where Mario was pointing. Not that she hadn't been aware of the mountains looming in the distance ever since the wagon train had crossed the Arkansas River into Mexican territory, over a week ago now. A parched dead plain had given way to a trail winding among barren hills until they had crossed the Purgatoire—River of Lost Souls, Mario had called it—and come into a land of scrubby piñon woods with the curious little nuts and their sweet, oily taste.

The trail had continued winding upward south and west of the river. The Raton Peak toward which they were heading thrust its jagged edges above the trail before them with the snow-capped mountain ranges of Sangre de Cristo—the Spanish Peaks—dark blue against the distant horizon. For two days the road had turned and risen and dipped dizzily, only to climb again. Except no one in his right mind would call this narrow, boulder-strewn trail clinging to the side of the mountain a road, Star thought. She could understand now why, although it was only fifteen miles through the Raton Pass, a caravan was lucky if they made the passage in a week. Six hundred yards a day was an achievement for the huge, cumbersome wagons lurching and swaying over that jumbled mass of rock.

"*Magnífico, si?*" Mario asked proudly, as if the mountains, with the opal clouds drifting over their peaks, were his own personal accomplishment.

Star eased back in the saddle, carefully avoiding looking downward into the dangerous precipice that dropped away below the wagons, at the double and triple-teamed oxen straining as they pulled the heavy wagons inch by inch upward. Drovers cursed as they cracked their whips and blocked the huge wheels with stones to prevent the wagons from crashing backward and crushing an unwary victim beneath their wheels.

Instead Star fastened her gaze upward, at the sky that seemed so close she felt she could reach up and touch the blue vault above her, at the breathtaking views everywhere she looked. "Magnificent," she agreed, restraining an impulse to fling her arms around the neck of her horse as a giddiness swept over her.

The Mexican boy glanced worriedly at the *señora*'s white face.

"It is the height, *señora*," he said sympathetically. "The air is difficult to breathe."

"Yes," Star said, and thought hopefully, yes, that must be it, the thin air in this high altitude making her dizzy. Since leaving the fort she had managed to convince herself that her fears about carrying a child were false. There had been no more nightmares about Charles's body, no nausea when she awoke in the morning. In fact, if it weren't for the unaccustomed exercise on horseback making her muscles stiff and sore, she had never felt better until this sudden attack of dizziness.

"I think I'll walk for a while, Mario," she said. Scrambling up and down this rocky trail on foot like a mountain goat left her gown and face covered with a layer of dust, but it was still preferable to riding on horseback. She thought wistfully of the Rockaway carriage that, at Michael Kelly's orders, had been left behind at Bent's Fort, along with the tent that had been her home ever since Independence.

The *carretilla* would never make it through the Raton, Michael had pointed out, when Star had objected. "And we need the mules and your driver to help with the wagons, not bothering with a carriage and your tent. We're shorthanded as it is, with a half dozen of the men joining the army at Fort Bent."

"Where will I sleep?" she asked indignantly. Surely he didn't expect her to curl up in a blanket beneath the wagons the way the drovers did at night. Or did he? Was he perhaps expecting her to join him in his blanket, she wondered, giving him a wary glance. Was he already forgetting his promise?

If he guessed what she was thinking, his indifferent expression didn't alter in the slightest. "You can sleep in the Dearborn," he said.

Where Theresa had slept with Charles, Star thought, mentally flinching. Still, it was better than sleeping on the ground. "Am I supposed to walk to Santa Fe?" she asked, annoyed at his high-handed manner.

"I've found you a horse." He lifted a quizzical eyebrow. "You can ride, can't you?"

Horseback riding had been taught at the convent school, but the horses had been gentle, stable-bred creatures. Still, she saw no need to explain this to Mr. Kelly, with his supercilious way of speaking to her as if she were an inconvenient piece of baggage he was forced to drag along with the caravan. "Of course I can ride," she snapped.

When she saw the horse he had selected for her, she had been even more annoyed. The small, shaggy animal with its short legs and rough coat was far from beautiful. Nevertheless, she had to grudgingly admit that the animal was amazingly surefooted on the rock-strewn trail, patiently ignoring her frantic seesawing at the reins as they clambered up and down the mountainside following the wagons.

Mario had reached out a hand to help her dismount when Michael Kelly suddenly appeared behind him. His dark face glistened with perspiration, and his shirt, open to the waist, showed an expanse of brown, muscular chest. He spoke sharply in Spanish to the boy. Mario gave the man a fearful glance, ducked his head, murmured, "*Si, si,* Don Miguel," and scuttled away toward the wagons.

Star slid awkwardly off the horse, the ground dipping beneath her feet for a moment. She grabbed at the bridle, and the dizziness passed.

Michael Kelly gave her a sharp glance. "Are you all right?"

She straightened her shoulders, giving him an aloof glance. "Of course."

"Then I'd appreciate your not bothering Mario when he's supposed to be working," he said curtly, before turning and striding away back to the wagons, calling out in a roar that echoed against the overhanging cliffs, "Find a bigger rock to block those wheels, man! Ramon, put your back into it!"

As if he'd already forgotten her existence, Star thought, staring after him angrily. Ever since they had begun the trip, if Mr. Kelly wasn't ignoring her, he was barking orders at her. Wearily she turned and began to scramble up the trail, clutching at shrubs as the rocky soil slid away beneath her feet. Well, at least Colonel Owens needn't have worried about her virtue, she thought ruefully, remembering how shocked the colonel had been when he had learned the Bradford wagons as well as Star herself were to accompany the Cordoba wagons to Santa Fe.

"My dear Mrs. Bradford," he sputtered. "I'm sure you haven't considered . . . the gossip . . . your good name . . . a young lady traveling alone with a party of men."

Michael Kelly had been standing quietly to one side. Now he spoke, his voice ominously quiet. "You're not insinuating, Colonel, that any harm would befall Mrs. Bradford while she was traveling under my protection?"

The colonel gave the man a troubled glance, then sighed. "No, no, of course not, Don Miguel. It's only—" He shrugged and turned pleadingly to Star. "With your father not here, child, I feel I must act in his place. I'm sure he'd never approve such an undertaking."

He had unfortunately said the wrong thing. Star had begun to waver, doubts assailing her. The colonel was right. The idea of a woman traveling alone with a group of men would certainly set tongues wagging in St. Louis. But mention of her father stiffened her backbone. Did she want instead to go crawling back to her father's home, and to his gimlet-eyed disapproval? After all, she wasn't in St. Louis now, so why should she care what a bunch of gossiping women said?

She remembered now how daring, how courageous she had felt, assuring the colonel that he was not to worry, that she would be perfectly safe. She stopped a moment to rest, trying to wipe some of the dust from her face with a kerchief that was already dust-coated, and looked down disgustedly at hands and arms that were equally coated with the fine brown dirt. She must look a sight, she thought, sighing. It was no wonder Mr. Kelly never gave her a second glance. Not, she thought quickly, that she wanted his attention, but it was rankling to be so completely ignored.

Perhaps that was why, when the wagons made camp that evening next to a rushing, clear mountain stream, instead of falling exhausted into her bed of blankets in the Dearborn as she usually did, Star bathed her face and arms in the cold, invigorating water. Then she slipped into a pale green-and-white-sprigged calico gown, brushed her hair until it gleamed, and tied it back from her face with a green satin ribbon.

Only then did she stroll over to the cookfire where the tantalizing fragrance of roast hare and freshly baked biscuits and boiling coffee mingled with the scent of pine and crisp, cool mountain air. Michael, who was having a cup of coffee, saw her approach and watched, frowning, as Mario rushed up with a campstool, upon which she sat, spreading her skirt over her ankles. The firelight caught in the sparkling gray eyes made them shine like crystal, and added even more fire to the depths of the gleaming auburn hair. The calico gown was buttoned modestly high, but a glimpse of shimmering white skin could be seen above the bodice, more tantalizing somehow than if the gown had been cut daringly low.

Despite his irritation, Michael was well aware that he was moved by the girl's vivid beauty, that if the situation had been different . . . But he was even more aware of the exhausted drovers haunched around the fire, their faces turned toward Star with a mixture of frustration, loneliness, and barely concealed lust. Deliberately, slowly, so there was no doubt that all could see, Michael's hand moved to rest on the pistol in a holster slung low over his hip. What was wrong with the woman, anyway? he thought exasperated. She wasn't some naive virgin, but a widow. Surely she should know the effect she would have on love-starved men who hadn't touched a woman since Independence, almost three months before. Or was she one of those women who couldn't help flaunting their charms before an audience of men?

Yet when she turned to him, there was no hint of such knowledge in the clear gray eyes, and her voice was innocently serene as she asked, "Will we be much longer, crossing the Raton, Mr. Kelly?"

"Another day to the top of the pass if we don't run into rain." He smiled tightly. "Then it's downhill all the way."

She nibbled delicately at a piece of the delicious fried rabbit, as if oblivious to the eyes watching her every movement. "And after the Raton, how long before we reach Santa Fe?"

He shrugged. "Depends on what lies between us and Santa Fe, Armijo's Lancers or Kearny's army." And couldn't resist adding, lifting an amused eyebrow, "Are you so anxious then, Mrs. Bradford, to reach Santa Fe?"

Star felt a flush rise in her face, remembering their agreement, the evening she had promised him in Santa Fe. With the distant way Michael Kelly had been behaving toward her ever since the start of the trip, she had begun to believe that it had all been a stupid jest, that of course he hadn't meant for her to take him seriously. Now, as that dark green gaze fastened on her face, like a hand reaching out, holding her entrapped so that she could not look away, she knew, with a faint sensation of alarm, that it was not a joke. She would be expected to keep her end of the bargain once they reached Santa Fe.

All at once, too, she became uncomfortably aware of the faces of the men around the fire, turned toward her hungrily. Something in those eyes, glistening as they watched her, reminded her frighteningly of Charles, how he had always looked at her before . . .

She got abruptly to her feet, her heart racing. "If you'll excuse me, I think I'll go—"

Then hesitated as hoofbeats sounded in the darkness outside the firelight, beyond the wagons pulled into a tight corral. Michael had heard the approaching horses before her, had already half risen, his hand now resting firmly on the pistol butt.

A half-dozen men in uniform rode into the camp. The officer in charge of the patrol, a yellow stripe running down his trouser leg, dismounted first, slapping the dust from his uniform. "Damn dusty road," he complained. "Hope you don't mind, we smelled your coffee. Couldn't resist stopping." Then he saw Star and broke off, giving her an incredulous glance, then swept his hat hastily off his head. "Sorry, ma'am, didn't know there was a lady present."

Michael saw the admiration leap into the captain's eyes and felt an irrational surge of anger. "You and your men are welcome to coffee, captain." He added stiffly, "The lady was just about to retire."

Star gave Michael a frigid glance. Did he think he could

send her off to bed, like a child ordered out of the room when company arrived? She smiled sweetly at the officer as she poured and handed him a tin cup of coffee. "Have you any news of Colonel Kearny?"

"General Kearny," he corrected her, his glance drifting back to rest, puzzled, on Michael's face. "The announcement of the promotion only reached us last week at Bent's Fort. As for other news—" He frowned unhappily. "There's a rumor that Armijo has gathered himself an army of sorts and is preparing to head off General Kearny at Apache Pass. But Kearny is continuing forward to Santa Fe."

Once again he bent a puzzled frown at Michael. "Have we met before, sir?" he asked. "There was a student at West Point, a plebe in the class before mine. You resemble him a good deal. I can't remember the fellow's name. There was some trouble and he—"

His voice faltered. He had the sudden uncomfortable sensation that looking into the wagon master's face was like looking into the business end of a Colt. "You and your men are welcome to spend the night," Michael said flatly.

The captain put down the coffee cup. "Thank you, but we'll be pushing on. There's a full moon so we'll have no trouble seeing the trail. We want to reach General Kearny before he runs into Armijo and we miss out on all the fighting." He grinned engagingly at Star. "Hate to come all this way for nothing. Thanks for the coffee, ma'am." He turned again to the wagon master, "I've been told to warn all traders to stay well behind the troops, Mr. . . . ."

Michael hesitated only a split second. "Kelly," he said, and a look of amusement for a moment flashed in the vibrant green eyes beneath the slanted brows as he added dryly, "You needn't worry. We don't plan to reach Santa Fe before the general."

Star noticed the startled look of recognition in the captain's face when Michael gave him his name, but the officer said nothing, touched his hand to his hat toward Star, and then disappeared with his men again into the darkness surrounding the camp.

Michael took Star's arm. "I'll walk you to the Dearborn," he said.

She nodded meekly enough, and walked quietly along beside him. But she couldn't resist saying teasingly, "What a surprise, Mr. Kelly, that a man as disapproving of the army as you are should have attended West Point."

She thought at first he wasn't going to answer her. Then he said, "When I turned fifteen, my father decided I should learn something of his country. He sent me to stay with an uncle in upper New York State. After two years, my uncle thought I needed the discipline of a military school, so he wangled me an appointment to West Point." Star could not see Michael's face in the darkness but she could hear the wry amusement in his voice. "Unfortunately, despite my uncle's fond hopes, I made an indifferent soldier. And there was a duel, I recall, over a lady who unhappily was married to the vice-commandant. The school frowned on that sort of thing. My parting, however, from the Point was amicable, with no regret on either side." They had reached the Dearborn and Michael stopped, his voice quiet. "Does that satisfy your curiosity, Mrs. Bradford?"

Star flushed. Did he think she had been prying into his personal life? As if she cared, she thought crossly. Still, it occurred to her to wonder how old Michael had been when he had been ransomed from the Indians. And then to be shipped off from his family again to a strange country, relatives he didn't know, who undoubtedly found the half-savage boy a handful, then shipped off again to a military school whose discipline he must have detested. How he must have hated all of it, the straitlaced uncle, the restrictions at the Point, after the free, untrammeled life he had led in the Indian camps. To her surprise, she found herself feeling sorry for that boy.

Until Michael lifted her suddenly in his arms and deposited her unceremoniously in the Dearborn. Even through the darkness she was aware of his eyes roaming insolently over the pretty flounced green-sprigged dress, and his voice was hard. "A word of advice, Mrs. Bradford: in the future I'd suggest you make yourself a little less . . . attractive. My men are drovers, not saints, and I don't care to have to bash one over the head just to prove to you the invincibility of your charms."

All feelings of warmth and sympathy for the young Michael Kelly left Star at once. How dare he insult her with his insinuations! Unfortunately, before Star could find the words to match her fury, the wagon master had walked away, and she was left with a good deal of unvented anger to spoil her night's rest.

She awoke the next morning still annoyed, but there was no time for recriminations. She dressed hastily in the crowded confines of the Dearborn while she could hear the call of "Catch up," echoing through the camp, oxen protesting as they were ruthlessly prodded forward up yet another almost perpendicular incline. Then, as Mr. Kelly had promised, they finally reached the top of the pass late in the afternoon.

For a few moments Star forgot her irritation, gazing at the magnificent vistas on all sides of her. All of New Mexico, coated with a golden molten sunlight, seemed to lay at her feet, green valleys and massed purple snow-capped mountains drawing the eye to immeasureable distances. Whether it was the altitude or the dazzling beauty she did not know, but she had never felt more alive and yet somehow, for the first time in months, more at peace with herself.

There was little time for reflection, though. The wagons were already beginning the descent, oxen and men braced against the wagons' careening to their destruction. Star watched, terrified, as a half dozen men held the weight of the huge wagon wheels back by sheer physical strength while the driver tried to hold the oxen steady as the wagon noisily, clumsily plunged forward. Star saw Michael Kelly take his place at the wheels with the rest of the men, the muscles straining like cords beneath his shirt as he braced himself to hold the wagon back from pitching down the incline. She saw the gigantic wheel turning too quickly, his swift leap aside at the last moment or the wheel would have caught and crushed him. She could not bear to look, at the same time she could not bear to tear her eyes away from those deadly wheels. For a second the dizziness returned, and she had to clutch at the saddle horn to stop the world from spinning around her. Thankfully, Mario and the rest were busy with the wagons and she managed to scramble off her horse, find a secluded haven behind a rock, and be violently sick without, thankfully, anyone noticing.

The next day the caravan left the Raton Pass behind. But not the mountains, which seemed to follow the lumbering wagons as they moved more quickly now through the violently colored land. The caravan passed baked red adobe hamlets nestled in the mountains, crossed rain-swollen streams that threatened to snap wagon tongues, inched through ocher and tawny yellow-streaked canyons that opened finally into green meadows.

The meadows, in time, though, became a broad rolling plain, where a scorching wind and blazing sun made Star remember longingly the pine-scented cool air of the Raton. She dug out the veiled bonnet she had worn on the prairie, and although the veil kept the stinging grit from blowing into her eyes, it did little to relieve the heat pushing down on her head like a weight. She could feel the perspiration trickling down her back, staining the bodice of her by now much-worn and dusty riding habit.

The wagoners wore kerchiefs over their lower faces and when Michael Kelly stopped beside Star, she saw he had a red kerchief tied over his nose and mouth. She lifted her veil and gestured, amused, toward the drovers. "They look like a ferocious bunch of *ladróns*."

"Your Spanish is improving rapidly, *señora*," he replied, smiling.

"Oh, I practice on Mario." She gave him a defiant glance. "Or do you object to the boy instructing me?"

"On the contrary, I'm only sorry I don't have the time to teach you myself." The kerchief had slipped down around his neck, and when he smiled, she was uncomfortably aware of the man's charm, the flashing white smile against the tanned face, the intimate way the clear green eyes touched and held hers. It was like physically snipping a taut line between them when she looked away, pretending to lean forward and soothe her horse when he had to sidestep sharply to avoid a gopher hole.

"Your horsemanship has improved also," he commented, amused. Despite her protestations, he had immediately guessed that she was not an accomplished horsewoman and had hand-picked the shaggy Indian pony for her as being the safest for a novice rider. He even had to give her credit for never once complaining about the sore muscles he knew she must have endured these last days. "It's too bad we can't find a more suitable mount," he murmured, thinking of a chestnut mare with sleekly beautiful lines he owned at the *rancho*. How lovely Star would look riding on the back of Perdito, in a green velvet riding habit, her own hair just a shade darker than Perdito's shining chestnut coat.

"Oh, I'm grown fond of my *caballo*," she said, patting the horse affectionately. "It's only that I worry about him in this heat."

"And you?" he asked, his glance all at once too penetrating. "How are you bearing the heat?"

She glanced at him warily. "Well enough."

"Back at Las Vegas," he persisted, "you looked as if you might be ill."

She remembered the small adobe village where they had stopped the day before. After the beauty of the mountains, its filth and ugliness had shocked her. At sight of the caravan the people had come streaming out into the narrow streets, littered with slops carelessly pitched from the open windows of the small, mean houses. "*Los americanos. Los carros.* Don Miguel . . ." they had shouted, surrounding the wagons.

The Mexican men wore torn cotton shirts and trousers and straw sombreros, but the women, Star noticed, embarrassed, wore only a chemise that barely covered their breasts and a skirt that often swung high enough so it was obvious the women didn't bother with underclothes. It was the women's faces, though, that made Star shrink away from them. They were coated with a thick flour paste or vermilion, like some sort of coquettish, hideous mask. And the children! There wasn't a stitch of clothing on any of them, young girls and boys, both, naked as the day they were born.

"It was the food," she said quickly. "It didn't agree with me."

The *alcalde* of the town had proudly insisted upon feeding Don Miguel and his *bonita señora*, serving tortillas wrapped in a dirty napkin, cheese with a black-flecked crust, earthen jars of chili verde that burned Star's throat as she forced herself to swallow so as not to offend the elderly official. Anxious to change the subject from the nausea that attacked her even at the memory of the food, she said hastily, "I didn't understand your conversation with the *alcalde*. Did he mention something about General Kearny? Has the army passed through here?"

"Over a week ago," Michael said, his gaze still thoughtful, resting on Star's face. "According to the *alcalde*, the 'small general,' as he called Kearny, climbed to the roof of the church and told the people that they were no longer subjects of Mexico but free citizens of the United States. Their religion and property would be respected, but they would be required to take an oath of loyalty to their new country." He finshed dryly, "And, oh yes, he also said that any of them who took arms against the United States would hang."

"Still, the people seemed pleased to see us," Star said, annoyed at the undertone of mockery in Michael's voice. It was true, then, she thought, what the newspapers in the United States had claimed, that the people of Mexico would welcome the American troops not as conquerors but deliverers.

Michael's mouth narrowed into a hard, bitter line, even as his eyes held a sardonic amusement. "The Indians and *mestizos* are used to being conquered and exploited, ever since the days of the Spanish Conquistadors. They've learned over the years it's better to be courteous and agreeable to their conquerors, at least on the surface, if they want to stay alive. No doubt they were delighted the Americans didn't desecrate their churches or ravage their women."

"American soldiers would never behave so dishonorably," Star protested. And then, proudly, "President Polk has promised to free the Mexicans from their bondage."

"I wouldn't put too much trust in the honor of soldiers, Mexican or American," Michael said grimly. "As for President Polk, perhaps he should first free from bondage the men and women in his own country. Or aren't you aware that the United States is one of the last civilized countries in the world to still practice and condone slavery? President Polk himself is a slave owner. As a matter of fact, I understand there are those Whigs in Washington who claim that the American invasion of Mexico is simply a pretext to bring another slave state, Texas, into the Union, as well as an excuse to seize the lands of California and New Mexico from Mexico."

Was it true? Star wondered uneasily. She remembered a dinner party at her father's home where the men at the table insisted that the Pacific Ocean and the Rio Grande were the natural boundaries of the United States. And she had read in the newspapers of the controversy over Texas entering the Union as a slave rather than a free state.

Quickly she thrust such disloyal thoughts from her mind, glancing up into Michael Kelly's face, the dark green eyes inherited from his American father and the swarthy skin and aquiline nose inherited from his Mexican forebears. Suddenly she wondered: Where did Michael Kelly y Cordoba's loyalties lie?

"Do you think General Kearny has reached Santa Fe?" she asked.

"It's possible, although Armijo's troops may have made a stand at Apache Canyon." Michael shrugged grimly. "Anyway, Kearny is running low on supplies and horses. He has to go forward. It would be disaster to retreat."

Star had noticed along the trail the remains of broken and abandoned army commissary wagons, the bleached bones of mules and horses, the discarded packs of foot soldiers. If this heat was hard on her, she realized, how much worse on weary men who had already marched over eight hundred miles through plains, mountains, and deserts.

Michael reached into his pocket and flipped a brass button from an army uniform into the air. "I'd say Kearny's army is running short of money, too, or the troopers wouldn't have been using these to try and buy food back there in Las Vegas." He smiled regretfully. "It's too bad. Soldiers with money in their pockets can buy a lot of trade goods."

"I don't intend to make a profit off of the army," Star said indignantly.

"No?" Michael's mouth twisted in a cynical smile. "I thought that was the reason for your trip, to make money by selling your trade goods. A soldier's money is as good as the next man's."

Star frowned unhappily. Of course that was what she had been counting on, making enough money from the sale of her trade goods in Santa Fe so that she could support herself. And not just herself. The money was even more important to her if, as she was beginning to fear more and more each day, she was carrying Charles's child.

Once again she tried to put the troubling thought aside. After all, she could still be mistaken. It could be this dreadful heat.

Her lips felt parched and her eyes burned against the glare of the sun splintering against the dry ground, so that the world seemed veiled in a shimmering haze. All at once she felt as if the sun were flattening the life out of her, pressing her down into nothingness.

"Mrs. Bradford."

She lifted her head, vaguely aware that the wagon master was speaking to her, but when she looked at him, he seemed to be receding, his cynical, twisted smile reminding her of the Cheshire cat in *Alice in Wonderland*, his face fading and fading until only the smile was left.

When she became aware of her surroundings again, she was lying in the Dearborn. As she wondered confusedly what she was doing here in the middle of the day, she became even more shockingly aware of hands at the bodice of her riding habit, undoing the row of pearl buttons from her neck to waist.

She struggled to sit up, pushed the hands furiously away. "How dare you? What do you think you're doing?"

Michael sat back, his glance flicking amused from the gaping jacket front to her flushed face. "Not what you have in mind, apparently. How are you feeling?"

"I fainted?" she asked uncertainly, clutching at the edges of the jacket and drawing it together across her breasts, only thinly covered by her chemise.

"And no wonder," he said, his voice irritated. "Don't you have anything cooler to wear than that heavy riding habit?"

"It's a perfectly good riding habit," she bristled.

"Perhaps for a jaunt in St. Louis," he said. "Not in the August heat on the plains of New Mexico."

"What do you expect me to wear, riding a horse?" she asked, irritably. "A dress?"

His face grew thoughtful. "Why not?"

"I . . . I can't," she sputtered, outraged. "The skirt of a dress, it'll ride up and my legs—my limbs will be exposed," she finished coldly.

He shrugged and left the wagon, calling for Mario. In a few moments he returned and tossed a pair of ragged but clean white pantaloons and a tattered blue shirt into her lap. "Wear these."

She picked them up gingerly. "These belong to Mario!"

"Not any longer. It's your new riding habit."

She gave him a startled glance. "You can't expect me to wear a boy's trousers and shirt."

"Why not? They'll certainly be cooler than what you've been wearing." A glint of amusement touched the hard green eyes. "And your limbs will be properly covered."

When she sat motionless, a mutinous look gathering in her eyes, he sighed and said slowly, "Look, Mrs. Bradford, I have a wagon train to get to Santa Fe. I haven't time to keep picking you up off the trail every time you pass out from the heat. Now you can either wear that outfit, or you can ride in the Dearborn the rest of the trip. Take your choice."

He had half turned away when she blurted angrily, "You can't—" then broke off abruptly when he turned again and she saw that his face had grown very still. The green eyes glittering coldly in controlled anger were somehow more frightening than open rage.

"I can't what?" he asked, very quietly. "Can't make you ride in the Dearborn? But you know I can." As his glance roved slowly over her frightened face, watched the rapid rise and fall of the pale creamy breasts, a warmth like a dancing green flame touched the narrowed eyes. But his voice remained cold, snapping like a bullwhip through the air between them. "Wear the pantaloons and shirt, Mrs. Bradford. You'll find them more comfortable than riding tied in the Dearborn the rest of the trip to Santa Fe."

Then he was gone and she stared after him, feeling the anger churn helplessly inside her. If only she could cuss like the drovers, she thought, her hands balling into fists. For the first time she understood the feeling of satisfaction the bullwhackers must experience, rolling off a stream of colorful obscenities when the oxen turned contrary—as contrary and bullheaded as Mr. Kelly, she thought, yanking off the riding habit and pulling on the soft cotton pants and worn blue shirt.

She could not see how she looked, but she felt foolish the next morning when she mounted her pony wearing Mario's clothes. The trousers had to be tied around her waist with a piece of rope and the sleeves rolled up so they didn't hang over her hands. Still, by the time the train reached Apache Canyon, she had to admit that the clothes were less constricting and cooler than the heavy riding habit.

At the narrow canyon, she was relieved to discover that there had evidently been no battle after all. According to a passing Mexican, astride a burro, the guns protecting the canyon had been spiked and Armijo and his dragoons had fled south to Chihuahua. General Kearny and his Army of the West had marched triumphantly into Santa Fe without a shot being fired.

It was another two days, however, before the caravan, following the base of a flat-topped mesa, finally began to climb again, crossing dry arroyos, then reached a rise overlooking the Royal City of the Holy Faith of Saint Francis. Rising eagerly in her stirrups, Star could see in the distance to her right the foothills of the Sangre de Cristo Mountain Range and to the left a vast plateau reaching to another range of blue mountains. And directly ahead of her, Santa Fe.

An exitement stirred within Star. At last she was to see the fabled city that she'd heard about ever since she was a small girl. And more importantly, she had made the trip against all odds, overcoming hardships that would have terrified and defeated her only six months ago. It was a personal sense of triumph that she hugged happily to her, making her forget for a moment Charles and the nightmare of her marriage. Even her father, she thought wistfully, would be proud of her.

The weary wagoners must have felt the same excitement, the same anticipation that she did, for the train stopped while the men shaved and washed and put on clean shirts. New crackers were fastened to the long whips. Star dug the riding habit out of her trunk, brushed it, and tied a fresh white scarf around her neck. After the pantaloons and shirt, the habit felt oddly heavy. As she climbed back on her horse, Mario came rushing over to her with a wide smile and an armful of dark rose-purple colored flowers, the petals delicately fringed, the flowers almost covering the long branches. "For the *señora*," he said.

"How beautiful." She gave the boy an appreciative smile. "What are they called?"

"Some call them gayfeathers, but the name I prefer is blazing star," Michael said.

She had not heard the wagon master come up beside her. Michael, too, had changed from his trail clothes into his tailored black frock coat, a white ruffled vest, and flat-brimmed plainsman's hat.

Star gazed at the blazing stars, delighted. So these were her namesake. She wondered if Michael Kelly knew. She looked up quickly and caught the dark green eyes studying her face, a flattering warmth in their depths.

"You don't object to my wearing my riding habit now?" she asked, lifting her chin defiantly.

He grinned and shook his head. "Though I must admit I miss the girl in the tattered pantaloons."

Star almost felt herself weakening beneath the winning charm of that smile, then reminded herself that Mr. Kelly should not be forgiven so quickly for his indifferent and high-handed treatment of her on the trail. She lowered her eyelids demurely, knowing that the admiring gaze had not left her face. She had been concerned about the evening she had promised to spend with Mr. Kelly. Now, seeing the bemused look in his eyes, she decided, pleased, that the evening might be amusing after all. It would be pleasant for a change to humble the man who had humbled her. He looked at the moment as smitten as Robert Donley, and shouldn't be any more difficult to handle, she decided.

Then there was no more time to contemplate the pleasure of repaying Michael Kelly for his overbearing rudeness. It had been a long, hard trip from Independence, and all the men were eager to reach Santa Fe and the company of the *señoritas* who were noted for their warm welcome of the traders, the big, virile *americanos*.

At first the outskirts of Santa Fe seemed to Star no more than a replica of the other adobe hamlets they had passed: unpaved, crooked streets, huts built of mud bricks, cornfields reaching into the very heart of the town. Then the caravan reached the plaza in the center of town. The first thing Star noticed was the American flag waving on a pole in the middle of the plaza and the American soldiers marching on guard duty, ignored by the residents of Santa Fe, who went about their business. Fruit and vegetable vendors sold their wares from the backs of burros. Indians and roughly dressed *rancheros* wandered in and out of the stores that fronted the square, and under the cottonwood trees that edged the stream running beside the plaza, monte dealers plied their trade on bright red serapes.

On the north end of the plaza stood the Governor's Palace, a grandiose name, Star decided, for what was only an unpretentious New Mexican dwelling with a portal across its front. As the caravan circled the plaza, whips cracking, wagoners strutting proudly, the people streamed out to meet them as they had in Las Vegas, calling, "*Los americanos! Los carros! La entrada de la caravana!*"

As in the other towns, the women were scantily dressed in skimpy *camisas* and short, flaring shirts. Their faces, bleaching under a coating of flour-paste, were filled with an obvious delight at the coming of the traders.

As Star drew to one side, watching the exuberant welcome the traders gave the women, she noticed a carriage that sat waiting before a store nearby. A woman came out of the store. Her dark exotic beauty was such that she made all the other women in the square seem dowdy. Instead of the usual Mexican costume, she wore a pale striped satin blue and white gown, with just the hint of a bustle, and a modish bonnet that looked as if it had just arrived from Paris the day before. She was carrying a pale blue silk parasol, and beneath the parasol Star caught a glimpse of glossy black hair and lustrous black eyes that at the moment were casting a smiling glance toward Michael Kelly.

Michael saw the woman and dismounted immediately. As he swept off his hat, the woman extended her right hand and Michael drew the woman gently toward him, his left arm around her waist, pulling her closer until his cheek lay against hers.

Pulling her eyes away from the tableau, Star turned to Mario, who was mounted on a mule beside her. "Who is that woman with Don Miguel?" she asked stiffly.

Mario looked surprised. "You do not know Señora de las Flores? Everyone in Santa Fe knows the *señora*. She is the richest woman, they say, in all of New Mexico."

Star was suddenly much too conscious of her dusty, worn riding habit, of the beautiful blazing star wildflowers, their rose-purple petals now lying wilted in her lap, of her own pale skin that, try as she might to protect it from the sun, she was sure had too much color now to be fashionable. As for the *señora*'s gown and bonnet, there wasn't a dress or bonnet in Star's own trunk that could match the lovely creation the *señora* wore.

It didn't help matters any when Star saw that the *señora* had stepped free of Michael's embrace and was studying Star with the same open curiosity. She spoke swiftly to Michael in a softly liquid voice. Star could understand only a portion of the words. *"Muy linda niña . . ."*

That much Star did understand and her hands tightened, annoyed, on the reins of her horse. Pretty child, indeed!

Then all at once she remembered where she had heard the name of the woman with Michael before. It was Charles. Charles had told her that la Señora de las Flores was Michael Kelly's mistress.

Chapter Ten

"*There* isn't any doubt, Mrs. Bradford. I'd say you were at least three months into your term. The baby will probably be born late in March." Major Hastings fell silent, staring curiously at the frozen-faced young woman sitting across from him. He knew who Mrs. Bradford was, of course. All of Santa Fe knew of Mrs. Charles Bradford, who, after her husband's death at the hands of the Comanche, had traveled to Santa Fe with the caravan of Michael Kelly y Cordoba. Fleetingly the major wondered if the child might not be, after all, Kelly's offspring. Don Miguel's reputation with the ladies was well known in and out of Santa Fe, and from all accounts, his caravan had been traveling with the Bradford wagons from Council Grove. Plenty of time for the wagon master to have had his way with the beautiful Mrs. Bradford. Why else should the newly bereaved widow look so desolate at the news of the impending birth? It certainly wasn't maternal joy the major saw in those bleak, dove-gray eyes.

"You're sure? There's no chance of a . . . a mistake?" she asked, her voice shaken.

The major shook his head, his voice taking on a forced joviality. "It's true I'm more accustomed to tending the wounds of soldiers, but I have delivered a baby or two in my time." He thought distastefully of the laundresses, a polite name for the camp followers who had accompanied the Army of the West to Santa Fe, women he had been forced to attend when they found themselves in the same predicament as Mrs. Bradford. The colonel's lady and Mrs. O'Grady, he reflected, gaz-

133

ing at the obviously well-bred young woman seated before him, all sisters under the skin.

Still, something in that vulnerable young face beneath the black mourning bonnet, a childish terror behind those remarkable gray eyes, softened the major's puritanical New England upbringing that divided all women simply into good women who didn't and bad women who did. He reached into a wall cabinet and brought out a vial of pills. "There's no reason to worry, you know," he said gruffly. "It's perfectly natural, having a child." No need to alarm Mrs. Bradford with the news that she had a narrow pelvis and the delivery of the baby would not be easy under the best of circumstances. "I want you to take one of these every night, especially if you find you have trouble sleeping. And of course, stay away from long jaunts in a carriage or horseback riding. No point in taking unnecessary chances at this time."

Almost automatically, Star took the pills and got to her feet. "Yes, thank you. I'm sorry to have bothered you but my Spanish isn't very good." She gestured helplessly. "I was afraid I wouldn't understand a Mexican doctor."

The major escorted her from his surgeon's quarters to her waiting carriage. "I'm glad to be of assistance, Mrs. Bradford. However, I should tell you the chances are I won't be in Santa Fe next March to assist you in your confinement." At the dismay he saw in the girl's face, he added, "A soldier's life, you know. We go where we're ordered."

So it was true, Star thought, the rumor that was swiftly making the rounds throughout Santa Fe, that having taken the New Mexico territory without a fight and set up a new territorial government under American laws, General Kearny would soon be following the remainder of his orders from Washington: to conquer California.

"Will all the soldiers be leaving Santa Fe?" she asked.

The major frowned. He supposed he shouldn't pass along military information, but he had no wish to alarm a woman in Mrs. Bradford's delicate condition. "Colonel Doniphan's Missouri troops will be staying," he assured her. "And I understand additional reinforcements under General Price are expected shortly. Very likely there will be an army surgeon with them."

He assisted Star into her carriage, and as he did so, he

couldn't help noticing how attractive the young widow looked in her widow's weeds. Several tendrils of auburn hair had slipped from beneath the black ruched bonnet, and her skin was a pale ivory with just a trace of apricot pink running along her cheekbones. Lucky devil, that Don Miguel, the major thought, with an envious pang, having a mistress like Mrs. Bradford, as well as that infamous town beauty Señora de las Flores at his beck and call. Of course a woman like Señora de las Flores, with her monte game, would be frowned upon back in Vermont, but the major had discovered that the women in Santa Fe and their openly lascivious behavior were a far cry from Vermont.

Star was oblivious to the admiration in the major's eyes; she was too involved in her own worries, as if her mind were a maze in which her thoughts raced, endlessly trapped. A child. Charles's child. It was as if in some last, cruel trick Charles had reached out from the grave and enslaved her again, that she hadn't escaped him at all. The child would be a constant reminder of Charles.

The carriage was driving slowly through the noise and confusion of the plaza, and lifting her gaze, Star stared absently at the colorful scene. Young women with bare legs strolled by the soldiers on guard duty, swinging their short skirts flirtatiously, even as their rebozos modestly covered their heads. A *caballero* in a tight, braided jacket, a silk kerchief around his neck and a long silken sash tied around the waist of his pantaloons, removed his enormous, gold-bedecked sombrero with a flourish as Star's carriage drove by. His liquid black eyes gazed admiringly after the beautiful red haired senora. Burros crowded the entrance to the plaza, backs piled high with baskets of fruit, grapes, yellow melons, loads of piñon fagots, while the patient burros twitched the flies away with their long ears. Here and there an Indian seemed to drift like a shadow on some mysterious business of his own.

As they drove by the Church of St. Francis, its bells were ringing. But then Star had discovered that church bells were always ringing in Santa Fe, so much a part of the scene she hardly heard them anymore. The bells rang with equal fervor for church services, fandangos, a *baile*, or a funeral.

Star had visited the adobe Church of St. Francis when she

first arrived in Santa Fe. She still remembered her shock at the rough pine floor, the dingy mud walls, tawdry altar, and candles set in brandy bottles. The musicians in the church balcony played the same tunes to accompany the mass that they had played the evening before at a fandango. Most of the worshippers had spent the night dancing, gambling, and brawling, and gone straight to early morning mass without yet going to bed.

What a study in contrasts the town was, Star thought, gazing around her, stirred momentarily from her lethargy. The narrow streets were filthy, and yet one could glimpse, through an open gate, a courtyard of rare beauty filled with glorious flowers. The Mexican people could be fun-loving one minute and filled with unbridled passion the next. They might have only a crude mud-brick hovel for a home but gladly shared its hospitality with a stranger at the door in an instinctive, gracious courtesy. Star was enthralled with Santa Fe and its sparkling, sunlit beauty one minute and appalled the next with its poverty and ugliness, by the ignorance and superstition of its people.

The carriage had stopped to allow a funeral procession to pass. A small, uncoffined corpse, a child of five or six, dressed in her Sunday finery, was being tenderly carried on a board on the shoulders of several men. A fiddler played a gay tune as the procession passed, while the parents followed their dead child, weeping and fingering their rosaries. The American soldiers had carried measles with them into Santa Fe and it had spread like wild fire through the beggar children who swarmed around the army camp.

Star, after one glance at the pitiful burden the men carried, shrank back in the carriage. For all that fresh snow lay on the rim of the Sangre de Cristo Mountains, it was an unseasonably warm October day, and she let the black shawl drop from her shoulders. The whalebone stays of her corset dug into the soft flesh of her breasts, making it difficult to breathe.

Her driver turned and smiled as he urged the mules forward again. "Now we go to the Alameda; *muy bonita*."

Star shook her head. "I've changed my mind. *Llévame a casa*."

The driver shrugged philosophically and turned the carriage down a side street. Star huddled in a corner of the carriage.

The dead child had shaken her out of her preoccupation with her own misery. She could no longer pretend the child she was carrying didn't exist. She must make some sort of plans for the future. She would need money, she thought, a great deal of money—more than it seemed she would get from the sale of her trade goods. Twice since she had arrived in Santa Fe, Mr. Kelly had come by Señora Delgado's home, where she was staying as a guest. He brought the ledgers from the store with him and carefully explained the figures to Star. There was money, yes, but not as much as Star had expected. It was the war, Michael had explained. None of the traders were making as much profit as they had expected.

"But Charles said the war would help the traders."

"We were expecting the army to buy goods from us. Unfortunately it seems the army here in Santa Fe hasn't enough money to buy food for their men, much less buy trade goods. They haven't seen a paymaster in months, and the war has cut off the usual travel between Chihuahua and Santa Fe. It was always the *ricos* from Chihuahua who bought most of our goods. Without the Chihuahua trade...." Michael shrugged his broad shoulders. "Of course we can store our goods till the war ends, or somehow manage to reach Chihuahua with our wagons."

But I can't wait, Star thought bleakly. Who knew how long the war would last? It was clear that those optimistic souls who thought the war would be ended in only one or two months had underestimated the Mexican determination to defend their homeland. As for her traveling the 600 miles to Chihuahua across the dreaded Jornada del Muerte, she doubted if the doctor would approve such a trip for an expectant mother. Not that she could tell Michael Kelly why she was unable to make such a trip. She could imagine the mocking amusement in his eyes— or would it simply be indifference, she wondered suddenly, with a sharp stab that might have been regret.

With all the beautiful women in Santa Fe eager to catch the eyes of the handsome and eligible Don Miguel, why should he have any interest in a woman who in another few months would be fat and shapeless and ugly, Star thought, her hands clenching into helpless fists in her lap.

She glanced up as the carriage drove by an elegant *casa*,

larger and more handsome than its neighbors. Because she had
been thinking of Mr. Kelly, at first she thought it was her
imagination when she caught a glimpse of familiar broad shoulders, that lithe, Indian stride, as a servant held open the heavy
carved door of the house. It was Michael, she thought, surprised. And that *casa*—surely she remembered someone had
pointed it out to her as a gaming house.

She leaned forward and caught the attention of the driver.
"Juan, whose home is that we just passed?"

"Casa de las Flores, *señora*. Doña Lupita has her monte
bank there, very private, very expensive."

So that explained the infrequency of Mr. Kelly's visits these
last weeks, Star thought. And why he had never bothered to
collect the evening together that she promised him for bringing
her to Santa Fe. Not that she wanted to spend an evening with
a man as arrogant and unprincipled as Mr. Kelly, she thought,
deliberately turning her eyes away from the *botiga*.

She was so intent on keeping her eyes fastened straight ahead
that she did not notice that the visitor to Casa de las Flores had
stopped a moment before entering the *botiga* and, turning, had
caught a glimpse of the back of the slowly moving carriage
and its occupant.

Michael frowned, annoyed, staring after the carriage. What
was Star doing riding alone? Hadn't he warned her never to
go outside the *casa* by herself? He thought of riding after her,
then realized that the carriage must be heading for Doña
Louisa's *casa*, just a few short streets away. And if he missed
this meeting with Lupita, she would have his hide, he thought
with a wry amusement.

The servant was waiting, and he turned and entered the *sala*
where, despite the hour of the morning, the game of monte
was still being played, the continuation of games that had
undoubtedly begun the evening before. The shutters were closed
over the windows, the candles burned brightly on the walls and
tables, and he was sure that none of the players, raptly engaged
in their cards, was even aware that it was morning.

Cigarette smoke hung like a blue mist in the air, along with
the smell of whiskey and brandy, as Michael moved slowly
through the *sala*, finally finding the table where Doña Lupita
sat, dealing monte. As always when she handled the monte

bank, Lupita dressed very simply, in a loose, comfortable black gown, with no jewelry on her long, graceful fingers. As Michael watched, lounging against the wall, he saw her hands sweep away a pile of gold coins from the table into a sack at her side, which was immediately removed by an attendant.

The player at Lupita's table, a bearded trader that Michael recognized, at once put another bag of gold on the table, poured out a pile of pieces, doubling his former stake, and commenced playing upon a new spot.

The cards left Lupita's fingers with skilled precision, but the expression on her beautiful face was almost that of boredom. For a few moments there was only the sound of the cards, slip, slip, slip, through her fingers onto the table. The trader, his face flushed, doubled and doubled again.

"Would you care for a new deck, *señor*?" the dealer asked, her voice soft in the silence that now fell upon all the tables in the room. The other dealers were already closing their games, drifting away, or gathering around Lupita's table.

The player shook his head, giving his dealer a suspicious glance. "We'll stick with the deck we have, *señora*. And keep your hands where I can see 'em."

Doña Lupita smiled graciously. Only Michael, who knew her so well, saw the contempt that flashed for a moment in the dark eyes as the pale hands dealt the cards, slowly, deliberately. In another half hour the dazzling heap of gold and Mexican dollars on the table were once against swept into an empty bag.

Now Doña Lupita paused, her hands resting on the table. "You wish to continue, *señor*?" she asked politely.

The trader let loose an oath and rose clumsily to his feet. "You know I ain't got any gold rascals left," he snorted. "You cleaned me out."

The woman rose serenely. "Then the game is ended, *señor*," she said, motioning to her attendant. He picked up the bag of gold and followed her as she disappeared through a side door.

Michael waited a few minutes to see if there might be any trouble, but the attendants knew their job well. Still grumbling, the trader and his friends were ushered out the front door politely but firmly by several oversized Mexicans.

Michael made his way to the side door, knocked lightly, then entered. The room he entered was richly furnished with a rug on the floor and banquettes, pushed up against the wall, were covered with handsome blankets. Lupita sat at her dressing table while a maid brushed her hair. She had changed from the black gown into a gauzy gold-and-white streaked robe, and her hands sparkled with ruby and diamond rings, while a heavy gold chain wound round her slim, white neck and nestled between the full breasts.

She was smoking a *cigarrito* when Michael entered the room, the blue smoke wreathing around her face, but when she saw him in the mirror, she gave a pleased cry and, dropping the *cigarrito*, ran into his arms. "*Mi alma!* How I've missed you."

She pulled his face down to hers, her lips caressing his mouth hungrily while her arms pulled him close. Almost automatically, Michael returned the kiss until the mouth on his became more teasing, more insistent, and his response not so automatic. Finally his hands slipped beneath the sheer robe to stroke the musk-scented, white satin skin.

When at last he pulled free, he reached around her to crush with his heel the cigarette, still smouldering on the rug. "Someday, *cara mia*, you'll burn the roof down over your head," he warned.

She shrugged indifferently as she pulled him down on one of the banquettes beside her. Her black eyes sparkled behind silken lashes as she smiled lazily up at him. "You still do not approve of my smoking? But all the ladies smoke, even the *ricos.*" Through lowered eyelids, she asked sulkily, "Doesn't your *niña*, Señora Bradford, smoke?"

"The *señora* is not my *niña*," Michael said shortly. Then, as Lupita began to unbutton his shirt, he caught her hands and said, "You didn't insist I come here to talk about Señora Bradford, did you?"

She pouted prettily. "Why shouldn't you come to see me? It's been a whole week. I am desolate without you. I cannot eat or sleep."

Michael grinned. "I saw how desolate you were out there." He jerked his chin toward the *sala.* "That was a whole season's profits that man lost in one night."

His companion shrugged. "If he playes, he must take the chance of losing. It is *en la mano de Diós.*"

"I've noticed God seemed to be mostly on your side of the house," Michael said dryly.

"Why not?" Lupita asked, her dark eyes widening. "I am a *Cristianos*; they—" her soft red mouth twisted contemptuously. "The traders are infidels, the soldiers heathens. They have come to despoil our country, to kill our people."

Michael got to his feet, his voice impatient. "You don't believe that. You care as little about this war as I do."

Slowly the woman got to her feet, studying her companion speculatively. "Is that so, *mi alma*? Sometimes I think you care a great deal. Your mother was, after all, a Cordoba."

"And my father was an American Irish trader from St. Louis," Michael said curtly. "Which makes me neither fish nor fowl, American or Mexican. I have no loyalty to a country, only to myself."

"Is it because Don Francisco left the *rancho* and the mine to Esteban?" Lupita asked. "The old man was angry with you because you defied him. It was you who should have married Doña Elena, as he wished, not Esteban."

Then a coldness in the dark jade green eyes staring at her made Lupita wisely decide not to pursue the matter further.

She reached for her bag of cornhusk wrappers and, using a pair of gold tongs, carefully spread the powdered tobacco within the cornhusk. The servant who had been crouched in a corner of the room rushed forward to light the *cigarrito*, and then flung herself to the floor before the divan so that Lupita could rest her tiny feet on the woman's prostrate body.

Watching the servant make a footstool of herself for her mistress, Michael frowned, annoyed. No matter if it was an accepted practice in Mexico for servants to behave in such a fashion, he had lived in the States too long not to find the custom distasteful, the same way he found the cigarette dangling from Lupita's red lips less than appealing.

Lupita saw the frown and said, petulantly, "You are angry with me, *querido*. It is the flame-haired *niña*. She has bewitched you."

Michael sighed and pushed aside his irritation. He had known Lupita too long and too well, so why should he expect her to change now, like expecting a playful kitten to suddenly have the manners and morals of a great lady. Lupita was clever in her own way, and always beautiful and tireless when making love. What more could any man want?

"I've told you before," he said patiently. "I brought the *señora* and her wagons down the trail from Bent's Fort and found her a *casa* in which to live. That's all."

"Everyone in Santa Fe knows you are lovers," she said jealously.

"Then everyone in Santa Fe is wrong," Michael snapped, not sure whether he was irritated with Lupita because of her suspicions, or even more annoyed with himself because, unfortunately, the suspicions were groundless. By now he should have long since bedded the beautiful widow. Instead, each time he had visited Star during the last weeks, to his own surprise he hadn't so much as touched her, as if those cool silver-gray eyes, that air of unconscious arrogant reserve about Star, threw up an invisible barrier between them, making him feel as awkward as some callow school boy.

"She is *muy linda*, your *niña*," Lupita said wistfully. She herself was a beautiful woman and knew it, but she was clever enough to know that her youth was behind her and that the young, vulnerable loveliness she had glimpsed in Senōra Bradford's face could defeat even her practiced charms.

"Senōra Bradford is hardly a child," Michael said. "She's been married and widowed." Remembering Star's behavior with Charles Bradford in St. Louis, he wasn't even sure how innocent she had been when she ran away to Independence and married Bradford. And she had willingly agreed to join his caravan to Santa Fe; he hadn't forced her to come along. Certainly no carefully brought up Mexican girl would have dreamed of accompanying a man alone on such a trip, nor many respectable American women either, he thought, his face hardening. And a few moments ago, when he had seen her alone in the carriage, where had she been? The town was filled with American officers, only too eager to enjoy the charms of a beautiful widow like Star Bradford.

Lupita saw the warmth burning in the vivid green eyes staring down at her and didn't know it was not her face Michael saw, but another woman's, a woman with flawless creamy skin, fire-lit hair, and cool, disdainful gray eyes that yet managed to promise, if one only looked deeply enough, untold pleasures.

"Mi alma," Lupita whispered, kicking aside the servant, who scurried from the room. The transparent robe drifted, forgotten, to the floor as her hands deftly removed the embroidered vest, the cambric shirt and trousers until finally, with a soft moan of rapture, her hands wound around Michael and pulled him against her, so that his hardness rested between her thighs.

As Michael gently lowered her beneath him on the banquette, just before desire wiped all else from his consciousness, he remembered thinking wryly if it wasn't a special sort of perversity to vent lust roused by one woman upon another.

"Señora, por favor." Doña Louisa's soft voice, always a little breathless, stopped Star as she walked toward the front door of the *casa* late one afternoon. "Surely you were not going out alone?"

Star felt a twinge of exasperation. She had grown very fond of her hostess in the weeks she had spent at the Delgado *casa*. Doña Louisa, plump as a robin and with a bright, eager liveliness, had welcomed Star into her home with as much warmth and affection as if Star had been her own daughter.

Nevertheless, there were times that Star couldn't help feeling that Doña Louisa took her duties as *dueña* much too seriously. Star could not leave the house without her hostess accompanying her in the carriage. That one morning when she had managed to slip off alone to visit the army surgeon, she had returned to the house to find Doña Louisa in a state of shock, the whole household in an uproar at Star's disappearance.

"I won't be gone long," Star said firmly. "I'm just going for a short walk."

"A walk!" Doña Louisa looked as startled as if Star had suggested running stark naked down the street. "With all the soldiers roaming the streets, that's most unwise, my dear. Let me call the carriage and I'll fetch my shawl."

"No." Star heard the irritation in her voice and forced herself to speak more calmly. "Those soldiers are Americans, Doña Louisa, not savages. They don't attack women. I'll be perfectly safe."

Doña Louisa's face clouded. It was true that the people of

Santa Fe had found General Kearny's army of occupation to be surprisingly well behaved. But General Kearny had left with his men for California, and the Missourians who had arrived with Colonel Price to replace General Kearny's men had been of a different caliber. Boisterous, contemptuous of the easy-going Mexicans, they seemed more eager to fight each other or anybody else handy, than to engage in military activities. And their unseasoned volunteer officers more often than not looked the other way, rather than try to enforce discipline.

In any case, Doña Louisa knew it was unheard of for a respectable woman to go out into the public streets without a *dueña*, especially a woman like Señora Bradford, who Dona Louisa had begun to suspect was carrying a child. Her small, rounded chin set stubbornly. "I am sorry, but it cannot be permitted, your leaving the house alone. Don Miguel was very angry the last time."

Beneath the black bonnet, Star's face stiffened. "What I do is none of Mr. Kelly's concern," she said sharply. "I am not accountable to him for my actions, and I will not be a prisoner in this house."

Doña Louisa gave a soft gasp of dismay. It was so difficult, understanding these foreigners with their strange, outlandish ways. Despite the fact that Don Miguel's visits were remarkably infrequent, she had, of course, taken it for granted that he was Señora Bradford's protector, possibly the father of her child. Why else should he be paying Doña Louisa so generously to house the young woman? How could the *señora* be so un-grateful as to flaunt herself on the public streets of the town like some common woman? On the other hand, short of calling the servants and having them drag her young guest to her room, how could she stop the *señora* from leaving?

As Doña Louisa hesitated, her small white hands fluttering nervously before her, a heavy knock at the front door for the moment at least delayed the need to solve her problem.

The servant returned from the entrance to announce to Doña Lousa, "There is an American officer, desiring to speak to Señora Bradford."

"The *señora* is not receiving callers," Doña Louisa answered quickly. The servant had spoken in Spanish and Doña Louisa had replied in Spanish but she had forgotten how clever her American guest was at picking up the language.

Star said quickly, *"Que entre el caballero en la sala."*

Dona Louisa opened her mouth to protest, but the stubborn tilt of Star Bradford's chin made her reconsider. Instead, she settled herself prominently on a chair in the *sala* next to Star as the servant ushered in the American officer.

A small, rusty-haired major with a skimpy beard, and a uniform that somehow seemed a size too large, he nodded to the two women, but it was to Star he spoke. "Please forgive the intrusion, Mrs. Bradford, but if I might have a few moments of your time?"

Star had removed her bonnet, and she gestured to a chair. "Please be seated, Major . . ." she hesitated.

"Jeremy Reston, ma'am, Quartermaster Corps."

He took the proffered seat, sitting uneasily on the edge of the fragile Louis IX chair.

"Would you care for tea?" Star asked. For all the man's unprepossessing appearance, it was pleasant to talk again to an American, she was discovering.

The major looked as if he would have preferred something stronger, but he nodded. "Tea would be fine, ma'am."

Star gave the order to the servant, who, when she returned, brought not tea but hot chocolate, which Star shoud have expected. After she poured the chocolate into beautiful, if cracked, Meissen cups, and exchanged pleasantries with the major for several minutes, she gave her guest a warm smile and asked, "And now how can I help you, Major Reston?"

The major put down the chocolate quickly. "Actually, it was both Mr. Kelly and yourself I wanted to see, ma'am. I couldn't find him at his place of business and I thought perhaps he might be here."

Star arched a questioning eyebrow, her voice distinctly cooling. "I don't understand, Major Reston. Why should you expect to find Mr. Kelly here?"

A flush crept up to the major's retreating hairline. What sort of cat and mouse game was the woman playing, he thought irritably. Everyone knew that the widow Bradford had been married to a traitor who had got himself killed by Comanches

just before the army could hang him, and that afterwards the
widow had come down the trail with Kelly; that he had set her
up in the fancy private home until presumably she bore his
half-breed brat.

He cleared his throat uncomfortably. "I'm sorry, ma'am,
but you and Mr. Kelly are . . . business partners? I thought that
as an American, you would be willing to talk to Mr. Kelly
about my . . . about the difficulty in which the army finds itself."

Star was beginning to regret that she had allowed the major
into the house. She didn't like the way he looked at her, or
what he had intimated about Mr. Kelly and herself. Curiosity,
though, got the better of her, and she asked, "What difficulty,
Major Reston?"

Stumbling a little over the words, the major explained that
the army was unhappily short of ready cash to pay its soldiers
or buy supplies. Even the recent arrival of a paymaster from
St. Louis had only helped a little. More gold was needed immediately or the army in Santa Fe would be in desperate straits.
The major had been ordered to approach the traders in town
for assistance to meet the army's payroll.

"Naturally, the traders will be given government drafts to
cover the loans," he said quickly. He did not think it necessary
to add that so far evey one of the traders he had approached
had flatly refused to take government paper for hard money.

"Couldn't you borrow from the local *ricos*?"

The major shook his head. "That wouldn't do at all, ma'am.
It would be admitting a weakness to the Mexican people, put
the American government in a bad light." As far as the major
was concerned, if he were in command, he would have seized
the necessary food supplies from the local people long ago,
but orders from Washington were that nothing was to be taken
from the Mexicans without proper and full payment.

"Since I understand you own half of the trade goods Mr.
Kelly has in his store," he continued, "I thought you would be
willing to assist your government in its hour of need, show
your patriotism and loyalty . . ." The major fell silent, his small,
deep-set eyes watching Star closely.

It occurred to Star to wonder if the major knew about Charles.
Was the major perhaps insinuating that her loaning the army

money would be a way of repayment for Charles's traitorous act?

"Are you suggesting Mrs. Bradford's loyalty is in question, Major Reston?"

Neither the major nor Star had heard Michael Kelly's approach. Star jumped nervously at his sudden appearance. How quietly the man moved, she thought, annoyed, and then gave Doña Louisa a suspicious glance. No doubt her hostess had sent a servant after Mr. Kelly the minute the major had arrived on the doorstep. And where had the servant found her business partner, she thought scornfully. Probably at the Casa de las Flores with Doña Lupita.

The major's face flushed a deeper red at the dark green eyes staring at him with an Indian's flat, obsidian stare. "I can assure you, Mrs. Bradford, I meant no disrespect." He scrambled to his feet, reached quickly for his hat. "If you should consider loaning the government—"

"You will have to look elsewhere for your money, major," Michael interrupted coldly. "Mrs. Bradford has no intention of giving gold for the army's worthless paper."

"You did not think the army so worthless, sir, when we guarded the traders' wagons from Bent's Fort to Santa Fe," the major retorted, stung to anger.

"Come now, major," Michael drawled, amused. "The Santa Fe traders have been taking their wagons safely to New Mexico long before the army came along." A smile twitched at the corners of his mouth. "And perhaps you've forgotten that it was a trader, James Magoffin, who was sent by Washington to Santa Fe ahead of the army and negotiated successfully with Armijo so that he withdrew his troops and Kearny was able to take New Mexico without a fight."

Star had not heard that story about Mr. Magoffin, but from the angry look on the major's face, she suspected it was the truth.

"I'll be saying good day, ma'am," the major said abruptly. Then, bowing over her hand, "The officers in Santa Fe are giving a *baile* at the Governor's Palace next month. We would be honored if you would attend."

Before Michael could speak for her again, Star said firmly,

"Thank you, Major Reston, but as you see, I'm in mourning."

"Yes, of course." The major's eyes sidled from his hostess to Michael Kelly, and the knowing look in the small eyes brought a stain of color to Star's cheeks.

"I'll see you to the door," she said, and felt Michael's hands tighten on her shoulder.

"You needn't bother," he said coldly. "Doña Louisa will take care of the major."

As soon as the major and Doña Louisa had left the *sala*, Star jerked herself free from Michael's grasp, whirling indignantly upon him. "How dare you? How dare you march in here and behave as if you owned this house, as if you owned me!"

Michael went to the sideboard and took his time mixing ice and lime juice and rum, before he turned again to Star, his face impassive. "It so happens that I do own this house. It was formerly in the possession of the Delgado family. Doña Louisa stayed on as my housekeeper. As for my interrupting your tête-à-tête with the major. . . . " He shrugged indifferently. "I would suggest you pick your guests more carefully. Major Reston has a less than savory reputation with the ladies."

"And your reputation is so much better?" Star asked cuttingly.

Michael smiled, lifting an amused eyebrow. "Worse, probably, but then I didn't realize you were interested in my prowess with the fair sex."

"I'm not," Star said coldly. "But the major seemed to think. . . . You let him believe . . . " Her voice faltered, embarrassed.

Michael put down his drink and came to stand in front of Star, laughter in his eyes as he saw the discomfiture in her face. "That we were lovers," he said softly. "Does the thought disturb you so?"

Star pulled her gaze away from those intense green eyes that saw too much. There was something different about Mr. Kelly today, she thought. There was the same flat hardness to his face, but behind the mocking amusement in his eyes she glimpsed a bleakness, almost a raw pain, that startled her. She moved a safe distance across the room. "Of course it disturbs me," she said hotly. "And you had no right making decisions for me about my own money. If I want to loan it to the army, it's my concern."

"Only you have precious little gold to loan to anybody," Michael said flatly. "Enough to get you safely back to St. Louis, and I have no intention of watching you squander that on some quixotic whim to make up somehow for what your husband tried to do with the guns and ammunition he had hidden in his wagons."

A stillness settled over the heart-shaped face, the silver-gray eyes remote as stars in a winter's sky. "I have no reason to discuss my husband with you, Mr. Kelly," she said coldly, but she was shaken. How had he guessed? How could he read her mind so easily? It was disconcerting that this man she hardly knew, whom she wasn't even sure she trusted, could know her so well.

She forced herself to look directly into that darkly handsome face. She felt the undeniable attraction of the man reach out to her, making her feel oddly breathless, as if she'd run a long distance. It was an effort to keep her voice composed as she said, "I think it's time we ended our business relationship, Mr. Kelly. If you'll give me the money that's owing me, I'll make arrangements for leaving Santa Fe as soon as possible."

She walked past him toward the door, but his hand reached out and caught her arm, turning her around to face him again. "But it's not ended, not yet," he said softly, but his eyes were hard and cold. "You haven't forgotten our agreement? I brought your wagons and you to Santa Fe, as I promised. Now I intend to hold you to your end of the bargain."

He turned away from her and snapped his fingers. A servant came into the room carrying a large box, elaborately wrapped with gilt paper and ribbons. He handed the package to Star with a flourish. "It isn't that you don't look charming in black," he said, smiling disarmingly. "However, for our last evening together, I prefer you in a more festive gown."

Except, she thought furiously, he wasn't asking her. He was ordering her to wear the gown, taking it for granted that she would spend the evening with him, as if she were his mistress, like that monte dealer. Before she could protest, though, he had touched his lips lightly to her hand and murmured, "You won't disappoint me, I'm sure."

Then he was gone and she was still clutching the box, her face frozen with anger. Well, he would cool his heels waiting for her, she thought, marching from the *sala* and flinging the box on the bed in her room. The maid had closed the shutters to keep the room cool but it felt all at once too cool, and she started a fire in the tiny beehive fireplace in a corner of the room, the fragrance of burning piñon logs soon scenting the air.

Taking off the black gown, she slipped into a cotton robe inset with strips of lace, and, sitting at her dressing table, began to brush her hair, carefully not looking at the unopened box on the bed.

It was her maid, Rosita, who opened the box and let out a pleased cry as she held the gown up before her. "*Ay*, it's so *hermosa*."

"Put the gown away, Rosita," Star said. "I'll be having dinner in my room."

Then, reluctantly, Star glanced toward the bed and felt a start of pleasure. It was a stunning gown, of some soft gauzy muslin material in a color that was the palest springlike green, with silver ribbons tying the small puffed sleeves and catching up the flounces of the embroidered skirt. Slowly, almost against her own volition, she reached out a hand and touched the soft material, which clung irresistibly to her fingertips.

"The *señora* will look like an angel," Rosita said proudly. "Don Miguel will be helpless in her hands."

Star got to her feet, pulled her robe tight around her waist, and studied herself thoughtfully in the mirror. She certainly didn't look as if she were carrying a child, she decided. Her waist was still tiny, her stomach flat, only her breasts were fuller, more rounded. And there was a definite bloom about her face, a soft radiance that had not been there before.

Her mouth quirked in a sudden, mischievous smile. Mr. Kelly was so sure that all he had to do was snap his fingers, give a woman a new gown, and she would tumble eagerly into his arms. Well, tonight he would learn differently, she thought.

She held the gown before her, her eyes calculating as she gazed at herself in the mirror.

"Shall I put the gown away, *señora*?" Rosita asked unhappily.

"No, I've changed my mind. I'll wear the gown to dinner after all." Star reached for her hairbrush. Rosita was right, she thought confidently. Mr. Kelly would be helpless in her hands. And when she had him helpless, she thought triumphantly, her eyes shining diamond bright, Mr. Kelly would be taught a lesson about women that he would not soon forget.

Chapter Eleven

Later, looking back on that evening at the Delgado casa, Star was unable to pinpoint the precise moment her carefully laid plans began to go awry. Certainly the evening had begun exactly as she had planned. She had watched, smugly, the flattering warmth leap into Michael's eyes when she walked into the candle-lit dining room, wearing the pale sea-green gown that drifted in deep flounces from her tiny, silver-beribboned waist and clung tightly above her waist in a low-cut bodice trimmed with Valenciennes lace. The lace moved as she did, revealing then artfully concealing the creamy skin and swell of her breasts. Silver slippers peeped from beneath the gown, and silver ribbons were wound through the coiled auburn hair.

All through the dinner, from the sopa de vermicelli to the several desserts, the caramel pudding and the coconut cake, to the chilled fruit, Star couldn't have asked for a more devoted, attentive dinner companion than Michael Kelly. Or a more amusing one. She had forgotten how long it had been since she laughed, really laughed, with a girlish abandon, breaking into helpless giggles at the humorous stories Michael told of his early days on the trail when he had been as much a greenhorn as Star had been.

Delicious local wines were served with each course of the meal, finishing with champagne with the desserts. Wine had never been allowed in her father's Presbyterian household, and now Star was discovering she liked the taste of it, especially the champagne that tickled deliciously going down her throat and made her feel delightfully light-headed.

After dinner, when Doña Louisa tactfully disappeared, and Michael suggested they walk out onto the patio, Star carried a glass of champagne with her. The servants had placed candles around the courtyard, but their flickering light was hardly needed, with a brilliant full moon and a scattering of stars flung across the deep blue sky. In the clear night air, the scent of aromatic piñon fagots mingled with the spicy fragrance of the oleander bushes and the tuberose flowering vines that tumbled from the terrace roof of the *casa* into the patio.

Star settled herself on a wrought-iron bench, sipping her champagne and studying Michael Kelly's face from beneath her lashes. The candlelight played across his features, accenting the flat planes of his face, the dark, slanted brows, and a mouth that could smile with such arrogant self-assurance one minute and then soften, as it did now, smiling down bemusedly at her like any smitten lover.

"Are you warm enough, *querida?*" he asked. "Shall I fetch your shawl?"

She shook her head. She felt deliciously warm. Perhaps it was the champagne, she thought blissfully, or the knowledge warming her that soon, very soon, her companion would attempt to make love to her. Oh, she would allow him a few favors, she decided magnanimously, just enough so that he would be even more crushed when, in her very best ladylike manner, the way she had been taught at the convent school, she would make it very plain that she had no intention at all of surrendering to his charms.

The sound of several guitars playing very near startled her out of her reverie. But then there were always guitars playing, men and women singing in the streets of Santa Fe, as one fandango followed after another, night after night, and the music of the waltz, the cuna, the reel, spilled loudly out of open windows into the street. These musicians, though, were not moving on. They must be standing right outside the patio wall. It was a love song they were playing, bitter sweet, liltingly lovely.

Star cast a questioning glance at Michael, her lips curving in a provocative half smile. "How disappointing, Mr. Kelly. I thought surely you'd serenade me yourself."

For a moment he looked abashed, then grinned broadly. "I must confess I'm all thumbs with a guitar. But no Mexican would ever consider an evening with a beautiful woman complete without music. And please," he coaxed, "surely we know each other well enough for first names." He paused. "How did you come by a name like Star?"

"My father named me after the blazing star, the wildflower that you told me is also called gayfeathers," Star explained. "Mother liked the name and kept it for me."

Thinking of her parents, both now lost to her, a wave of homesickness swept over her, followed by a panic like a hand squeezing at her heart. Suddenly the lovely night surrounding Star was no longer filled with music, fragrance, and laughter, but with bleak despair. Everything she had been desperately trying to forget suddenly came rushing back into her mind. The child was there, growing just beneath her heart. She couldn't run away from it. Yet how could she take care of it when she wasn't sure how she was going to take care of herself, alone in a foreign land, in the middle of a war?

The musicians had begun to play a waltz, gay and inviting. Michael was standing before her, holding out his hands. "May I have the honor, madam?"

The next moment she was in his arms. At first she held herself warily, but then as his arm rested lightly but firmly around her waist, guiding her expertly through the fashionable steps of the waltz, she began to relax in his arms. She moved lightly over the stone floor of the patio, her skirt swirling like the petals of a flower around her, her eyes half-closed, dreamy.

She was sorry when the music stopped, only vaguely aware that Michael still had his arms around her, until his arms tightened, drawing her closer. Her eyes flew open, startled, to find his face so near her own she could see the dark flecks in the green eyes. His voice was warm against her face as he whispered, "Someday you will dance the tarantella for me, *querida*, with your red hair hanging down to your waist, barefoot like a *gitana*, wearing only a skirt and a *camisa*, but dancing only for me, for my eyes."

"No, I mean, I couldn't," she said, flustered, thinking that it was time now to step back, out of harm's way, except somehow, with his lips lightly caressing her eyelids, the curve of her cheek, then moving softly over her mouth, the words wouldn't come. In a minute, she thought, feeling a delightful languor take possession of her, as his lips moved down the graceful line of her throat. Then he bent her back in his arms so they could claim the curved roundness of her breasts.

Wherever his mouth touched she could feel a warmth start, a trembling deep inside her. Without even knowing how it had happened, her own lips were parting, responding. She hadn't dreamed a kiss could be this way, so tender, teasing at her senses, promising ever more pleasure, not at all the way Charles had ever kissed her or even the brutal way Michael had kissed her so long ago that night in the Kirkland garden.

Then, to her surprise, it was Michael who suddenly pulled away. She was even more shocked when she looked up into his face and saw that he was darkly scowling down at her. Feeling strangely nervous under that fierce frown, she turned away, tugging at the neckline of her gown, which had fallen off one shoulder, reaching for the glass of half-finished champagne. She swallowed the rest of the champagne and held out the empty glass to Michael, murmuring, "Is there more?"

He took the glass from her hand, his voice oddly flat. "You've had enough."

"What is it?" she asked, puzzled at his anger. And then, laughing a little brittlely. "I would have thought champagne was part of the seduction you had in mind."

He looked down into her pale face lifted to his, the moonlight brushing lightly with silver the creamy skin, the gray eyes shining like stars caught behind the dark, smudged lashes. Damn it, what was wrong with him, he brooded. In another few moments they would have been in the bedroom, he would have been taking off her gown, savoring the loveliness that lay waiting beneath the flounces and petticoats, and the torment of desire she had roused in him since the first moment they had met would have been slaked, fiercely, once and for all.

Yet, all at once, he knew he didn't want her, not that way, half-giddy from too much wine, swept off her feet by a carefully staged romantic evening, by caresses that were equally staged and calculated to awaken her passion, so that she wouldn't think, only feel when he presented his proposition to her.

"I want to marry you," he said harshly.

She sat down on the iron bench, her eyes widening, shocked. "You—what?" she blurted.

"I want to marry you," he repeated, his voice softening, and then, with mock gravity, "Shall I get down on my knees to you and make a proper proposal? Unfortunately, I've no time for a conventional courtship. As a matter of fact, if you wish, you need not consider it a conventional marriage at all, rather an extension of our business partnership."

Looking into those intense green eyes that no longer held the warmth of a besotted lover, Star wished she did have a shawl for her shoulders—the night suddenly seemed chill. "Perhaps you'd better explain," she said carefully.

He nodded, moving away from her to stand by a trellised rosebush. "Yes, I want you to know the whole story. I received word yesterday that my half brother, Esteban, had left the *rancho* and joined General Pedro de Ampudia's army."

"Ampudia," Star said, frowning, trying to remember. "Wasn't that the general that General Taylor fought at Monterrey just a few weeks ago? Was your brother in that battle?"

"He was killed at Monterrey," Michael said. For a moment the impassive face was contorted, twisted with a terrible, wrenching pain, before it once more became blankly hard again.

"I'm sorry," Star said softly, realizing that it had never occurred to her that Michael Kelly, with his arrogant ruthlessness, could be hurt like any other man. And then, puzzled, "But I don't see why your brother's death should mean that you must marry."

Michael shrugged wryly. "It goes back to when my father, James Kelly, married my mother. She had been married before, to an older man carefully picked for her by her father. Her husband died a year after their marriage, the same year that Esteban was born. A year later my mother, against her father's wishes, married my father, a *gringo* marrying the daughter of Francisco Diaz y Cordoba." Michael smiled bitterly. "My grandfather accepted the marriage because he had no choice. I was on the way into the world. But he never forgave my mother, and when she died giving birth to me, his feelings never changed. My father was always the outsider, and though in time my grandfather grew to tolerate, perhaps even love me, Esteban was always his favorite."

"What of your own father?"

"I hardly knew him. He was away a good deal of the time, conducting his business on the Santa Fe trail. One day he came to visit the ranch and, taking a good look at me, was shocked to discover I was growing up more Mexican than American. That was when he sent me to live with his brother in New York. While I was in the States, my father was killed in an Apache raid. And when I returned to the *rancho*, I found that my grandfather had made arrangements for me to marry Elena Moreno, the daughter of a good friend of his." At Star's surprised glance, he smiled thinly. "It's not unusual in Mexico, arranged marriages. It's seldom a young Mexican man or woman has any choice in whom they are to marry. It's for their family to decide, to keep the bloodlines untainted, and," he added grimly, "to make sure the marriage is profitable to both families."

Only, he remembered, he had been young and wild and quick-tempered and had had no intention of anyone picking out a bride for him, or even of marrying at all. He had argued with his grandfather, always a mistake with that mercurial, arrogant man with a temper as vitriolic as Michael's own.

"I refused to marry the young woman my grandfather had selected for me. I seem to recall I told him I had no intention of marrying at all. My brother married Elena instead, but my grandfather never forgave me for bringing dishonor to the Cordoba name. He died five years later and in his will he left all the Cordoba holdings to Esteban. If Esteban died and left no heirs, then the *rancho* and the estates would come to me— only, however, if I were a respectably married man. I never thought much about the will. Esteban was young and healthy and married and would eventually have children. And he was happy to have me manage the ranch and the mine and occasionally the trading end of the business. Esteban was . . ." Michael chose his words carefully, "a scholar, interested in his books and music, not a businessman, but I never dreamed he'd be foolish or romantic enough to join the Mexican army, and get himself killed in the bargain."

Star was quiet a few moments, thinking about what Michael had told her, sorting out the complex relationships of people she didn't even know. "Suppose," she said, "you didn't marry. What happens then?"

"There is a cousin, Alfredo Cordoba y Ortega, who has a ranch adjacent to the Cordoba *rancho*. The Cordoba holdings will pass to him." A coldness in Michael's voice when he spoke his cousin's name sent a shiver through Star. His mouth twisted cruelly. "There is no way I will allow Alfredo to take over the Cordoba lands."

"But why me?" Star asked. "Surely you must know other women." She fell silent, thinking of Señora de las Flores. She supposed Michael might hesitate to marry a woman with Doña Lupita's reputation. Still, there had to be other women, respectable Mexican women of good families, only too happy to marry a man of Michael's wealth when he inherited the Cordoba estate, not to mention the devastating charm that Michael could turn on when it pleased him.

Why indeed, Michael thought, studying the young woman sitting so quietly, only her face alive, with that quick intelligence that irritated and yet pleased him. Star would never be the typical Mexican wife, passive, submissive, bending her will to his without question. Perhaps he had been too long among American women, he thought. Perhaps that was why she intrigued him—that, and her beauty that never failed to stir him, as if he were seeing her for the first time. He didn't delude himself that it was love he felt. He wasn't even sure that he believed in that will-o'-the-wisp emotion. In the end there was only a mutual shared desire between a man and woman in bed, and mutual tolerance of each other's faults out of bed.

When Star remained mute, her gaze fastened on the flagstone floor of the patio, a hardness pulled at the muscles in his face and his eyes narrowed to icy slits. "Is it because I'm a breed?" he demanded coldly. "Is that why you won't marry me? Look at me, Star." He reached down, forced her chin up so that her eyes had to meet his. "Is it because you can't see yourself married to a Mexican—a greaser," he said harshly.

Surprise flooded her face. "Of course that's not it," she said, startled. "It's only . . ." She pulled her face free from his grasp. "It's just that I never intend to marry again," she said firmly.

Had she loved Bradford so much then, Michael thought, disconcerted by the sharp jab of jealousy the thought brought him. Then the look in those wide gray eyes, a mixture of pain and vulnerability, made him reach out and draw her gently into his arms. "Is that wise, *querida?*" he asked quietly. "A woman in your condition needs a husband."

He felt her stiffen in his arms. "You know?" she asked, shocked. "You know I'm carrying another man's child and you still want to marry me?"

"Why not?" he asked, indifferently. "I like children, and the ranch is large enough for a great many." He wondered what Star would think if she knew that half the people in Santa Fe believed that the child she was carrying was his own.

His arms pulled her closer, his hands and then his lips caressing her hair, speaking to her softly now in Spanish, sweet endearments that she didn't understand but sounded somehow so much more romantic in Spanish. Gradually she felt the stiffness, the wariness leave her body. It was crazy, of course, Michael's proposal, not to be thought of for a moment. Still, she sighed and rested her head against shoulders that felt so hard and strong, as if within the circle of those arms nothing could ever harm her again. Even the fear she had lived with these past weeks, the lonely, panicky feeling that would waken her in the middle of the night and sit like a stone on her chest, seemed to fade. If she were married, she would be safe, the baby would have a home, would grow up like any other child with a mother and father.

As Michael's hands, sensing her weakening, began to move slowly over her body, lightly caressing the delicate bones of her spine, then resting just above her waist, the thumbs moving upward to stroke the swell of her breasts, she felt a different, more terrifying, fear suddenly return, sending shock waves of panic through her. Had she forgotten so quickly what always followed the deceptively tender caresses: the humiliation, the pain and degradation.

Abruptly she thrust Michael away from her and stepped back, trying to think. She reminded herself that he was the one who had started out suggesting that the marriage be one of convenience, a business arrangement. If it were that, nothing more, wouldn't that still solve her problems?

"Did you mean it?" she asked, holding her body rigidly erect. "Did you mean that the marriage would be the same as a business partnership?"

Now it was his turn to stare at her bewildered, not understanding.

Quickly she hurried on, before he could speak, before she lost her nerve. "I'll agree to marry you, Michael, but only if it is just that, a marriage of convenience, nothing more. You'll have the wife you need so that the Cordoba estates will be yours, and I'll have a home for myself and my child."

"I see." Nothing in Michael's carefully guarded voice betrayed the anger erupting within him like a volcano. So that was all she was interested in, he thought coldly, a make-believe marriage that would bring her wealth and security, without the need to endure his lovemaking. And he had almost been fool enough to betray to her how much he wanted, desired her. He shrugged carelessly, his sardonic gaze raking her face. "I don't see why not, if that's what you want. I can always find my . . . comforts elsewhere."

Star winced, thinking of Doña Lupita, but then, straightening her shoulders, she lifted her chin haughtily. "And there should be something in writing, some monetary arrangement, so that if the marriage doesn't work out, my child and I won't be left destitute." Never again, she thought, clenching her hands into fists at her side. Never again would she allow herself to be left in the completely helpless position she had found herself in after Charles's death.

Michael's mouth thinned to a hard, cynical smile. "You strike a hard bargain, *mi querida*," he said. "But if it's what you wish . . ."

"I do," she said firmly, although she was trembling inside and it was only with the greatest effort of will that she kept her eyes fastened on that impassive face, the contempt glittering in those narrowed green eyes.

"Very well. I'll have the papers drawn up the first thing in the morning and then see the priest about the wedding arrangements. It will have to be a Catholic wedding," he warned. "No other marriage would be considered valid in a Mexican court of law, or in accordance with my grandfather's will."

"I have no objection to a Catholic wedding," Star said. She wet her suddenly dry lips. "When . . . when would the wedding be?"

"I don't want to appear to be sweeping you off your feet," he said dryly, "but if it can be arranged, will the day after tomorrow be too soon? I'm most anxious to return to the ranch as soon as possible, after stopping at Chihuahua to sell the rest of the trade goods."

So soon, Star thought, her heart pounding. Still, what difference would a few days make? She had made up her mind, and it would be better to get it over with before she lost her nerve.

"That will be fine," she said coolly, holding out her hand to Michael.

As if he were a stranger she were bidding good night, Michael thought, enraged. He lowered his eyelids so that she could not see the anger flaring there. He remembered the way she had danced, how she had moved, so soft and pliant in his arms, how warm and inviting her skin had felt beneath his lips when he had kissed her. He could wait, he thought coldly, feeling the hand tremble when he lifted it deliberately, turning it over to place a long, lingering kiss in the palm. No woman had ever bested him, he thought coldly. It should, he thought grimly, be an interesting wedding night.

The wedding of Margaret McFarland Bradford to Michael Roberto Kelly y Cordoba took place three days later. During those three days, Star's moods alternated between a relief that she would no longer have to worry about the future of herself and her baby, and pure panic at the thought of marrying again and going off to live with a man she scarcely knew. She reminded herself that she had the legal papers, which had arrived promptly the morning after Michael's proposal, giving her financial security no matter what happened in her unorthodox marriage. The terms were more generous than Star had thought to ask, making her feel vaguely guilty.

The wedding itself took place in a small adobe church on the outskirts of Santa Fe, before a simple, lovingly carved wooden altar, on a rush floor that had been swept scrupulously clean. The priest had an ascetic, pale face and he spoke beautiful Latin as he smiled gently at Star during the service, as if aware of her fears and trying to reassure her. Doña Louisa and an officer friend of Michael's, Captain Lauren Curtis, were the only guests at the wedding. Doña Louisa cried softly all through the ceremony, but Star's eyes were dry. Once she stole a look at Michael's face but could glimpse only his profile, sharp-edged, the small jagged scar standing out whitely against the dark skin, his mouth a cold, thin line. His hand, though, when he slipped the ring on Star's finger, was warm. Where, she wondered, had he found the ring? It looked like a family heirloom, set with tiny garnets. Suddenly she remembered that other wedding with Charles, the minister with the sly eyes and the wife with the dirty dress, and Charles's mouth on hers, dry and hard. Her hand began to tremble so that Michael had to hold it tightly before he could slip the ring into place.

After the wedding, Doña Louisa insisted upon a small wedding party at the *casa*, with champagne and tiny fruit cakes, while she bemoaned the fact that there were no more livelier festivities and so few guests.

The captain had had too much champagne, and as he toasted the bride and groom he insisted that Michael must bring his new wife to the *baile* at the Governor's Palace the next week, so that all could admire her loveliness.

"I don't think we—" Star began but felt Michael slip a warning arm around her waist as he interrupted smoothly.

"We'd be honored to attend, Lauren, that is, if we're still in town."

The captain frowned, worried. "You're not thinking of taking your wagons to Chihuahua, Michael, at least not until Doniphan makes his move south, clearing the trail. The Navajos and Utes have been busy sending out war parties against caravans and Mexican settlements, not to mention the possibility of your running into Mexican dragoons."

"I thought General Taylor had signed an eight-week armistice at Monterrey," Michael said.

"Damn fool thing to do," the captain mourned. "Won't last, especially when President Polk hears of it." He laughed shortly. "Jimmy Polk knows that old Rough-and-Ready Taylor is using the war as a political platform for his own presidential campaign against Polk. Anyway, Taylor should have had the sense to wipe out the Mexicans at Monterrey while he had the chance, instead of letting Ampudia march out with his army still intact."

Star felt Michael's arm tighten around her waist. She did not look up, but she could imagine the anger gathered in those narrowed eyes. "My half brother died at Monterrey," Michael said quietly, "fighting with General Ampudia."

The captain's face went ashen, his voice stammering apologetically. "My God, Michael, I'm sorry. I didn't know. I hear Ampudia put up a damn good fight. It took three days for Taylor to get him and his men cornered, and the dragoons had to fight from house to house, inch by inch." A professional's scorn for the amateur crept into his voice. "Taylor would never have won the battle at all if it hadn't been for Colonel Worth and his regulars, and Taylor's brother-in-law Jefferson Davis, and his First Mississippi Rifles."

"I never understood the reason to take Monterrey at all," Michael said. "It has no military importance and could easily have been bypassed."

"Winning battles come in handy when a man's running for president," the captain said cynically. "I'll wager the newspapers back home are already filled with Taylor's great military victory at Monterrey." He twirled his empty champagne glass, then changed the subject abruptly. "You're friends with Ortiz and Archuleto, aren't you, Michael?"

Michael's expression did not alter, but his voice sharpened warily. "I know both of the gentlemen. The Ortiz and the Archuleto families are old and respected in Santa Fe."

"Stay clear of them, Michael," the captain said abruptly. "The army's heard rumors that there's talk of a rebellion, something happening up in the hills where Ortiz and Archuleto are hiding out. I wouldn't want you to get involved in their troubles."

Michael lifted an amused eyebrow. "You should know me better than that, Lauren. I'm a trader, not a soldier. My only concern is to get my goods safely to Chihuahua."

Star glanced swiftly up at Michael's face. She knew that mocking note in his voice too well to be fooled by it, and from the uneasy look on the captain's face, she knew he wasn't convinced either. Swiftly she leaned forward and asked, "May I get you more champagne, captain? Your glass is empty."

She hardly sipped her own glass of champagne. The strain of the last three days was beginning to tell on her, and a headache had begun to throb in her temple. She was relieved when Doña Louisa and the captain finally tactfully withdrew. While Michael accompanied the captain to the front gate, she went quickly to her bedroom, where Rosita was placing a white, lacy gown and robe across the bed.

She did not recognize either the gown or the robe. "Where did they come from?" she asked Rosita sharply.

The girl gave her mistress a sly, pleased glance. "A wedding present from Don Miguel. *Muy linda,* yes?"

She held up the gown, and Star could clearly see the girl's hand through the sheer fabric. She felt her face grow hot. She almost ordered the girl to take the gown away but stopped herself in time. There was no need for the whole household to know that she was planning to spend her wedding night alone.

"I'll undress myself, Rosita," she said. "You can go along to bed."

Giggling, the girl scurried from the room. Star undressed quickly, reaching for her cotton nightgown, hanging on a hook in the wall, then paused, gazing wistfully at the bed, at the gown still stretched out there, delicate as spun moonbeams. It wouldn't do any harm just to try it on. Of course she had no intention of keeping it. It wasn't the sort of nightgown that a respectable woman wore to bed.

Oh, but it was beautiful, she thought, her eyes glowing with delight when she had slipped the gown over her head, the sheer material clinging to her breasts and hips, falling as airy as cobwebs to her ankles. The tiniest of straps secured the filmy, tucked bodice to her shoulders so that she felt positively indecent.

"You are even lovelier than I thought you'd be, *mi querida.*"

Star spun around, startled. Michael stood in the doorway of her room, watching her, a half smile on his face. His broad shoulders seemed to fill the doorway, his head almost touching the lintel of the door.

Snatching up the robe from the bed, she hastily wrapped it around her, although the robe was hardly less sheer than the gown. "What are you doing here?" she demanded, more angry than frightened by his sudden appearance. And then, coldly,

"Our agreement didn't include your visiting me in my bedroom."

Michael stepped into the room, closing the door softly behind him. "As I recall, it was to be a marriage of convenience, if that's what you wanted." The smile deepened as the dark green eyes, looking a pure translucent green in the candlelight, traveled over the slim figure standing before him, as if even the sheer gown didn't exist. The warmth in those eyes stirred an uneasy answering warmth in Star's own body, causing a peachlike flush to spread under the creamy skin. He laughed softly, and walked with his pantherish Indian's stride toward her. "But I'm not convinced it's what you want, *amor mia*, not the way you look in that gown, and not after I remember how you kissed me the other evening."

Then, before she could cry out, his arms were around her and his lips were on hers, not with the teasing gentleness of the kiss on the patio, but crushing her mouth beneath his. She was too shocked to struggle at first. Then the sheer bodice of the gown was being roughly pushed aside while his hand impatiently sought and found her breast, the peak velvety soft beneath his stroking fingers. Terror whipsawed through her. For one nightmarish moment it was happening all over again. It was Charles with his hands hurting her, humiliating her, the nerves in her skin jerking spasmodically in painful memory. A whimper of protest started deep in her throat and she was struggling frantically like wild thing, trying to push him away as Michael forced her back onto the bed.

She could hear her voice as if from a great distance, pleading, low, rotelike, "No, please, no!"

Michael drew back, puzzled. He had thought that the trembling body beneath the silken gown was caught up in the driving throes of passion, as his was, but he saw now that the wide gray eyes staring up at him were not soft and blurred with desire but filled with fear and loathing.

Michael rolled away from Star and got swiftly to his feet. For a long moment he stared down at the woman on the bed, at the body held rigid, at the frozen white mask of a face. His own face became dangerously still, so that only the dark green eyes seemed alive as they flicked contemptuously across Star. "I see that I was mistaken, *senōra*," he said harshly. "My apologies. The agreement will stand, as you wish. Exactly as you wish."

Then he was gone. For several moments Star lay still, every muscle in her body pulled taut. It was true then, she thought, wincing as she remembered the way Michael had looked at her. She was only half a woman, just as Charles had told her. Whatever it was a man wanted from a woman, she was unable to give.

Wearily, she got out of bed and, taking off the beautiful gown of moonbeams, slipped into her practical cambric gown and, finally, slept.

Chapter Twelve

Rosita put the final touch on Star's hairdo. The rich auburn hair swept up in waves on top of her head was held in place by a high Spanish comb of silver set with clusters of emeralds, matching the emerald-colored shimmering velvet gown that Star wore. The emeralds that glittered in the earrings and necklace flashed like green fire against her creamy skin.

Rosita adjusted a lace mantilla over Star's head, then stepped back and sighed happily. "The *señora* looks like a Spanish *aristo*, a *grande señora*. She will be the most beautiful *señora* at the ball."

Star touched the exquisite necklace uneasily. The necklace, earrings, and comb must be worth a small fortune and had belonged to Michael's mother. He had insisted that she wear the jewelry to the ball, along with the gown he had bought for her. At first Star had protested, but had finally agreed to a compromise: she wouldn't wear mourning to the ball, but she would not dance.

"As you please," Michael had shrugged, as if it were a matter of indifference to him if she joined in the dancing. As if whatever she did was of no great concern to him, Star thought, although when they were in public, he played the perfect husband, courteous and attentive to her every wish. Even when they were alone together here at the *casa*—which seldom happened, since Michael spent most of his days hiring men and preparing the wagons and goods for their trip south—not by word or look did he express any disappointment in his marriage, or any resentment of that disastrous wedding night.

Star quickly turned her attention back to her toilette. She

did not want to think about that night. At times she almost succeeded in blotting it out of her memory, as if it had never happened. She smiled at her maid. "You must take the evening off, Rosita. I can undress myself when I come home."

"Gracias, señora." Rosita gave her mistress a wide, childish smile of delight. She was a few years older than Star, but despite her full breasts and hips, she seemed much younger with her round face and guileless black eyes. "I will be attending a fandango with *mi soldado."*

Star knew Rosita was seeing a soldier, an American she guessed from the girl's rapturous description. But then most of the young Mexican women in Santa Fe had boyfriends among Doniphan's or Price's regiment.

"What does Jose have to say about your new friend?" she asked curiously. Jose was the young gardener at the *casa,* who had spent a lot of time gazing longingly at Rosita when Star had first come to live with Doña Louisa.

The smile dimmed. "Oh, Jose! He went to visit his parents near Parral and the soldiers came through the village and took all the young men there for the army." Her face brightened. "My *gringo* is much handsomer than Jose, with his blue eyes and fair hair. And so strong, like a young bull. All night we make love and he never grows tired."

Listening to the girl's happy artless chatter left an acrid taste like alum in Star's mouth. Why should it be so simple for a girl like Rosita to fall into bed with a man, she thought bitterly, to welcome what passed between a man and a woman as effortlessly and eagerly as she ate or drank, and think no more of it, while Star herself . . . Irritably she got to her feet. After all, she wasn't some stupid peasant girl who found pleasure in rutting with any man who came along. "Bring me my shawl, Rosita," she said sharply. "I'm already late."

She hurried out into the patio. But if Michael had grown impatient with waiting, he didn't show it. He rose smoothly in one graceful movement, grinding out the cheroot he had been smoking in a silver ashtray. As she walked toward him, Star couldn't help thinking resentfully, why did he have to be so handsome?

The fine broadcloth of his black jacket fit smoothly over his shoulders, and his trousers were cut in the Spanish style, almost too tight over the muscular thighs. The white ruffled shirtfront contrasted with the dark skin of a face whose features were chiseled to a classical sharpness. The lashes hiding the green eyes were almost indecently long for a man's.

He smiled a greeting at Star's approach, his gaze moving swiftly from the green satin dancing shoes to the mantilla, frothy white and lacy, around her face. He said nothing, however, only murmuring, "It's a chill evening," and, reaching for her shawl, wrapped it around her shoulders.

As he did so, his hand brushed her shoulder where the gown fell away at the neckline, and he felt a muscle under her skin jerk at his touch. For a second his mouth tightened into a hard, cruel line, feeling a flicker of anger lick at his nerves. Or was it only injured pride, he thought ruefully, pulling his emotions swiftly back under control. It was discomfiting to be married to a woman who cringed at your slightest touch, an experience that was not only new to Michael but bewildering as well. Had she loved Charles Bradford so much that even the touch of another man offended her? Well, let her sleep alone in her narrow widow's bed, he thought coldly. He had no interest in competing with a ghost.

They walked slowly through the gate and out into the street where a servant holding a torch lit the way. Michael carefully handed her up into the waiting carriage, making sure she was completely settled before swinging up beside her and signaling the coachman to drive on. As the carrige turned into the plaza, church bells were clanging, announcing fandangos and *bailes*, the din making Star's ears ring.

The carriage stopped before the palace. The building was brightly lit with torches set in silver holders at the door and hundreds of candles burning inside the great *sala*. The candlelight glittered against gilt epaulettes on the officer's blue dress uniforms, gold buttons and satin and gold sword belts. As Star's eyes became accustomed to the brightness, to the noise and confusion, she became aware that the women guests from the *aristo* families in Santa Fe were all gathered on one side of the great room. Some of the women, with their feet resting on the backs of servants, stared openly at Star as she walked down the hall, her hand resting on Michael's arm. She was thankful that a chair had been arranged for her so that she did not have to join the rest of the women on the banquette, or spend the evening trying to understand their rapid-fire Spanish conversation and inhaling their *cigaritto* smoke.

When Colonel Doniphan, a tall, red-haired man with a craggy face, took his chair, the red-coated musicians began to play loudly and raucously. Star watched, fascinated, as men and women chose partners seemingly at random and danced with a careless abandon. It was a waltz tune the musicians were playing, but the Mexican women danced in a distinctly carefree, almost shocking fashion, skirts flying around their legs, dark eyes flashing at their partners.

In spite of her decision not to dance, Star found her own feet tapping time to the infectious rhythm as she watched the officers swing their partners eagerly around the floor. Michael leaned over her, his eyes bright with amusement. "You're sure you won't change your mind?"

She almost relented, then reminded herself it was shocking enough that, newly widowed as she was, she should be attending a ball. Or was it another reason that made her shake her head firmly, she wondered uncomfortably. Was it the disturbing thought of Michael's arms around her, his hands holding her, remembering how she had felt on the patio when Michael had danced with her. Michael's face darkened, as if he guessed what she was thinking, then he bowed and said shortly, "As you wish. If you'll excuse me, I'll find us some refreshments. It's growing warm in here."

She felt ill at ease when he left her alone and, taking her fan, began to move it restlessly. The room was too warm, the air too close. Over her fan, she watched Colonel Doniphan across the room from her. He seemed bored with the festivities and uncomfortable in his dress uniform. She remembered hearing he had been a small-town lawyer in Missouri before joining the army. Although his volunteers swore by him, some of the regular army officers thought his behavior too casual and easygoing for a military man.

He was talking to a captain who had his back to Star, yet something about the man seemed vaguely familiar. Then, as if feeling her eyes on him, the man turned, and Star found herself staring across the room at Robert Donley. She saw a quick flush rise beneath the man's fair skin, reaching up to the ginger hair retreating from the broad forehead. Then he was striding across the room to her, the slight stammer still in his voice as he bowed and said, "Good evening, Mrs. Bradford." Then smiling, he shook his head. "I'm . . . I'm sorry. It's Mrs. Kelly now, isn't it?"

There was no reproach in his voice. Star, embarrassed, almost wished there had been. She deserved any recriminations he wanted to heap upon her. Beneath her embarrassment, though, she discovered she was pleased to see Robert, and she gave him such a dazzling smile of welcome that Robert promptly forgot all the pain and humiliation she had caused him when she had run off to marry Charles Bradford.

"It's good to see you, Robert," she said, giving him her hand. "I didn't know you were in Santa Fe."

"I only arrived this morning. I'm to be attached to Colonel Doniphan's regiment. I would have arrived sooner with General Kearny's army, but I took sick at Fort Leavenworth and had to stay behind. I . . . I was sorry to hear about Mr. Bradford," he said, his soft eyes genuinely sympathetic. "It must have been a terrible shock for you."

"I'm the one who should apologize," Star said softly. "I treated you very badly, I'm afraid."

And all at once she found herself thinking, suppose Robert had been at Fort Bent with Kearny's men when she was there, frightened and alone, after Charles's death. Would she have married Robert then, she wondered, instead of accepting Michael's proposal to go down the trail with him? Certainly it would have been a safe, comfortable marriage. She was sure Robert would have been a gentle, undemanding husband.

Then she looked up and discovered that Michael had returned. Disconcerted, she saw the narrowed, black-flecked eyes studying her face and suspected that he knew exactly what she was thinking, and was startled by the rage she saw flare in the depths of those narrowed eyes before, just as abruptly, his face was wiped clear of all expression. "Captain Donley, isn't it?" he asked. "And of course you know my wife, don't you?"

At the gibing amusement in Michael's voice Robert gave the man an uneasy glance, then said stiffly, "You're to be congratulated, Mr. Kelly, on your marriage. I only heard of it when I arrived in Santa Fe this morning."

"Oh, yes," Michael said, laughing softly as he handed Star a glass of champagne. "We count our blessings nightly, don't we, my love?" Then he added, casually, "But I forget, captain. You must already be aware of my wife's many . . . charms."

Star straightened, giving Michael a furious glance. Why was he baiting Robert this way? And suddenly she wondered how many glasses of wine Michael had had. His eyes were bright and hard, his mouth twisted and cruel.

Then she became aware of a stir on the dance floor, like a disrupting breeze moving through the *sala*. Glancing up, she saw a woman had entered the room on the arm of Major Jeremy Reston. It was Señora de las Flores, in a scarlet velvet gown, a striking foil to her camellia white skin and glossy blue-black hair.

Both of the men had turned to stare, too. Robert said, shocked, "Isn't that the . . . the woman who runs the monte games? How do you suppose she was allowed to attend the ball?"

"It appears that Major Reston is escorting her," Michael said, his eyes glinting, amused.

"But it's outrageous," Robert sputtered indignantly. "A woman like that, here. I never would have believed Major Reston was serious when he told me his plan."

"What plan is that?" Michael asked curiously, his eyes following the new arrivals, the center of attention as they made their way across the room. Major Reston was quite obviously drunk and seemed to be hanging on Lupita's arm as much for support as anything else. A few of the women watching from the sideline tittered with laughter.

Robert glanced toward Star, then shrugged unhappily. "It had something to do with Reston needing money to pay the soldiers. Evidently the, ah, the lady offered to lend the major the necessary gold if he escorted her to the dance tonight. I never dreamed the major would accept her offer. No gentleman would."

"Evidently the major decided the *señora*'s gold was above reproach, even if Doña Lupita's social position isn't," Michael said dryly.

The musicians, evidently hoping to cover up an awkward situation, swung into another waltz. The major turned to his

partner and took her in his arms, but it was plain he was in no
condition to dance. He lurched and would have fallen if the
woman hadn't caught his arm and steadied him. Watching, Star
felt almost sorry for Doña Lupita, who, although she held
herself proudly, her beautiful face cool and composed, was
obviously as embarrassed as the major was drunk. Then Star
took a closer look at the woman, and her pity dissolved into
rage. The scarlet dress Doña Lupita wore was an exact copy
of her own green velvet gown, down to the fringed overskirt
and gold binding on the bodice and hem. She was sure that
the other women present were noticing the similarity of the
two gowns, too. She felt her face grow hot.

"You'll excuse me, *querida*," she heard Michael murmur.
"I'm sure the good captain will look after you."

In another moment he had crossed the floor to Doña Lupita's
side, and before the befuddled major even realized what was
happening, Michael had removed the major's dance partner
from his arms and was waltzing her across the floor. Lupita's
scarlet skirt swung gracefully around her tiny gold slippers as
she lifted her smiling face to her partner, oblivious to everyone
else in the *sala*. Star felt her breath catch painfully in her throat,
watching that small white hand resting possessively on Michael's arm.

Robert Donley looked unhappily down at Star's pale face.
It had been decent of Mr. Kelly to help the Mexican woman,
he thought. No matter the woman's lack of morals, she didn't
deserve such treatment at the hands of a boor like Reston. Still,
he didn't suppose he could expect Kelly's wife to take the same
charitable attitude.

Star rose to her feet, her voice clear and cool as a mountain
spring, only her eyes were dark and stormy. "I'll be leaving
now, Robert."

He cleared his throat uncomfortably. "I don't think . . . really,
Star, you shouldn't make a scene, not here."

But Star had already turned and disappeared into the crowd
of men and women on the edge of the dance floor. She had
noticed a door in the back of the *sala*. She could make an
inconspicuous exit, she thought. She didn't intend to stay and
be humiliated by her husband's openly consorting with Doña
Lupita. Even if all of Santa Fe undoubtedly knew of the re-

lationship between Michael and that woman, he had no right to flaunt his mistress in her face, much less embarrass his wife by dressing his mistress in an identical gown.

The back door led down a short flight of stairs and out into the courtyard of the palace, where cottonwood trees towered in the darkness. Once outside, Star took a deep breath of the heavily scented night air. She realized she had forgotten her shawl, but it didn't matter. It could only be a short walk to the front of the palace where the carriages waited in the plaza. If only it weren't so pitch black, she thought, peering around her, trying to distinguish some sort of familiar landmark. Finally she found the gate that led out of the patio, but the street was even darker than the courtyard area, with only an occasional dim yellow lamplight piercing through an open, unpaned window.

She lifted her velvet skirt fastidiously, remembering the deplorable condition of most of the Santa Fe streets. There was, of course, no such thing as a sidewalk. She started walking in the direction she thought the carriages should be, and had gone only a short distance when she realized she must be walking in the wrong direction. Then she heard the sound of footsteps coming toward her. With the darkness pressing in on her from all sides like walls, it was impossible to distinguish shapes, much less faces, but she assumed it was Mexicans and she asked, hesitantly, *"Perdóneme. Estoy perdida. Donde está—?"*

Before she had a chance to finish her question, she was aware of several things: the cheap smell of whiskey and that it was several men, not Mexicans but American soldiers gathering around her in a swaggering, gleeful circle. She felt an arm reach out and grasp her around the waist, a voice muttering thickly, "Hey, look what we got here, a pretty little *señorita*. You looking for *amigos, señorita?* You found 'em for sure. First give us a kiss, honey, then we'll get down to business."

Star let out a shocked cry that was more like an indignant squeal before she felt a mouth, hot and moist, cover her own lips so she could not breathe. A huge body pinned her own slim body back against a wall. She could still struggle, though, and she did. When she could not free her legs from the full, entangling skirt to kick at the man's shin, she raked his face with her fingernails.

Abruptly the man drew back, staring blearily down at her through the darkness. Then, with a growl of rage, he lifted his hand and cuffed her across the face. Her head snapped back and hit the wall of the building behind her, so that the darkness was suddenly shot full with shooting stars.

One of the other men chortled, "Little hellfire, ain't she, Joe? Let me have a crack at her. Maybe you ain't her style."

Gasping, half crying from the pain, Star turned to run, but again her skirt betrayed her. She tripped over the hem and felt herself staggering, falling hard to the street, the breath knocked out of her, a queer pain twisting, like a hot poker, just beneath her waist.

She felt hands at her shoulders, tearing at her dress, felt cold air slide across her breasts as the soft material ripped. Then she did scream, over and over, all the while she felt herself being dragged off the street into a muddy side alley where the smells of garbage, human and animal excrement, sent waves of nausea through her.

One of the men grumbled, "Stop your bellowing. Hold still. We ain't going to hurt you. You be good to us, we'll be good to you. Ain't you got a room we can go to?"

The pain was worse now, like a steel vice tightening around her middle, so that she could only whisper, "I'm not . . . let me go . . ."

The darkness was invading her brain, a misty grayness rising before her eyes. She mustn't faint, she thought, or she'd be completely at their mercy. She mustn't lose consciousness. She was still weakly struggling, trying to force the rough, calloused hands away from her breasts, when she heard a shout, footsteps, a man's voice cursing, giving orders. She heard the flat of a sword striking against hard muscular backs. The men crouching over her were jerked to their feet and stared drunkenly at the officer who had suddenly appeared in the alleyway.

Then someone was kneeling beside her, a man's arms lifting her gently away from the filth of the street, a voice . . . Was it Robert's, she wondered, dazed. Where had Robert come from? She thought he was in St. Louis. "Are you all right, Star?" he asked anxiously. "They didn't hurt you?"

One of the men shuffled his feet uncomfortably. "Hell, captain, we didn't know she was white. We thought she was a *puta*. You know how the Mex women are always asking for it, any man they can get their hands on."

"Shut up!" Robert Donley turned his attention back to Star, easing her carefully to her feet. "I'll take you home, Star."

She clutched at his hand, as once again the pain ripped through her body. "A doctor," she gasped. "Hurry. A doctor."

Mercifully she remembered very little of the rest of that night, the jouncing carriage ride to the *casa*, Doña Louisa undressing her gently. But even the touch of those soft hands on her body, how they hurt. And finally she knew she was in her own bed, but there was no way she could lie that the pain didn't pursue her. Then there was another face, a man's face, a stranger but with a soothing voice, who gave her something to help the pain, he said. But it didn't help. Nothing helped. The pain was the only thing in the whole nightmare she remembered clearly, as if it were an ax physically splitting her body. Once she thought she saw Michael's face, but it seemed to float above her. Oddly, the pain she felt seemed to be in his face, too. Perspiration glistened on his forehead, and the muscles in his jaw were knotted. Finally, whatever it was the doctor had given her took hold, and she slipped into a blessed oblivion.

When she awoke again, Doña Louisa was dozing in a chair beside her bed and a small fire in the beehive fireplace filled the room with the fragrance of piñon. The pain was gone, but there was an emptiness, like an ache, inside of Star. She gave a small moan, and Doña Louisa came instantly awake.

"My baby?" But she already saw the answer in Doña Louisa's dark eyes, shining with tears.

"God was good, *niña*," she shispered, patting the girl's hand. "We almost lost you, too."

"My fault," Star said dully. "I killed my baby."

"That's not true," Doña Louisa said. "It was those burros who attacked you. They should be shot like dogs."

Star shook her head listlessly. "No, you don't understand. I never wanted Charles's baby. I hated the thought of any part of him growing inside of me."

"Shhh, *niña*." Doña Louisa hastily made the sign of the cross, her eyes round with shock. "You don't know what you're saying. Every woman wants her baby. It would be a sin not to."

Star turned her head toward the wall, her face bloodless, her gray eyes drained almost as colorless as her face. Lost, lost forever, she thought bleakly. Not Charles's baby, the way she had always unconsciously called it. For at the end, she had known it was her child, too, and she had wanted it desperately. She had fought to save it, would have given her life to save it. Only it was too late. And that was the guilt she knew she would have to live with for the rest of her life.

Doña Louisa said soothingly, "You're young. They'll be other children."

Star did not answer. Faintly she remembered something the doctor had told her, that she had been hurt inside, that she might not be able to bear any more children. Or had she imagined that, too? What did it matter? she thought. What did anything matter now?

"*Señora*..." Rosita crept softly into the bedroom where Star sat by the fireplace, a colorful woven serape thrown across her lap. "You have a visitor."

Star shook her head. "I don't want to see anybody, Rosita."

Rosita rolled her eyes upward. "But it is a handsome *soldado, señora,*" she protested. "A Captain Donley. He is leaving Santa Fe and wants to say good-bye."

Star remembered then that it was Robert who had saved her from the soldiers, and she had never thanked him. Remembering those hands grabbing at her breasts, she shivered. Suppose Robert hadn't come along when he did?

"I'll see the captain, Rosita," she said. Her hair hung loosely around her face and she brushed it back, not really caring how she looked but feeling absently that she must make some sort of effort to be presentable.

By the time Robert came to the door, Rosita had brushed Star's hair gently back from her face, tied it with a ribbon, and coaxed her mistress into draping a soft rose-colored shawl over her shoulders. At the door Robert paused uncertainly, until Star held out her hand, smiling faintly. "Please, Robert, come sit down. I haven't had a chance to thank you."

"I'm sorry I didn't find you sooner," he said unhappily. "I looked for you at once, of course, when I realized you'd left the palace, but it wasn't until you screamed..." He fell silent, embarrassed, remembering how Star had looked when he had found her, the bodice of her gown torn, revealing one white gleaming breast, her skirt pushed up around her hips, and even more embarrassed to realize uncomfortably that the memory had the power to excite him. Hastily he thrust the thought away as he made apologies for the soldiers who had tried to rape her. "I'm afraid the volunteers make good fighters but poor soldiers. They get drunk on cheap *pulque*, gamble away their horses, won't clean their carbines, and their sabers are rusty in their scabbards. I'm sure, though, they never would have harmed you if—"

"If they had known I was white and not Mexican," Star finished dryly.

Robert flushed. "Of course the men's behavior was reprehensible in any case. I didn't mean . . ." He shrugged helplessly. "Still, you must admit the Mexican women are inclined to be immoral, the way they dress and behave toward our soldiers."

An angry retort leaped to Star's lips but she bit it back, remembering just in time that Robert was newly arrived in New Mexico and that she had thought much the same thing when she had first seen the Mexican women at Las Vegas—before she had known the warmth and kindness of Doña Louisa and the childish sweetness of Rosita. How easy it was, she thought, to look down upon people you don't know, people who seem different from yourself.

She leaned back in her chair, too tired to argue. "Rosita told me you were leaving. Will you be going south with Colonel Doniphan to Chihuahua?"

"How did you know?" Robert asked, startled, then frowned. "Naturally, I should know there's no such thing as a military secret in Santa Fe. I imagine old Santa Anna knows our plans before we even make them."

Star drew the serape closer over her lap as if against a sudden chill. "General Santa Anna is back in Mexico?" she asked. Even the name, she thought, was enough to cause goose bumps to rise on her flesh. Santa Anna, the butcher of the Alamo and Goliad, who had murdered wounded American prisoners without mercy, and whose corruption and venality had finally outraged even the citizens of his own country so that he had been exiled to Cuba.

Robert nodded glumly. "He arrived at Vera Cruz in August

and was greeted by the people like a long-lost hero. He's already taken control of the Mexican army. They say he's the only man who can make the Mexicans stand and fight. Now he's stomping around Mexico City on his peg leg like Mexico's savior, swearing to tear the star of Texas from the American flag." Robert's soft blue eyes blazed with anger. "And the damnable part of it all is that President Polk himself allowed Santa Anna to leave Cuba and slip through the American blockade into Mexico. It's even claimed that Santa Anna made some sort of secret deal with the president. If he were allowed to return to power in Mexico, he would end the war with the United States. But our spies say Santa Anna's scouring the country, raising troops, even forcing the *aristos* and the church into giving him gold to supply his army." Robert snorted disgusted. "Jimmy Polk's a bigger fool than even I thought he was."

Star remembered that her father, a Whig like Robert Donley, had also had little liking or respect for the president. "A little man with a little mind," he had said at dinner one evening. Remembering her father, Star suddenly thought, how odd that her father had lost a grandchild and would never know. And if he did know, would he care? Or did he still despise her for running off and leaving him?

Robert noticed the droop to Star's mouth, the sadness shadowing the too pale face, and was immediately contrite. "I'm sorry, Star. I shouldn't be upsetting you with talk of politics and war. I wouldn't have come here at all today, except—" He cast his companion a worried glance. "I learned in town today that your husband is preparing to move his wagons south to the markets at Chihuahua. Surely you won't be accompanying him? No one knows what our troops will run into between here and Chihuahua. If not a skirmish with Mexican dragoons, then there are the *bandidos* and Indians always ready to jump any wagons trying to cross the Jornada del Muerte. I can't believe your husband would take you into such dangers and hardships."

Star wondered what Robert would think if he knew that she had no idea at all of her husband's plans. She hadn't seen Michael since the night of the *baile* at the palace, unless . . . Had it been Michael's pain-wracked face she thought she had seen in her delirium? She knew that Doña Louisa had been shocked when Star had said that she did not want her husband to visit her while she had been recovering from her miscarriage. She could only assume that Michael felt the same. She knew that if he had wanted to visit her, nothing she would have said would have stopped him. Yet now, unaccountably, she found herself bristling at Robert's criticism of her husband.

"I'm sure Mr. Kelly will do what he thinks is best," she said coolly. "There are . . . family problems that make it important that he return to the Cordoba *rancho* as soon as possible. And I gather other traders are leaving Santa Fe, too, for Chihuahua, so we won't be alone on the trail."

If Michael planned to take her with him, she thought suddenly. Perhaps he had already realized that their marriage was a travesty. And he had their wedding lines to prove their marriage when he claimed the Cordoba estate. Did he really need her presence, she wondered. Would he perhaps be just as happy to be rid of her?

Later, though, after Robert had left, Star sat, gazing, into the small piñon fire, her thoughts tangled and confused. She had been surprised herself at how quickly she had sprung to her husband's defense. Surely after the way Michael had behaved at the *baile* he was deserving of no consideration. Unwillingly, she saw in her mind's eyes again Doña Lupita's white hand holding Michael's arm lightly, possessively, as they waltzed, his face smiling down into those lustrous black eyes. And the queer, choking sensation she had felt at the *baile*, watching them, suddenly returned. And just as suddenly she knew, with a sense of shock, that it wasn't hurt pride or injured dignity that had sent her rushing from the *sala* into the night. It was a jealous rage at the woman Michael held in his arms— had held how many nights in his arms. It was almost as if she could see that soft white body entwined against Michael's hard, tanned limbs.

With a half sob, Star sprang to her feet, the serape falling to the floor. Good God, what was the matter with her? Surely she didn't want to endure again what she had suffered with Charles. How could she forget the pain and humiliation that had almost destroyed her? Even thinking of those nights with

Charles made her stomach muscles tighten and a trembling wave of nausea sweep over her.

Rosita had brought in a bottle of wine and glasses when Charles had arrived. Star's glass was still untouched. Now she picked it up and drank it quickly, then poured herself another from the decanter.

The wine sent a warmth through her body, and she could feel the knot of tension ease, the bad memories shoved back into the shadowy corners of her mind. After a third, she returned to bed and fell instantly into the first dreamless sleep she'd had in weeks.

She wasn't sure how long she slept. It was dark when she awakened again, a faint pale moonlight drifting in through the shuttered windows. When she sat up in bed and lit the lamp, she was aware of being terribly thirsty, longing for a cool glass of water. She reached for the water decanter beside the bed and discovered to her dismay that it was empty. Well, there was always water on the sideboard in the *sala*, she thought, slipping into her robe against the faint chill of the room now that the flames in the fireplace had died out.

She had grown accustomed enough to the *casa* so that even without a lamp she was able to walk along the gallery that circled the patio and into the *sala*. There was even enough light from the moon so that she could locate the heavy crystal decanter of water and a glass. She had taken only a sip of the water, though, when she heard footsteps and the soft murmur of voices coming her way, a man's voice and a woman's speaking in a quick, liquid Spanish. There was no way Star could retreat without revealing herself. She could only shrink back against the wall on one side of the high sideboard, hoping it would conceal her.

The footsteps passed through the *sala* and stopped at the door into the courtyard. For a second Star could see Doña Lupita de las Flores in a black gown, leaning forward in the moonlight, whispering earnestly to Michael, whose back was to Star. Star's Spanish was not yet good enough to understand all the words, but she caught the names "Ortiz . . . Archuleta . . . Pueblo. . . ." and then a soft whisper, like a sigh, *"Vaya con Dios."* The woman pulled a black rebozo over her head, reached

up, and kissed Michael, and then in the next minute seemed
to meld with the darkness around her.

Star waited until the footsteps completely faded away from
the courtyard. They must have left by the gate from the patio
to the street, she decided. Then she ventured out of the *sala*
to the gallery.

She was hurrying along the gallery at the edge of the patio
when a voice came out of the darkness. "Aren't you up late,
Star?"

She turned, her eyes becoming accustomed to the darkness
so that she could see the darker shadow that was Michael,
moving toward her from the patio.

"I . . . I was thirsty," she stammered, wondering if he could
possibly know she had been eavesdropping. Andthen thought,
annoyed, why should she be the one to be embarrassed? After
all, it was Michael who had brought his mistress into their
home for a clandestine rendezvous.

"You're not running a fever?" Michael asked sharply. She
felt his hand on her forehead before she could draw away from
its disturbing warmth resting against her face.

She saw Michael's mouth tighten at her instinctive with-
drawal from his touch. When he spoke again, his voice was
brittle. "No, there's no fever. If anything, I'd say you were
suffering from a chill." He glanced down at her feet. "You
shouldn't be roaming around without slippers."

Star realized that her feet were cold and that her thin silk
wrapper was little protection against the chill of the night breeze
coming down from the mountains.

Michael saw her pull the ridiculously ineffectual wrapper
closer around her and said irritably, "This is no time for you
to come down with a cold."

Then he picked her up in his arms and was carrying her
through the gallery toward her bedroom. "There's no need,"
Star protested. "I'm perfectly able to walk."

He didn't bother to answer. She was held pressed so tightly
against his chest that she could hear the slow, steady beat of
his heart, catch the faint scent of tobacco and whiskey and
another scent, a woman's perfume, clinging to his clothes.
Doña Lupita's, she thought, suddenly furious. But it was as
foolish to struggle against those arms holding her as it was to

push away a rock. She was being carried into her bedroom and lowered onto her bed. Her robe had loosened, and she snatched at it with one hand while with the other she yanked the coverlet up over her, glaring up at Michael, speechless with exasperation.

He grinned down at her, thinking absently that at least anger had brought some color to her face, stirred her out of the troubling lethargy that had held her in its grip ever since that night when she had lost her child and he had stood by her bed, helpless, watching her body wracked with pain and unable to do anything to ease the agony. Memory of that night brought back his own sense of guilt, like a knife thrust between his ribs. If he hadn't felt sorry for Lupita standing in the center of the *baile* room, the target of all eyes, with that stupid oaf falling all over her, if he hadn't shown Lupita the gown he had bought for Star to wear to the ball and she had mischievously had it copied, stitch for stitch, perhaps then Star wouldn't have foolishly run off from the palace into the hands of those drunken soldiers. She might still be carrying her child.

The knife twisted, turned, making his voice harsh. "You needn't look so alarmed, *querida*. I have no intention of climbing into your bed."

Abruptly he turned away and knelt beside the fireplace, coaxing the fagots into burning to take the chill from the room. And knew angrily that that was exactly what he wanted to do, despite all his firm resolutions, despite the fact that he knew she must surely despise him, must blame him for her miscarriage. Yet he still wanted her, had felt the desire leap in him when he had carried her to her bed, the way she had fit so easily into his arms, the yielding softness of that slender body beneath the silk wrapper, even her special fragrance that had none of the cloying sweetness of the perfume that Lupita always wore—her fragrance that was so familiar to him now that he had known at once that she had been in the *sala* earlier.

By the time he rose again and turned to face her, his emotions were once again tightly under control, his face, impassive. "I assume your friend Captain Donley, when he visited you this afternoon, told you our wagons are ready to leave Santa Fe for Chihuahua."

Her eyes widened. "How did you know?"

He shrugged. "Some of my drovers told me the captain had been asking questions, and Doña Louisa said he was here this afternoon." He lifted a mocking eyebrow. "I assume to bid you a fond farewell, since he'll be pulling out with Doniphan."

"How soon will you be leaving?" Star asked slowly.

"We'll be leaving," he corrected her sharply. "And it should be within a day or two."

"I'm going with you?" Star asked, surprised.

He tried to read past the surprise, to discover what she was thinking, but her lashes hid the revealing gray eyes that usually so easily and vulnerably exposed her every emotion.

"I spoke to your doctor yesterday. He said you were recovered enough to travel." What was the point of telling her, he decided, that in fact he had planned to leave her behind in Santa Fe. Better than Robert Donley he knew the dangers that waited below the Rio Bravo, bad enough in peacetime, much worse with a war throwing the countryside into turmoil. Yet after what Lupita had told him this evening, he knew there would be even greater danger in leaving Star behind in Santa Fe.

"Suppose I refuse to go with you?" she said, lifting her gaze steadily to study his face. Would he force her to accompany him, she wondered, knowing how quickly those impassive features could fill with menace. She remembered how he had forced her on the trail to wear Mario's clothes or ride tied in the Dearborn. He had meant the threat, too, she knew, and she had no doubt that, if it suited him, he would force her just as easily to come along with him to Chihuahua.

For a moment she saw the green eyes darken with anger, then he drawled indifferently, "I assumed we had a marriage agreement. Of course, if you don't plan to honor it, if you're afraid to make the trip to Chihuahua . . ." His voice trailed away contemptuously.

A flush rose in Star's face, her pride stung. Did he have so little opinion of her that he thought it was fear of the trip that made her hesitate to accompany him? She had come down the trail from Santa Fe without once complaining about the hardships, hadn't she? Surely the road to Chihuahua couldn't be worse than traveling the Raton Pass. And no one had ever accused a McFarland of breaking their word. Isn't that what her father had always taught her?

She lifted her chin with an unconscious arrogance as she turned a haughty profile to him. "I have no intention of not honoring our agreement," she said coldly. "I'll be ready to leave Santa Fe when you are."

Chapter Thirteen

"*Is it much farther, señora, to Chihuahua?*"

Star stifled a feeling of irritation. Rosita had asked the same question in the same plaintive tone of voice every day since they had left Albuquerque. Then, glancing at the girl's woebegone face, she saw that Rosita's fair skin was painfully reddened by the sun despite her riding in the *carretilla* and being swaddled constantly by a black rebozo. She reminded herself that Rosita was certainly a much more pleasant maid and traveling companion than Theresa had been, and said patiently, "Don't you remember? Don Miguel told us it's at least a forty-day trip from Santa Fe to Chihuahua, and we haven't even reached El Paso del Norte yet."

"And the Jornada del Muerte," Rosita asked, with a shudder. "When will we reach there? They say that those who don't die of thirst in the Jornada are murdered by the Apaches." She crossed herself, rolling her eyes skyward as she moaned, "*Madre de Dios*, I will never live to see my sweet Jaime."

Star sighed to herself. She supposed it wouldn't do any good to remind the girl that she was the one who had pleaded to be allowed to travel with Star and the caravan to Chihuahua so she could join her soldier lover in Doniphan's army. Much to Star's surprise, Michael had agreed to Rosita's request.

"I've talked it over with Doña Louisa. She says if we don't take the girl, she's foolish enough to run away and become a *señorita soldadera* with Doniphan's dragoons. At least with our wagons she'll have a better chance of reaching her boy friend alive." Then added, almost off handedly, "And she's small enough to ride in the *carretilla* with you."

189

"Carretilla?" Star had echoed, pleased. She had assumed that she would be riding horseback to Chihuahua or riding in the Dearborn, as she had coming down from Bent's Fort. She had been even more delighted the morning she had said her tearful farewells to Doña Louisa and saw the trim little carriage, trimmed in gold, standing before the *casa*. The interior of the buggy was a luxurious padded scarlet velvet with gold fringe on the pillows.

"Where did you ever find such a carriage here in Santa Fe?" she had asked Michael, amazed. It was the sort of elegant buggy one would expect to find on the streets of St. Louis. Then she had noticed the gold filigreed initials embroidered on the scarlet pillows, and her glance flew indignantly to Michael. He smiled down at her, the sunlight sparkling in his eyes. "Call it a wedding present from Doña Lupita, or an apology for a ball gown."

Star had been about to step into the carriage. Now she drew back, her voice icy. "Tell Doña Lupita thank you, but I prefer to ride horseback."

"And I prefer that you ride in the *carretilla*," Michael said. Although his voice did not raise in the slightest, Rosita took one look at Don Miguel's face and scrambled into the buggy. Star followed more slowly, still seething. She remembered that evening in the *sala* when she had watched Lupita cling to Michael so their two shadows had been one. The effrontery of the woman, to have an assignation with her lover under the same roof as her lover's wife.

Of course she had to admit that it was much more pleasant riding in the carriage than on horseback, the pillows cushioning her back so she could even nap a little at times, as the buggy followed the Rio Bravo del Norte. A poor excuse for a river, Star thought. The Rio Bravo was muddy and so sluggish one could almost walk from one side to another on the low, sandy islands. Then they had reached the country below the river, green, lush valleys with cornfields and herds of sheep, and orchards and great rich haciendas surrounding the town of Albuquerque.

It was after they left Albuquerque that the thriving settlements began to thin out and the mountains lining the valley, dark and forbidding, seemed to move in closer. The ground was sandy now, and there were monstrous cacti and prickly pears with spoiling fruits and spiny yuccas.

"That cactus, *señora*, over there," Rosita suddenly giggled, her fears forgotten as her usual good nature quickly returned. "Doesn't it look like Señor Baldwyn?"

Laughing, Star had to agree that the hairy, fat plant did have a resemblance to the caravan's wagon boss, Jim Baldwyn. All it needed was a straggly white beard and pale blue eyes that uncomfortably had a way of twinkling jovially while the mouth did not smile at all.

Rosita's voice dropped to a horrified, yet delighted, whisper. "Did you know that Señor Baldwyn worked for the Governor of Chihuahua as an Apache scalp hunter? I heard the other men talking. They say he got fifty dollars for a man's hair and half that amount for a woman or child!"

Star had not known, but she had no trouble believing the story. All the men Michael had hired as drovers and *arrieros* for the caravan looked like cutthroats to her. She had said as much to Michael the first night the caravan had camped.

"That's because they *are* cutthroats and *ladróns*," he said. "That's why I hired them."

"How can you trust men like that?"

"I don't. But they know how to fight and kill, if necessary, without asking questions." He smiled mirthlessly. "Indians, bandits, Mexican or American dragoons, they're not particular."

When Star still looked outraged, he said with forced patience, "Chihuahua is over five hundred miles to the south. If it's all the same to you, I'd like to arrive there with our goods and hides intact."

"Your *rancho?*" Star asked, curiously. "Is it near Chihuahua?"

"No, it's closer to Mexico City. After we reach Chihuahua, I'll arrange passage at Brazos by boat to Vera Cruz. Then we'll travel overland by *diligencia* to the ranch."

Star listened, bewildered, realizing she hadn't the vaguest notion where the towns he mentioned were located, and only the most rudimentary idea at all of the geography of Mexico. "On what coast is Vera Cruz?" she asked, embarrassed at her ignorance.

"The east coast, and there's no need to look embarrassed."
He smiled grimly. "I'm sure that among all those American
soldiers so anxious to storm the halls of Montezuma, only a
few have any idea at all where Mexico City is."

Leaning down, he picked up a stick and, in the soft dirt,
drew a crude map of Mexico, showing her the route they would
follow from Santa Fe to the Cordoba ranch. Gazing at the map,
Star saw with a sharp feeling of dismay that the route they
would travel from Chihuahua to Mexico City was more than
twice as long as the trail from Santa Fe to Chihuahua. "I . . . I
hadn't realized it was so far to the ranch," she said faintly.

"Are you afraid, *querida?*" he asked softly.

So softly that she thought she must have misunderstood the
murmured term of endearment. She looked up quickly, but she
could catch no hint of tenderness in the hard lines of his face.
The shadows cast by the campfire only emphasized the flat
slant of his cheekbones, the opaque darkness of the narrowed
eyes watching her. "If you are afraid, it's not too late to change
your mind," he said. "I'll see that you get back safely to St.
Louis, and the money promised you in our agreement will still
be yours."

"I haven't changed my mind," she said quickly, annoyed
at her own momentary weakness. Or was it the casual way he
spoke of her leaving the caravan, as if it were a matter of
complete indifference to him. Did he care at all whether or not
she accompanied him to the ranch? she wondered. Still, why
should he? She was, after all, wife in name only, a useful ploy
to gain his inheritance.

She stared out at the sparse dusty land she could glimpse
from the *carretilla*, the endless stretches of mesquite and chaparral, and thought about the rest of that first night the caravan
had camped beside the Rio Bravo. Rosita had retired to the
baggage wagon where she was to sleep, and Star had curled
up in a blanket in the Dearborn, wondering if Michael would
join her. When he had appeared, he moved so quietly and
swiftly that he had swung into the Dearborn and spread out his
blanket beside her before she knew he was there.

Pretending sleep, she had lain curled inside her blanket, her
back to Michael, all the muscles in her body pulled taut. In
the still not complete darkness, Michael studied the blanket-

wrapped woman, frowning slightly. He knew by the too quick sound of her breathing, by the tension he could sense in her body curled as far away from him as possible, that Star was feigning sleep. For his benefit, he thought angrily.

"Can you handle a pistol, Star?" he asked abruptly.

Surprised, she sat upright, clutching her blanket around her, and stared at him.

He took a revolver from his belt and placed it in the space between their bedrolls. She glanced at it in the dim light. It looked much like the gun Charles had taught her to use that afternoon on the prairie, the day, she remembered with a shudder, that Charles had murdered the Indian and left him lying there, his blood staining the tall grass.

"Yes," she whispered. "My husband—" and then seeing Michael's mouth tighten, amended herself quickly. "Charles taught me."

"Good." Michael thrust the gun toward her. "It's loaded, so be careful. Keep it beside you all the time. If anyone . . . uninvited should attempt to climb into the Dearborn or buggy, don't be afraid to use it." A flicker of amusement touched the green eyes. "I would appreciate it, though, if you'd make sure first that I wasn't your target."

Without another word he wrapped himself in his blanket, and in a few minutes Star realized from his steady breathing that he was sound asleep. In the nights that followed, he would often come to the Dearborn after she was asleep, and was always gone when she awoke in the morning. When he did touch her, to help her in and out of the *carretilla*, his hand never lingered around her waist or on her arm a moment longer than necessary. As if, she thought bitterly, her presence was as welcome as those spiny cacti along the trail. And contrarily, as terrified as she was of the thought of her husband's sharing her bed, Star realized that she was equally offended that Michael could so quickly and easily be uninterested in making love to his new bride.

"*Señora*, what is it? Why are we stopping?"

Rosita's voice, pulled thin with fear, drew Star back to the present, to the realization that the caravan had indeed stopped, and the *carretilla* with it.

"Is it Indians?" Rosita asked, her voice quavering.

"No, of course not," Star said, climbing out of the buggy to get a better look. "It's a man on horseback." The wagoners had crowded around the man. She could hear excited voices shouting. She caught the words, "California . . . ours . . . didn't fire a shot . . ." Men were slapping each other on the back; a few took out their guns and shot them into the air.

She saw Michael ride up to the circle of men and lean forward in his saddle to ask some questions. Then he turned and rode back toward the carriage where the women stood.

"What is it?" Star asked. And then, bewildered, "Surely General Kearny can't have reached California yet?"

"Not Kearny," Michael replied, dismounting and joining the women. "Fitzpatrick's a scout from Kearny's command. Kearny hadn't even reached the Gila River when Kit Carson brought him the news from California. American settlers in California revolted against Mexican rule last summer, and in August, Commodore Sloat sailed into Monterey and raised the American flag over the port."

"Do you suppose General Kearny will be turning back?"

"Not according to Fitzpatrick. He says the general's following his orders to proceed to California, although he has sent back some of his men to join Price in Santa Fe. No doubt the general has heard the rumors—"

When he broke off abruptly, Star asked, "What rumors?"

For a moment she thought Michael wasn't going to answer her, then he said, smiling thinly, "It seems that not all Mexicans are happy with the American conquest of New Mexico. There's a group of insurgents stirring up rebellion aginst the American rule. Right now it's no more than a smoldering brushfire, but it's only waiting for a torch to send all New Mexico up in flames."

Star found herself remembering her wedding party, and that captain friend of Michael's who had been his best man. Hadn't the captain warned Michael about staying away from certain friends . . . Ortiz . . . Archuleto? Was it because he was afraid Michael was involved in the insurgent's cause? And that night she had hidden in the *sala*, she thought suddenly. She had heard those names again.

She gave her husband a suspicious glance. "Señors Ortiz and Archuleto are part of the conspiracy to overthrow the Americans, aren't they? And Doña Lupita—is she part of it, too?"

"So you were hiding in the *sala* that evening," Michael said, one eyebrow lifting mockingly. "How flattering to discover you care enough to spy on me."

Star's gray eyes were bright with anger as she glared at him. As if she cared how many women he slept with! "You should have told General Price if you knew anything about those men," she said indignantly. "They should be arrested as traitors."

"Traitors against whom?" Michael asked, amused. "Is it treason for men to want to free their country from foreign invaders? Anyway, it's the military's concern, not mine. I always find it's more practical to mind my own business." A harsh note of warning crept into his voice. "And I strongly advise you, *querida*, to do the same."

Rosita glanced uneasily from her mistress to Don Miguel. Although her knowledge of English was not good enough to understand all of the conversation, she sensed the friction that always seemed to leap in the air between Doña Estrella and her husband. Now, glancing into Michael's glowering face, she asked timidly, "Señor Colonel Doniphan and *mi amor* Jaime, what of them? Will they be marching still to Chihuahua?"

Michael smiled sympathetically at the eager young woman. "Not right away, it seems. The latest reports that Fitzpatrick brought are that Doniphan and his army have been sent to chase the Navajos and the Utes in the valleys of the San Juan and the Little Colorado before marching on Chihuahua."

"What of the trade caravans?" Star asked. "Will the army allow us to continue?" With all of New Mexico threatening to erupt into violence behind them, and the army of Santa Anna growing stronger every day to the south, the caravans would be caught in the middle, unable to retreat or to go forward.

"The rest of the trading wagons are only a few days ahead of us," Michael said. "We'll find out what the army has planned for us soon enough."

At Valverde, in the green valley of the Rio Grande, the Bradford-Cordoba wagons caught up with the rest of the caravans. Over three hundred wagons were encamped near a ruined and crumbling hacienda. "Indians wiped out most of this valley years ago," Jim Baldwyn told Star and Rosita as he spit a stream of tobacco inexpertly so that his white beard became even more tobacco-stained.

"What will happen to the traders?" Star asked impatiently. Michael and his wagon master had left for the traders' camp earlier that afternoon, and Baldwyn had returned later alone.

"They're jittery as a bunch of nervous hens sitting on their nests," the wagon master said, grinning. "Doniphan has sent orders that no wagons are to move into enemy territory before the army arrives. So there they are, sitting on merchandise they know they can sell in Chihuahua for ten times what they paid for it. Old Governor Trias, the governor of Chihuahua, even sent the traders a cordial invitation to ignore Doniphan's orders, and offered them safe passage to Chihuahua."

"Did any of them go?"

"A few tried. The army caught some and turned them back. If I know Trias, the others are probably cooling their heels in a prison cell in Chihuahua by now."

"When do they expect Colonel Doniphan to arrive?"

The white beard waggled thoughtfully. "No way of knowing. Some of the traders have been waiting here since October. May have to wait all winter. Anyway, Don Miguel has found a house for you and your girl to stay in while we wait for Doniphan to make his move. I'm to take you there. It ain't much," he warned. "But better than sleeping in a wagon or the ground."

When Star saw the rude adobe house, she tried not to let her feeling of dismay show in her face. There were only three rooms, a bedroom, a small *sala*, and a *comisa* smelling redolently of green peppers and garlic. The walls of the bedroom were whitewashed, and cloth was hung halfway up the walls to keep the whitewash from flaking off on anyone leaning against the wall. And there were, of course, the inevitable vividly colored saint's statues in niches and cracked bits of mirror hanging on the wall.

"I warned you it wasn't much," Baldwyn said, squashing with one big foot a scorpion that was scuttling across the floor.

Star swallowed hard. "It will do fine," she murmured, "after a bit of cleaning up, won't it, Rosita?"

Cheerfully, the girl agreed. After Star and Rosita had spent several hours scrubbing and dusting and airing out linen, the

house may not have been sparkling, but it was reasonably clean.
When Michael arrived late in the afternoon, Rosita had started
cooking dinner, and the house smelled of tortillas and cooked
green peppers. Star had been helping make biscuits and she
was still wearing an apron when Michael entered. Snatching a
quick look at herself in a bit of mirror, she hastily wiped a
smudge of flour from her nose and smoothed back her hair,
which, in the heat of the kitchen, had curled in tiny auburn
ringlets around her face.

"Perhaps you'd care to stay for dinner?" she asked Michael.
"Or do you have to return to camp?"

"Later will do," Michael said, eyeing appreciatively the food
Rosita was bringing to the table. After they had finished eating,
he leaned back in his chair and lit a *cigarrito*, studying Star
across the table from under half-lowered eyelids. How domestic
we look, he thought, amused. We might be any ordinary husband and wife exchanging small talk across a dinner table.

His gaze drifted regretfully toward the bedroom. It was
difficult enough in the cramped space of the Dearborn, wrapped
in his blanket, listening to Star's measured breathing, knowing
he had only to reach out a few inches to touch her, to imagine
his hands moving slowly over the soft, inviting curves, the
dark valleys and warm peaks of that body, to watch her eyes
grow wide and bright with desire at his touch.

Only, he reminded himself sourly, it would not be desire
he saw in those eyes, but disgust and loathing in the deep gray
depths.

Abruptly, he rose to his feet. "I'll be getting back to the
camp now. All the men are taking turns at guard duty, so I'll
be spending my nights there."

"Oh." Star felt a twinge of disappointment, but her cool
gray eyes revealed nothing as she walked with him to the door
and said her polite good-bye, as if to an acquaintance who had
happened to drop by the house. But she stood at the door,
watching for several minutes until his tall figure in the saddle
merged in the darkness. It was much later that night that she
woke up suddenly, her heart pounding, in the unfamiliar black-
ness of the tiny bedroom.

Almost unconsciously, still half asleep, she reached out for
Michael's sleeping figure. Although their bodies had never

touched during the nights they spent together in the Dearborn, she had always been aware that the blanketed figure was there, a darker, reassuring shadow in the darkness, giving her a sense of reassurance that all was well. Now there was no one, and she was sure she heard something, someone, moving outside the house.

Her hands trembling, she lit the candle beside the bed, debating whether or not to awaken Rosita, who she could hear snoring peacefully on her cot in the kitchen. For all she knew the noise might only be her imagination. There was no point in frightening Rosita.

She found the revolver Michael had given her, and moving quietly, the gun awkward and heavy in her hand, she opened the front door and peered out into the blue-black night. A first glimmer of sunrise was turning the horizon a pale pink and cream color. Then she drew back, startled, as a man suddenly stepped out of the shadows and she recognized Manuel, a mestizo, more Indian than Mexican, who was one of the wagoners Michael had hired for the caravan. Star had noticed that Manuel seldom talked with the other men in the caravan, staying to himself, his face with its high-beaked nose and oddly flat black eyes holding a deep stillness like the surface of a pond in a dark woods.

"Manuel? What are you doing here?"

He spoke haltingly, as if words were alien things to be regarded suspiciously. "Don Miguel says... at night... I stay... guard..."

"Oh." Feeling all at once foolish, she let the gun fall to her side and, as she returned to her room, wondered if, after all, she would have found the courage to use it.

During the next weeks, through the rest of November and into December, her life in the small *poblado* of San Rosa fell into a pleasant if quietly domestic routine. In the mornings, basket in hand, with Rosita close behind her, she shopped for food, fresh fruit and vegetables, and milk from the townspeople. At first she felt alarmingly conspicuous, knowing that eyes were following her as she walked through the plaza. She was the first *gringa* most of the people had ever seen. Always, though, she was greeted with courtesy, and murmured greetings in a liquid Mexican following her as she passed.

Poverty was painfully evident everywhere in the village. Even the cassock the village priest wore was worn and ragged. But when Star was finally invited into the rude homes of the townspeople, it was with a hospitality as gracious as if she were being invited into a mansion. More and more, as she grew to know them, she respected the quiet courage of the people of San Rosa. Twice the *poblado* had been attacked by the Apaches, houses and cornfields burned, several families had had children carried off, never to be seen again. But like the rocks, the rich red adobe walls, the arid soil itself, the village somehow survived. The precious cornfields were replanted, the church rebuilt.

Star began stopping at the small church after her daily shopping expeditions, sitting quietly in the cool darkness, not praying, but letting the quiet and peace touch her with soothing hands. Once she watched a simple wedding in the church between a plain-faced but glowing bride and her proud bridegroom. She had already learned from Rosita that many Mexican couples never married but simply lived together because they could not afford the fees the priests charged for a marriage. Here in San Rosa, though, Father Roja, as poor as his parishioners—and almost as illiterate—had none of the venality of the priests that Star had met in Santa Fe. The couple did not kiss at the altar, but their eyes clung together in a happy daze. As they left the church hand in hand, the groom spoke softly to his new bride and she smiled up at him shyly, with such a look of adoration in her eyes that Star felt a thrust of pain and her breath caught in her throat. Watching the two young lovers together, she was aware of the great emptiness in her own life, like a numbness at the center of her existence. When she went from the church into the glaring sunlight, her eyes burned with unshed tears.

Although Michael continued to drop by every few days, she was sure his visits were only through a sense of duty, to see how she and Rosita were faring. Occasionally he stayed for dinner and would bring the two women the latest rumors from the Valverde traders' encampment. General Wool and his Texas troops had already taken Chihuahua, it was said; equally firm rumors declared that General Wool and his men had been destroyed by a Mexican army under General Urrea; that the same

General Urrea and one thousand Mexican regulars were already marching north to attack the traders' encampment. There was an even more disturbing rumor that Colonel Doniphan's troops would soon be under attack.

"Do you suppose it's true?" Star asked, trying to hide her fear at the thought of standing in the path of a Mexican army. "Will Colonel Doniphan retreat north?"

"Probably not," Michael said calmly. "With an insurrection brewing behind him, the only way he can go is forward. I only wish it would be soon," he added irritably. "At this rate it will be spring before we reach Vera Cruz."

Although Star was content living in the village, she knew that Michael was impatient at the delay.

"Is there any news at all from Doniphan's camp?"

"Only what we hear from his men that sometimes drift down from the mountains to Valverde. They're afraid Wool's men will get to Chihuahua before them and hog all the glory while Doniphan is negotiating peace terms with the Navajos." He suddenly grinned. "Apparently the Navajos can't understand why the Americans want them to stop raiding Mexican settlements when American soldiers are at war with Mexico."

He got to his feet and knelt before the fireplace, poking restlessly at the small piñon fire. The evening had turned cool and there was a storm building, rain splattering against the shuttered windows. Inside the *sala*, though, it was a pleasantly warm and cozy world. Star sat on the banquette, forgetting formality enough to tuck her feet under her, as she drowsily observed the man across the room from her.

Hunkered down as he was in front of the fireplace, Michael reminded her even more of an Indian, with something of Manuel's stillness about him. Yet she knew her husband well enough to know that he was not as relaxed as he seemed. She could sense unseen disturbing vibrations in the air, the coiled tension in the man. And what was even more troubling, she sensed that Michael's carefully banked frustration was somehow aimed at her.

She wondered whether, if she and Rosita hadn't been with the caravan, Michael wouldn't have long since defied the army and headed into the dangerous *jornada* alone. Was he perhaps blaming her for keeping him and the wagons at Valverde when by now he could be halfway to his ranch?

It was raining harder, a distant roll of thunder moving steadily closer. Michael got to his feet, cocking his head toward the sound. "I should be getting back to the camp before the storm gets any worse."

He'd be soaked, Star thought, even with a poncho, the way the wind and rain were blowing. Impulsively she blurted, "Why don't you stay the night?"

When he turned toward her, lifting a questioning eyebrow, she felt a rush of color to her face and added quickly, gesturing toward the banquette, "You could sleep here."

Michael's face remained still, but the green eyes narrowed as he studied Star, the pale flush of color beneath the flawless skin, the way the calico dress clung to her small waist, her young proud breasts thrust upward without the need for stays. The pent-up frustration he had been feeling all evening twisted inside of him, watching her across the table from him earlier, the way she cocked her head a little to one side as she listened intently, the play of emotions across her features and the unexpected, musical peal of laughter, so that for a moment that reserved, wary look disappeared from her face. And the way she walked across the room with an unconscious, provocative swing to her hips; even the drowsy half smile on her lips now as she sat curled up on the banquette. The glow from the firelight made her eyes shine with an inviting softness, the look of a woman wanting, anticipating love. Frustration exploded into anger. Damn it, he was her husband, wasn't he? How long did she expect him to continue this hands-off charade between them?

"As I recall, *querida*," he said slowly, "the bed is large enough for two."

He saw her gray eyes flare wide beneath the delicately arched brows, but as he walked across the room toward her, she did not retreat. Suddenly he was reminded of a time years ago when he had been hunting in the mountains. There had been a doe he had caught in the sights of his rifle. The creature had faced him, too, in the same fashion, her beautiful graceful body frozen in midmotion, her eyes wide and frightened, as

Star's were now, and yet somehow resigned to whatever fate he would inflict upon her. For a split second the predator and the victim had stared at each other. Michael had lowered his rifle, unable to fire the fatal shot, and the doe, without a backward glance, had bounded away into the underbrush.

He stopped a few inches from Star, gazing down into her face, close enough to see the trembling at the corners of her mouth. He sensed that if he insisted, she would submit to him, not fighting him off as she had on their wedding night, giving herself to him, but without joy, through a sense of duty. And he knew he couldn't take her that way, any more than he had been able to shoot the doe. She must come to him of her own free will, wanting him as much as he wanted her, with the same aching need and joyous abandon she surely must have felt for her first husband.

He reached out and tugged gently at an auburn curl that had slipped from the chignon and hung over one shoulder. "It's all right," he said quietly. "Go to bed. I'll sleep out here."

He saw the relief flooding her face, followed for only a fleeting instant by disappointment, sadness, he could not be sure, for, like the doe, she had turned and fled.

The next morning when Star awoke early and came out into the *sala*, she found that Michael was already gone. The banquette looked untouched, so that she wondered if he had slept there at all but instead had returned to the camp the night before.

A week went by, and he did not return. In the face of Rosita's growing curiosity, Star determinedly hid her disappointment. She hadn't realized how much she had come to depend upon Michael's visits, or how much she had enjoyed their conversations over dinner. She had begun to feel at ease with Michael in those quiet evenings in a way she had never felt with Charles, even in those early days when she thought she had loved him.

Then, in the middle of December, while she was returning from a shopping trip in town, she heard the sound of hoofbeats, the clatter of scabbards, men's voices raised in raucous song. With the rest of the townspeople, she hurried to the edge of the small village.

A troop of Doniphan's men were riding south, not bothering to skirt the town but riding straight through, trampling down the precious cornfields. Star was shocked at the appearance of the soldiers. Their dirty, ragged pieces of clothing in no way resembled uniforms, and the young unshaven faces were gaunt from the weeks of staving off starvation and frostbite as they pursued the Navajos.

There was eagerness in their faces, too, and they yelled boisterously, whooping like young boys on a holiday. Finally they were off to fight the Mexicans at Chihuahua, they hoped, before Wool's men got there and stole all the glory.

They waved at the villagers staring quietly at them, and some of the young men sang lustily:

> "Old Zac's at Monterey
> Bring out your Santa Anner,
> For every time we raise a gun,
> Down goes a Mexicaner."

The children of the village, with no knowledge of English, waved happily back at the soldiers. Father Roja came to stand beside Star, staring soberly at the young men. His voice was bewildered. *"Los pobres niños.* They have come so far, only to fight and perhaps die. *Porqué?* I hear your country is very rich, very large. Mexico is poor. Yet you want our land. *No comprendo."*

Star was no longer sure she understood either. In the beginning it had all seemed so plain to her, the reasons behind the war, the newspapers talking proudly of manifest destiny, of bringing the blessings of liberty and democracy to the poor, enslaved Mexicans. Yet now that she had shared the life of San Rosa, she knew that, for all their poverty, the people of the village were contented and happy. Was it just, she wondered uneasily, for one people, even with the best of intentions, to inflict their way of life upon the people of another country?

The priest in his shabby robes sensed Star's discomfort and was at once apologetic for offending a guest in his village. "Forgive me, *señora.* It is the way of war and the wickedness of all men, this greed for land and gold."

The next day more of Doniphan's regiment passed through San Rosa, more dragoons and foot soldiers, hurrying south.

"No artillery. Doniphan's going to need artillery to lick the Mexicans at El Paso Del Norte."

Star turned to see that the white-bearded wagon boss had joined her and was watching the passing soldiers with a skeptical eye. Then, as if remembering why he was at San Rosa, he turned to Star and smiled, exposing a full range of tobacco-stained teeth. "Got a message for you, *señora*, from your husband. He said to pack up, *pronto*. Our wagons are heading south in the morning."

Chapter Fourteen

*A*lways *afterward, when Star thought about the car*avan trek south from Valverde, across the Jornada del Muerte, she could never decide which part of the journey was the worse: the lack of water, making her mouth and throat constantly parched so that it was an effort just to swallow; the unceasing wind, blowing a powdery grit across the high plain, filtering into the *carretilla,* into her hair and eyes and the folds of her gown, despite the closed curtains; or the constant jouncing of the carriage itself over the rough trail, making every bone in her body ache. Or was the worst of all the fear, pushed to a back corner of her mind. For now the caravan had entered the country of the dark people, the Apaches.

"Be sure you fire and reload your pistol each day," Michael had ordered, stopping by the *carretilla* when the wagons reached Fray Cristobal. It was just below this burned and deserted mission that the Rio Bravo and the Camino Real road to El Paso parted company. The river swung west in a great curve, while the wagons would follow the most direct passage south through the mountain barrier and across eighty miles of desert.

Star had drawn aside the curtain to look out at the desolate landscape, at withered brown grass and spiny cactus, dust swirls, and a black buzzard wheeling lazily in the blank, pale blue sky. And in the distance, the jagged brooding mountains.

"How long will it take to cross the Jornada?" she asked.

"Three days, if we're lucky. There was a man once who tried to cross it in one day. He ran out of water and gave the Jornada its name: "The Journey of Death," Michael said grimly. He ran his glance over the small carriage, grimy, battered, no

longer the elegant buggy that had left Santa Fe. "We'll be
traveling mostly at night. It's better for the animals. Keep an
eye on your driver so that he doesn't fall asleep and go off the
road. We don't need another accident."

A day south of Valverde a wheel of the *carretilla* had broken
off, sending the carriage crashing to the ground. Star and Rosita
had been only bruised and jostled in the accident, but it had
taken a day to repair the wheel and the carriage, forcing the
Bradford-Cordoba wagons to fall dangerously behind the rest
of the caravan.

Now as Star clutched the side of the buggy seat for support,
peering anxiously out into the darkness while the *carretilla*
lurched in and out of yet another hole, she couldn't help thinking wearily; What road? And how long had they been traveling
since they had entered the Jornada late that afternoon? Or had
it been yesterday afternoon? Time seemed to stretch endlessly.

She remembered they had stopped only briefly for supper:
cold meat and brackish water—because Michael said they
couldn't chance a fire. The grass around them was too dry. A
flame could spread in seconds through this sandy, seared land,
engulfing the wagon train. Or was it that he didn't want anyone
to see their campfires, she wondered uneasily. With the rest
of the caravan a day's travel ahead, their dozen wagons could
be easy prey for a roving Apache band.

The buggy wheel hit a rock, the impact flinging Star hard
against the carriage frame. She bit back a groan, wondering if
there were any part of her body that wasn't black and blue,
first from the carriage accident and now this interminable jolting
ride. Almost resentfully she looked at the other corner of the
carriage where Rosita slept, making soft, snoring sounds.

A cold, piercing wind, howling outside the *carretilla*, snaked
in under the curtains. Star shivered and pulled the buffalo robe
closer around her. How strange that in the desert the day should
be so hot and the nights so cold, she thought, as she tried to
find a comfortable position so she could sleep.

Later, when the night was almost over and the wagons did
stop for a few hours' rest, Star crawled gratefully into the back
of the Dearborn. She was too exhausted to do more than remove
her dress and wrap herself in her blanket, before falling immediately asleep. It was the cold that awakened her, and the

wind. She curled up in as small a ball as possible beneath her blanket, wishing that she had brought the buffalo robe from the carriage. Even a double blanket wasn't protection against the chill that crept into the Dearborn. She was dimly aware that Michael had joined her, only a hand's breadth away.

It might have been a mile, she thought dismally, the distance that had stretched between them since that last night he had visited her in San Rosa. He hardly spoke to her now unless it was absolutely necessary, and his glance slid over her face like water over a stone. Perhaps, she thought, if he had stayed with her that night, had made the first move to break the wall that seemed to surround her . . . Only he wouldn't make that move, she sensed now. His pride was as great as the paralyzing fear that gripped her. She shivered, pulling the blanket tighter around her. It wasn't only cold she felt, but her own loneliness and the loneliness of this desolate land.

When she awoke again, she realized that sometime during what little remained of the night, she must have instinctively moved closer to Michael's warmth. She was under his blanket, her body curved like a spoon against his back, absorbing the heat from his body. For a moment she felt drowsily content to stay where she was, sliding off again into sleep, when she felt her shoulders being shaken gently. She looked up into Michael's face, his voice softly amused. "If you wanted to share my blanket, *querida*, you had only to ask."

Hurriedly she sat bolt upright. Surely he didn't think that she had deliberately planned . . . "I was cold," she said defiantly. She saw that the sun was high in the sky; she could hear the sounds of the wagons being readied to move, the crack of a whip, the bawling protests of the oxen. Her own body was still stiff from yesterday's ride, and if she were tired, she could imagine the exhaustion of the wagoners, who had endured so much more of the heat and scouring wind than she had in the comparative comfort of the buggy. It was inhuman to drive the men this way, she thought indignantly.

"We're not leaving already?" she protested.

"We've stopped too long as it is," Michael said, and that blank indifference was back in his gaze.

Star glimpsed her face in the scrap of a looking glass she had tied to the canvas of the Dearborn. Her face appeared as blurred and dust-coated as the mirror. Distastefully she picked up her dress and shook it, sending clouds of powdery yellow dust flying from its folds. "I want to wash my face and brush my hair," she said rebelliously. "And I'm hungry."

"We'll be pulling out in five minutes," Michael said, his face hard and stained deeply brown as hickory. The green eyes glittered impatiently. "Be ready."

Then he strode away from the wagon before she could reply. As if he'd pay any attention to what she said anyway, Star thought, annoyed. Hastily she struggled again into her dress, twisting her hair back from her face into some semblance of order. Then she squashed her bonnet down over her hair and scrambled for the carriage just as Rosita began to look around nervously for her.

The second day in the Jornada was even worse than the first, if that was possible, Star reflected miserably, huddling in a corner of the carriage, trying to breathe past the powderlike dryness in her mouth and throat. It hurt her body to move in any direction, even to lift her arm to unfasten the curtains to glance out. The scenery never changed. Sand hills rolled like sculptured waves across the barren land. It was as if they were moving across the face of some alien, dead world, with no beginning and no end.

Late in the afternoon they stopped at the Laguna del Muerto, which, to Star's bitter disappointment, was not a lake, but only a sink in the plains filled with stagnant water good only for the animals to drink. Once more the wagons rested a short time to allow the beasts to graze in the dried grass. This time Michael allowed a small campfire to be lit to boil coffee, using dried grass and soapweed for kindling since there were no trees or wood in sight.

Still irritated with Michael, Star sipped at the coffee, holding the liquid as long as possible in her mouth before swallowing. Now that it was getting closer to evening, she moved nearer to the tiny fire for warmth. "I . . . don't know why we couldn't have had a fire last night," she complained to Rosita. It seemed to her there was just as much danger from fire in the dry grass here as there had been the night before.

Jim Baldwyn was hunched down by the fire, holding a cup of coffee in his two sausagelike hands. Like all the other men, his face and beard were dust coated, his eyes bloodshot, his lips cracked. He glanced thoughtfully up toward the oppressive hills, gathering the darkness into their valleys. "Reckon Don Miguel knows there's ain't any more use pretending the *indios* don't know we're here. They must have sniffed us out last night."

Indians! Star's glance flew toward the mountains, which suddenly seemed even more menacing. Rosita gave a wail of fear, then flung her rebozo over her face and fell to her knees, mumbling a long, involved prayer.

"I . . . I don't see anything," Star said. "Are you sure?"

"Yes'm." The man made a disagreeable sound sucking at his coffee before he spoke again. "You won't see the devils till they they want you to. Then it's usually too late." He nodded with grudging admiration toward Michael, who was off to one side of the wagons talking to Manuel. "He smelled them out even before I did. Guess they must be right when they say he's half Comanche."

"Why don't they attack, then?" Star asked, gazing at a dust cloud swirling, rising in the distance. Dust raised by the whining wind—or did it hide a pack of Indians racing toward the wagon train, she wondered apprehensively.

Her companion's mouth, cracked and raw, smiled painfully. "Ain't no use trying to make sense of those red niggers. Maybe their *puha* ain't right. Who knows?" He put down his coffee cup and took out his knife, thin and evil looking, while he ran his finger down its edge, almost affectionately. "In a way it's too bad they can't make up their mind. I'd favor lifting a few scalps. Too bad it's probably a war party. No women with them," he said regretfully.

Star swallowed. "You'd kill women?"

The wagon boss looked up at her, as if surprised at the question. "Hell, they're meaner than the braves and hate *tejanos* even more. They'll spread-eagle a captive on the ground, man, woman, or child, don't matter, and cut 'em up little by little, and the more the poor devils scream in agony, the more they laugh and jump around, like they was at a hoedown." The pale blue eyes were glazed with a quiet, terrible fury. "I seen 'em cut up my family that way back in Texas, my mother and sister and baby brother. They made me watch. I was big and strong for my age so they didn't kill me. They ran me through the chaparral, figuring they'd take the fight out of me." He smiled derisively. "But they ain't knowing old Jim Baldwyn. A year later, I lit out one night, took two of their best ponies, but first I clubbed to death a couple of the old crones, the ones that tortured and killed my family, and lifted their scalps, the way they had taught me." A wolfish grin split the man's face as he gazed at Rosita. "Might say it's been my profession ever since. Even lifted the hair of some greasers. The fool Mexicans that paid me for scalps never knew the difference."

Rosita had stopped her prayers to gaze, horrified, at the wagon master, while Star wondered, sickened, if that was what had happened to Michael. Had he endured the same horrors as young Jim Baldwyn when he had been a captive of the Comanches? Did that explain the times when a sudden ruthlessness appeared in his face, as if he had reverted back to those savage boyhood days.

"You run off too much at the mouth, *compadre*."

Star had not heard Michael approach, but she did see the white-bearded man stiffen. His hand tightened on the wicked-looking knife, a dull anger flooding the pale blue eyes as he gazed at Michael, whose own hand rested lightly, almost casually, at his belt.

Then the older man shrugged and got slowly to his feet. "Reckon I do at times." He gestured toward the mountains. "What you goin' to do about them?"

"Nothing. We'll keep moving." Michael turned to Star. "We'll be traveling most of the night again. You'd better get back to the *carretilla*."

This time Star did not protest as she climbed in beside Rosita. Somehow it seemed safer moving on through the night in a jolting carriage, rather than sitting and waiting for an Indian attack.

"*Tejano diablo*, that Jim Baldwyn," Rosita hissed as the carriage moved slowly forward through the night.

Star had known that the Mexicans and the Texans hated each other but she hadn't realized before how much. Rosita was right, the wagon master was a devil, she thought, remembering the pleasure in Jim Baldwyn's voice when he talked of scalping Indians and Mexicans. It was as if, ironically, the hatred festering in the man had turned him into as much of a savage as the Indians he despised.

She was too tired, though, to bother to reply to Rosita's muttered invectives, and finally her companion fell into an exhausted silence as the carriage jolted its way through the night. Once or twice Star managed to doze off but always jerked awake, her heart pounding, listening intently above the whining sound of the wind, the rattle and creaking of the carriage wheels and the groaning of the wagons moving painfully slow through the deepening sand. She could almost see the Indians, like shadows moving through the night, lances raised, demons out of a nightmare. Once she even unfastened the curtains to look out, but there was only the arid empty stretch of land, Spanish bayonets and mesquite glistening silver-white in the pale moonlight.

When she awoke again, she was dimly aware that the carriage had stopped. It was still night, and as if from a great distance, she heard someone speaking to her. Her lips were so dry she felt as if they would split if she spoke, and her eyes were swollen shut. She felt arms lifting her, carrying her to the Dearborn, hands removing her shoes, unfastening her collar, pulling blankets over her.

For a bewildered moment, time was jumbled, rushed backwards. Whose hands were touching her? "Charles?" she croaked. And then thought, no, not Charles. Charles's hands had never been so gentle. Before she could speak further, she had once again fallen asleep.

The sound of gunfire awakened her, exploding all around her, rifles and revolvers and muskets and the hullabaloo of men shouting. Indians! She sat up, pushing aside the Dearborn curtains. The heat of the sun reflecting against the land hit her face like a blow.

"Is it Indians?" she asked Michael, as she hurriedly pulled on her slippers and rushed to the tiny campfire. Michael poured out a half cup of coffee and handed it to her. "Not Indians," he said, smiling. "It's Christmas Day. Sorry if it alarmed you but the men had to have their celebration."

Star realized she had lost all track of the days since they

had left Valverde. How strange, she thought, not to even know it was Christmas.

Michael lifted a cup of coffee to her. *"Feliz Navidad.* I'm afraid I haven't any Christmas gift for you, except that you'll be happy to know our friends who have been following us have gone."

Star glanced toward the hills. Everything looked exactly the same. "How do you know?"

"I know." Michael did not elaborate on how he had left the train last night and gone up into the mountains. He had tracked the band of Apaches in the moonlight by the crushed grasses and leaves in the soft earth, found the cold campfire the Indians would never have had if they had planned an attack, even moccasin tracks of squaws, who wouldn't have been traveling with a raiding party. "We'll have to keep moving, though," he warned. "The animals need water, and the river's only a day's travel away now. We should reach it by this evening."

He looked at Star, as if waiting for her cries of protest at being shut up in the airless carriage for another day beneath the broiling sun. She clenched her teeth and stubbornly pushed back the groan of weariness that rose in her throat. What good would it do? The caravan would still move on, and if the men could stand the torturous heat, then she could, too.

"I'll tell Rosita," she said and, almost triumphantly, saw the fleeting look of respect touch the dark green eyes watching her from that impassive face.

Rosita, however, vociferously protested, moaning she was being roasted alive, as the carriage moved slowly under the baleful sun, its rays splintering, dazzling against the ground, hurting the eyes to look at it. If they opened the curtains to let in some air, the dust blew in, making them choke and cough. When they closed the curtains, the two women sat limp, soaked with perspiration, gasping for breath in the ovenlike heat. Finally they reached a point where they both drifted into a semiconsciousness that was like a drugged sleep where all sensations, good and bad, ceased.

The *carretilla* had stopped for several minutes before Star was groggily aware of the lack of movement. When Michael unfastened the curtains, she stared at him blankly, hardly recognizing him with the powdery dust coating his dark hair and stubble of a beard. Even his eyelashes and brows were coated a yellowish gray.

"We made it to the river, *señora*," he said, his voice rasping through raw, cracked lips.

Rosita had already pushed by her, half stumbling, half running to the river's edge, where the men were already flinging themselves, fully clothed, into the water. When Star stepped from the carriage, her legs, stiff and cramped, crumpled under her, and she would have fallen if Michael hadn't held her. Then she, too, was at the water's edge. Never in her life had anything felt as wonderful as the cool water splashing over her face and arms. She didn't even care that she was drinking the same water as the thirsty animals.

For several days the wagons rested beside the river at the camp called Robledo. Star and Rosita found a private place downstream where they bathed and washed their hair while, a short distance away, Manual stood guard. Back at the camp, Rosita brushed Star's hair dry. The hair, unbound, hung in auburn waves to Star's waist, and caught glints of flame as Rosita moved the brush slowly through it.

"*Ay, bonita*," Rosita sighed. "It is a sin to hide such hair beneath a bonnet."

"Well, if I don't wear a bonnet, I'll be dark as an Apache," Star replied, gazing into the mirror she had removed from the Dearborn and hung on a nearby tree. Her skin had already taken on entirely too much color, she thought regretfully, remembering how in St. Louis Cousin Sophia had always washed Star's face in buttermilk during the summers to keep her face a ladylike white. Suddenly Star giggled, thinking how shocked Cousin Sophia would be if she could see her now, brushing her hair in full sight of a camp full of men, after taking a bath in a river with a half-Indian on guard.

"*Madre de Dios!*" Rosita breathed.

Star followed the maid's wide-eyed gaze, and her blood seemed to freeze in her veins. A party of Indians had appeared on the outskirts of the camp as if they had sprung out of the ground. The wagoners had seen them, too, and had snatched up the rifles and pistols and taken their positions within the half circle of the wagons. Two of the Indians separated from the rest of the group and rode swiftly forward toward the camp, the lances glittering in the sunlight.

One of the wagoners lifted his rifle. Michael suddenly appeared beside him and knocked the rifle downward, his voice coldly furious. "Don't be a fool! Can't you see they want to talk."

"I thought you said they had gone," Star whispered, unable to take her eyes off the approaching Indians.

"It's not the same band. These are Comanches," Michael replied, without turning his head. "Give me your mirror, Star."

She stared at him, mystified. "My mirror?"

"A Comanche will trade his pony for a piece of mirror, and the chief looks as if he's in the mood for trading, not fighting."

She snatched the mirror off the tree and handed it to him.

"Now get into the Dearborn, quick," he ordered.

But it was already too late to follow Rosita, who had immediately scurried off to the wagon. The lead Indian deliberately placed his horse between Star and the Dearborn. Too frightened to move, she watched as the man spoke over her head to Michael, disdainfully ignoring the other men with raised guns.

When the Indian slid off his horse, Star saw that he was not as tall as he had appeared. He wore only a breech clout and moccasins and leggings of deerskin, painted blue. He was deep chested with short, squat legs, and his black eyes were heavily bloodshot, his features, massive. It was the Indian's hair, though, that held Star's fascinated gaze. Parted in the middle of the skull, long, greasy braids hung down below the man's shoulders. Each braid was intertwined with bits of silver, scarlet and yellow cloth, colored beads, and broken shards of glass. It must have taken the man hours to complete such an elaborate hairdressing, Star thought.

As fascinated as she was by the man's hair, the Indian was apparently as captivated by Star's. His black eyes shone with greed and an awed wonder as he reached out a hand to touch, then lift a gleaming mass of her hair, letting it ripple like water through his fingers.

Star instinctively started to step away from that dirty, reaching hand. Michael said sharply, "Don't move!"

Star discovered it wasn't fear she felt as much as nausea. Close up, it was clear that what the man had used to grease his hair was bear fat or buffalo dung, or both. The foul odor from the hair, along with the man's unwashed body, made her choke, trying desperately not to breathe. If he touches me, I'll scream, she thought, feeling the hysteria bubbling up in her throat.

But the Indian did not lower his shining eyes from her hair. Then he turned to Michael again, speaking quickly, in a strange, guttural tongue. Michael shrugged and gestured toward a cleared area of the camp, where the Indian hunkered down. Michael said softly to Star, without looking at her, "Go to the Dearborn. Walk slowly. Don't run. Stay there, no matter what happens."

Star did as she was told, but was unable to resist one backward glance. Michael had joined the Indian, squatting on the ground beside him, and they were talking long and earnestly. The other Indians stayed outside the camp. She could see puffs of dust as their horses moved restlessly. The Indians themselves were still as statues.

"What is it?" Rosita asked as soon as Star climbed into the Dearborn, where Rosita crouched, her rosary in her hand. "We will all be scalped!"

Now that she was safe inside the Dearborn, Star discovered she was trembling. She clasped her hands tightly together. The stench of the Indian was still in her nostrils. Through a slit in the canvas drawn across the Dearborn, she could glimpse Michael and the Indian. Their conversation had taken on a leisurely air, with long, companionable silences in between.

Finally, curiosity overcoming her fear, Rosita joined Star. "What are they doing?" she asked. And then, surprised, "Don Miguel has his dice out."

Another half hour passed as the game continued, the dice changing hands frequently with little or no conversation, both men intent upon the game. At last, the Indian picked up the dice and flung them upon the ground with a surprisingly childish display of temper. Then he got to his feet and stalked back to his horse. After he had mounted, Michael said something to him, then smiled, and handed him the mirror. The man clutched

Star's mirror beneath his arm and rode out to join the other Indians. In a few moments they, too, were gone, as quietly as they had appeared. The landscape was once more empty of anything except mesquite and the cottonwoods clustered by the river.

Michael spoke to the men, who quickly began to yoke the oxen while the *arrieros* gathered and loaded the mules. At last Michael came to the Dearborn. "We're pulling out. I don't expect that band will be back, but no point taking chances." He cast an amused glance at Star. "Especially since the chief seems to have taken quite a fancy to you."

"To me?"

"He much admired your red hair," Michael said. "He seemed to feel that a squaw with hair of flame in his tipi would bring him powerful *puha*. He offered me six ponies for you." He laughed at the indignation flooding Star's face, then arched a mocking eyebrow. "You should be flattered. Most squaws bring one, two ponies at the most."

Star glared at him. She had been frightened half out of her wits and he was making fun of the whole episode. "I'm surprised you didn't accept his offer," she said coldly, jumping out of the Dearborn and straightening her skirt with one angry twist of her hand.

Michael walked beside her to the buggy, assisting her inside with elaborate care. "Your constant distrust wounds me, *querida*," he said with feigned chagrin. "I didn't want to offend the chief, though, by turning down his generous offer, so I offered to throw the dice for you instead."

Star's head jerked around. "You were gambling over me!"

"Comanches love to gamble. They'll roll dice for anything they own except their medicine bags," Michael said. "I knew the chief wouldn't refuse."

"Suppose you had lost?"

Michael took the dice from the red and gold leather pouch, tossing them thoughtfully into the air, a wicked gleam in his eyes. The dice were a gift from Doña Lupita. There was, he knew, no possible way he could lose playing with dice from Señora de las Flores. He shrugged philosophically. "Someone always loses in a dice game. Fortunately, I won."

He placed the dice back in the bag and handed it, with a

flourish, to Star. "Perhaps you'd like to keep the dice as a memento of the time you almost became a Comanche chief's squaw." He saw her hand tighten on the pouch as if she would dearly love to throw it in his face.

Before she could do so, he grinned and stepped back quickly, calling to her driver, *"Hola, Tomas. Vamos, pronto . . ."*

Chapter Fifteen

It was late the next afternoon when the wagon train was halted again as a cloud of dust appeared on the horizon. This time, however, it was no threatening band of Indians. They were soldiers in bright green coats, the uniforms of Mexican dragoons. Only, as they rode closer, Star saw at once that the three men were not Mexicans, but Americans. "Couriers," Michael said, waving a rifle high above his head, signaling that they were recognized and welcome.

"Aren't you heading the wrong direction for a battle?" he asked as the three men rode into camp. "I thought Doniphan was to the south of us."

"We've already had a battle," the corporal said as he dismounted. "Fifteen miles from here, at a place called Brazito."

Star moved closer. There was something familiar about the giant of a man, despite the odd hodgepodge of uniforms he wore, half Mexican green coat and the blue trousers of an American uniform. "Mr. Malone," she said, holding out her hands to him. "It's so good to see you again."

The rough, red face became redder, as he snatched off his hat at sight of Star. "Mrs. Brad—" He broke off with a sideways glance at Michael. "But it's Señora Kelly now, or so I heard in Santa Fe. It's grand to see you looking so fine. I felt bad, leaving you at the fort without a proper good-bye."

Star brushed aside the apology. "Tell us about the battle," she said eagerly. "When did it happen?"

"Christmas Day." The man coughed loudly, giving Michael another sideways glance, then muttered, "This riding is dusty work, makes it hard for a man to talk."

Michael grinned and brought out a bottle of pass whisky, which the corporal swallowed from freely before handing to the other two men. Then he wiped his mouth with the back of his hand and reached for the bottle again. Michael took what was left of the bottle into his own hand and said pointedly, "You were telling us about the battle, Corporal Malone."

"Not much to tell. It was over in half an hour," the man said cheerfully. "Riled Colonel Doniphan somewhat, the Mexicans arriving unexpectedly and him in his tent enjoying a game of poker and holding a winning hand. The Mexicans had set up battle lines half a mile away, behind a low bank of hills. They sent in an officer carrying a black flag with a death's head on it, inviting Doniphan to surrender or the Mexicans would charge." Ben Malone grinned widely. "Old Doniphan told them to go to hell—begging your pardon, ma'am—then lined us up and told us to squat on the ground and not to fire until he gave the signal. So there we squatted, waiting, and here comes the Mexicans, looking in their fancy coats and cockaded hats like they was going to a fancy ball, the dragoons in the front, shooting their carbines as they came. Bullets whistled over our heads like hail. They were about a hundred and fifty yards away when the colonel shouts, 'Take your pick, boys, and fire!'

"I tell you, I never heard any sound sweeter than those Missouri rifles letting off all at once! The dragoons that didn't get blasted off their horses by the first volley, broke after the second, and those following behind them took off running, throwing aside their helmets, carbines, wine bottles, sabers, not even stopping to carry off their wounded."

"A glorious victory," Michael said dryly.

The corporal shuffled his big feet uncomfortably. "Well, if truth were to be told, it was plain, when we buried the poor sods, that there wasn't a regular among them. When we rode into El Paso, we found that the young men had been rounded up the day of the battle and marched off to El Brazito. Except for the dragoons in the front of the line, the men probably never had a gun in their hands before in their lives, and no officer worth a tinker's damn to lead them."

Michael frowned. "Are you saying that Doniphan's taken El Paso del Norte?"

"Without a fight. We just waltzed right into the town two days later, and all the leading citizens came out to greet us like long-lost brothers."

Rosita, who had been listening impatiently, now pressed forward, her large dark eyes anxiously searching the corporal's face. "My Jaime, *mi amor*. He is not *muerto*?"

"None of our men was killed, *señorita*," Ben assured her.

"And the traders and the caravan ahead of us?" Michael asked.

"Safe in El Paso, except for the few who bolted for Chihuahua. Doniphan sent troops after them, but they got away. The traders that are left are being armed and formed into a battalion under Colonel Owens." At Michael's lifted eyebrow, the corporal grinned, abashed. "It may not be exactly military, arming civilians, but Colonel Doniphan's never been one to run a war by the book. And most of the soldiers figure the traders have been a pain in the rear to us from the beginning. Some of the men even say it's a trader's war, so why shouldn't they fight alongside us? Anyway, I figure the colonel's going to need all the help he can get when he marches on Chihuahua. It won't be a picnic like Brazito, more like walking into a hornet's nest."

"I thought Colonel Doniphan was joining up with General Wool," Star said. Surely Colonel Doniphan with his small force wasn't planning to take on the whole Mexican army that was already forming to the south to stop any further invasion into Mexican territory.

"Well, it seems no one's exactly sure where General Wool is," Ben admitted. "In the meantime, Doniphan's waiting for his artillery to come down from Santa Fe. That's where I'm heading, to see what's holding up Major Clark, and to pass the word along about Doniphan's taking El Paso del Norte."

"How long do you think it will be before Doniphan gets his artillery?" Michael asked.

The corporal's face took on a sudden, carefully guarded look. "I wouldn't be knowing that, sir. Can't be too soon, though, for the men. Not that El Paso ain't a pretty town with lots of willing *señoritas*, but the men are restless, impatient-like, up to all sorts of foolery, if you know what I mean. The colonel's having a hard time keeping them in hand." The man glanced from Star to Michael, and an uncertain look crept into the bright blue eyes. "It's none of my business, but it might be more sensible-like if you didn't bring your wagons and Mrs. Kelly into El Paso."

Michael studied the corporal's face. "There's more, isn't there?" he asked quietly.

Ben nodded reluctantly. "Oh, the town's peaceful enough on the surface, but underneath, well, there's some Mexicans not happy about what's been happening in their country. There's a priest, Ramon Ortiz, and some others, been stirring up rebellion in El Paso. Doniphan's had Ortiz arrested, along with some of his compatriots."

Michael stiffened. "That won't make Doniphan many friends in El Paso, arresting a priest."

"That's what I mean, sir," the corporal said unhappily. "And Colonel Doniphan already knows that your sentiments, well, ain't exactly with the Americans here in Mexico. And that you was friends with some of those in Santa Fe who caused the trouble up there." At Star's small gasp of dismay, he said, "But then maybe you ain't heard that all hell's broken loose in Santa Fe. We don't know the whole story yet, just rumors, but Doniphan's not taking any chances of the same thing happening in El Paso."

"No, I hadn't heard," Michael said slowly. "Are you saying that I'll be arrested if I take my wagons into El Paso?"

Ben Malone shook his head. "That's not for me to say, sir. It's just a friendly bit of advice I'm offering you." He glanced up at the sky, at the sun beginning to cast long shadows across the valley. "We'd best be moving on if we want to make the river crossing by nightfall."

"Thanks for the advice, corporal." Michael shoved several bottles of *aguardiente* into the man's arms, adding, with a smile, "It gets chilly in the Jornada at night."

Star held out her hand. "Take care of yourself, Ben," she said, giving the man a warm smile. And then guiltily, all at once remembering, "Major Donley wasn't hurt in the battle, was he?"

"No, ma'am. He's fine." Ben stuffed the bottles into his saddlebag and swung up into the saddle, taking a last look down at Star. Strange about women, he thought, the way they seemed so weak and helpless. He remembered the first time he had met Star Bradford, how lost and childlike she had looked, her eyes wide and frightened when her husband so much as glanced at her. He had expected that, after her husband's death, she would go scurrying home to her father. Yet here she was, still in Mexico, in the middle of a war, had crossed a Jornada that had killed strong men, and, if anything, she was more beautiful than ever. Thinner perhaps, that soft baby-fat gone from her face and body, with eyes that now had a hint of gray flint behind those thick, black lashes, a new firmness to that softly curved mouth. He supposed it was just that some women, like some men, were survivors, while others simply curled up and quit when faced by adversity. Star McFarland Kelly had the courage to match her flaming hair, he decided, and a lot of her father's stamina and grit.

He jerked his head toward Michael, standing a short distance away. "Your man there. Does he treat you all right?" he asked gruffly.

Star smiled at the hostility in the man's voice. "He treats me fine, Ben," she assured him.

The red-haired giant frowned again, still hesitating. "Well, if he don't, you let me know." He touched his hand to his hat in a salute. "Maybe we'll meet again, in Chihuahua."

As Star walked back to the *carretilla*, Michael fell into step beside her. "Another admirer, *querida?*" he murmured, looking back at the dust cloud the soldiers' horses made in the distance.

"A friend," Star said. Then couldn't resist asking, "What about Doña Lupita? Aren't you concerned what may be happening to her in Santa Fe, that she may be in prison?"

Michael laughed. "Lupita? You underestimate her if you think she's languishing in *el calabozo*. She's either seduced her way free or bribed her way out."

The amused affection in his voice when he spoke of his former mistress sent a whiplash of anger through Star.

As if he guessed what she was feeling, Michael smiled tauntingly down at her. "Jealous, *querida?*"

Star jerked her arm free of his touch. What an impossible man he was, she thought, annoyed. "I'm not jealous," she assured him. "But I am curious. What are you planning to do now? Will we be going into El Paso?"

"I think not," Michael said thoughtfully. "It could be weeks or months before Doniphan gets his artillery and marches south. And I've had a stomach full of the military deciding when and where I can move my wagons. The Diaz family have a ranch about twenty miles outside of El Paso del Norte. Don Ramon and his wife are old friends of my family, and they'll be happy to put us up. Don Ramon can help me dispose of the wagon goods and buy fresh supplies for the rest of our trip south."

"Wouldn't the goods bring a better price in Chihuahua?"

"Probably, but I'd rather get rid of as much of the trade goods as possible in El Paso. With fewer wagons, we can travel faster to Chihuahua."

Star was relieved to know that they wouldn't be pressing on immediately to Chihuahua. From the stories she'd heard, she suspected the trail south of El Paso wasn't much easier than the road from Valverde.

For the next week she luxuriated in the hospitality the Diaz ranch offered. It was heavenly to sleep again in a soft bed, to bathe in warm water, and have Rosita rub aloe oil into her face and body, to soften skin dried by the sun and dust of the trail. Most of all, she couldn't get enough of simply enjoying the lush greenery of the El Paso valley, the sight of cornfields and vineyards and fruit orchards after desert and prickly pear and cactus, or the taste of fresh grapes and melons and oranges, fresher and more delicious than any she had ever tasted.

It was Rosita, though, who was unhappy, who moaned and complained about not being able to see her precious Jaime in El Paso after coming so far, until finally Michael sent her into town with the wagons and their host, El Señor Ramon Diaz, who had offered to try and sell as much of the trade goods as possible for Michael.

After a few days, when Rosita returned from El Paso, Star couldn't help noticing how blooming the girl looked, how soft and dreamy the dark eyes had become. And how irritating the way the girl chattered on incessantly about her lover.

"Jaime says soon we will be married," Rosita said proudly one morning as she brought Star a cup of chocolate in the inner courtyard of the Diaz hacienda. "Once this foolish war is over."

"Doesn't it bother you, Rosita, that Jaime is your country's enemy?" Star asked curiously.

Rosita shrugged. "War is a stupid business, to be sure, but then men are often stupid, like boys, testing always their manhood."

Star had learned that Private James Kinsley came from a small farm town in Missouri. "Do you plan to live in Missouri?" she asked Rosita, trying to imagine the ebullient, exotic-looking Rosita fitting into a provincial farm community.

Rosita looked startled. "Oh, no. We will live here in Mexico. Jaime will buy a small *rancho* and we will have many children to help with the work." She patted her stomach smugly. "Perhaps he already has planted a child in me."

The girl's smug complacency, the swell of the full white breasts above her unlaced *camisa*, only seeming to emphasize the girl's delight in her immorality, grated suddenly on Star's nerves. She said sharply, "Lace up your *camisa.* You look like a shameless *puta!*"

"But all the women in El Paso wear their *camisas* unlaced," Rosita protested. "It is the fashion."

"Well, it's not the fashion here," Star retorted. "I will not have a maid who dresses like a whore."

Tears immediately drenched Rosita's eyes. She gave a wail of misery and ran from the courtyard. Immediately ashamed of her sharpness, Star started after her, then remembered that her hostess, Doña Carlota, was seated in the courtyard with her. It would not do to rush off and leave her.

"I'm sorry, Doña Carlota," she said, embarrassed, as she glanced at her hostess, whose sleek dark head was bent over her sewing. Although Doña Carlota was plump to the point of obesity, scarcely seeming to move at all on her remarkably tiny feet, and was so quiet that one often forgot she was in the same room, nevertheless she managed the *casa* and servants as efficiently as if she were constantly on the go. It was also plain that her husband adored her, and that the feeling was mutual.

The older woman smiled at Star. *"No importa."* Then in an unusual burst of loquacity, she added, "Do not judge the girl too harshly. She is young and in love. And love is a sort of madness."

"But it's a sin, isn't it?" Star asked. "To sleep with a man before marriage."

"Oh, yes," her hostess said, nodding placidly, making several chins jostle in unison. "Still, sometimes I wonder why the good lord gave us such pleasure in union with a man, if he did not expect us to enjoy his special gift."

Pleasure, Star thought bitterly, remembering those brutal moments in bed with Charles. What pleasure? And then wondered, uncomfortably, if Doña Carlota was aware that Michael and his wife did not share the same bed, much less the same room. And then thought wryly, of course Doña Carlota knew, as she knew everything that happened within her household. What Star didn't know was that Doña Carlota and her husband had puzzled over the matter in their own bedroom at night, the strange fact that Don Miguel and his wife occupied separate bedrooms.

"It is the fault of his father," Señor Diaz said, sighing heavily. "The boy should never have been sent to live in the United States for so long. It has turned him into a *Yanqui*. Or perhaps it is true what they say, that *Yanqui* women have ice water in their veins."

Studying the unhappy face of the young woman across from her, Doña Carlota disagreed with her husband. Whatever the trouble was between Don Miguel and his wife, it was not because the girl lacked passion. Why else should she flare up at her servant that way if it was not because she was jealous of Rosita's open joy in her lover.

"The only real sin, I think," she said softly, "is to enter into the act without love. But you are blessed, are you not, Señora Cordoba? Your husband loves you deeply. I can see it in his eyes when he looks at you."

Star's eyes widened, startled. Doña Carlota was mistaken, of course. Michael didn't love her. Oh, he might have wanted her in his bed at one time, as he would want any pretty woman. But love? Michael had never ever given any indication that he loved her.

"And you love him, too," Doña Carlota smiled. "Or why would you accompany him on such a dangerous journey?" She gave a little shiver. "As much as I adore my Ramon, I cannot imagine venturing into lands of the *banditos* and the Apaches as you will be doing on your trip to Chihuahua. We have heard tales of one *bandito* captain, they call him El Güero. They say he is worse than the Apache; those he captures scream for the mercy of death." She crossed herself rapidly. "May God protect us from such."

Star hardly heard the woman. She was still caught up in what Doña Carlota had said. Was it possible? she wondered slowly. Did she love Michael? She enjoyed his company and his conversation, for all that so often he seemed to be mocking, laughing at her. The days and evenings tasted flat, like a dish without salt, when he was away. And when she looked up and found his eyes upon her, even from across a room, she felt a tightness in her stomach, a warmth that made her cheeks flush and even her breasts feel warm and somehow heavier against the bodice of her gown.

That night, at the late Spanish-style dinner with her host and hostess, she barely touched the delicious, light tortillas, the crisp banana and cinnamon fritters, or the fruit punch made from grapes that grew in the valley and provided the country with its famous *aguardiente*. This evening she found herself studying Michael's face surreptitiously, as if she could catch the truth in what Doña Carlota had said, there. But Michael seemed the same as always. He was unerringly polite and attentive to her needs, but his glance touched her face lightly, quickly turning away, to listen to what Don Ramon was telling him of his trip to El Paso.

"I'm sorry that I could not dispose of all your goods, my friend," the man apologized. "Unfortunately, the city is in a state of turmoil. The American soldiers are being sent from house to house, confiscating food, guns, ammunition, whatever can be found. Evidently it is months since they received any supplies from the American government, and the soldiers have not been paid since they left the United States. They are in a surly humor. Colonel Doniphan does what he can to control them, but the news from the north, which arrived just before I left the city, has not calmed matters any."

"What news is that?" Michael asked. He had been listening without any change of expression on his face, but now at once he was alert, his full attention upon Don Ramon.

"It is bad, Don Miguel. The revolt in Santa Fe has spread to Taos. The Indians have joined with the Mexican insurgents, killing those who cooperated with the Americans in their government of New Mexico. Governor Bent was attacked in his home in Taos and killed and scalped before the eyes of his family. It is only by God's mercy that the family managed to avoid being massacred, too."

"There will be reprisals," Michael said.

Señor Diaz nodded sadly. "General Price has already moved against the insurgents with the army. Many have been killed already, and I fear it is only the beginning. Now your Colonel Doniphan is even more wary of Mexican sympathizers in his midst. It is good that you stayed away from El Paso."

Star's Spanish was fluent enough now so that she understood most of what Don Ramon had been saying, and she was quiet as Michael escorted her back to her room after dinner. This night, though, to her surprise, he did not immediately wish her a good evening and leave. Instead he lingered at the door, then said abruptly, "We need to talk."

"Of course." She opened the door and he followed her inside, closing the door behind them.

She let her shawl fall from her shoulders as she lit the lamp and turned to the decanter of brandy that Rosita always brought to the bedroom each evening, presumably for Don Miguel to drink, a deception, Star thought, that fooled nobody. She started to pour some of the brandy into one of the crystal glasses, but Michael shook his head. "Don't bother. I'll only be a minute."

"Oh." She placed the stopper in the decanter, composing her face, hoping the stab of disappointment she felt hadn't been reflected there.

Michael stood by the door, far enough from the lamp so that his face was in shadow. "I've made arrangements for you to stay here with the Diaz family when I leave for Chihuahua," he said. "Since it seems Don Ramon won't be able to sell any more of the trade goods, there's no reason to delay my journey to Chihuahua any longer."

"I see." Star felt a pulse of anger begin to beat in her throat. "And I'm to be left behind, with no more say in the matter than a sack of flour," she said bitterly.

"You heard your friend Corporal Malone," Michael said impatiently. "Doniphan will soon be marching south to take

Chihuahua, and Santa Anna has no doubt gathered an army to stop him. There's bound to be a battle. It's too dangerous, a woman traveling with the caravan at a time like this. You'll be safe here at the Diaz *rancho*."

"It was dangerous traveling from Bent's Fort and from Santa Fe," she pointed out, her gray eyes brilliant with anger. "It didn't stop you from taking me along. As I recall, you insisted I accompany you."

He scowled, knowing, infuriatingly enough, that she was right. He could not even be sure that she would be completely safe here at the *rancho*. All the *rancheros* around El Paso lived in constant dread of Indian attacks, as well as the chance of American army patrols from El Paso, bored and restless, attacking local *ranchos*, looking for women, whiskey, or food. The regular army officers might deplore the violent, undisciplined actions of the volunteers, but they were helpless to stop them.

"It isn't only the possibility of running into a battle," he said. "All of Central Mexico has been torn apart by this war, *banditos* calling themselves guerrillas, as well as Indians, plundering and burning and killing. The countryside we'll be traveling through is already filled with the bones of murdered men and women, bleaching in the sun." His face darkened. "Are you so anxious to add yours to the rest?"

Star flinched as memory swept back. The caravan had crossed the Brazito battleground on their way to the Diaz ranch. Scattered shells and rusting muskets, the discarded flotsam and jetsam of a battle, covered the sandy soil. But what still haunted Star was the sight of human bones thrust obscenely out of the dry earth, a few with enough flesh on them so that the vultures still gathered. And the red ants were busily finishing the job of polishing the bones of what the vultures had left. The American soldiers had buried the fallen Mexicans, as Ben Malone had said, but not deeply enough. The wolves had dug the bodies up, feasting on the remains.

She swayed, remembering the horror of that day, her face draining of all color. Michael slipped a hand under her elbow, supporting her. She lifted her eyes to the dark, familiar planes of his face, saw the fine white lines splaying out from his narrowed eyes gazing down at her, the slight indentation in the lower lip. A dizziness washed over her, not from the memory of Brazito, but from the sudden, startling knowledge that possessed her between one breath and the next. How could she possibly let Michael go without her? How could she bear living for months on end, here at the ranch, never knowing if his bones had been added to the bloody soil of Mexico, whether he was alive or dead? And worse, live with the bitter knowledge that he would never know how much she cared, how much she needed him? Was this love then, she wondered, dazed. It was nothing at all like the infatuation she had felt for Charles. An excitement ran along her nerve endings, as if she knew she were venturing into a land about whose geography she knew nothing, and that she had taken the last step across the last threshold and knew she could never turn back. Yet beneath the excitement, there was a deep, unquestioning contentment at the very core of her being, simply knowing that she could reach out and touch Michael.

"It's settled, then," Michael said flatly. "You'll stay here at the ranch."

"No!" Star blurted, and watched as Michael's face grew dangerously still at his orders being challenged. She was vaguely astonished herself at her courage in standing up to him. "You're forgetting," she said, desperation driving her to find some excuse, any excuse, to accompany Michael to Chihuahua. "The wagons and trade goods are still half mine. I have the right to go with them and protect my interests."

She saw surprise and then anger flare up in the glittering green eyes. Michael's voice was hard, all the liquid Spanish softness gone. "There's more of your father's Scotch blood in you than I thought, *querida*, if money means more to you than your life. And your trust in my honesty is truly touching," he added sarcastically. "Did you think I planned to run off with your share of the gold from the sale of the goods?"

Star licked her dry lips, her whole mouth felt parched, as if she were back on the Jornada, unable to swallow past the dry, powdery fear in her throat.

Michael smiled coldly down at her. "The truth is, you have no financial interest in the wagon train, and I needn't pay you one *centavo*. As your husband, I have complete control over all your financial affairs." His glance traveled with a deliberate proprietorial air over the smoothly shining auburn hair, past the slim waist to her satin slippers. "The same way, as your husband, everything else you own is mine to do with as I please, when I please."

Then his mouth was on hers, moving with the same deliberation, forcing her lips apart, bending her head back against the crook of his arm. For a moment, at his touch, she felt shaken, as if something deep inside of her had wrenched free and an urgency, a need she hadn't even known she possessed, raced like fire through her blood. Her own mouth became soft and yielding beneath his questing, insistent tongue. Until she felt a hand cup and imprison her breast, felt the heat of that hand through the stiff moire material of her gown, and it was as if her very flesh and nerve ends had a memory of their own. She felt the icy terror like a black cloud, rushing into her mind. Somehow she forced her body to stillness, not to pull away or struggle against those stroking hands. She would endure his lovemaking; she must, she thought helplessly, or there would never be any hope of a real marriage between Michael and her. She closed her eyes, her body bracing as if against a merciless, battering wind.

Michael felt the slender body stiffen in his arms and looked down into a face so very beautiful, and so very closed to him, the eyelids shut, the lashes dark as silken fans against her cheeks. A martyr's face, he thought bitterly. And if he took her now, whose name would she cry out when he caressed her. Charles? As she had that time on the Jornada when he had carried her, half unconscious, to the Dearborn and tried to make her comfortable. Would she lie with him and pretend it was her dead husband holding her?

So abruptly that she swayed and had to clutch a chair to keep from falling, Michael's arms fell away from her. She watched as he turned and walked to the door. "You're not—" She swallowed hard, embarrassed. "You're not staying?"

He turned and bowed, his mouth twisting in a sardonic smile. "You'll forgive me, *mi querida*. The offer's tempting, but I've never found much enjoyment in sharing a woman's bed with the ghost of a dead husband."

She shook her head, biting at her lower lip to keep it from trembling. "I . . . I don't understand. I never meant—"

But the door had already closed behind him, and the room was very quiet around her.

Chapter Sixteen

*W*hen the wagons departed from the Diaz hacienda two days later, the *carretilla* with Star and Rosita inside was part of the caravan. Star was not sure what had made Michael change his mind. Perhaps it was the news brought to the Diaz *rancho* by a *vaquero* the morning before and the telltale pillar of smoke that could be seen in the sky in the distance. A band of Apaches had raided a neighboring *rancho*, burning the house and carrying off half a dozen women and children working at the ranch.

Michael had offered to join the posse of *vaqueros* who were preparing to start out in pursuit of the Indians and their captives, but Don Ramon wouldn't hear of it. He shook his head sadly, "You know only too well how little chance there is the Indians will be tracked down. And your grandmother would never forgive me if I delayed you any longer."

At the last moment, saying good-bye to Star seated inside the buggy, Doña Carlota had given her a silver medallion, the Virgin of Guadalupe. *"Vaya con Dios,* my child. My prayers go with you."

Star's eyes burned and she grasped the woman's hand tightly through the window, unable to speak for fear she would burst into tears. Then the caravan stretched out, a much smaller caravan this time, only two wagons of trade goods, the baggage wagon, and the Dearborn and the *carretilla*. Several of the wagoners had refused to continue the dangerous trip to Chihuahua and remained behind in El Paso. Jim Baldwyn and Manuel, however, were still part of the drovers accompanying the train, but Star suspected they were not acting as teamsters but guards.

233

Baldwyn looked like a *bandito* himself, carrying a *lazo*, two huge pistols, a Mexican sword, and a double-barreled shotgun hanging in a saddle scabbard.

"It is not so bad, this road," Rosita commented, the second day out from the Diaz *rancho*. She glanced around the arid countryside, then hastily crossed herself as the caravan passed another crude wooden cross thrust into the ground beside the trail to indicate an unfortunate wayfarer's death. Murdered, no doubt, Star thought, wondering if anyone in this country ever died except by violence.

They had already passed several deserted *ranchos*, raided and burned out by Indian attackers, with a few cottonwood trees still standing lonely guard over the crumbling blackened walls of what had once been a home. Occasionally a black vulture could be seen slowly circling over the gutted remains of a hacienda. Star shuddered, knowing the attack must have been recent enough for the turkey buzzards and vultures to linger over the ruins and the dead bodies, which must be what was attracting their greedy attention.

She had been surprised that Rosita had insisted upon going with the caravan to Chihuahua when she could have stayed behind in El Paso with her soldier lover.

"What would you do without me to take care of you?" Rosita had asked, and then shrugged practically. "Anyway, if I march with Jaime and the *soldados* to Chihuahua, I would have to walk. This way I can ride in comfort, no?" She gave Star a companionable smile. Star's sharp words to the girl at the Diaz ranch were long since forgotten. Rosita was too good-natured to bear a grudge, and between the two women had sprung up a friendly alliance rather than a mistress-maid relationship.

Two days later, when the caravan reached a passage of sand dunes rolling like waves to the horizon, Rosita was to change her mind about the road to Chihuahua. The sand was fine and deep and the oxen were unable to pull the wagons, so the mules took their place at the arduous task of dragging the wagons forward an inch at a time, with the men taking turns pushing at the wheels, sunk hub deep in the soft sand. To lighten the load, Star and Rosita took turns walking beside the *carretilla*. The hot sand quickly burned through the soles of Star's thin slippers, and she felt as if she were walking through burning

coals. The sun blazed down on her head, and though she kept
her veil pulled down over her face, the searing wind made her
eyes burn and her tongue felt swollen in her mouth. Perspiration
turned her dress black with dampness; each step forward was
a painful effort.

After two days of stumbling along next to the *carretilla*,
hanging on to a rope for support, and when she was sure that
she could not walk another step, that the sand hills would never
end, the wagons reached an ancient spring, Ojo Caliente, surrounded by crumbling rocks. Although the water was blood
warm and smelled strangely of minerals, at least it was wet.
Once again Manuel stood guard while Star and Rosita bathed,
Rosita stripping to the buff without a second thought, while
Star more modestly kept her chemise on. Gratefully she slipped
her head as well as her body beneath the surface of the water,
washing away the accumulation of days of sand and dust. She
had just begun to wash her hair when she felt an arm around
her waist, jerking her, sputtering, from the water.

"Bath time's over, ladies," Michael said, with a glance at
Rosita that sent the girl scurrying from the water, gleaming
silver drops outlining the full breasts and cascading down the
plump hips and buttocks.

"We've only begun," Star protested, annoyed. Michael
grinned, his glance roaming over the water-soaked chemise
that clung revealingly to Star's breasts and long, slender legs,
somehow making her body more tantalizing than if she'd been
as naked as Rosita. "You make a pretty picture, *querida*," he
drawled, tossing her a towel. "I'm sure our friends up there in
the hills are enjoying the view."

Star gasped and spun around, but all she could see were the
stark, barren hills around them, no sign of the dreaded smoke
or dust that meant unwelcome visitors. Nevertheless, she and
Rosita snatched up their clothes and hurried to the waiting
carretilla. The caravan pulled out quickly, with the buggy in
the lead position. The sand dunes were behind them now and
the wagons moved more quickly, but the land was still barren
of wood or water.

Star had struggled into her dress and arranged her damp hair
in some sort of order as the sand and heat once more began to
filter into the carriage. Longingly she thought of the spring

they had just left behind so abruptly. It was Rosita who first saw the man sprawled in the road in front of the buggy.

The startled driver halted the mules. Star, pushing aside the curtains, could hear the terrible moaning cries of the man. *"Por favor . . . help . . . I am dying. Nombre de Dios . . ."*

"Señora, wait!"

Ignoring Rosita's cry of alarm, Star had already scrambled from the carriage and was hurrying toward the man whose body twitched horribly as if in mortal agony. She had almost reached the slumped figure when she heard Michael's voice crack like a bullwhip around her, jerking her around. He was only a few paces behind her, a drawn revolver in his hand pointed at the man in the road.

"Get down, Star!"

"But he's hurt, you can't—"

And then horrified, disbelieving, heard the explosion as Michael fired. She felt the air stir as the bullet missed her by inches, then heard the sound of splintering bone, saw the body of the man in the road jerk once, shudder, and lie still. And she saw Michael's face with no more expression on it than if he had stepped on an insect in the road.

The next instant she, too, was flung violently into the road, the breath knocked out of her as Michael thrust her to the ground, his own body landing on top of hers.

She struggled to free herself, sobbing with rage. "You animal! Oh, God, you're worse than a savage . . ."

She was being half carried, half dragged, the jagged rocks in the road ripping at her skirt, slashing at her skin, her arm feeling as if it were being wrenched from its socket. Then she was pushed into Rosita's arms. Dimly she was aware that Rosita, her eyes round with fright, was crouched behind one of the wagons, and that the caravan had been formed into a protective half circle.

Rosita's arms closed around her comfortingly. "It is a trick the *banditos* use, *señora*," she said. "A man lies in the road and pretends to be wounded. Then when you stop—see!" She gestured toward a low ridge of rocks. Star saw movement in the rocks as men scuttled into position, then a dirty white cloth was being waved at the end of a bayonet. A man's voice called out cheerfully in Spanish, "Ho, *gringos*, we talk, yes? You keep your money. Give us the girl, the *señorita* with the hair of fire. Or you all die slowly, word of honor."

"No harm in talking, *hombres*," Michael answered. Star was startled at how hollow, almost frightened, he sounded.

The man with the white cloth raised his head cautiously over the rocks. Star caught a glimpse of a leather-clad body, a flat-brimmed hat pushed back on a dark head. Then all at once there was a deafening explosion and the head seemed to dissolve, while the rest of the man's body fell slowly, clumsily, down over the rocks.

Howls of outrage rose from behind the rocks and several other leather-clad bodies appeared near their fallen leader, shouting, *"Yanqui burros! Hijos de putas!"* as they fired their *escopettes* down into the wagon train.

Star and Rosita crouched even lower, while musket balls whined overhead or plowed harmlessly into the wooden wagon sides. Jim Baldwyn, leaning against a wagon, chewing contemplatively, growled disgustedly, "Damn greasers, couldn't hit the side of a barn with a rock." The reverberations from the barrage hadn't died away when Michael gave a signal and the wagoners, as one man, returned the fire. This barrage was deadly accurate.

Three of the guerrillas joined their leader, tumbling to the bottom of the slope of rocks. One man stumbled to his feet clutching at his *escopette* and, cursing loudly, staggered toward the wagon.

Baldwyn raised his rifle, took aim almost casually, and fired. The man spun in his tracks and fell to the ground.

"I count maybe only four or five of them left," Baldwyn said to Michael, grinning loosely. "If you keep them busy, me and Manuel can go round those rocks and take care of the rest."

Michael nodded. "Bring one of them back alive," he said. "I've got some questions I want answered."

The two men slipped away from the train. The remaining drovers showered the boulders with continuous rifle fire, making splinters of rock fly through the air. Star pressed her hands to her ears to try and shut away the deafening din.

Five minutes later shots from a carbine could be heard, then a silence, and more screams of rage and fury, and curses, and finally the beat of horses' hooves racing away over the rocky road. It was fifteen minutes before Jim Baldwyn and Manuel returned, alone.

Michael met them in the road, glancing swiftly from Jim's belt, where a fresh scalp hung, to the man's slack, grinning face. Anger simmered beneath the surface of his voice as he asked, "No prisoners?"

Manuel stalked away, and for a moment the wagon boss's grin seemed to hang suspended on his bearded face as he said hurriedly, "There was one, still alive, willing to do some talking. I meant to bring him back, but he up and died on me."

Michael restrained his fury with an almost physical effort, although his face remained hard and expressionless. "What did he say before he died?"

Jim frowned. "Funny thing, it was like those bandits knew your missus was part of the caravan. Even knew her name, called her *Estrella*, Star—that's right, ain't it? Knew *your* name, too." He gave Michael a sly glance. "Makes you wonder, don't it?"

So that was why the band hadn't raided the caravan in the sand dunes when they would have been completely vulnerable, Michael thought. They had wanted to make sure that Star was in the caravan before they attacked. Why? There was something here that he didn't understand, and that always made him feel edgy. If only he could have questioned the *bandito* before that bloodthirsty idiot Baldwyn had gotten his hands on him, he thought, repressing the desire to smash his fist into the man's stupid, grinning face. But that would solve nothing, and he needed Baldwyn's gun, at least until they reached Chihuahua.

Anger was still roiling inside of him as he strode back to the wagons and stopped in front of Star. Her skirt was torn and dusty, and there was a scratch on her arm and a smudge of dirt across one pale cheek.

He could see the fear bright in her eyes, but her voice was steady as she asked, "It was me they wanted, wasn't it?"

He shrugged. "They saw you bathing. I guess you took their fancy, that's all. They won't be back."

She could not hold back the shudder that passed through her body at the thought of those horrible men watching her, wanting her.

Michael saw the shiver of fear, her arms folding tightly

under her breasts. She *should* be afraid, he thought, his anger at Baldwyn finding an outlet in Star. She could have been killed out there on the road. In another second the derringer the man sprawled in the dirt had held hidden beneath him would have sent a ball into that beautiful, trusting face.

Star was remembering that moment, too, and the angry words she had flung at Michael. She said guiltily, "I'm sorry. What I said—" She lifted her hands to him helplessly. "I didn't know."

He shrugged again, indifferently. "I've been called worse." His voice suddenly dropped, so that only she heard the menace in the softness, saw the raw anger in the slitted eyes. "Only next time, when I say drop, you drop! I don't want to have to say it twice. *Comprendes?*"

She nodded meekly enough, but she stared after Michael as he strode away from her, her face thoughtful. There was more, she suspected, something about the *banditos* that Michael wasn't telling her.

The next few days, though, there was no chance to query Michael further about the guerrillas. The caravan entered into a series of *jornadas* across a high sandy desert, each trek across the waterless wasteland seeming to Star more painful and exhausting than the ones that had gone before. There was no water for the animals and only warm, brackish, carefully measured-out water from a rubber canteen for the humans. The hot wind never ceased blowing, and at night Star would fall asleep to the sound of coyotes howling in the distance and the pitiful moans of the thirsty oxens. Michael had to throw out some of the trade goods to lighten the wagon loads, and at last the Dearborn itself and most of Star's baggage had to be abandoned after two more of the oxen died.

Rosita and Star now slept under the wagons, the same as the men. Always Star would shake out her blanket carefully to make sure there were no scorpions in the folds and carefully place a lasso in a circle around the blanket, which, Rosita insisted, kept snakes away. And once more they walked alongside the *carretilla* instead of riding inside. Often Star felt her legs give way beneath her and she would have to drag herself to her feet, the dust clogging her throat and nostrils till it was a painful effort just to breathe. She lost all track of time, day and night seeming to run together in a dull, hazy blur, the nights perhaps a little cooler.

Watching the two women, Michael knew they couldn't last much longer without rest and fresh water. With their fair skins and small frames, both Star and Rosita were becoming dangerously dehydrated.

"There's a small *rancho* about two miles off the trail," he told Manuel. "We'll stop there." He did not say it aloud, but both men knew that the hacienda could now be only a blackened, gutted ruin, the spring poisoned as the Indians often did after a raid.

Only the hacienda wasn't burned, Michael saw, relieved, as the caravan made its weary way past stunted willows and cottonwoods and, riding ahead of the wagons, he could see the house before them. The hacienda was built like a square fort, with a flat roof and portholes for wary riflemen on guard against intruders. He gestured to Manuel that it was safe to bring the wagons forward.

After tasting the water and finding it pure, the members of the caravan stumbled to the well, pulling up buckets of water, scooping it up with their hands, swallowing it greedily. Finally buckets of water were drawn for the animals, with the drovers watching so that the animals didn't drink too much, too quickly, and flounder and die.

After she had drunk her fill, and washed her hands and face, Star wandered away from the group toward the rear of the hacienda, wondering idly why its owners should have abandoned a *rancho* where there was good water and grass. It looked like a sturdy home, loved and cared for. She saw the cloud of vultures swooping lazily in the milky-blue sky overhead almost at the same moment she saw the three dead men tied to wooden posts, stuck into the hard, unyielding ground. There was a bullet hole neatly in each man's forehead. And on the ground before the posts were two women, one middle-aged, one not much past sixteen, their clothing stipped away, their eyes staring in blank, unseeing horror up at the cloudless sky, a lance thrust through their bodies pinning them to the earth.

Star heard someone screaming, shrill, mindless screams, over and over again, and didn't know the screams came from her own throat. Her body shook wildly and her wide gray eyes had almost the same blank look of horror as the raped and murdered women.

She didn't so much feel the palm of Michael's hand, flat and stinging hard, against her face, as hear the sound of the blow ringing in her ears. She blinked, staring up at him, dazed, her voice low, uncomprehending, "How could they..." She took a deep, gasping breath. "How could anyone..." She began to cry helplessly, the tears streaming down her cheeks, tasting of salt in her mouth. "This land! This cruel, heartless land. How I hate it!"

"Not the land, *querida*," Michael said quietly. "It was men."

"Indians?" she asked, horror-stricken, not wanting to look at the dead men, the ravaged women, but unable to tear her eyes away.

Baldwyn squatted down almost a hundred feet from the three posts, his hand shifting through the dust, picking up shell casings. "Colt revolver," he said. "Not Indians and not *banditos*. They ain't carrying Colts. Whoever it was knelt here and took slow, careful aim, one man at a time. Three dead men, three shells. Damn good marksman," he said admiringly. "Couldn't have happened more than an hour or two ago, or the buzzards would have had them by now."

Michael's mouth tightened to a hard, narrow line as he saw Star flinch, and sensed the hysteria building up inside the slim, tense body. "Bury them," he said brusquely to the wagon boss. "Get them buried, and then let's get the hell out of here. Whoever they were could still be hanging around."

Rosita had fallen to her knees and, head bowed, murmured hasty prayers for the murdered family, then made sure that crosses, if only primitive pieces of wood tied together, were placed over the five graves. As the caravan pulled away from the *rancho*, Star took one last look back. Five more crosses she thought, and a weariness seemed to settle into her bones, the flesh of her face pulled taut so that the cheekbones seemed to stand out in bold relief.

The weariness stayed with her as the caravan traveled slowly forward out of the dry arid plains into a more habitable land. Men in straw sombreros and ragged ponchos astride burros suddenly appeared. There were haciendas and even small crumbling wayside chapels with tiled domes in a frame of trees.

The two women rode in the *carretilla* again, and there was more than enough water for washing and drinking. But neither food nor water seemed to agree with Star. She pretended to eat and drink when Rosita was watching, but the food nauseated her and she felt hot and cold by turns, as if she couldn't get cool or warm enough.

It was the second day after the wagons left the last *jornada* and the caravan had stopped for the nooning by a stream, that a band of horsemen could be seen riding toward the wagons from the direction of the *jornada*. Although it was obvious from their bold approach that the approaching riders were neither Indians nor guerrillas, each man in the caravan reached for a rifle or his carbine. As the band drew closer to the camp, Star could see that the men were not in uniform but wearing long black coats, slouch felt hats, and leather vests. Almost all the men had beards, and all were heavily armed.

"That's far enough," Michael warned, stepping forward. "State your business."

The lead man swung off his horse. When he saw Star, he doffed his hat and made a graceful bow in her direction. "My apologies for interrupting your meal, ma'am." He had a clear, high voice, and for all that he was slight and slim hipped, there was an air of command about the young man. He turned, inclining his head toward Michael. "Captain Richard Masey of the Texas Rangers at your service, sir. We're attached to Ben McCulloch's company with General Wool at Saltillo."

"You're a long way from your base," Michael said, and then, lifting a quizzical eyebrow, "Am I to understand the Texas Rangers are working for the military now?"

"We're under orders from General Taylor to clear the area of guerrillas that have been harassing the movement of the army's troops and supplies," the young man said stiffly. His glance moved casually over the gathered wagoners. "You have taken a terrible gamble bringing your wagons through the *jornadas* at this time, *señor*..." He hesitated, his own glance questioning now.

"Kelly. Michael Kelly." He did not introduce Star, and she was sure that Captain Masey noticed the affront. Michael's voice was unruffled. "We're bringing trade goods to Chihuhua."

"You met no *banditos* then, during your journey?"

"There was one attack. We drove them off."

"The leader of the band that attacked you, his name was not El Güero? We have been searching for him for a month now, although he usually operates farther south. We thought we had his band cornered at a *rancho* several days back, but they got away."

"The bandits didn't give us any names," Michael said. His face hardened as he studied the slender man before him. "We stopped for water at the ranch you visited with your men. I assume that was your handiwork, what happened there."

Star stared, horror-struck, at the young man with his lovely manners, his face that looked young enough to be beardless. "It was your men who murdered those people?" she said accusingly.

"We are at war with Mexico," the man said. "That *rancho* was well known for sheltering guerrillas."

"The women, too?" Michael asked, not trying to hide the contempt in his voice.

A faint flush rose beneath the young man's fair skin. "One of the leaders in El Güero's band is a woman. She's the most savage of the lot." He turned to Star. "I appreciate your naturally tender feelings, ma'am. But some of my men had relatives at Mier. And you are undoubtedly not aware how the guerrillas treat the American soldiers they catch straggling behind their units. They strip them naked and pull them through the chaparral until their bodies are covered with cactus spines. Then they cut out their tongues and leave them, still half alive, for the buzzards to finish. They take no prisoners and show no mercy. Neither do we."

Star swallowed around the sour taste of nausea rising in her throat. She would not, she thought fiercely, give that murderously pleasant young man the satisfaction of weakly fainting before his eyes.

"Was there anything else, captain?" Michael asked softly. The slash of the black brows over the icy, narrowed eyes made the young Texan reconsider whatever else he might have said.

"Nothing, sir. My apologies again for intruding, ma'am."

Then he lifted his hat in a farewell gesture, signaled to his men, and they rode out of the camp.

Michael walked Star back to the carriage. "What did the captain mean when he said some of his men had relatives at Mier?" Star asked curiously.

Michael hesitated, frowning before he spoke slowly. "It's not a story you'd want to hear." Then, when Star stood, her chin set stubbornly, waiting, he sighed and said. "Back in '41, several hundred Texans, civilians and dragoons, were captured after attacking the town of Mier on the Rio Grande. When they tried to escape, seventeen were executed, after drawing lots, as an example to the others. The rest were sent on a death march two thousand miles to Mexico City. Many more died of thirst and starvation along the way. Those who couldn't keep up were shot. Those still alive at the end of the march were imprisoned in filthy dungeons, along with lepers and hardened criminals." He shrugged grimly. "As you can imagine, the Texans have never forgotten Mier, any more than the Alamo or Goliad."

Star's shoulders drooped. So much horror piled on horror, she thought. Would there never be an end to the hating, the cruelty, she wondered, as Michael lifted her gently into the carriage.

"If we keep moving, we should make Chihuahua by nightfall," he said. "If you're not up to it, though, we can rest awhile." He gave Star a searching glance, disturbed by the glistening waxy pallor in her face, the feverish, too-brilliant eyes.

Star thought longingly of a bed beneath her, a real bed, instead of the hard ground. Every bone in her body ached and even her flesh hurt at her waist where Michael's hands had rested lightly. "I'll be fine once we reach Chihuahua," she assured him. "Will we be staying at a hotel?"

Michael grinned. "Not unless you have a liking for fleas. No, I always stay with Don Felipe Alvarez and his family when I'm in Chihuahua. They have a comfortable hacienda on the outskirts of town."

"More friends of your grandmother's?" Star asked, smiling faintly.

"Distant relations, as a matter of fact. The daughter of the family, Francesca, is engaged to Alfredo, the cousin who has the *rancho* near the Cordoba ranch." For a moment, a glint of amusement touched the green eyes. "I imagine Don Felipe and his family will be surprised when I show up with a bride."

But it wasn't surprise that Star saw in Francesca Alvarez's face when, late that evening, the *carretilla* finally pulled with a clatter into the cobblestoned courtyard of the Alvarez home. Servants came running from the house with torches to greet the visitors. An exhausted Star, her head swimming with fatigue, stepped from the *carretilla* and saw that the hacienda was huge, almost a small palace. A fountain cascaded noisily in the center of the court. Bougainvillea climbed the walls, the flowers such a bright red that it hurt her eyes to look at the vibrant color.

The major domo had come out the great double door, a thin, tall man in black, very much aware of his high position among the other servants as he greeted Michael warmly.

"Don Felipe will be pleased to hear of your arrival, Don Miguel."

Then from behind him, a young woman dashed out into the courtyard in a flurry of flounced skirts. A white lace rebozo dropped away from a thin, pointed face whose skin had the texture and color of camellia petals.

She would have flung herself into Michael's arms, but she suddenly saw Star standing behind Michael, and she stopped abruptly. Her glossy black eyes flashed arrogantly in the lamplight as she turned, gesturing imperiously toward Star. "Who is . . . this, Michael?"

Michael took Star's hand, pulling her forward. "Francesca, may I present my wife. Star, this impetuous young woman whose manners are so deplorable is Francesca Alvarez."

No, Star thought, gripping at Michael's hand tightly, it wasn't surprise she saw in the girl's face. It was more like pure, unadulterated hatred.

Except, of course, later she wasn't at all sure what she had seen in the girl's face in that split second, and what she had imagined. She dropped Michael's hand and extended her own hand to the girl. But she never touched the girl, for in the next moment the giddiness that had plagued her for the last days suddenly swept over her in a dizzying wave, lifting her, then dropping her down like a dead weight, into darkness.

She heard Michael call out her name sharply. It was the last thing she heard before she fell unconscious to the cobblestones of the courtyard.

Chapter Seventeen

She awoke slowly, *as if she were fighting her way* upward through layers of gauze. It was a tremendous effort to lift her eyelids, to move her head on the pillow and stare, bewildered, around her. She didn't recognize the room, large and luxurious, with Brussels carpeting on the floor, full-blown roses in a crystal vase, a silver pitcher and basin on a washstand, and delicate lace embroidery on the coverlet over the bed.

Then a familiar face leaned over the bed, a soft anxious voice asking, "You are feeling better, Doña Estrella?"

"Rosita." She managed to lift her arm and touched the hand that grasped hers warmly. "I've been sick?"

"It was the fever," Rosita said. "At first the doctor thought it was the cholera. You were burning up and you couldn't swallow, not even a drop of water. The doctor said there was nothing more he could do and the priest should be sent for. Only Don Miguel would not allow it." Rosita's eyes widened, awestruck, in memory. "He was like a mad man, Don Miguel. He cursed the doctor and called him a fool and would not allow the priest, or anyone else, in your room."

"Who, who nursed me then?"

"It was Don Miguel. He would not even allow me in the room. Sometimes, though, I would come to the door and watch him, oh, so patiently—who would believe he could be so patient?—place a few drops of water on your lips, then, time and time again, stroke your throat, so gently, to make you swallow. And all the time talking to you, as if you could hear what he said."

Vaguely now, snatches of memory were returning. The terrible retching with nothing in her stomach to bring up, the fire that consumed her body, and someone removing her gown, placing cool, wet clothes against her skin, so that for a while at least the flames licking at her flesh were cooled, the pain made bearable.

She gave Rosita a startled glance. "Don Miguel, he did everything?"

"Everything," Rosita said solemnly. "Then yesterday you kept down a few drops of broth, and I knew you would recover. So I asked Don Miguel if I could not come in and sit beside you." She got to her feet. "I promised Don Miguel, as soon as you awoke completely, I would make you take some more broth, or would you rather have custard, *señora*?"

Star didn't want either but Rosita insisted, and so obediently she forced herself to swallow the custard, discovering after a few spoonsful that she was hungry, after all.

After she had finished eating, Rosita helped her sit up in bed. She was shocked at how weak she was, like a baby, hardly able to hold up her head.

"Where is Don Miguel?" she asked.

"In the room next to this one, sleeping. It is the first time he has put his head down since you took sick. Shall I fetch him?"

"No, let him rest," Star said quickly, then glancing around her. "Are we still at the Alvarez hacienda?"

"*Si, señora.*" Rosita's voice dropped to a respectful whisper. "You would not believe the magnificence of this *casa, señora*. There are more rooms and servants than one can count, and a great marble bathing pool off of the patio."

"Are the Alvarez a large family then?"

"Only Don Felipe and Doña Maria, his wife, and a daughter, Francesca. The servants say it is a great sadness to Doña Maria that she has no other children."

Star remembered then the girl in the courtyard the night she arrived, the easy familiarity with which she greeted Michael and the angry look in her eyes when she had met Michael's wife. "She is very beautiful, Doña Francesca," she said slowly.

"*Muy linda,*" Rosita agreed and then, pursing her lips critically, "but very spoiled by her parents, I think. All the servants fear the young one's temper. Once Doña Francesca even took a whip to her *dueña,* and the servants say she comes and goes as she pleases. The *dueña* is afraid to tell her parents of the girl's wicked behavior with men."

Star smiled to herself. Rosita's own behavior around men could hardly be called proper, but she supposed Rosita considered the behavior of the daughter of an *aristo* family like the Alvarezes should be above reproach. At the moment, though, she wasn't interested in listening to gossip about the Alvarez household. All she was interested in was sleep.

For several days she drifted in and out of periods of wakefulness. The third day, when she woke up, Michael was standing beside her bed. There were lines of strain around his eyes that disappeared when he smiled down at her. "They tell me you're feeling better."

"Yes, thank you. I seem to have been a great bother." She was aware that in her sleep she had pushed aside the coverlet, and that the gown she wore was almost transparent. Whose gown, she wondered, tugging the coverlet over her as Michael watched, amused. "I understand I have you to thank for my excellent nursing care," she said stiffly.

He inclined his head, his voice equally formal. "Naturally, I could not take the chance, if it were cholera, of having it spread to the rest of the household. You are, after all, my responsibility."

Not his beloved, not his wife, she noticed, with a stab of pain: his responsibility. Just as the trade goods, the oxen and mules, were his responsibility.

"What day is it?" she asked, realizing she had lost all track of time.

"February the tenth."

She gasped. That meant she had been sick almost two weeks. "I never realized I'd delayed you so long," she said unhappily.

He shrugged. *"No importa.* I've rented a *tienda* in town and am doing a good business. All the trade goods should be sold in a week or so. In the meantime, you are to rest and grow strong. The Alvarez family have great plans for a *baile* when you are feeling better, to introduce you to Chihuahua society. You mustn't disappoint them."

He was at the door when her voice, uncertain, stopped him. "You will come by to see me?"

His eyes were suddenly too probing at her face, and she said quickly, "I . . . I don't know anyone here."

He nodded politely. "Of course, if you wish."

For two days, though, he did not visit her. Rosita told her he was busy in town at the shop and arranging for their transportation to Mexico City. Then, the third day, when she was alone in the room, a knock came at the door. Almost before she could call out, *"Entre,"* the door was pushed open and Francesca glided into the room with an unhurried arrogance, as if she were quite sure she would be welcomed wherever she wished to be. She was affecting the wearing of a Mexican peasant's dress, but her skirt was not of simple cotton but a beautifully and heavily embroidered scarlet woven material, with a white silk *camisa* worn low in the bodice, and a scarlet rebozo flung carelessly over her shoulders.

Close up, Star saw that the girl was older than she had first thought, perhaps only a year or two younger than Star herself. But she had a voluptuous figure that belied her years. The dark hair was tied smoothly back from the thin face with the sharply etched features. The girl would have been a great beauty, Star decided, if it were not for a discontented droop to her full lips and a certain hardness in the gleaming black eyes.

As closely as she was observing the girl, Francesca was studying her. Now she spoke disdainfully, in Spanish. "You are little more than skin and bones. I never thought Don Miguel would take a skinny wife. And for myself, I think red hair is common."

Star felt an amused anger. It was clear the girl had a crush on Michael and would resent any wife he took. She answered slowly, in Spanish. "You'll have to speak more slowly, Doña Francesca, if I am to understand you."

Francesca looked startled that Star had understood her, then tossed her head. "I did not know you spoke Spanish, *señora.* Still, you speak it very badly."

"As well, perhaps, as you speak English," Star replied coolly, and decided that Rosita was right. The girl was spoiled. Certainly no well brought up young Spanish girl of a good family would treat a guest so discourteously.

A flush of color ran across the girl's face as she almost spat out the words. "Never! I would never speak the language of the barbarians from the north who have invaded my country. When the *gringo* burros march down upon Chihuahua, papa has promised me that I can drive with him in the carriage and watch our brave dragoons slaughter every *Yanqui* soldier that dares set foot on Mexican soil. Already General Jose Heredia has 20,000 men under his command," she bragged. "How many men does your Colonel Doniphan have?"

Star had no idea, though she suspected not more than a thousand at most. She didn't blame the girl for her hatred for Americans; no doubt she would feel the same if the Mexican army had invaded Missouri. But if the rest of the family felt like Francesca, her stay with the Alvarez family wouldn't be too pleasant. "I'm sorry you feel as you do about Americans," she said slowly, and couldn't resist adding, "But your friend, Don Miguel, is half American, is he not?"

"In his heart, Don Miguel is Mexican," the girl said staunchly. "Through his grandfather, Don Miguel's family goes back to the conquistadores."

"Have you known Don Miguel long?"

"Since I was a small child," the girl said airily. "There was some talk that we might marry, but his grandmother said I was too young. And there was another girl that his grandfather wanted him to marry. He was very angry when Miguel refused, and Michael's half brother, Esteban, married Elena instead. I have met Elena," she said, her voice disparaging. "She is pretty enough, but afraid of her own shadow." Francesca's mouth drooped petulantly. "It is not fair that a *gringa* like you should have had two husbands, and I have none."

"How did you know I was married before?" Star asked, startled.

The girl's glance did not meet Star's, sliding evasively away. "Oh, when you were sick, you called out his name, the servants tell me. Carlos, is that not his name?"

Ignoring the girl's question, Star said instead, "I understand you are to be married to Michael's cousin Don Alfredo, so soon you will have a husband, too."

Francesca's mouth drooped even further, her voice became childishly petulant. "Not any longer. Papa says Don Alfredo has gambled away his estates. It did not matter when it was thought he would inherit the Cordoba lands after Esteban's death, but now that Don Miguel has taken a wife, all the Cordoba wealth passes to him. Poor Alfredo is left with nothing, so papa says now I must marry Don Antonio. I hate him! He is old and fat and spends all his time on his *rancho*."

Star understood then the look of hatred on the girl's face that first night. The news that Michael had taken a wife not only deprived Francesca of Michael, but of her fiancé Don Alfredo as well.

"Perhaps it is just as well," she said, remembering the hostility she had heard in Michael's voice when he spoke of his cousin. "You may not have liked Don Alfredo."

"But, of course, I would," Francesca said. "We met once when I was fifteen and traveled to Mexico City with my parents. He is handsome, like a marquis, and no doubt would be an excellent lover." She glanced slyly at Star. "Not as good a lover, perhaps, as Miguel." And then boldly, deliberately insulting, "Or perhaps you would not know about that, *señora?* I understand you do not share your husband's bed."

Star struggled to keep her composure, but she could feel anger stiffening her face. How could the girl know that she and Michael didn't share the same bed? Surely Michael wouldn't have told her. No, it must have been Rosita, gossiping with the servants.

Before she could think of a reply to the girl's rude outburst, a woman, tall and thin, with a harassed look on her bony face, hurried into the room. Her voice was affectionately scolding as she said, "Francesca, what are you doing here? And without your *dueña*, as usual. Doña Dolores has been looking all over for you. Run along. The seamstress has arrived to fit your gown for the *baile*."

She dropped a fond kiss on the girl's face and gave her a gentle shove. "You can talk with our guest later."

After the girl left the room, she turned with a sigh to Star. "I hope the child hasn't upset you, my dear."

Hardly a child, Star thought, and then realizing that she must be in the presence of her hostess, she said quickly, "No, she didn't upset me. And it's very good of you, taking me in this way. I hope it hasn't been a great inconvenience to you, my being ill."

"Certainly not," Doña Maria assured her, and there was no

doubting the sincerity in the woman's voice. "Our house is your house for as long as you and Don Miguel care to stay. You are feeling better, I hope. We were all so concerned for you."

"Much better. I thought perhaps tomorrow I might get up."

"Then you must join us for dinner tomorrow evening. And when you are completely recovered, Don Miguel thought you might enjoy seeing the city of Chihuahua. It is not as old as Santa Fe, but many say it is much more beautiful," her hostess said proudly. "And, of course, our friends are most eager to meet Don Miguel's wife. We thought perhaps a small *baile*." She gestured absently. "Only a few hundred guests."

"It's very kind of you, Doña Maria," Star said, hoping the consternation she felt didn't show in her face. "I'm afraid, though, I have no suitable gown. Most of my clothes had to be left behind on the trail."

Her hostess was already fluttering toward the door. "Don't concern yourself, my dear. Your husband has some beautiful silks among his trade goods. You must pick out what you like and my seamstress will take care of the rest. She is really very clever. Of course, with the Americans blockading our ports, we no longer receive news of the latest Parisian styles. Still, as my husband continually reminds me, we are fighting a war and must make sacrifices."

Star, with Rosita's help, dressed very carefully for her first dinner with the Alvarez family. She wore the one good dress she still owned, a yellow figured silk, its oval décolletage filled in with a chemisette and neck frill of cream-colored muslin, matching the inner sleeve, which had a frill of the same material at the wrist. The waist was cut low, and Rosita had had to take it in to fit Star, who stared unhappily at her figure in the mirror. She had lost weight during her illness, so much so that the fragile bones in her face and shoulders were clearly visible. Rosita hinted at some subtle camouflage to fill out the bodice of the gown, but Star rejected the suggestion.

At least her hair had regained its former vibrant glory, and Rosita arranged it, caught up on top of her head with a silver comb, ringlets slipping free at the nape of her neck and at her temple, softening the too thin lines of her face.

"I will just have to eat more," Star decided firmly, which

wasn't difficult in a Mexican household with the early morning
cups of rich chocolate, full six-course meal at lunchtime early
in the afternoon, then rolls, pastries, and shiny yellow custard,
along with candied fruits, for the late-afternoon snack to stave
off starvation since dinner was always served late, at nine or
ten o'clock.

At eight thirty Michael arrived to escort her to the *sala*,
where the family always met before dinner. It was the first
time Star had seen the rest of the hacienda, which was arranged
in much the same style as the Delgado hacienda, the house
built around a spacious courtyard, with the family living quarters on three sides and the fourth used for the servants' living
quarters and kitchen. All the family quarters were connected
by a long gallery circling the patio that contained beautifully
tended flower beds, vines of night-blooming jasmine and cle-
matis, a softly bubbling fountain, and a grilled gate through
which Star glimpsed the large bathing pool of white marble
that Rosita had mentioned.

The *sala* was much more magnificent than any Star had
ever seen, a high-ceilinged room with the ceiling ornately decorated with gold leaf, and gold-framed Venetian mirrors hanging everywhere Star looked. There was a small platform at one
end of the thickly carpeted room where velvet-clad musicians
played, and the major domo circulated with crystal goblets of
wine on a silver tray.

Star had not realized there would be other guests at dinner,
but evidently this was not unusual. Guests as well as relatives,
she discovered, were always coming and going from the Alvarez hacienda. There were at least a dozen people in the room
when she entered. Michael introduced her to her host, Don
Felipe, a tall, distinguished-looking man with a sharp, bony
face much like his wife's. He was dressed in a heavily embroidered black jacket and trousers that fit so perfectly not a
wrinkle could be seen anywhere.

He greeted Star warmly, and his dark eyes gave no hint of
his real feelings, which, Star suspected, were dismay and bewilderment at Michael's choice of a *Yanqui* wife.

At dinner, Star was seated next to Don Antonio, whom she
remembered as being Francesca's intended. After a few minutes' stilted conversation, she could understand why the girl

was not happy about her father's choice of a husband. Don Antonio, almost as old as Don Felipe, had little charm or small talk, and his small eyes, set deep in folds of fat, had a stubborn, intractable look.

She was just as happy, though, not to have to carry on a conversation, and she concentrated on her food, which was delicious, one delicately seasoned course following another. Francesca sat next to Michael, which Star was sure had been deliberately planned by the girl, and she was trying to tease Michael into going riding with her the next morning. Francesca was dressed in white muslim with a pale blue girlish sash and blue ribbons at the short puffed sleeves, but there was nothing girlish about the décolletage, which revealed gleaming white shoulders and the ripe, crescent curve of young breasts. Star noticed that her dinner partner's small black eyes had a way of fastening greedily on his fiancée's flesh as it spilled out above the tightly fitted bodice. Francesca, however, ignored Don Antonio, her flashing smile and sparkling eyes for Michael only.

"We always ride together out to the *rancho* when you visit Chihuahua," she was protesting, her rose-red mouth pouting prettily.

"But there wasn't the possibility of running into a full-scale battle then," Michael said, refusing to rise to her bait. "The rumors in town are that Colonel Doniphan and his dragoons and artillery left El Paso over a week ago."

"It is not rumor but fact," their host said. "General Heredia's scouts have reported that the *Yanquis* are experiencing great difficulty in crossing the second *jornada*. Many of their big guns have had to be left behind, and the soldiers are so desperate for water, they have tossed away their swords and are carrying water in their scabbards."

"Even if the *yanqui* burros by some miracle should cross the *jornadas*, there is no cause for alarm," Don Antonio said importantly. "I have visited the fortifications that General Heredia has built where the El Paso road crosses the Rio Sacramento. The fortifications cover all approaches to the city and the general has over three thousand men manning the defenses. The cowardly *gringos* will never pass. They will turn and run, you will see."

Michael sipped his wine thoughtfully, a wicked gleam in his eyes as he stared across the table at Don Antonio. "I don't recall the *gringos* running at Monterrey or El Brazito."

A dull red swept over Don Antonio's face, a vein in his temple enlarging and throbbing angrily.

Don Felipe interrupted hastily. "What you say is unhappily true, Don Miguel, but always before it was peons fighting, with no trained officers to lead them. General Heredia is a brave, professional officer. I do not think that from now on the Americans will have it so easy. And, too, there is the fact that General Santa Anna is leading a force of twenty thousand men north from San Luis Potosi, no doubt to destroy General Taylor and his army at Saltillo. The American supply lines are already dangerously long. When they are forced to retreat, the countryside will rise up against them."

"If Mexico must rely on such men as Santa Anna, then her cause is indeed lost," Michael said, disgusted. "That strutting charletan should have been hung after San Jacinto."

"President Antonio Lopez de Santa Anna is a great leader," Don Antonio said angrily. "He has sworn to devote himself to the death to the cause of independence for the republic of Mexico."

"Santa Anna's only devotion is to himself, his gamecocks, and his gambling," Michael replied curtly.

Their host was still determined to smooth troubled waters between his two guests. "I am not a political man myself, as you know, Don Miguel, but you must agree that *el presidente* has a talent for raising armies and money to outfit them."

"Oh, I give the old rascal credit for forcing the church to support his army, though I don't imagine seizing and selling church properties, as he's been threatening to do, will make him many friends with the church authorities in Mexico City."

"It takes money to raise an army," Don Antonio said. "There must be arms manufactured and supplies bought and uniforms for the officers and soldiers." His thick lips twisted in a scornful sneer. "But then perhaps, Don Miguel, you haven't seen the American soldiers. My nephew fought with much honor at El Brazito. He said the *Yanqui* soldiers, even the officers, were dressed like wild men, in buckskins and torn trousers, not a uniform among them. And the American General Taylor, I have heard, wears a common shirt and trousers and a straw hat." He laughed harshly. "Still, what can one expect from a race of heretics and uncouth barbarians."

Michael put down his wine glass. In the candlelight, his face held a smooth stillness, only his green eyes, narrowed, caught and reflected the candleshine. He spoke softly. "I am sure you are forgetting, Don Antonio, that my wife is American and my father was, also. I will accept an apology for your rudeness and would demand more, if you were not a guest in this house."

Star saw the wormlike vein in Don Antonio's temple begin to throb again, and, sensing the man's explosive temper, began to be sorry for Francesca's future as his wife. At the moment, though, she was more concerned about Michael's future.

With a deep sigh, she let her fork drop to the table, swaying slightly backward in her chair. "I am sorry, *mi alma*," she sighed faintly. "I am not as strong as I thought, I'm afraid. If I could be helped to my room..."

At once, Don Felipe and Doña Maria were all apologies and concern. Servants were ordered to assist Star, but it was Michael who took her arm, against which she leaned weakly, her head resting on his shoulder, as he escorted her from the room and through the gallery to her bedroom.

Once in her room, he sent one of the servants to fetch Rosita, then stood staring down at Star, one eyebrow cocked thoughtfully. For someone about to faint, she had a good color in her face. "You have a habit of fainting at inconvenient moments, *querida*. I seem to recall you had a similar attack of weakness in St. Louis at the parade ground when your friend Captain Donley and I were having a... a disagreement."

Star's mouth curved in a half smile. "Well, it worked, didn't it?" And then, her face sobering, "Are the Mexican fortifications as strong as Don Antonio said? Francesca told me that General Heredia had over twenty thousand men in his command!"

The corners of Michael's mouth quirked in a skeptical smile. "Francesca is inclined to exaggerate. The general has nowhere near that many men. I must admit the people of Chihuahua, though, are convinced that the Americans will be defeated." Michael smiled wryly. "They've been busy gathering coffles

of rope with which to tie the *Yanqui* prisoners after the battle
and drag them back to Chihuahua. There's even talk of building
grandstand seats so the citizens of Chihuahua can drive out and
watch the glorious victory." He did not mention an unsavory
rumor he'd heard around the plaza, that the citizens had also
been promised that they would be allowed to beat Doniphan
and his men to death when they were dragged, prisoners, back
to town. Several American traders in town had already been
attacked by angry mobs and had had to go into hiding, for fear
of their lives.

At the dismay he saw cross Star's face, he added quickly,
"I wouldn't underestimate Colonel Doniphan. He may not be
regular army, but the man has a remarkable genius for military
tactics. And the American guns and artillery have always been
much better than the Mexican firepower."

Star sat down on the edge of the bed, her eyes clouded with
unhappiness. "I hate this war! In the beginning, it was different.
I never doubted we were in the right. But now . . ." She shook
her head, bewildered. "Now I'm not sure who's right and who's
wrong. Everything's so mixed up in my mind."

For a moment, as she lifted her troubled gaze to Michael,
she saw something flicker in the dark impassive face, as if her
words had touched an emotion that he had immediately sup-
pressed.

"But then it's worse for you, isn't it?" she asked softly,
understanding taking hold of her. "It always has been."

Michael frowned as if he would not allow her pity to touch
him, and his voice was cold. "There's never any point in trying
to figure out the right and wrong of a war. It's a sort of . . . insanity
that takes hold of men, always has, perhaps it always will. The
sensible man stays clear of the madness, and minds his own
business. For myself, I'm a—"

"Trader, not a soldier," Star finished for him, smiling faintly.
"Isn't that what you always say?" But it wasn't true, she saw
now. Michael did care, passionately. She had heard it in his
voice at the dinner table with Don Antonio, and remembered
just as clearly his defense of the Mexican people at the Kirkland
party. How difficult to live like Michael, she thought, with
your loyalties divided, two countries, two peoples, straddling

two worlds. And knowing always that someday he would have to take a stand, turn his back on one of the worlds, his father's or his mother's.

All at once, a weariness pressed down upon her, a weakness that was real, not pretended. It had been too much for her first day out of bed, the effort of dressing, the strain of the dinner.

Michael saw the exhaustion shadowing her face and pushed her gently back against the pillows. "You should be resting, not talking," he scolded, as his hands deftly removed her slippers. "I'll see what's keeping Rosita."

When he almost reached the door, she called out, "Don't go."

Her body ached with wanting him to stay, to have him lie down beside her and hold her in his arms so that her fears and worries could be forgotten in his hard embrace. Only she stopped herself from calling his name, knowing that Michael wouldn't just want to hold her quietly in his arms. He would want more than that, more than she was able to give to him, to any man.

It was late that night before she finally fell asleep, yet she awoke early, aroused by noises in the courtyard. She went to the window and opened it. She could catch only a glimpse of the patio, the flowers heavy-headed with morning dew, the sun beginning to trace shadows on the adobe wall. She saw Francesca in a modish black riding habit crossing the patio and Michael, also in riding clothes, slip an arm around the girl's waist, his dark head bent toward the girl, smiling teasingly down at her. Star watched the couple, her gray eyes stormy, as they disappeared in the direction of the stable yard.

Two weeks later, Doña Maria took Star riding into Chihuahua in the Alvarez carriage, with two liveried footmen and blooded horses with silver bridles pulling the coach. As they drove through the *Alameda*, shaded by orange and fig and banana trees, and around the marble-rimmed plaza with its enormous stone fountain, Doña Maria proudly pointed out the marble Governor's palace and the handsome cathedral. There were statues of the twelve Apostles in niches in the elaborate facade of the marble-fronted cathedral, and Star, after one quick glance, pretended not to see that the statues were festooned with the long-haired scalps of Indians. Beyond the city she could see the lilac-tinted mountains and the great stone arches of the ancient aqueducts that carried water from the mountains into the city.

At the monument to Miguel Hidalgo y Costilla in the plaza, Doña Maria had the carriage stop. After saying a silent prayer, she turned, smiling, to Star. "It was Father Hidalgo who led the first fight for Mexican independence against Spain in 1810. With the help of the Indians who rose in revolt with him, they captured Mexico City, but were finally defeated by the Spanish Army. The good father was shot here at the site of this monument, but his memory is much revered as a courageous and saintly man. Don Miguel's father, El Señor Kelly, admired Father Hidalgo greatly. He said he was much like your George Washington, who led a revolution in your own country."

"You knew Michael's father?" Star asked, interested.

"Oh, he always visited us during his yearly caravans, as Michael did later, after his father's death. For a while I had hopes that he and Francesca—" She broke off abruptly, afraid she was being tactless with her guest.

Star pretended not to notice and said innocently, "I understand Francesca is to marry Don Antonio."

"Her father has made the arrangements, yes, but Francesca..." Her mother shook her head half proudly, half in despair. "My daughter can be very willful, I'm afraid. She has set herself to marry Don Alfredo, and of course now, without any promise of an inheritance, that is impossible."

"But if she loves Don Alfredo," Star protested.

Her companion gave her a shocked glance. "What does a young innocent girl know of such things? It is for her father to decide what is best for her. I myself saw my husband only once before our marriage," she said smugly. "No woman could ask for a kinder, more loving husband. It will be the same for Francesca."

Star thought of Doña Maria's words the night of the Alvarez *baile*. The *sala* of the hacienda was literally glittering with hundreds of candles, reflecting against crystal chandeliers and golden mirrors. Although many of the guests wore European costumes, at least half of the men wore Mexican attire, black velvet jackets with silver ornaments and taggles, and rows of silver buttons running down the side seams of tightly fitted trousers, with colorful sashes cinched around their waist. Here and there the green and gold uniforms of Mexican lancers competed with the vividly colored gowns of the women guests. Jewelry dripped from the womens' ears and gleamed around their necks, and more gemstones were tucked into their hair and gathered around their waists.

Star glanced down at her own gown of dark green changeable silk inset with strips of matching lace, her low-cut neckline filled in by the emerald and diamond necklace she had worn in Santa Fe. She had thought the dress too flamboyant, but now she felt almost subdued next to the gowns and jewels of the other women in the room.

She remembered she had tugged embarrassedly at the low-cut bodice that made it abundantly clear that she had regained the figure she had lost during her illness. "It will be a scandal if I bend over, Rosita!" she had protested.

Her maid was arranging the auburn curls in an apparently random but in fact carefully contrived fashion around Star's slim neck and pale white shoulders. "It is not as low-cut as Doña Francesca's," she sniffed. "You should keep your eye on that one, *señora*," she warned darkly. "Her servants tell me she is already bragging how she will be in Don Miguel's bed tonight."

Glancing around the crowded *sala*, where the musicians on the raised dais had already begun playing, Star frowned as she saw Francesca float by in the arms of Michael. Francesca's gown was white, befitting a young, unmarried woman, but there all innocence ended, Star thought wryly. The bodice of the gown was scooped so low that one could almost, but not quite, see the rosy nipples of the girl's breasts, and the demure red ribbons at the sleeves and waist matched the flash of scarlet petticoat that could be seen as the girl twirled gracefully. Doña Maria, Star noticed, was casting nervous glances toward her daughter, and Francesca's father was glowering at his daughter's shocking gown, but without making a scene, there was little they could do.

"You do not look as if you are enjoying the *baile*, Señora Kelly."

Star smiled automatically up at Don Antonio, who had appeared beside her. Although there was still something about the look in the man's tiny eyes that she disliked, she had to admit that the black *caballero*'s jacket he wore suited him well, making his fleshy face and stocky figure seem almost handsome.

Deliberately she looked away from Michael, who was laughing down at Francesca, and waving her gold lace fan gracefully, she murmured, smiling, "I am surprised that you would show any concern for an enemy, Don Antonio, a barbarian from the north like myself."

Don Antonio laughed heartily, his small eyes roaming delightedly over the splendid creature standing at his side. How odd that she had appeared so quiet, so pale at the dinner table the other evening, he thought. How had he missed that ravishing smile, those astonishing silvery gray eyes, and that red hair catching the gleam of the candlelight. "No true Mexican would ever consider a beautiful woman his enemy," he protested, sweeping her out onto the floor.

He danced well for all his heaviness so that Star found it easy to follow the intricate steps of the bolero, while flirting with him at the same time, as he paid her extravagant compliments. She had almost forgotten how it felt to have a man look at her as if he thought she were desirable beyond belief, to see eyes gazing upon her filled with warmth and not polite indifference. Soon other *caballeros* took Don Antonio's place in her arms, and when she grew warm from the dancing, there were always servants threading among the guests with goblets of cool sparkling wine mixed with fruit juices for the ladies. Star drank several glasses, and the hurt that the sight of Francesca in Michael's arms had caused lessened as the magic of the wine, the swirling dancers, and the rhythm of the music seemed to throb in her veins. Once as she whirled around in Don Antonio's arms, she saw Michael watching her, his eyes narrowed to angry slits in his dark face. She pretended not to see him, thinking airily that what was sauce for the goose was sauce for the gander. If he found his pleasure with other women, then she would find her own enjoyment.

Toward the end of the evening, a man and woman and several musicians in colorful gypsy costumes played and danced for the guests. It was the first time Star had ever heard *gitano* music, or watched a gypsy woman dance the bolero Tzigane, the woman moving her body with such grace and primitive abandon that Star felt her breath catch in her throat.

Then, as the music ended and the guests started to drift away, Star saw Francesca go up to the gypsy musicians and whisper in their ears. Once again the gypsy musicians touched their instruments, filling the *sala* with flamenca music. This time, though, it was not the gypsy woman who danced but Francesca, at first spinning slowly, almost dreamily, on the points of her tiny scarlet slippers, while her slim white arms with castenets in her hands kept rhythm with the music. Then, as the guests watched, spellbound, the girl's body spun faster and faster to the passionate music, her white skirt swirling, billowing up higher and higher, showing the scarlet flounce of skirt beneath. A look of complete wanton abandonment softened the girl's face, her dark hair, released, tumbled over her shoulders. Finally, on the last chords of the wild music, the gown billowed almost shoulder high, and for a brief second, Francesca's slim, nude body flashed white to the young, proud breasts. A hushed, shocked silence fell over the room.

Beside her, Star could hear Don Antonio draw in his breath sharply through clenched teeth; his face was a bright purple red. Star saw servants, Francesca's *dueña*, the major domo, rush forward to hurry the girl out. The regular musicians immediately reappeared and the gypsies hustled away. Dancing was begun again, and shortly thereafter a late dinner was served.

Star decided she didn't want anything to eat and considered the possibility that she might have drunk too much wine, as she walked carefully from the *sala* out into the courtyard, past the orange trees on the terrace and the rose garden. For a moment she paused in the garden, the air brushing cool and refreshing against her heated face.

When Don Antonio slipped an arm around her waist and turned her around to face him, she was at first too startled to protest. "*Mi amor,* I knew you'd be waiting for me," he whispered thickly, his breath hot and smelling of wine against her mouth. Furious, then, she tried to push him away. The touch of his mouth on hers, moist and warm, sickened her, and when his hand tried to push aside the silken material of her gown, she fought him with her elbows and fingernails, half sobbing with anger, but too embarrassed to call for help.

Then, abruptly, Don Antonio had stepped away from her. At first, she was too busy snatching at the torn bodice of her gown, to notice that Michael had stepped out of the shadows until he spoke, his voice filled with an icy amusement. "It seems my wife does not care for your embraces, Don Antonio."

Star took a great deal of satisfaction in seeing Don Antonio's face grow pale, the Adam's apple in the man's throat rising and falling rapidly in his panic, as he stammered, "A thousand . . . pardons, Don Miguel. No insult was intended, I assure you."

"And none taken," Michael said calmly, slipping an arm around Star's waist. "My wife, however, has had a full evening. You will excuse us, *señor*."

At the door to her bedroom, Star pulled free, furious as much at Michael now as at herself. She still felt soiled from the touch of Don Antonio's mouth on hers. Anger made her voice tremble, "You should have killed him! The *canaille!*"

"Your Spanish is improving, *mi bella*," Michael said. Opening the door behind her, he almost pushed her into the room, his voice cold. "Why should I kill a man for trying to take what you were so evidently willing to give?"

Rosita, who had been dozing in the chair by the fireplace, leapt to her feet, staring from Star to Michael. Then she murmured uncertainly. "Shall I help you undress, *señora?*"

"No," Star blurted.

"By all means," Michael said, setting comfortably in a chair, his long legs stretched out before him. One eyebrow lifted tauntingly. "Unless you prefer that I undress you, *querida mia*."

Star stiffened. Surely he wasn't going to sit there watching her disrobe. Then, realizing that that was exactly what he was going to do, and that there was no way she could force him to leave her room, short of making a scene in front of the maid, she turned her back on him indignantly. Rosita quickly unhooked the row of tiny gilt buttons that ran down the back of her gown. The changeable silk fell in a wash of color to the floor, followed by a half dozen lacy petticoats, and cambric drawers. After Rosita removed her beribboned linen corset, Star snatched up her robe and flung it hastily over her delicately embroidered chemise, pulling the robe's silken sash tight around her waist before turning and angrily facing Michael.

Rosita scooped up the undergarments and the gown into her arms and stood, waiting. "Was there anything else, *señora?*"

"That will be all for this evening, Rosita," Michael said. "You can go now."

Star stared at Michael, at the scar, bone-white, the eyes glittering emerald-green against the hickory brown face. It was a face whose every plane, every expression, she thought she knew as well as her own, but suddenly it was the face of a stranger. She reached out her hand to her maid. "No, stay, Rosita."

Michael said nothing, simply nodding his head toward the door. Rosita, with one last startled, and yet pleased glance toward her mistress, scurried quickly from the room. The door closed quietly behind Rosita and Star stared, mesmerized, as Michael rose from the chair and walked with his lithe, Indian-like stride across the room toward her.

Chapter Eighteen

S*tar took several steps backwards away from the* violence barely concealed in Michael's face, the hard brilliance of the eyes looking almost black as he moved away from the lamp. "You should have told me how you longed for a man's embrace, *querida,*" he drawled. "Or is it only my touch that turns you to stone?"

"That's . . . that's not true," she whispered and cast a despairing glance toward the door. But even if she could make her escape, she could hardly go rushing out into the gallery in her nightgown. The servants would surely know, and it would be all over the hacienda in the morning, and then the town itself, the whispers and laughter and coarse jokes about Don Miguel's wife fleeing from his bed in the middle of the night.

She had come up hard against the wall and could move no farther. Michael halted before her, his pitiless glance moving slowly over her tense, slender figure. "To think of all the months we've wasted, while you indulged in your childish game of touch-me-not. Did it amuse you, playing the vestal virgin, or was it the lovelorn widow? Or are you one of those women who find their pleasure in teasing, leading a man on, the way you did tonight with those poor fools on the dance floor, with Don Antonio." His voice suddenly slashed angrily at her. "And myself, of course, your beloved husband, the greatest fool of them all."

"Stop it!" Anger lent her a courage that she thought had deserted her. Her gray eyes flared darkly, a gathering storm in her pale face. "You have no right to say such things!"

His hands gripped her arms cruelly. "I have every right,

267

querida. I'm your husband, remember? And I've suddenly run out of patience. I think it's time we lay the ghost of your late, lamented husband to rest."

When she tried to pull away, his hand caught her jaw and held her imprisoned, while his mouth slowly descended on hers. She was held motionless in his embrace, his lips clamped on hers, hard and bruising, so that the breath seemed to rush from her body and the room swam dizzily around her. When she thought that her lungs would burst, and her knees grew weak, he released her abruptly, while his hands reached out to the ribbons at the bodice of her robe.

For a moment she thought of thrusting the hands away, but then thought wearily, what would be the use? He was stronger than she was, just as Charles had been. And perhaps, like Charles, her feeble attempts to fight him off would only give him greater pleasure. Perhaps it was the same with all men, the need to inflict their will upon someone weaker than themselves, a means of proving their manhood.

She forced herself to stand quietly while he slipped the robe off her arms, letting it fall with a soft, sibilant sound to the floor. Then he untied the tiny satin ribbon that bound her chemise. It was only when he reached up and undid her hair, pulling out the pins, so that the auburn coils fell heavily over her shoulders, making her feel suddenly completely vulnerable, that the helpless tears stung her eyes like vinegar.

Michael looked down at her stricken face and frowned, annoyed, at the knife stab of guilt that almost unmanned him before he said warily, "Oh, no, *mi querida,* it won't work, not this time, the trembling lips, the tears of the bereaved widow. Tonight, I promise you, there'll only be two sharing our bed."

Then he swept her up in his arms and was carrying her through the darkness to the bed, away from the lamplight. She lay stiffly, listening to the sounds of Michael undressing quickly, tossing his clothes carelessly onto a chair. If only, she thought, it could be different this time, if just this once she could enjoy the alien feel of a man's hands exploring her body with searching intimacy. She remembered how frantic she had been when she thought Michael would leave El Paso without her, how watching him with Lupita, Francesca, or with any woman, turned her sick with jealousy. How could she feel that way about him and yet retreat in shame and fear when he held her? At least, she thought desperately, she could pretend to enjoy his lovemaking. Surely she wouldn't be the first wife who feigned desire and passion to salvage her marriage and keep a husband.

Michael stood beside the bed, and her eyes fastened on his face, then downward, for the first time seeing the long, scimitar-shaped scar on his chest where black hair curled crisply. And between his muscular thighs—a coldness entered her body and she averted her eyes quickly.

"Don't look away from me, *mi amor*," he said softly, but she heard the threat behind the quiet voice. As his gaze traveled slowly over the red hair splayed over the pillow, the breasts pulled taut, the rounded hips, and the faint swell of her stomach, she felt her skin crawl, the same feeling she had had with Charles, of being physically violated although he made no move to touch her.

When he slid into the bed beside her, she felt a momentary shock at the hardness of his body along the length of hers, but she made herself turn toward him, resting a hand timidly in the mat of hair at his chest as her lips found his mouth in the darkness. At first it wasn't difficult, pretending. It had never been unpleasant, she remembered, kissing Michael. Her mouth moved softly against his, feeling a delightful warmth spreading through her body when the pressure on her mouth was returned.

It was only when he pulled her beneath him and she felt his hardness between her thighs and his mouth moved downward, his tongue teasing the velvet-soft nipple, that she had to fight the terror, like a beast struggling to escape from inside of her. She forced herself to remember, like recalling the fragments of a nightmare, the instructions Charles had coldly given her when they had made love, what she must do with her body to accommodate him, the words that she must say to him that made her face burn and she could only whisper in the darkness.

Now she closed her eyes and moved her hands and body as she had been taught, mimicking the soft moans of passion, simulating an ecstasy that had always excited Charles, brought him to fulfillment.

When Michael suddenly flung her away from him and slipped out of the bed, turning up the lamp in the wall sconce beside the bed, she stared up at him, shivering, her gray eyes dilated, enormous in her pale face. "What is it?" she asked bewildered. "What's wrong?"

His face was expressionless, only his eyes, darkly opaque, held a withering contempt as they moved over her body, half sprawled on the silken coverlet. "I prefer my acting in the theater, not in bed, *señora,"* he said coldly.

He pulled on his trousers, was stuffing his shirt into his waist band when Star scrambled out of bed. "Where . . . where are you going?"

He turned to look at her. "Not that it's any of your damn business," he said flatly, "but I have a bad taste in my mouth. I think first a bottle of excellent brandy, and then—" he shrugged carelessly. "Chihuahua offers a great variety of entertainments for a lonely *caballero.*"

A coldness gathered in Star as she stared at the closed face of the man across the room from her, listened to the harsh finality in his voice.

He had half turned again to the door when she whispered, "Wait . . . please."

He hesitated, caught in spite of himself by the pleading note he had never heard in her voice before. She had always been too independent, too proud to humble herself by begging for anything from him. He scowled blackly. What trickery was she up to now? For months she had acted as if she couldn't bear to have a man touch her, and then, only a few minutes before in his arms, she had mouthed words, behaved with the lewd, if practiced, abandonment of a *puta* in the lowest of bordellos.

She moved hesitantly toward him. He watched the convulsive movement of her throat before she spoke, as if the words were being dredged from deep inside her, her voice softly beseeching, "Don't go, please. Don't leave me."

Michael was annoyed to discover that instead of feeling a sense of triumph that she finally had become the humble supplicant, he felt only a sense of outrage that she should abase herself so meekly before him.

"Stop it, Star!" he said harshly. "Don't beg. Don't ever beg for a man's favors."

With a groan, he swept her up in his arms and carried her

back to the bed, catching the scent of her fragrance that was peculiarly her own. And yet as he once again tossed his clothes aside and slipped into the bed beside her, he was almost unconsciously aware of another, more disturbing scent, the scent of fear, the terror of a cornered animal. When he pulled her gently against him, he could feel her body shaking as if with a chill, her eyes wide and glazed with fear.

Her hand caught his as she whispered with a feverish intensity. "You won't leave me. You promise."

"Be still, *querida*," he murmured softly. "Be still, my love."

For several moments he held her quietly in his arms, his hands stroking her body gently, soothingly, until the trembling stopped and she gave a sigh of contentment and cuddled closer to him, her breath warm against his face. It was only when his hands became bolder, more insistent on the silken peaks of her breasts, moving lightly downward to explore the petal softness between her thighs, that he felt the alarm shudder through her body, a stiffness settling like a mask over her features.

Startled, he lifted himself on his elbow to look down at her, at the terror glistening in her eyes before they became shuttered, staring up at him as if he were a frightening, hurtful stranger.

"What is it, *mi amor?*" he asked. "Why are you afraid?"

After all, he thought mystified, she wasn't a virgin who'd never known a man's touch. And she certainly wasn't a cold, passionless woman. He could sense only too disturbingly the banked fires within that cool, silken body, the passion behind those luminous gray eyes, so that the effort of not possessing her swiftly, immediately, in answer to his own pressing need, was like a knife thrust into his loins—it made perspiration break out on his forehead.

She turned her face away so that it was shadowed, hidden in the darkness. She didn't want to think, much less talk, about Charles. Not here, not now. Not ever to Michael. "It's me," she said bleakly. "I have nothing to give."

He took her chin in his hand and forced her gaze back to him. "Who told you such a pack of lies?" he growled.

His mouth descended on hers again, at first, as before, moving teasingly, coaxingly, and then gently urging her lips apart, as his hand trailed downward over the peaks and hollows of her body till it rested on the silken softness of her inner thigh. At once he felt her shudder and try to draw away, but he would not let her, holding her pinioned gently against the bed so that she could not move. His mouth continued its seductive assault on her lips while his hand stroked surely, skillfully, as if knowing exactly where the trailing fingers could bring the most pleasure, until he felt the tautness leaving her body, and she turned blindly toward him, soft and supple in his arms, while her tongue moved at first timidly, then more ardently in his mouth, as if seeking a deeper, deeper pleasure.

It was Michael who finally pulled away, laughing softly down into her flushed face, her eyes like quicksilver, her lips still half parted, quivering.

"Are you sure, *mi alma*," he asked, his voice gently mocking. "Are you so sure you have nothing to give?"

Star was startled herself at the warmth racing like fire through her veins, at the aching in her breasts, at the delicious, yet painful, pressure between her thighs so that when Michael touched her there, caressing her gently, then more urgently, reaching deeper, a soft, incoherent cry rose in her throat. The only fear possessing her now was that he would stop, that the almost unbearably delightful sensations flooding her body would end. When his mouth found her breast, his tongue coaxing its peak to hardness, the pleasure only increased, rising to a crescendo that made her gasp with delight, so that at first she wasn't even aware that her body was beneath Michael's until she felt his hardness suddenly inside of her. She felt him grow still, waiting, and she whispered, uncertainly, "I'm not sure . . . what should I do?"

Once more Michael's laugh came softly through the darkness. "Don't worry, *querida mia*," he whispered. "You'll know."

Then he was moving within her and the pleasure she had felt before was only a prelude; the only pain was that she could not get close enough to the flat hardness of his body. Her whole body moved instinctively with his, giving and taking pleasure, trying greedily to prolong the sensations indefinitely, but finally, suddenly, she felt an explosion of joy within her, leaving her limp with happiness and, to her surprise, weeping quietly.

Michael settled her back into his arms beside him, brushing

her hair from her face and the tears from her cheeks. "It's good, to cry afterwards," he said, smiling at her confusion.

She rested her head on his chest, feeling spent and yet completely alive, as she had never felt before in her life. "Will it ever be the same again?" she asked wistfully. And then, flushing, as Michael lifted a quizzical eyebrow, "I mean," she added hastily, "not right away." And then, worried. "But soon—again?"

Michael grinned, his face relaxed, his green eyes bright with laughter. "It will happen again, my greedy *poca amor*," he promised. "And it will be even better."

Through her drowsiness, it occurred to Star that it was the first time she had seen Michael's face so completely open and vulnerable, without the guarded, impassive mask it usually wore. For protection? she wondered suddenly. Was Michael, in his own way, afraid of being hurt, too, as if very young, he had been taught never to expose his true feelings to others.

She ran her fingers lightly across his chest, touching the scars there, between the crisp dark hair. Michael watched her, his voice quiet, "Do they offend you, the scars?"

"Of course not," she replied indignantly, reaching up to caress with her lips the white etched scar on his cheek. "I was only thinking how terrible it must have been for you, a young boy forced to live with the Comanches."

For a moment Michael did not answer, then he said slowly, "At first, it was bad, the testing to separate the strong from the weak, but it made a sort of sense. A warrior had to have his courage proven before a battle or the whole tribe could be destroyed by his cowardice."

She shivered at the pictures that leaped to mind, the terrible ordeals the young Michael must have endured to leave such scars on his body. "And the weak captives? Those who didn't pass the testing?"

A hardness crept into Michael's voice. "Those that survived the torture were treated much like slaves. They tended the horses, the old women tormented them, the braves ridiculed them. And no young woman would allow them beneath her blanket."

"But you were only a boy," Star said, shocked.

Michael's mouth thinned in a mirthless smile. "Indian women mature early. Many are brides by age twelve, old women by thirty."

Star felt the bitter taste of jealousy on her tongue as she asked, "Was there? Did you . . ." Then fell silent, embarrassed.

"There was a girl, a woman, rather," Michael said. Once again the mirthless smile flickered across the long mouth. "A year after I was captured, she made it clear that she wanted me to share her blanket. I had never been with a woman, but she was an excellent teacher, and I turned out to be an apt pupil."

"Was she . . . very beautiful?"

"No, not beautiful at all," Michael said reflectively. "There were pox marks on her face, but *Madre Dios*, she was warm and loving and patient."

"Did you love her? Did you marry her?"

"No, I don't suppose I loved her, and she was already married. Unfortunately her husband found out about us."

"What, what happened?" Star asked, not sure by the look on Michael's face that she wanted to know.

"The Comanches have a custom of punishing unfaithful wives by cutting off their noses," Michael said dryly. "A woman mutilated in that fashion is no longer accepted by her family. She loses all caste and becomes what we would call a prostitute, available to any man who wants her."

"Oh." Star couldn't hide the revulsion in her voice. "How cruel."

Michael lifted himself on his arm, gazing down at her, his face thoughtful. "To your mind, yes, but then you don't think like a Comanche." He dropped a kiss into the soft, dark hollow of Star's throat, felt the pulse beating there beneath his lips. "I wonder, *mi querida*," he murmured, a wicked look in his eyes, "what I would do if I discovered you were unfaithful. Not cut off your nose, that would be a sacrilege, but if I thought any other man had held you . . ."

His voice roughened and he pulled her back into his arms, his mouth burning like a brand against her lips, then moving downward, tracing a path from the drowsy smile on her mouth to the rosy tip of her breast and downward still, over the slight curve of her stomach, and lower still, to the cool, silken thighs.

Almost, she cried out against this new, uncharted intimacy, but the cry turned into a moan of pleasure, when his mouth found her softness, and her body arched upward, her hands tightening around his head, caressing the crisp curls, pulling him closer.

And he was right. When he possessed her again, it was, if possible, even better the second time, her body responding swiftly, passionately, reaching eagerly for each peak of delight, lifting her to only another, more exciting, plateau.

"*Despacio, mi amor*—slowly, my love," Michael murmured. "We have all night."

But then he was as impatient as she was, and afterward, as they lay entwined in each other's arms, he said huskily, "Blazing star. It suits you. You blaze in my arms and afterwards, you are as cool and beautiful as some distant star, *mi esposa.*"

"Say it again," she said sleepily, curling closer to him.

"What again?"

"*Mi esposa*—my wife." She sighed happily. "It has a lovely sound."

"*Señora.* Doña Estrella." A soft scratching at the door, the sound of Rosita calling her name, awakened Star. She stretched languoruously, still half asleep, then noticed, surprised, that she hadn't a stitch of clothes on. Memory of the evening before rushed back, bringing a blissful smile to her face. How different everything seemed this morning, all her senses sharpened, so that the air seemed sweeter, the color of the roses in the crystal vase more vivid.

"*Señora, por favor.*" Rosita's voice was beginning to sound desperate.

Hastily Star reached for her robe, wondering what time it was, and, more importantly, where was Michael? She pulled open the door and Rosita slid into the room, balancing a tray, her black eyes fairly popping with excitement. "I thought the *señora* might be hungry."

Star took the tray, discovering that she was starved. Never had chocolate and honey cakes looked so appetizing. "What time is it, Rosita?" she asked, sitting down by the small table near the fireplace.

"Almost seven."

In the evening, Star thought shocked. That meant she had slept the whole day away. Not the whole day, she remembered, smiling. It was well past daybreak, the last time she had awakened and turned to Michael and teased him awake with her kisses, and he had gazed at her through narrowed, sleep-filled eyes, grumbling, *"Mi amor,* you are insatiable." But then he had reached for her, and . . . Star saw that Rosita was watching her curiously, a knowing smirk on her face, and she asked hastily, "Where is Don Miguel?"

"He left early this afternoon when the news of the battle came, but he left strict orders that you were not to be disturbed."

"Battle?" Star put down her cup quickly. "What battle?"

"The Americans, *señora."* Rosita's voice bubbled with excitement. "They attacked the fortifications at the Rio Sacramento. Don Felipe, along with many other families, have driven out in their carriages, with picnic baskets and wine, to watch the battle. Señorita Francesca is sulking in her room because she is in disgrace and her father would not allow her to leave her room, so she cannot watch the battle, too." Rosita's voice dropped to a fascinated whisper. "Is it true, *señora,* that Doña Francesca danced naked at the *baile?"*

"No, of course not," Star said, sure that the gossip about Francesca's scandalous behavior had already spread through Chihuahua without her adding to it. "Has there been any news of the battle?" she asked anxiously.

"Only that General Heredia's army has won a great victory, or so the priests said at the special services held this afternoon to pray for victory over the barbarians from the north." A glint of shrewdness appeared in Rosita's soft black eyes and she shrugged philosophically. "Still, the priests would say that, would they not, *señora?* And my Jaime is *muy bravo.* He would never run," she added indignantly.

When Michael returned late that evening, Rosita's suspicions turned out to be true. The Mexican army had not, after all, won a great victory but sustained another defeat at the hands of General Doniphan and his Missourians. "It was El Brazito all over again," Michael told Star, as they shared a late meal in their bedroom. "The American artillery tore the Mexican line to shreds, and when the lancers tried to charge the rear of the American lines, the traders ran them off. After several companies of American cavalry stormed the Mexican redoubts and killed the defenders or drove them off, that was the end of the battle." Michael's mouth tightened grimly. "There must be hundreds of Mexican dead and wounded still lying on the battlefield."

Star shivered, remembering the dead she had seen on the battleground at El Brazito, and found she could not eat a morsel of the food on her tray. She doubted if anyone in the hacienda was eating that evening. The whole household was in a state of confusion. Don Felipe, as well as the other spectators who had driven out to watch the battle, had been forced to flee back to Chihuahua. Carriages and picnic lunches had been abandoned, with many fleeing on foot back to their homes in the city, to await, in terror, the occupying army of the barbarians. Stores were boarded shut, the streets were empty. All huddled within their homes, waiting. Having seen the murderous fury of the Americans, who had fought like wild men, what horrors could they expect from such victorious heretic conquerors?

"What will happen now?" Star asked unhappily. Although Michael's hand rested in hers, she was aware that his thoughts were elsewhere. She could only guess at what he was feeling, the bitterness, the wounded pride of that part of him that gloried in his Mexican heritage. She wished there was something she could say to ease the hurt, but she couldn't find the words. After all, the hated victors were her people. Was it possible, she thought, growing cold at the thought, that Michael might come to hate her, too?

There was no hatred in Michael's eyes, though, when he turned to her, only frustration and bitterness. "Doniphan will take Chihuahua, of course. After that, who knows? There's been rumors for days of a battle around Buena Vista between General Taylor and Santa Anna, but no one knows for sure. One thing I have heard and know to be true is that General Winfield Scott and a new American army have landed at Tampico, which means we'll have to make new travel plans."

Star had heard, of course, of General Winfield Scott, the brave hero of the war with England in 1812 and later Indian wars. "You've given up the idea of traveling to your ranch?" she asked.

"No, it's as dangerous for us to stay here, but we won't be

going by way of Vera Cruz. That's bound to be the route General Scott will take, first capturing Vera Cruz, then marching over the royal highway to Mexico City. It's the route that the conquistadors took under Cortez. Scott knows that Mexico will never be conquered until Mexico City is taken."

"Is it possible?" Star asked, uncertainly. She knew very little of the capital city except that it had been built by the Aztecs on lakes and marshes surrounded by mountains and long extinct volcanoes, and that it had been captured by the Spanish in the sixteenth century.

Michael shrugged. "It's a mountainous stretch of road between Vera Cruz and Mexico City, and no doubt Mexican troops will be fighting the invading army every inch of the way. Even Santa Anna must realize it's his last chance to save Mexico, and he's good at raising and training armies, if nothing else. And if Scott stays too long in the lowlands around Vera Cruz, he'll lose half his men to the *vómito*. I've seen yellow fever wipe out whole villages, and the Americans are particularly vulnerable to the disease. Still, if anyone can get his men to Mexico City, it's Scott. He's not a man to give up easily."

"But the Mexicans will keep fighting, won't they?"

Michael poured himself a glass of wine, downing it quickly before exploding angrily, "Oh, yes, they'll fight. And they'll lose, in the end. This war is already lost." He turned to Star, his eyes blazing with anger. "My God, you should have seen the Mexican guns and powder they had at the battle today, the powder badly manufactured, the guns the same ones used by Mexican soldiers fifty years ago. When they fired shot at the American lines, the Americans could see the balls coming, ricocheting on the ground so that the American soldiers could dodge them like billiard balls. All the Mexican army has are too damn many officers in pretty uniforms, playing at being soldiers."

Hesitantly, Star reached up a hand to brush a lock of dark hair from Michael's scowling face. *"Mi alma,"* she said softly, "I'm sorry."

At her touch, the hard anger in the greenish black eyes softened, the scowl disappearing as he saw her worried face. "I'm the one that's sorry, *querida,"* he said huskily. "For stupidly dragging you into the middle of this war. I should have left you behind with the Delgados in El Paso."

"I wouldn't have stayed," Star said promptly. "I would have followed you." And then, lightly, "And you needn't frown at me that way, my love. I'm not afraid of your scowls anymore." Except, of course, she knew she would always be a little uneasy at the streak of ruthlessness in Michael, his passionate, stubborn pride that nothing could bend or sway.

Michael got to his feet, pulling her up beside him. "Nevertheless, I want you safely out of Chihuahua," he said firmly. "Don Felipe is sending Francesca to their country estate for safety. You're to accompany her."

"I won't leave you," Star protested indignantly.

And then fell silent under Michael's fierce gaze, even as he spoke quietly. "You will go, Star. You saw what happened in Santa Fe when the Americans took over. It will be worse here in Chihuahua. I've never forgiven myself for what happened to you the night of the *baile*, when those bastards attacked you. Do you think I'd take the chance of your being hurt again?" Then when Star's chin lifted stubbornly, the rebellion back in her cool, gray glance, he took her shoulders gently in his hands. "It will only be for a few days. It shouldn't take any longer than that to hire guards and transportation for us across the Sierra Madre Occidentals to Mazatlán. We'll take a boat there for Acapulco and then overland by carriage to Mexico City and the ranch. It won't be an easy trip, but at least we shouldn't run into any battles on the way," he said wryly.

Star still continued to protest, but it was useless; Michael would not be swayed. And perhaps he had been right, she decided two days later as she traveled in the Alvarez carriage, with Rosita beside her, over the makeshift road that led to the Alvarez country estate. Even though she knew Michael would have been furious with her, early that morning, wrapped in a black rebozo, hiding her hair, and dressed in an old gown, she had crept out of the Alvarez hacienda to watch Colonel Doniphan, at the head of his small army, march victoriously into Chihuahua.

Star had watched, shocked, the ragged, wild-looking soldiers, unshaven, dressed like Indians in many cases, who swaggered behind Doniphan into the plaza. Several agreeable *señoritas* had already rushed to the soldiers, offering coffee laced with *aguardiente*, and she had no doubt that the ragged army would be celebrating its victory soon with *pulque* and women and brawls in the streets. It was certainly no place for a respectable woman to linger.

She had turned to hurry back to the hacienda when an arm reached out and grabbed her. For a moment, cold terror seized her, but when she turned, she found herself looking into the sun-burned face and pale blue eyes of Robert Donley. Captain Donley's ragged uniform was not quite as threadbare as the dragoons but his jacket was torn and there was a bandage on his arm. He wore an unkempt beard that made him look unlike the gentle Robert Donley she had known.

"I couldn't believe my eyes," he said now, smiling happily down at Star, "when I saw that glimpse of red hair under your rebozo. Are you living in Chihuahua now? The last I heard you were at El Paso."

"For a few more days only," she said. "Then my husband and I will be leaving for his ranch." She glanced at the bandage. "Is your wound bad?"

"Just a scratch from a lance," he answered. "The surgeon says I'll be fine in a week or so. We were damn lucky," he said gravely. "Only one of our men died of his wounds, and Colonel Owens, the trader, was killed in the attack."

At Star's sharp gasp of dismay, he said, "I'm sorry. Did you know him?"

"Yes, we met on the trail from Independence, and he was a friend of my father's. He was . . . very kind to me after Charles's death. How did it happen?"

"He charged directly at the Mexican redoubts, almost as if he wanted to be killed," Robert said, shaking his head. Taking Star's arm, he drew her into a side street where there were less people crowding around. "How are you, Star? Are you all right?"

But of course he could see that she was. She was more beautiful than ever, with a new softness to her face, a glow deep in the gray eyes. The look of a woman satisfied, a woman in love, Robert thought dourly. She hadn't looked that way in Santa Fe, he remembered. He had thought—well, truth to tell, hoped—her marriage was not going well. He had even dreamed foolishly that when the war was over, he would find her again, take her back to St. Louis with him where she belonged.

"You're happy?"

She nodded, smiling. "Very. What of you, Robert? Will you be staying with the army? Where will they go next?"

"No one knows. Colonel Doniphan received word, finally, that General Wool is at Saltillo. General Taylor may decide to order us there, now that he's defeated Santa Anna at Buena Vista."

"Michael said he'd heard there'd been a battle to the south," Star said slowly.

"We haven't had official word, but our Mexican spies tell us that Taylor's men weren't as fortunate at Buena Vista as we were at the Rio Sacramento," Robert said soberly. "Taylor almost lost the battle. It was the artillery that pulled him through. Not even Doniphan knows what General Taylor plans next, especially with General Scott's arrival on the scene, upstaging Taylor, so to speak. In any case, the enlistments of most of the men in Doniphan's regiment are up in another month or two and we'll be heading home."

Home. Star felt an unexpected lump of homesickness in her throat.

"Home to Sarah and the children," Robert grinned. "That's what Colonel Doniphan said when he was asked where he wanted to go next. Now all the men are saying it, even those without a wife and children, like myself. We all feel we've done our fair share of the fighting," he said. "By the time we reach the coast we'll have marched over three thousand miles, and the men haven't drawn a day's pay since they left Fort Leavenworth." He scratched at his beard uncomfortably. "For myself," he said ruefully, "I never want to fire another shot except at a wild turkey or squirrel."

"You'll be seeing my father when you reach St. Louis, won't you?" Star asked.

Robert nodded. "I'd plan to. I know he'll be pleased to hear that I've seen you. Do you have any message for him?"

"Tell him I love him," Star said slowly. "And I'm sorry to have been such a disappointment to him."

"Do you suppose you'll ever come back to St. Louis?" Robert asked wistfully.

"Perhaps, for a visit, when the war is over." She stood on tiptoe and kissed his bearded cheek fondly. "Good-bye, Robert."

But it wasn't just Robert she had said good-bye to, Star realized, settling back in the carriage seat, watching the fields of blue-green maguey pass by the window. She was saying good-bye to her old life, cutting the ties binding her to everybody she had once held dear. Mexico was her home now. Not as comfortable and familiar as Missouri, but beautiful in its own untamed way.

Like Francesca, she thought, a smile flickering across her mouth as she watched the girl riding gracefully on her dappled mare, not far from the carriage. The girl had haughtily refused to ride in the carriage with Star. Ever since the night of the *baile*, Francesca had been openly hostile towards Star. It was obvious that Michael was no longer paying her any attention; that his whole concentration now was on his wife, and Francesca was not used to being ignored.

Well, let her sulk, Star thought indifferently. It would be uncomfortable the few days she would have to spend in the country with the girl, but at least Rosita would be there with her. She cast a fond glance at her maid, who was sleeping, her mouth open, a rebozo pulled over her raven hair.

No doubt dreaming of Jaime, Star thought. It had already been arranged that Jaime would leave the army at Chihuahua and buy a farm and settle down with Rosita, as soon as the girl returned from accompanying her mistress to the country. Star suspected, although he had not said so, that it was Michael who had given Private James Kinsley the money to buy the farm.

Watching the girl made Star sleepy. They had left Chihuahua early, and it must be now almost noon. She wondered whether they would stop for lunch and if Michael was already missing her as much as she missed him. It would be two days before she would see him again. A lifetime, she thought. She smiled dreamily, remembering how she had fallen asleep in Michael's arms last night, how it would be when she saw him again and his arms held her close.

Still smiling, she fell asleep.

At first the sound of approaching riders did not alarm her.

After all, there were four armed servants riding alongside the coach. But the sound of exploding rifle fire drove the last vestige of sleep from her mind. Rosita, too, came wide awake, staring out of the window at the dozen men in leather jackets, riding wiry mustangs, racing up to the carriage in great clouds of dust.

After that, everything happened so quickly that Star had only confused impressions of the guards being shot from their horses, their bodies dragging along behind their mounts, and the coach grinding so abruptly to a halt that both she and Rosita were flung to the floor. Then there were arms pulling at her, something hot and scratchy flung over her head. Just before the darkness descended around her she caught a glimpse of Francesca, racing back down the road toward Chihuahua, riding with the skill of a born horsewoman on her blooded mare that could outrun any wild mustang the bandits rode. At least, Star thought gratefully, Francesca will get away and sound the alarm.

Then there was no more time to think of Francesca. It was enough to concentrate on her own survival. She felt herself flung across a horse, the thud of hooves jolting beneath her. She had no idea in which direction she rode. Once they crossed a chaparral, the thorns slashing at her legs. With the blanket cutting off the air, she gradually lost consciousness. When she came to again there was darkness still around her, but the blanket had been loosened so that she could breathe.

Twice when the horses were stopped to let them rest, she was allowed to slump exhausted to the ground. She longed for even a drop of water, but when she pleaded, *"Agua, por favor,"* the bandits ignored her and she was bundled on the horse again. Finally, when it became dark the blanket was removed, but her captors' faces were hidden in shadow. By peering intently through the darkness, though, she determined that Rosita was on a nearby horse. The girl's head was slumped forward, but she seemed to be alive. Why? Star wondered, as if it were somehow necessary to make sense out of the illogical. Why not just take her jewels and valuables, or just kill Rosita and her, rather than bother kidnapping them?

The moon had risen and was almost directly overhead when the band of men rode into a deserted courtyard behind a high adobe wall. Without a word being said Star was lifted off the horse, and when her numb legs would not support her, she was picked up roughly and carried through another courtyard into a hacienda. A door was opened and she was pushed into a dark room that smelled stale and dank, as if it had been long unused.

She found a bed and sank down upon it, although there were rope springs only, and no bed coverings. She wondered where Rosita had been taken, and, finally, forced herself to walk, back and forth, to force the blood back through her legs.

When the door opened behind her, she turned slowly. She could not at first see the face of the man standing in the doorway, only that he was tall and dressed much as the other bandits had been. Then he lifted the candle and his face flared up in the flickering flame, seemingly almost disembodied. The amber gold eyes, the sun-streaked hair, and that boyish smile quirking at the corners of a mouth that she remembered so well.

The room swam dizzily around her and when she spoke, her voice was a thin, horrified whisper. "Charles, my God, it can't be! You're dead!"

Chapter Nineteen

Charles came into the room, closing the door behind him. "That's not a very affectionate greeting for a husband returned from the dead, my sweet."

Star could only stare at him incredulously. "But I saw your body!"

He grinned, a small boy's triumphant smirk. "You didn't look too closely, did you? I made sure of that. And Dutch and I had a certain similarity in build and coloring, don't you agree? Putting my clothes on him helped, of course. His voice was regretful. "It was too bad I had to give up my gold ring," but it couldn't be helped. It added an authentic touch."

Horror flooded Star's eyes as she remembered how savagely mutilated the body she thought was Charles had been, how she had only been able to look at it for a few seconds before turning away, nauseated. Her voice trembled. "How could you? He was your friend."

"My employee," Charles said indifferently. "You hardly expected me to hang around and be arrested for carrying contraband to the enemy, did you? It seemed more . . . discreet . . . to disappear permanently, even if it meant leaving my beautiful bride a widow."

He crossed the room to her side, holding the candle so the light shone down into her face. "Still, you didn't grieve too long, did you, Mrs. Bradford?" His hand picked up a coil of the rich auburn hair that had been torn loose in the wild ride to the hacienda and now fell in disarray around her shoulders. "It wasn't very flattering, you know, when I heard how quickly you had forsaken your widow's weeds in Santa Fe to jump into Michael Kelly's bed." He laughed, pleased, at her start of surprise. "Oh, yes, I've always managed to keep track of you. After all, I'd always planned to have you back." His voice turned bitter. "My wife and the six wagon loads of trade goods that belong to me!"

In the flickering candlelight, she saw that his face was fleshier, more dissipated, not as boyishly handsome as she remembered. But the amber-shaded eyes were still those of a predator's; if anything, they held a frightening rabid glitter, as if the thin veneer of morality that had always set lightly on Charles's conscience had fallen away completely.

His hand suddenly tightened on the coil of Star's hair and jerked her face toward his. "Or had you crawled into that greaser's bed even before my untimely death?" he snarled.

"No," she gasped, biting back a cry of pain, forcing herself to stillness, remembering how any sign of resistance only excited Charles to further cruelties. "I was never unfaithful. When I married Michael, I was carrying your child."

The hand relaxed its torturous grip. "Now that's something I hadn't heard," Charles said, startled, studying Star's face as if trying to determine if she was lying.

"I lost the baby, a few weeks after my marriage," Star said, and for a moment the hurt returned, along with the guilt that was so much a part of her sense of loss. "I don't know how I would have managed, afterwards, without Michael."

She glanced around her at the dark, evil-smelling room, at Charles, who had always been so fastidious about his clothes and now was wearing a worn leather jacket, Mexican trousers, his face unshaven. She spread her hands helplessly. "I don't understand any of this, Charles. Why have you brought me here? It won't do you any good. They're sure to hunt you down."

"That's been tried before," he said, grinning cockily. "Even the Texas Rangers haven't come close to catching El Güero."

Of course, Star thought, annoyed at her own stupidity. El Güero. In Spanish, the fair one. And leading a band of cutthroats and ruffians was just the sort of life Charles would find amusing as well as profitable. It all began to make a horrible

kind of sense. She remembered suddenly the attack on the
caravan by the *banditos* outside of Chihuahua. It was her they
had wanted, the woman with the red hair, because Charles
must have ordered them to bring her back. "Those were your
cutthroats that attacked the caravan in the *jornada?*" she said
accusingly.

Charles smiled cheerfully. "Not cutthroats, my sweet. We're
Mexican patriots, fighting for our country."

"You're murderers and thieves." She flung the words at him
bitterly. "You haven't any country."

"Ah, well," Charles said, shrugging. "Patriotism is only a
matter of whose side you're on, anyway. And evidently General
Taylor doesn't have your low opinion of our brave guerrilla
fighters. I understand he's hired one of the most nefarious bands
of brigands to act as scouts for him."

"Francesca got away," Star said, trying to quell the panic
spreading through her limbs. "She's probably already raised
the alarm. You'll never get away with kidnapping two women."

"Dear Francesca," Charles murmured. "I don't think you
need worry about her raising an alarm. How do you think my
banditos knew that you would be on the road to the Alvarez
country hacienda today?" He smiled at the dismay that charged
Star's gray eyes at the knowledge that it was Francesca who
had deliberately led Rosita and her into a trap of Charles's
making. No wonder the girl had been able to ride away un-
harmed. "In any case," Charles continued briskly, "it's hardly
kidnapping when a wife decides to return to her long-lost husband."

"I'm not—" Star blurted, then fell silent, as the even more
appalling realization struck her. She was still Mrs. Charles
Bradford. With Charles alive, her marriage to Michael was no
doubt invalid. And the realization that she wasn't Michael's
wife sent shock waves of pain through her, so that she could
no longer control the anguish in her voice as she cried, "Why,
Charles? You never loved me, not really. Why do you want
me back?"

"We'll have plenty of time to discuss that later," he said
coldly. "Right now there's a letter I want you to write."

His hand fastened on her arm, pulled her toward the bed,

where he roughly thrust her down. When he placed the candle on the table by the bed, she saw there was paper and a pen and ink, waiting. The message he wanted her to write was very simple, he explained. Michael was to deliver $50,000 in gold in a wagon to the ruins of the San Bonita Chapel ten miles south of Chihuahua by sunset of the following day. Michael was to bring the gold alone, and if any attempts to rescue Star were made, he would never see her alive again.

"But that's twice what the trade goods were worth when you bought them," Star protested indignantly. "I won't write any such thing! You can't make me."

Charles jerked her to her feet, his face contorted with rage. "You'll write exactly what I say," he stormed. His amber eyes gleamed as his gaze ran swiftly over the disheveled woman standing before him, her skirt torn by the chaparral, a rip in her bodice that let him see the pale silken skin beneath. A smile jerked at the corner of his mouth. "You seem to have forgotten the lessons I taught you, my pet. Shall I refresh your memory?"

His one arm held her while his other hand reached out and gripped her breast savagely, his fingers biting into the soft flesh. His smile never wavered as he watched her face, confident that in a moment her mouth would tremble, her eyes fill with submissive terror as they always had. To his annoyance, though, her mouth remained steady, and although her eyes shimmered with pain, there was no fear in the glance that met his directly. "I won't write that letter, Charles," she said quietly.

Cursing, he pulled her toward the door. "Unfortunately, I've no time to waste on your foolish heroics." They were halfway down the dark hallway, his hands pushing her roughly ahead of him, when she heard a woman's screams, agonized, harrowing screams, making her flesh crawl. Then they were at another door and Charles kicked it open with his foot. A dim light spilled from the room, enough light so that Star could see Rosita's naked, writhing body, tied to a bed by her arms and legs. Six or seven men, half dressed, stood around the bed, one man with a long, thin knife that dripped blood red in the lamplight. Rosita's moans rose higher, pulled shrill into a crescendo of pleading, *"Madre Dios, no, por favor, no."*

"Stop it!" Frantically Star tried to get into the room but Charles's arms around her were too strong, pulling her back into the hall as she kicked and clawed against him like a mad woman.

"You'll write the letter, Star?" Charles asked, as he half carried, half pulled her back to the dark bedroom. "Unless you're not interested in your little maid remaining alive."

She reached swiftly for the pen, choking on the anger and hatred like bile in her mouth. Then stopped, the pen half to the paper. "But first I want Rosita in here with me, so I'm sure she'll be safe from those filthy animals." When Charles hesitated, frowning, she put down the pen. "You know those carrion will kill Rosita otherwise."

Charles shrugged. "You have developed an alarmingly distrustful nature, my sweet. But very well. It will make my men very unhappy, though. Your maid is a *Yankedo,* a *Yanqui* lover. It's known she sleeps with the American soldiers. No Mexican man can forgive such a blow to his pride and honor. She's fortunate she's still alive. Other *Yankedos* have been killed, very slowly."

Star waited until Rosita was carried, half unconscious, into the room and placed on the bed, before she quickly wrote the letter and handed it disdainfully to Charles. "There. You'll get your gold. Don't worry." Then she turned to tend to the maid, and flinched with horror when she saw that the girl's ear had been severed from her head. "It's the punishment for *Yankedos,*" Charles said, peering down at the young woman. "First the ears, then they slit their throats."

Star gave him an imploring glance. "Please, Charles, she needs bandages, medicine."

He scowled, then said irritably, "Oh, very well. She'll be no use to me dead." He went out into the hall. She could hear him calling out to someone and in a few moments he returned with what at first, Star thought was a slender young man, wearing the costume of the other guerrillas. Until the young bandit began to tend Rosita, and Star saw the long, glossy hair in a ropelike braid, the dark face that had once held a disturbing beauty but was now hard, almost haggard looking.

"Theresa," she said hesitantly. "Theresa, it is you, isn't it?"

Her former maid gave her a glance filled with deadly venom from her sloe-black eyes, and without answering, returned to her task at hand.

Charles lounged at the door, his thumbs caught in his belt, a jeering note of amusement in his voice. "I'm afraid Theresa's never been overly fond of you, Star. I can't imagine why." He came over to the bed, ran his hand casually down the Indian girl's back. "Theresa's the best captain I've got. She never gives quarter or mercy, do you, *mi bella?*"

The endearment was lightly jeering, too, but Star saw the look of tenderness, like feather strokes, softening Theresa's hard features as the woman glanced upward toward Charles. For a moment, she almost did look beautiful again. Then she jerked her thumb toward Star, her voice vicious. "We should kill her, now."

Charles laughed but shook his head. "Oh, no, my murderous one. You are not to harm her. I told you that I need her alive, in Mexico City." And then, cruelly, "Besides, unlike you, she is still beautiful. And it might be amusing to discover what tricks her greaser lover has taught her in bed."

Intent upon anxiously watching Rosita, Star caught only a part of the conversation between Charles and Theresa. It occurred to her to wonder, though, if Theresa might not be the woman guerrilla leader that the Texas Ranger had described who was more bloodthirsty than any man. And why should Charles need her alive in Mexico City?

Then she turned her full attention to Rosita, who mercifully had slipped into complete unconsciousness. She wasn't even aware when Theresa and Charles left the room, though she heard the lock turning in the door. Finally, when she saw there was nothing more she could do for Rosita, she pulled a blanket over the girl and laid down beside her in the bed. She had thought she would be too wound up, too worried about Rosita, to sleep, but exhaustion took over from her keyed-up nerves, and she slipped into a fitful, restless slumber.

There was, however, no sleep at the Alvarez *casa* in Chihuahua. Ever since Francesca had returned at dusk, her horse lathered, with her story of the guerrillas killing the guards and carrying off Star and Rosita, the household had been in an uproar. The authorities were notified and *vaqueros* had been sent out at once to track down the bandits. It was only by an almost physical effort that Don Felipe had restrained Michael from riding with them. "You know better than I, my friend, that not even a Comanche can track at night," he said. "Wait till morning, then we shall know better what to do."

At the first light the next morning Michael was in the courtyard, waiting impatiently for the stableboys to bring his horse, when Don Felipe joined him. Michael's face was drained of all expression. Only his dark green eyes were murderously alive. They stared right through Don Felipe as if he didn't exist for him, as if at that moment nothing existed but his own memories, images playing over and over tortuously in his mind. Star curled up in his arms, her eyes silver-gray, blurred with lovemaking, the way her pointed chin tilted haughtily, the childishly open way she laughed, and the picture that wounded him the most: Star clinging to him that last morning, begging him not to send her away to the country. If only he had listened to her... if only he hadn't stubbornly insisted...

"Don Miguel, we must talk, in my study." Don Felipe repeated the words twice until, like a man possessed, Michael turned his face blindly toward him.

"Talk? Talk about what?"

"A message arrived for you only a few moments ago. I haven't opened it, but I would think it's from the *banditos*."

"The messenger? Have you held him?"

His host shook his head regretfully. "The gate porter took the box. He said it was a man who handed it to him. It was still dark. He couldn't see his face, and then the man was gone."

The study where he took Michael was a light, airy room, filled with books and wall maps of the Alvarez holdings. Don Felipe went to his desk and handed a small box to Michael.

The box was wrapped clumsily. The wrappings fell apart quickly under Michael's hands. He took out the letter, read it, then reread it before handing it to Don Felipe without a word.

"At least we know your wife is still alive," Don Felipe said, trying to offer some comfort to his friend. "If you need gold for the ransom, you have only to ask." Then when Michael still said nothing, he added uncertainly, "You do plan to pay the ransom?"

"Of course I'll pay," Michael said, his voice flat. "They made sure I would by enclosing this." He reached into the box and brought out a tiny severed woman's ear.

Don Felipe's face went white and he crossed himself quickly. "*Dios mio!*" he murmured appalled.

But it was another sound from the doorway, a thin moan of horror, that echoed through the suddenly quiet room. Francesca, still in her nightclothes, swayed in the doorway, her black eyes wide and distended with shock as she stared at the ear. "He . . . he promised," she whispered brokenly. "He promised he wouldn't hurt her."

It was Michael who reached Francesca first, who yanked her into the room, a murderous rage in his eyes as his hands shook her so that her head snapped back and forth, her black hair flying around her face. "What man?" His voice was merciless, and his hands lowered, tightened around the slim, white throat. "You know who took Star, don't you? Don't you?"

Francesca felt her windpipe being crushed; there was no breath left in her lungs that felt as if they were bursting, gasping for air. She tried to cry out but no sound came and, terrified, for the first time in her life, looking into Michael's pitiless face, she knew she was only a few moments from death.

It was Don Felipe and two servants who managed to pull Michael away from the girl. Francesca sank to the floor, gagging, making small whimpering sounds. "No, I swear. I know nothing." But it was useless. She could see in her own father's cold, disbelieving stare that it was useless. She began to cry, rubbing her eyes childishly with her fists. "El Güero promised," she cried. "How could I know . . ."

Her father's icy voice cut off her wails of self-pity. "Who is this El Güero? Where did you meet this man?"

"At the country house months ago. He stopped me one day when I was out riding alone. He was going to rob me, instead we—" she cast an apprehensive glance at her father. "We . . . talked, a long time. He was so handsome and romantic, like a blond god. Afterwards, whenever I was in the country, we met whenever I could get away from my *dueña*. He found out that I knew Don Miguel, that he always stopped at our *casa* whenever he came through Chihuahua on a trading trip. He even knew that Don Miguel had taken a wife and that she would be staying at our house, too."

Michael stared at the girl, his narrowed eyes filled with loathing. "You arranged that this, this El Güero knew Star would be on the road yesterday. That's why you were able to get away from the bandits, because you had helped arrange the ambush."

Don Felipe shook his head, his voice broken. "I can't believe it. How could you, child? The guards wounded, one man killed, Don Miguel's wife taken prisoner, and her maid, both subject to God knows what atrocities. Why? How could you do such a terrible evil?"

Francesca pulled herself to her feet, some of the old bravado slowly returning to her face as she faced her accusers. "It's not the way you think, papa. I'm sorry about the guards. I didn't know they'd be shot, but as for Doña Estrella." She flashed Michael a defiant glance. "How can it be wrong for a man to reclaim his own wife?"

"What lies are you telling now?" her father asked sharply.

"No lies. It's the truth. Doña Estrella is the wife of El Güero, only his real name is Charles Bradford. He told me so. He was married to Star McFarland in Independence last June." She turned to Michael. "That's true, isn't it, Don Miguel? You seduced that, that trollop away from her husband. Señor Bradford has the right to take her back. He's her legal husband, not you."

Don Felipe gazed at his friend, bewildered. "Is this so? Do you know this man, this Charles Bradford?"

Michael nodded slowly. "I know him, and yes, it's partly true." His thoughts were racing backwards, to the morning they had brought Bradford's dead body back to the caravan. He remembered now how something about the body had bothered him, something not right, the ring on Charles's hand, for example. Indians liked bright geegaws like a flashy gold ring. It was unusual they would have killed and then left such a ring on the corpse. Still, when Star had identified the body as that of her husband, he had put his misgivings aside. It was, after all, none of his business. He hadn't been in love with Star then—or perhaps the unpleasant truth was, he already was in love with her and didn't want to accept any uncomfortable truth that might keep him from her.

Don Felipe turned again to his daughter. "What you have done is still unforgivable," he said, his face frightening in its coldness. "You have brought dishonor upon your name. I should turn you over to the authorities, but I will give you a choice. You will either enter the convent at San Gabriel, or you will marry Don Antonio within the week, if he will still have you. Perhaps he can curb your wickedness. God knows, your mother and I have failed."

"No, papa!" Francesca ran to her father, flinging her arms around him and smiling pleadingly up at him in a way that always before had brought her forgiveness for her acts of mischief, for her misbehavior. "I promise I'll be good. I can't marry Don Antonio. I can't stand for him to touch me. And I'd die in a convent."

Don Felipe gazed down at his daughter, a fleeting sadness touching his face that made him suddenly appear years older. Then he pushed her away wearily, his voice coldly unwavering. "Until you are married or in the convent, you will be kept in your room, out of my sight. It sickens me to look at you."

When Star awoke again, it was to the sound of the door being unlocked. Theresa brought in some food, tortillas that were cold, and placed them beside the bed. When Star asked if she could have some water so that she could wash herself, Theresa did not even bother to answer her.

After making sure that Rosita was no longer unconscious but sleeping, and that there was some color again in her face, Star turned her attention to the food, forcing herself to eat although she had no appetite.

By the slant of the light coming in the barred window, she assumed it was close to noon, but when she surveyed her surroundings from the window, it was impossible to see beyond the empty high-walled courtyard and the mountains, looming dark and forbidding in the distance. She had no idea how far they were from Chihauhau, or in what direction, but if Charles expected the ransom to be paid by sunset that day, she decided they couldn't be too far.

After Theresa, there were no more visitors until evening. Then once again the Indian woman returned with more of the same food she had served for breakfast, except this time she also brought a bottle of *mesquel,* and then left without a word. Rosita had drifted in and out of sleep all day. Now she awakened, and Star coaxed her into eating some of the tortillas and drinking a little of the *mesquel.*

Rosita stared, in frightened confusion, around the room. "What has happened, *señora?* Where are we?" Then, her voice trembling hysterically as she remembered the torture she had endured in that small room the day before, she clutched at Star's hand. "Do you know what they did to me? You will not let them near me again, you must promise. Oh, *señora,* how they hurt me."

"It will be all right, Rosita. I promise you. We mustn't lose courage," Star said with a calmness she was far from feeling, holding the girl's hand tightly until she once again fell into a troubled sleep.

Star's own sleep was equally troubled. She kept waking up, bathed in cold perspiration, tormented with memories of Michael, fear and longing pulling equally at her nerves, until she ached to cry great angry sobs but dared not, for fear of disturbing and frightening Rosita even more.

The next afternoon Charles arrived at the door, bearing a bottle of wine and a basket of fresh fruit. He had put aside the worn leather garments and was dressed in a dashing *caballero's* clothes, silver-trimmed trousers and jacket of an expensive broadcloth, tailored to show off to advantage his broad shoulders and still slender body. His face was clean-shaven and his eyes sparkled engagingly at Star as he set the tray down and said, "A little celebration, I think, is in order, my sweet."

Almost casually, he dropped a kiss on her cheek. Star looked at him with disgust. In an odd way she resented most of all his cleanliness when she felt so soiled and grubby. "I'd rather have warm water to wash in, than wine," she said sharply.

Charles grinned. "I'll speak to Theresa. She's never understood this great love for cleanliness that the *gringos* have. Now drink your wine, my pet. It isn't every day your husband comes into fifty thousand dollars."

"Michael paid the ransom?" Star asked, relief surging through her.

"Down to the last centavo," Charles said, nodding smugly.

"Then we're free to go," Star said eagerly.

Charles frowned, his face darkening. "It isn't very complimentary for a wife to be so impatient to leave her husband."

Rosita was watching from the bed, bewildered. Why had her *señora* allowed the bandit chief to kiss her so familiarly, and although Rosita's knowledge of English was limited, she could sense they were speaking not like two strangers, but as if they had known each other a long time.

Then, as if suddenly remembering there was a third party in the room, Charles took Star's arm. "Come along. We can discuss this better in private."

He took her across the hall to another bedroom that, Star noted bitterly, was comfortably furnished. There was a bed that had silken sheets and coverlet, and a desk by the window with a decanter and crystal goblets and a silver desk set, including, she noticed absently, a silver letter opener with a gold handle.

Charles took a seat in one of the comfortable chairs, while Star remained standing. "You aren't seriously considering holding me, Charles, now that the ransom's paid," Star said immediately.

He smiled, in mock surprise. "Holding you? But you're my wife. Of course you'll stay with me."

Star stared at him, at first too shaken to believe what she was hearing. Then she blurted, "No!" She clenched her hands at her side to stop their trembling, forced her voice to calmness. "Michael will keep looking for me. He'll never stop." She lifted her chin defiantly. "You don't know him as I do."

At the warmth in her voice when she spoke Michael's name, Charles's mouth tightened. He had never heard her speak his own name with that special softness in her voice. "Oh, I don't underestimate Mr. Kelly," he said coldly. "That's why you're going to write him another letter, this time telling him that, having discovered your husband is still alive, you have also discovered that you are still in love with him, and that you have decided to stay with him. That you never want to see Michael Kelly again."

"I won't," Star said, outraged. "I'll never write Michael a letter like that."

Charles got slowly to his feet. "Oh, I think you will, my pet. For two reasons. First, if you don't, I'll make my own arrangements with friends of mine in Chihuahua to get rid of Mr. Kelly. Nothing fancy, you understand. A poison slipped into his wine, a knife in the back in a dark alley. And the second reason is: if you refuse to write the letter, my men would still love to get their hands on your little Rosita. And this time, I assure you, I'll let them finish the job they started." His gold eyes ran thoughtfully over Star. "I might even let them have a turn with you. I'm sure, after a few hours of their attentions, you'd be much more . . . amenable."

She stared at him, too appalled to speak, her mind refusing to believe that even Charles could be so bestial.

When she didn't respond at once, Charles shrugged impatiently. "Don't be a fool, Star. How can you think of going back to Kelly? Soon everyone will know that you're not his wife. Is that what you want, to be Kelly's mistress? And do you expect that, as his mistress, Kelly will take you to live with him at his ranch with his very respectable family?"

He saw the doubts, the uncertainty, struggling in the wide gray eyes and pressed his advantage. Moving closer, he said softly, "You belong with me, Star. You're my wife. And you'll love living in Mexico City. It's very sophisticated, with a proper society. Once we get you some decent clothes, you'll be the most beautiful woman there."

He had, he thought, pleased, forgotten how incredibly beautiful Star was, that great mass of red hair against those dark-lashed, silver gray eyes, the slender elegance of her figure that even the rumpled dress couldn't hide. He remembered, suddenly, urgently, how delectably soft and silken that skin had been to his touch. Now, moving swiftly, he thrust his hand through the opening in the gown, felt his excitement grow as his hand groped for and found a soft, yielding breast. "I think tonight, my pet, you'll sleep in here with me," he said thickly. "It's been too long."

He felt the shudder that passed through her body but, mistakenly, thought it was fear or perhaps even desire. What it was instead was anger, an icy implacable rage, as Star suddenly pushed him away from her and stepped quickly to the desk. Before he could move, she had picked up the sharply honed letter opener and held it clasped in a businesslike fashion in her hand.

Charles stepped forward, then stopped, laughing a little uneasily. "Do you plan to kill me . . . again? It's much easier with a gun, I assure you."

Star took the knife and deliberately turned it inward, pressing it against her ribs. Through the rent in the gown, he could see the point of the knife drawing blood against the pale skin.

Her voice was very quiet. "Not you, Charles. The knife is for me. I'll write your letter. Only Rosita must take it to Chihuahua herself. I'll convince her that it's my decision, that I want to stay with you. She'll believe me, and Michael will believe Rosita. I'll go to Mexico City as your wife. But if you try to touch me again, I'll kill myself. I swear I will."

Charles laughed, a little shrilly. "You'd never have the nerve."

But he saw quite clearly in her face that she would. There was no indecision there, only an odd composure, the soft gray eyes serene, almost happy, as if she would welcome the escape the knife would bring.

He moved then, lunging across the room at her, gripping her wrist and twisting it cruelly so that the knife fell to the floor from her numb fingers. Then he struck her hard across the face with the back of his hand so that she staggered and came up hard against the desk.

She didn't fall. Even with a trickle of blood running from the corner of her mouth, Charles saw, infuriated, that she still possessed that innate self-reserve and dignity that had never left her, he remembered, even during those times when he had most abused and degraded her.

"It's a long journey to Mexico City, Charles," she said with a small smile. "You can't keep me bound and watched every minute, all the way. If you so much as touch me, I'll find some way to kill myself, I promise you. And from what I overheard you say to Theresa, I gather it's very important to you that I reach Mexico City alive."

He stared at her, his face black with anger, then turned and stormed out of the room. But she knew she had won. For whatever reasons—and she couldn't imagine why—it was necessary that Charles reach Mexico City with a live wife, not a dead one. And this way, at least both Rosita and Michael would be safe from Charles.

She sank down in a chair, her knees suddenly weakly giving way beneath her. And for the first time since the guerrillas had dragged her from the Alvarez carriage, Star allowed herself the luxury of crying.

Chapter Twenty

Six weeks later, when Star, with Charles and Theresa, rode into Mexico City, they found the capital verging on chaos. Late in March General Scott had captured the port of Vera Cruz after a five-day naval bombardment that had left over half the city in blackened ruins. Then, to avoid the deadly yellow fever, Scott had hurried his troops away from the unhealthy lowlands up into the mountains. In mid April the American army had faced General Santa Anna at Cerro Gordo, a fortified position on a hill surrounded by deep ravines and woods. The area was so impregnable that Santa Anna had boasted "not even a rabbit could get through."

General Scott's West Point–trained engineer, Captain Robert E. Lee, however, had managed to drag heavy artillery siege guns across the ravines and through the almost inpenetrable woods, attacking the entrenched Mexican troops from the rear. Caught in a crossfire, the Mexicans were cut to pieces. The survivors scrambled in wild disorder back to the capital, with General Santa Anna among the first to retreat.

Star wasn't aware of the disaster that had struck the Mexican army, or that the American troops were resting, waiting for reinforcements, at Puebla, only seventy-five miles from the capital city. All she was conscious of as the *diligencia* rumbled its way slowly over stone-covered pavements was her own bone-weary exhaustion after weeks of hard, constant travel.

First, there had been the days of hot, dusty travel from the hacienda where she had been kept captive. The small band, including a half dozen of the guerrillas, Charles, Theresa, and Star, crossed a mile-high plateau, avoiding the main trail and

301

the cities of Parral and Durango, taking a roundabout route through sleepy, backwater Mexican villages. Then had begun the incredible dizzying, winding trek upwards into the deep barrancas of the Sierre Madre mountains. Ridges stacked on top of one another in endless confusion, each one higher and steeper than the one before. When Star was sure they could go no higher, when each breath became a painful stab in the lungs in the thin, clear air and white clouds closed around the travelers, they finally reached the highest peak, "The Devil's Backbone."

The trip down was even more dangerous and terrifying. The path was little more than a goat's trail that hugged the jagged cliffs, falling off abruptly, dropping thousands of feet into dark, shadowy gloom. One misstep could send the unwary traveler plunging down into that darkness. Star found herself staring as if mesmerized into those deep shadows. Charles, frowning, came up behind her and, holding her arm, shoved her forward down the trail. When they reached the lower slopes at last, there was a softness to the air after the chill heights. Scarlet-flowered vines hung from lush trees, and everywhere crept a thick, tropical undergrowth.

The seaport of Mazatlán was one of the prettiest and cleanest towns Star had seen in Mexico. She took a deep breath of the fresh ocean air, delighting in the salty taste in her mouth, the quarreling sea gulls, the tiny fishing boats bobbing in the harbor, the colorful marketplace. If the company with her had been different, if missing Michael didn't rub painfully at her raw nerves, she would have enjoyed their short stay in Mazatlán, even the three-day boat trip to Acapulco with the boat never far from the green-fringed shores with its palm trees and majestic mountains brushing constantly at a blue sky.

At Acapulco, they had boarded the coach that ran between the port and Mexico City. The half-dozen *banditos* who had been traveling with them suddenly disappeared. As the *diligencia* stopped for the night at various *fondas*, at Chilpancango, Taxco, Cuernavaca, the views became breathtaking, while the road steadily climbed upward. As the days passed, Star noticed that Charles's clothes became less flamboyant. He began wearing sober black broadcloth frock coats and starched white shirts, while Theresa gave up the leather jacket and trousers and wore a white *camisa,* colorful skirt, and black rebozo. Strangely enough, Star saw that these clothes didn't suit her as well as the bandit outfit. From somewhere Charles came up with a gray merino gown for Star, a frilly white jabot at the throat and a dark gray bonnet with white ostrich feathers. Anyone looking at the three of them riding in the carriage would never suspect they were anything but people of quality, a husband, wife, and servant, she thought wryly, certainly not *banditos*.

Now, as the carriage passed over one of the many ancient causeways that led into the capital, finally passing through the heavily fortified San Antonio gate, Star forgot her weariness and stared, fascinated, around her at a city that was already old when the United States was founded. Through the gathering dusk, she could see long, spacious streets, handsome colonial-styled buildings of opalescent rose and gray volcanic rock, rising five and six stories high, with iron grills covering windows and balconies. In spite of the late hour, the sidewalks were crowded with pedestrians. There were priests and friars and monks in somber habits, military men in showy regimental uniforms, half-naked *leperos* or beggars plying their trade, as well as men in long black cloaks and women in the inevitable rebozos and colorful skirts over bare legs.

In the last glow of sunset the turrets and domes and spires of the city caught fire, and from churches and monasteries and convents within the city bells began to ring out. Star remembered that when she had complained about the constant bell-ringing in Mexico, Rosita had explained reproachfully that while the bells pealed, souls in purgatory had peace from torment. Now Star crossed herself and said a silent prayer that Charles had kept his word and that Rosita, at least, was safe with her Jaime.

Watching the unconscious gesture, Charles murmured, tauntingly, "Don't tell me you've taken up the Roman Catholic faith, Star. How shocked your father would be if he knew."

Star was saved from answering by the carriage rumbling to a stop before an impressive gray stone building, much more ornate than its neighbors on the street. As usual, there was the barred doors of a porte cochere and a grilled peephole, finally opened after much banging on the door by the coachman. After they were carefully examined, the door itself was opened and the porter, a wizened, grumbling old man, conducted the visitors across a patio and past well-kept stables. More servants appeared and a fancily dressed major domo with obsequious fawning airs, reminding Star of the major domo in the Alvarez home. He led the way into the *casa* and up a magnificent staircase to the family apartments above.

A thin woman with prominent eyes and a dark, sallow complexion showed Star to a bedroom. The room, although lavishly decorated, with gilt on the ceilings and a velvet coverlet on the bed, seemed to Star as cold and gloomy as the rest of the mansion.

At least the bed was comfortable, she thought as she sank down into it, and the fruit and wine punch the servant brought her had ice floating in the goblet. When asked, the servant reluctantly explained that the ice came from the snowy peak of the volcano, Popocatepetl, brought over forty miles by Indians who sold the ice to the *ricos* in the city.

When Star asked the woman who owned the *casa*—although Charles had greeted several of the servants by name, Star sensed it wasn't his house—the servant fell into a sullen silence. Whoever was the master of the house, his servants were certainly unfriendly, almost fearful, was Star's last thought before falling asleep.

The next morning she was awakened by the same servant who reluctantly volunteered the information that her name was Josefa. She brought Star chocolate in a silver pot and told her that the French modiste, Madame Corrinne, was waiting on the Señora Bradford's pleasure. When Star had the dressmaker sent up to her room, she discovered that Madame Corrinne, although approaching middle age, was sprightly and loquacious, dressing and acting much younger than her years. She informed Star that Señor Bradford has given her carte blanche to prepare a completely new wardrobe for his wife. Star noticed that Josefa had not left the room with the arrival of the modiste, but settled in a corner, her face wreathed in perpetual discontentment. Star suspected she had been ordered not to leave Señora Bradford alone.

The dressmaker circled Star for several seconds, her glance assessing, then she smiled and nodded, pleased. "Madam has a *très elegante* figure. It will be a pleasure to sew for her."

"Do not the Mexican women have excellent figures?" Star asked the woman in French and, from the blank. look on the servant's face, felt secretly triumphant, sure that Josefa didn't understand French.

Madame Corrinne's smile grew wide at her delight that her customer spoke French. Not good French, of course, but passable. "Mexican *señoras*, their hands and feet are tiny and beautiful, but the rest . . ." She winked, indicating her waist and hips. "Not so tiny, you understand. But then, poor things, they never exercise, much less walk. They stand behind their grilled windows all morning, watching the street and gossiping with their friends. In the evenings they drive in their carriages on the paseo or the Alameda, and flirt with the *caballeros*, then attend a late supper, theater, and home. Each day it is the same."

It was from Madame Corrinne that Star learned of the surrender of Vera Cruz to General Scott and the Mexican defeat at Cerro Gordo. The modiste said scornfully, "When General Santa Anna left the capital for Cerro Gordo, he issued a proclamation, stating that 'My duty is to sacrifice myself. . . . I am decided to die fighting.'" The dressmaker sniffed. "Always he makes these grand promises and always he is the first one to flee the battlefield. This time they say he left so quickly, he left one of his wooden legs behind. In the streets they are calling him a coward and traitor. There are even rumors that the general has been bribed by the American President Polk to deliver Mexico into the hands of the enemy. Why else was he allowed to slip through the American blockade?"

"Yet the Mexican people always take Santa Anna back," Star said, puzzled.

The modiste gave a Gallic shrug. "Who can understand the Mexicans? Myself, I have lived here for fifteen years and they say it has been no different since the Spanish viceroys left in 1821. One *pronunciamento*, one revolution, one president, follows another. Constitutions are adopted and abolished. Sometimes it seems all the various political factions, the Federalists and Centralists, the Moderates and the Puros are more interested in fighting each other than the enemies who invade their country. Just last month a regiment of young dandies, called the Polkos, revolted against the government because of the confiscation of church property, instead of marching to the defense of Vera Cruz." Madame Corrinne shook her head. "It is all beyond my comprehension."

"Why do you stay?" Star asked. "Why don't you return to France?"

The seamstress sat back on her heels from taking measurements and gave Star a startled glance. "Why should I leave? It is *très joyeux*, you understand, between revolutions." She added, with a shrewd glint in her eyes, "And the Mexican *señoras* love to spend their gold on pretty gowns and expensive jewels. What other pleasure do their husbands provide them?"

"When a revolution comes, though, isn't it dangerous?"

The woman reached for her scissors and pins. "Oh, I always visit a friend who has a hacienda in the country until the fighting in the city is finished. Of course, this time it is different, with the American army waiting to attack the city." She gave Star a questioning glance. "But Madame and her husband are Americans, yes? You should have nothing to fear from the enemy."

"Do you know my husband?"

The woman shook her head. "I have seen him once or twice at the theater and on the *paseo*. He is very *distingué*. But he does not stay in the city long, and when he is here, he always lives at this *casa*."

"Whose house is this?"

If the modiste seemed surprised that her customer did not even know in whose house she was staying, she gave no sign. "Señor Alfredo Cordoba y Ortega. It was his father's and grandfather's before him, although Don Alfredo, of course, has a large *rancho* outside of the city."

"Is Don Alfredo married?"

Madame Corrinne shook her head, a curious smile playing around her mouth as she murmured, "His tastes, they say, lie elsewhere. He spends most of his time at the gaming tables in La Plaza Mayor. It is common knowledge that he has had to sell off many valuable works of art from this *casa* to cover his losses."

At mention of Don Alfredo's name, Star saw that the watchful Josefa was stirring uneasily, and she quickly changed the subject. Yet, now that she knew that her host was Michael's cousin, she was even more bewildered. Why should Charles have brought her here?

The next few weeks Madame Corrinne, who came to the house almost daily to fit the new gowns, became Star's only contact with the outside world. Neither Charles nor Theresa made an appearance at the meals Star was served in the huge, cold dining room at a table large enough to seat a banquet. Although the *casa* was enormous enough so that she supposed Charles and Theresa might be somewhere hidden in its depths, Star had no desire to explore the dark, drafty halls. She did quickly discover that she wasn't allowed to leave the *casa*. A stocky guard with a villainous face at the front door made that very clear, and when she ventured from her room, she had the uncomfortable feeling that eyes were always following her from the shadowy passageways.

She did use the library, which was well supplied with books in both English and Spanish, and she was allowed, morning and evening, to mount the stairs to the *azotea* of the casa. She found that other families in neighboring homes used their roofs for the same purpose, to take the air, to entertain friends, or be entertained by the never-ending dramas in the streets below, or to simply gaze upon the lovely vistas that met the eye on all sides. To the southwest the stone walls of the castle of Chapultapec brooded on its hilltop. Once the summer home of the Aztec, Montezuma, and later, of the Spanish viceroys, the castle was now a military school, heavily fortified and bristling with cannon. To the north of the city loomed the mountains, the snow-capped head of Popocatépetl soaring above the rest.

It was the street scenes, though, that caught Star's attention, always changing, always noisy, with the vendors calling their wares from early in the morning to late at night. Flocks of *leperos* in their filthy rags plied their trade, begging loudly for charity. Lancers paraded by with their gold-edged uniforms and glittering scabbards flashing in the sunlight, and almost every hour, a carriage would drive by with a priest carrying the Host on his way to bless some departing soul. The bells would peal and a dozen friars with lighted candles would follow the carriage, crying *"Dios viene! Dios viene!"* alerting passersby, who would fall on their knees and remain kneeling until the carriage passed.

One morning an ornate carriage, decorated in crimson and gold, surrounded by fifty hussars prancing alongside, passed on the street below the *azotea*. Star could not see the occupant, just a gold-headed cane and a hand waving gracefully in response to rather half-hearted "Vivas" of the crowds on the sidewalks.

That afternoon Madame Corrinne told her that yes, General Santa Anna had returned to the capital. Once more he had seized the Presidency and was issuing proclamations that the capital never would be surrendered, that he would sacrifice his life first.

"Always he says how much he will sacrifice for the country," the modiste said tartly. "All he has sacrificed so far is a leg during the French campaign. And he never for a moment lets anyone forget it. Did you know he had his leg buried with a high mass and full military honors under an elaborate tomb? Of course, in one of the next revolutions the insurgents destroyed the tomb and threw the leg away."

"Have you heard any more about the American army?" Star asked. "Are they still at Puebla?"

The modiste skillfully adjusted the fold of the skirt of a pale blue silk ball gown cut low in the waistline, so that the smallness of Star's waist was emphasized. A garland of matching blue silk roses at the bodice and over one shoulder led the eye discreetly to the perfectly shaped breasts and the elegant column of Star's throat. Talking with her mouth full of pins was no problem to the Frenchwoman, who nodded energetically. "Oh, yes, they are still there. Only it is most strange. The American General Scott is sending home thousands of his soldiers whose enlistments are finished. You would think he would need every one of his soldiers when he marches on the capital."

"How do you know these things, Corrinne?"

"From the newspapers. They carry stories all the time on the *Yanqui* soldiers, even copies of letters the soldiers have written home, complaining of how eager they are to leave Camp Misery, which is what they call Puebla."

"How could the newspapers get their hands on such private letters?"

"The guerrillas, madame. The *Yanqui* soldiers hold Puebla, but the guerrilla bands control the highway between the American camp and Vera Cruz. They raid the American supply trains as they will. Of course it is not mail they seek. Santa Anna has offered the *banditos* one half of whatever plunder they can take from the Americans." She made a moue of dismay as Star jerked suddenly and a pin stuck into soft flesh. "I am sorry, Señora Bradford." She glanced anxiously at Star, whose face had gone suddenly white. "You have been standing too long. Perhaps you should sit."

"No, I'm all right." Star straightened her shoulders, told herself it could not be, and yet all at once knew where Charles and Theresa had been these last weeks. El Güero and his band of murderers had simply transferred their base of operations from Chihuahua to Puebla.

The dressmaker climbed to her feet, satisfied with the gown, and said hopefully, "The *señora* will be wearing this gown to the ball the Presidente is giving at the National Palace next week. There will be no *señora* there as beautiful."

Star shook her head. "No, I don't believe we're invited." She knew that Corrinne was consumed with curiosity about her customer who was having such a splendid wardrobe sewn for her and yet never accepted any social engagements, and in fact, apparently never left the house.

Star elaborated no further, and from the cool, reserved look in the gray eyes, Corrinne knew she would get no more information. She sighed and said regretfully, "That is the last gown, madam. I will leave my bill with the major domo." She glanced down the dark passageway as Star stood with her at the bedroom door. "I will be sorry our little tête-à-têtes are finished." She gave a small shiver of distaste. "But I will not miss this *casa*. It is disagreeable, yes? There is a story that the grandfather of Don Alfredo, when he discovered his bride for whom he built the *casa* had been unfaithful to him, he locked her in one of the rooms in this house and she was never seen again until years later when she died. And then her hair was snow white and they say she had gone mad." At the shocked look on Star's face, she added hastily, "Of course, it is only a story. Old houses are always filled with tales, are they not?"

And then she was gone, the darkness of the passageway swallowing her as if she had never been.

A week later, the second week in July, Charles returned. He found Star reading in the library and, dropping a kiss on the auburn hair, said, frowning, "You are much too pale, my pet. You shouldn't bury yourself in this dark library."

As if, Star thought, annoyed, he had never been away at all but had left her only an hour before. She slammed the book shut and got to her feet. "It's difficult to go outdoors when I'm kept a prisoner in this house."

"Not a prisoner," Charles said. His smile was patronizing, as if she were childishly throwing a tantrum. "Naturally, I could not allow you to ride the streets of the city alone. It would be improper, as well as dangerous. This afternoon, though, we will take a carriage ride on the *paseo*. You will wear one of your new gowns, and later we'll attend the theater and have a late supper with friends. It is time the society of the city meets my lovely wife."

Star was too surprised to object, even if she would have passed up the chance to finally see the city she had only caught in glimpses from the *azotea*. Charles turned out to be a witty, informative guide. Although Star was skeptical of the charm he could bestow so readily, remembering too well the dark underside of that charm, nevertheless, she found herself relaxing and, for the first time in months, enjoying herself.

The carriage drove down the *paseo*, a long, broad avenue edged by trees and fountains with water dancing in the sunlight. Rows of handsome carriages were already driving slowly down the avenue. Inside the carriages, women in silks and satins, but without the usual mantillas covering their heads, gossiped or nodded to friends as one carriage passed another. The glass windows of the carriages were rolled down so they could better see and be seen. The women with languorous yet intricate movements of their fans indicated their interest in *caballeros* who paced their horses beside the carriages. The gentlemen equestrians wore jackets embroidered with gold and silver, and their fiery little horses performed graceful caracoles or curvets at command to impress the occupants of the carriages. It was,

Star thought, staring delighted at the scene, as if she had stepped from the nineteenth back to the eighteenth century.

They drove by the Alameda, a walled, tree-shaded park, and finally the carriage rolled into the Plaza Mayor. Star's eyes widened in amazement at the size of the square. An army could have paraded in the plaza with room to spare. The National Palace and the towering ancient cathedral took up one side of the square, while smart shops and cafes, under shaded arched portales, lined the other three sides.

As they drove by the cathedral, Star asked if she might visit inside. Charles looked as if he wanted to object, then shrugged and followed her inside the massive doors of the cathedral, his nose wrinkling at the smells and sights that met his eyes. Star tried not to show her own sense of shock at the contrast between the altar and shrines decorated with gold and silver and a fortune in precious stones, and the filthy, half-clad *leperos* and Indian women calmly searching their children's hair for lice as they knelt. Dogs ran up and down the aisles, and babies screamed. She started to kneel, then saw how thick with dirt the floor was and, rising swiftly, hurried back to the carriage. Charles helped her inside, a cynical smile on his face. "An edifying Christian spectacle, isn't it, my sweet?" he asked.

"How could the priests allow them to treat the House of God that way?" Star asked indignantly.

"You're being too harsh, my pet," Charles murmured. "For myself, I've always had the greatest respect for the Clericals, their ability to keep the peons in poverty and bondage while living lives of luxury themselves. One must admire such shrewdness."

"They're not all like that," Star objected, remembering the hard-working, poverty-stricken priest in San Rosa patiently tending to the needs of his flock, and Father Hidalgo, who had raised an army to try and free the Indians from the ruthless government.

"Perhaps not," Charles said. An oily gleam touched the amber eyes as he smiled reminiscently. "There are certain aspects of the faith I find intriguing. One evening I was privileged to visit services at the church of San Augustin. After all the lights were extinguished, and as the organ struck up the Miserere, the worshippers, men and women, stripped and began to beat themselves and each other with scourges. One could hear distinctly, even from the gallery, the sound of flesh being torn, even the splashing from the blood, and the monk encouraging them to greater violence, while reading aloud from the scriptures. Even when the bell was rung to end the scourging, the lashing continued."

Star turned away, sickened by the sheen in Charles's eyes when he spoke of the penitent self-flagellation, moving as far away from him as possible to the open window. The revulsion stayed with her the rest of the day, dulling the pleasure she had been feeling. The theater performance that evening did little to distract or amuse her. The actors were stilted, amateurish, and the theater, although lavishly decorated, had a distinctly unpleasant odor. The audience was more interested in gossiping with each other than watching the performance on the stage. Between acts Charles kept bringing a stream of people to their box for her to meet until faces and names began to blur, although she was well aware of the curiosity in the eyes of Charles's friends when they were introduced to her.

She had noticed that heads had turned in the audience to look toward her box. At first she had felt uncomfortable at the attention she was receiving, then decided to ignore the stares and let her own gaze travel over the women in the audience. Diamonds clustered in their hair, dripping around their necks, glittering in their ears. She remembered Madame Corrinne had told her that Mexican women adored diamonds above all other jewels. Colored stones were considered trashy. A wealthy Mexican matron often wore diamonds worth several fortunes, as casually as she wore her mantilla.

As her gaze traveled, bemused, over the dazzling display, her glance was caught by the head of a man who was leaning toward one side, talking to the woman sitting beside him. Although the man's back was toward her, there was something familiar about the set of the shoulders, the shape of the head. Of course, it couldn't be Michael, Star told herself, even as she felt her heart racing, her hands gripping the railing before her. The man was in uniform and Michael, if he had continued his journey south, would be at his *rancho*.

"What is it, my sweet?" Charles asked. "You're not ill?"

"It's . . . it's the smoke," Star said faintly. "It's given me a headache." Everyone in the theater, men and women, smoked, even the performers and the promptor on the stage. A thin blue haze hung in the air.

Charles insisted then upon taking her home, but at the Plaza Mayor the carriage stopped in front of the Merchant's Exchange. Above the Exchange the brightly lit gambling houses sent slivers of light out into the dark plaza. Charles turned to Star. "The coachman will see you safely home, Star." Lightly his hand stroked her shoulder, caressed the slender neck. He felt her body stiffen at his touch, even as her lovely face remained still, unresponsive. "I must find other diversions this evening or I'm afraid the temptation at home would be too inviting. And I want you to have a good night's rest so you'll be at your best tomorrow."

Before Star could ask him what he meant, he had left the carriage. By the time the carriage reached the house her headache had become very real, and she was too wrapped up in her own misery to wonder about Charles's cryptic words. These past weeks she had almost convinced herself that she had built a barrier in her mind high enough to wall off all memories of Michael. She had moved from the pain and helpless yearnings that gnawed at her into a safe, dull, gray limbo where neither sadness nor happiness existed, and each gray day followed another. And now, to her dismay, just one brief glimpse of a man that had looked like Michael had brought the pain and misery flooding back, so that her whole body ached with the most monstrous pain she had ever known. She wept helplessly, rocking back and forth, until there were no more tears and the pain became an exhausted emptiness. Finally there was the merciful oblivion of sleep.

The next morning it took an hour at her dressing table to repair her ravaged, tear-stained face. Even so, when Charles came to her room he frowned, annoyed at the shadows like pale bruises below the wide, lusterless gray eyes.

"You need a bit of rouge, my pet," he said coldly. "I have no intention of having my wife looking like a bedraggled waif when I introduce her to our host."

"Don Alfredo is here?" she asked, surprised, but obediently reached for the rouge pot, a cosmetic she seldom needed but that did add a blush of color to her wan face.

When she followed Charles down to the library, she hesitated uneasily at the doorway. The drapes at the windows had not been pulled and the room was crowded with men, all garbed in black, so that the library seemed filled with unrelenting gloom.

One of the men separated from the others and came forward to take her hand and pull her into the room. He wore black, too, but she saw at once it was of a more expensive material than the other men, the jacket edged with a delicate silver embroidery. He was tall but slightly built, with features too heavy for his thin face, and his neatly trimmed beard and hair were such a shining black that Star, repressing a nervous giggle, wondered if he used bootblack on them.

Don Alfredo's voice was softly modulated as he bowed over her hand and apologized profusely. "I am desolate I could not be here to greet you sooner, Señora Bradford, but affairs at the *rancho* kept me away. I hope you have been made comfortable."

"Yes, thank you. It was very kind of you to offer your hospitality," Star said, wishing the man's hooded eyes would not gaze at her intensely as if he were studying her for some hidden flaw.

"*Mi casa es su casa,*" he insisted. "My poor house, and all in it, even myself, though of no value and including all I have, is yours." Then ensued several more minutes of the exchange of courteous formalities that Star had already learned was an essential part of greetings and farewells in Mexico.

Finally, the courtesies attended to, Don Alfredo introduced the other men present, who turned out to be several family solicitors, an alcalde, a judge and a bishop.

At the look of bewilderment she turned upon Charles, he stepped to her side and said quickly. "There's no need to be alarmed, my sweet," he murmured, his hand resting lightly around her waist. "These gentlemen are anxious to clear up the matter of your marriage—or rather supposed marriage— to Michael Kelly y Cordoba. You have only to answer their questions truthfully and openly."

And if she didn't cooperate, she could expect no mercy from Charles, she thought, gazing into the slitted pale gold eyes fastened warningly on her face. At least now she understood why she was here, why it was so important that Charles keep her alive. A dead wife would never be able to swear that she was, in fact, married to Charles Bradford and that therefore her marriage to Michael, and subsequently his claim to the vast Cordoba estate, was nonexistent. She glanced thoughtfully from Charles to Don Alfredo, wondering how much money he was paying Charles to make sure his wife swore to her fraudulent marriage so that he, Don Alfredo, could be declared the rightful heir.

"We understand how painful this must be for you, *señora*," Don Alfredo said, a faint malicious smile touching the thin red lips. "Certainly no one blames you for your hasty marriage to my cousin Michael. I well know from his past behavior that my cousin can be most persuasive with women. And of course, to inherit, he needed a wife immediately."

Star felt her cheeks flame. Perhaps it had started out that way, she thought, a marriage of convenience on both sides, but at the end, she and Michael had been man and wife in a much deeper sense than any marriage document could join her to Charles. Furthermore, she disliked the contemptuous note in Don Alfredo's voice when he spoke of Michael.

The angry retort that sprang to her lips was held back by Charles's hand squeezing painfully around her waist. She inclined her head cooly toward Don Alfredo. "I did, after all, believe Charles was dead. I had seen his body."

Now the black-garbed men glided foward, surrounding her, questioning her. Had she, in fact, thought the body was her husband's? What was the exact date of her marriage to Charles Bradford? Where had it taken place? The questioning seemed endless, but in matter of fact, the inquisition was over in less than fifteen minutes. A document with gold and scarlet seals was drawn up, which she signed, although she had no time to read it thoroughly. As far as she could tell, it attested that her marriage to Michael was invalid because she had had a husband living at the time.

Then the black-robed men, reminding her of a group of scrawny black crows, murmured their elaborate courteous farewells, kissed her hand, and fluttered from the room. Don Alfredo brought her a chair and a glass of wine and she sat down, sipping the wine gratefully before asking Don Alfredo, "What will happen now to Michael's grandmother and his sister-in-law . . . and Michael?"

"Doña Elena and my esteemed grandmother, Doña Isobel, will, of course, continue living at the hacienda for as long as they wish," he said, as if surprised she should ask. "As for Michael," he shrugged. "*Quien sabe?* Now that he has joined General Francisco Perez's brigade."

"Michael, a soldier!" Star almost spilled the wine on her frock with the shock of the news.

"A grandiose gesture," Don Alfredo replied disdainfully. "No doubt to impress his women friends with his manly courage."

"At least he will be fighting his country's enemies," Star said, as she gazed scornfully at the man standing before her in civilian dress. A dull flush suffused Don Alfredo's face, and for all his foppish airs, Star realized uneasily that this was not a man to cross lightly.

In another moment her host had regained control of himself, his voice more amused than annoyed as he said, "We cannot all be romantic heroes, Señora Bradford, but I can assure you, if Mexico needs defending, I will fight at the *garitas* with the rest of the *soldados.*" He waved a languid hand. "However, I cannot conceive that a few thousand *Yanqui* burros will be able to penetrate the fortifications that surround our sacred city."

As if in after thought, he turned to Charles with a smile. "You must allow me to entertain your beautiful wife while you're away on business, my friend. There is a *baile* being given by the English legation tomorrow evening. It will be my pleasure to escort her, *con su permiso.*"

Star had the disconcerting impression, however, that Don Alfredo was not so much asking Charles's permission as telling him. A muscle jerked in Charles's cheek and she suspected he was annoyed at Don Alfredo's high-handedness, but apparently he had no wish to antagonize their host.

Therefore, the next evening Star found herself being escorted by Don Alfredo into a courtyard illuminated with colored lamps hung between gilded columns, and passing up a great marble staircase on his arm. She wore the gold-shaded ballgown that Madame Corrinne had designed for her, with its overskirt of deep flounces of Mechlin lace and a bodice embroidered with gold-beaded flowers. A gold lace mantilla covered her auburn hair, which was worn Spanish style, parted in the middle and pulled back from her face in soft waves. When he had seen she wore no jewelry with her gown, Don Alfredo had insisted she must borrow his late mother's diamond parure and earrings, along with a diamond-studded lace fan. Star did not care for diamonds, especially not worn with a gown already as opulently decorated as hers was, but she soon realized that for her not to wear diamonds to the ball was to Don Alfredo's mind as shocking as if she did not wear a ball gown. She did draw the line, though, at the diamond brooch and diadem he tried to press upon her, feeling already almost vulgarly over-dressed.

They were met at the first landing by the British ambassador and the other members of the British legation to Mexico, then led upstairs to the ballroom, where she was introduced to Pres-ident Santa Anna. Star was not sure what she had expected after the tales she had heard of Santa Anna, but the president did not appear the beast nor the dandy she had expected, but a quietly dressed gentleman with a scholarly face and rather sad, fine dark eyes.

Once in the ballroom, Star understood why Don Alfredo had insisted that she wear his mother's jewelry. There wasn't a woman present who didn't have diamonds around her neck, waist, or in her hair or ears. Some women wore diamond rings on every finger, and as they swayed gracefully in their partner's arms to a gay waltz, the diamonds caught and reflected in the light from the crystal chandeliers overhead, splintered into a multitude of dazzling rays.

As Star stood, watching the brilliant scene and listening to the laughter and music, she found it hard to remember that the enemy was lined up not seventy miles from the city, poised for the attack. Did the war exist at all in the minds of these merrymakers? she wondered, as the music stopped and the laughing couples began to leave the floor.

Don Alfredo was standing beside her, greeting and being greeted by his friends, his hand resting lightly on Star's arm. Suddenly she felt the hand tighten and a note of spiteful amuse-ment crept into his voice as he said, "And, of course, Doña Estrella, here is someone to whom you need no introduction."

Star turned with an automatic smile of greeting on her lips, then felt the smile freeze as she looked full into Michael's dark, impassive face.

Chapter Twenty-one

*F*or a second Star saw a blaze of hatred in the dark green eyes, then the eyelids lowered and all expression was wiped away from Michael's face. Only the muscles around his mouth remained taut.

He nodded, barely acknowledging her presence, then turned to his companion. "Elena, I don't believe you've met Señora Bradford. My sister-in-law, Señora Triaz y Moreno Cordoba."

The young woman stepped forward, and in the customary greeting between Mexican women, she slipped an arm around Star's waist and pressed her cheek to Star's lightly before stepping back. Elena's hair had the fragrance of tuberoses, Star thought irrelevantly, and at the moment the young, finely boned face beneath a black lace mantilla looked, embarrassed, from Michael to Star.

It was evident that Alfredo did not share in the general discomfort. There was a look of ill-concealed malice in his thin face, that made Star realize that Don Alfredo must have known Michael would be here tonight and had deliberately planned to embarrass his cousin by bringing Star to the ball.

Don Alfredo reached for Doña Elena's arm. "You must do me the honor of dancing with me, Elena," he said, smiling brightly.

The young woman drew back a little from his touch, her low, musical voice flustered. "You forget, I am in mourning, Don Alfredo."

"And you look most attractive in your widow's weeds, dear cousin," Alfredo said gallantly. A speculative look touched his eyes as his glance traveled over the woman's slim figure. "I'm sure once your mourning period is over, the young *caballeros* will be fighting for one of your smiles, don't you agree, Señora Bradford?"

Star tore her eyes away from Michael to give her full attention to his companion. Doña Elena had an ethereal beauty, with her small, pale oval face and large black luminous eyes framed to perfection by the black lace mantilla and the unadorned high-necked black silk gown she wore. At the moment, Star noticed that the large black eyes were fastened anxiously upon Michael, one small hand reaching out to clutch at his arm, an intimate, loving gesture that sent a jagged pain through Star.

"If not a dance, then you must keep me company while I fetch an ice for Señora Bradford," Alfredo insisted. The malicious smile twitched across the thin red lips. "I'm sure Michael and the *señora* have much to talk about."

Before the young woman could protest he had pulled her away beside him, the crowd swallowing them up. Star took a deep breath to still the trembling inside of her as she turned to face Michael, hugging her arms hard against her side as if afraid that against her own volition, they would obey the terrible yearning to reach out and touch Michael—the way she had dreamed of doing for so many sleepless nights. And if she touched him, even for a moment, she knew she would be lost.

"I'm sorry," she said, amazed herself at how composed her voice sounded. "I didn't plan this, you know, our meeting this way."

"I didn't think you had," Michael said dryly. "Cousin Alfredo has a flair for the dramatic. And since his solicitors served papers on me this afternoon, I suppose he couldn't resist his moment of triumph. I'm to remove my possessions from the *rancho* with all due speed. Elena and my grandmother have already moved to a hacienda here in town."

"But Don Alfredo promised that your sister-in-law and grandmother were to be allowed to keep their home at the *rancho*."

"Oh, I'm sure he'd be happy to have them stay, particularly Elena. She's the honey that will draw the pretty young men that Don Alfredo fancies." His voice roughened. "You don't really suppose I'd allow Elena to stay on at the *rancho*, accepting Alfredo's charity. As for my grandmother, she will do as she pleases. She always has."

"I'm sorry," Star said again, and then helplessly, "I had to sign the papers, Michael. Charles is my lawful husband. There was nothing else I could do." Then, powerless to resist any longer, the need to make some physical contact too great, she reached out her hand to touch Michael's arm as Elena had done. But her hand never reached him. Swiftly he stepped back, away from her. As if he couldn't bear to have her touch him, she thought, and a desolation, a grief worse than any pain she had felt when she thought she would never see him again, cut through her body. His eyes on her face were hard and brilliant as the diamonds she wore, and just as cold. How he must hate me, Star thought, struggling to keep her face from showing her anguish.

"Where is your esteemed husband?" Michael asked, glancing around him. "I wouldn't have thought Charles would let you out of his sight."

Star's throat tightened. "He's away . . . on business."

A sardonic smile flitted across Michael's mouth. "Ah, yes," he said softly. "I'd forgotten your husband's very profitable business."

Star remembered then the $50,000 ransom in gold Michael had paid for her safe return. No doubt he thought she had been part of that, too, she thought wearily. That she had written the ransom note willingly. After all, wasn't that what she had wanted him to think?

The music had started again, but Michael did not ask her to dance. An awkward silence stretched between the man and the woman studying each other warily. Like two strangers, Star thought, only worse than strangers, because strangers at least could attempt to find some common meeting ground. And it didn't help matters any that Michael had never looked as handsome or dashing as he did at that moment, resplendent in a gold-braided, dark green uniform faced with scarlet, belt white as snow, fringed gold epaulettes glittering on his broad shoulders.

Misery turned her voice sharp. "What a surprise to find you in uniform, Michael. And fighting for a lost cause. Isn't that what you told me, that Mexico could never win this war."

He shrugged aside her dartlike words. "Perhaps I've developed a fondness for lost causes. Or grown tired of straddling a fence. It's a damn uncomfortable position. And I'll have the satisfaction of serving with a general I know will stand and fight."

And die, Star thought, an icy hand squeezing her heart with a sudden premonition of disaster, as if she saw death standing at Michael's shoulder. Gazing into that still face, that obsidian gaze, she sensed that with an Indian's stoicism, Michael had already accepted the fact that he wouldn't survive the battle for Mexico City.

Michael saw the stricken look in the velvet-soft gray eyes and his smile taunted her. "I'd be more touched at your concern, only unfortunately I can't help remembering Rosita. Or have you forgotten her so quickly?"

"No, I haven't forgotten," Star said, and then frightened by the anger in Michael's eyes, she asked anxiously, "She's all right, isn't she? Rosita's alive?"

"Oh, she's alive. No thanks to your husband and his ...business associates," he said, and then, brutally, "Was it your idea or Charles's to send the girl's ear with the ransom letter?"

He saw Star flinch as if he had struck her, the blood draining from her face so that even her lips were colorless, and, for a moment, almost regretted his cruelty. Not even when Rosita had stumbled half-alive into the Alvarez hacienda and he had read the letter from Star she brought with her, driving him *loco* with rage, had he believed that Star, for all her duplicity, had actually been a party to the torture and mutilation of her maid. After Rosita's wounds had been tended, he had questioned the girl closely. Baffled, crying softly, her dark eyes bewildered and guileless so that he was sure she was not lying, she admitted that, yes, the *señora* wrote the letter willingly, that she was apparently fond of the brigand who had kidnapped them. Rosita had seen them exchange caresses. Then, frightened, she had looked away from Don Miguel's face, the blazing anger in the greenish-black eyes.

Now, staring down at Star, at the long, graceful line of her throat, the crescent curve of her breasts above the gold lace bodice, the creamy softness of her skin, he remembered his lips tracing the path from her sweetly upcurved mouth to those silken breasts, tasting the saltiness of her tears after they had made love, the scent of her flesh in his nostrils.

And the rage came back, smashing at him like a fist in his rib cage, so that he almost forgot himself and wanted to shout; "Why? For God's sake, why?" Only his pride, the fierce pride that she had so casually ground under her tiny, satin-shod feet, held him back. He gripped the reins of his emotions with an iron hand. This wasn't the time or the place, he thought bitterly. Someday, if he lived through the coming battle, he would have his reckoning with Star on his terms, and she would pay dearly for her betrayal.

Then suddenly he was unable to bear her nearness any longer. That cool, arrogant half smile was back on her face, and her beauty was an affront, a painful reminder of what a fool she had made of him, and the anger threatened to erupt again inside of him so that he had to get away from her.

He glanced over his shoulder. "You'll excuse me," he said. "I must find Elena."

Then he was gone. In a few minutes Don Alfredo returned alone. He took a quick look at Star's face, then handed her a wine glass filled with a pale golden liquor. "Drink this. You look as if you could use it."

The liquor tasted like flowers and ice in her mouth, then fire going down her throat. Alfredo's glance roamed, pleased, over the colorful assemblage, his foot tapping time to the music. "It is an interesting party, is it not?"

"Yes," Star said and took another swallow of the wine. "Very interesting."

During the next two weeks, Charles and Theresa continued to be absent from the *casa*. Following the *baile*, Alfredo became Star's constant escort. Although her host's unexpected flashes of spitefulness and his childish flare-ups of temper with the servants left Star feeling vaguely uneasy, still, Alfredo, most of the time, was an agreeable companion. There were even moments when she managed to forget Michael, and the dull ache she carried around inside of her ever since the night of the *baile*. Perhaps it had been for the best, her seeing Michael again, she thought wearily. Always before there had been that

secret spark of hope that somehow, someday, she would find
her way back to Michael. Now she had to face the fact that
even if by some miracle she could be freed of her marriage to
Charles, there was no way back, ever, to what she and Michael
had shared. In a way the knowing, the final acceptance of the
knowledge, was more merciful than her tormenting herself with
impossible hopes and dreamlike fantasies, like tearing at a
wound, refusing to let it heal.

Alfredo was an even more knowledgeable guide to Mexico
City than Charles. Slowly, as the days passed, Star began to
regain some of her insatiable curiosity about the colorful stream
of life that passed through the streets of Mexico City, not only
the poverty-stricken Indians who hawked their wares on street
corners, the crippled *leperos*, but the wealthy families Alfredo
took her to visit in their luxurious mansions. Many of the
families still bore titles of nobility given them in the days of
the Spanish viceroys.

One afternoon Alfredo took her to visit Chapultapec hill.
Their carriage drove through ancient cypress groves with hanging gray beards of moss, trees that had been old even when
Chapultapec had been the summer home of the Aztec ruler
Montezuma. The carriage ascended through the woods to the
castle itself, now a military academy, perched on top of the
craggy hill.

The commandant of the school, a friend of Alfredo's, introduced them to several of the young, fresh-faced cadets, then
took them on a tour of the thick walls and parapets of the castle,
proudly pointing out the great moats and cannon bristling everywhere. As they strolled along the wide, open gallery that ran
around the castle, Star could see for miles over the great valley
of Mexico, its lakes and woods and fields, surrounded on all
sides by snow-tipped mountains.

The commandant indicated with a wave of his hand the
breathtaking perpendicular drops on all sides of the castle. "As
you can see, *señora*, Chapultapec, like Mexico City, is invin-
cible."

Two soldiers walking near them overheard the remark, and
the one turned to the other with an ironic smile, muttering,
"Bedammed if old Ampudia didn't say the same at Monterrey."

The unmistakably American accent beneath the Irish brogue,

the reddish hair and bright blue eyes beneath the Mexican shako uniform hats, caused Star to give the commandant a wondering look. "They're members of the San Patricio Battalion," the man explained stiffly. "They are visitors here today like yourself."

"Surely you've heard of the Irish-Americans, as well as other foreign-born *Yanquis,* who have left the American Army and formed their own battalion within the Mexican Army." Alfredo's smile was disdainful as he spoke. "Of course, Santa Anna offered them free land and money to desert."

"The San Patricio Battalion has proven its courage in battle, Don Alfredo," the commandant said quickly. "And it wasn't only for land or money they left the *Yanqui* army. Many were brutally mistreated by their officers. Others are devout Catholics who didn't realize they would be fighting a war against the Holy Church."

Alfredo made a sweeping, mocking bow of apology. "I stand corrected, General Bravo." His glance rested with pride and affection on the church spires, the broad avenues and rose stone buildings at his feet, as Mexico City spread out beneath them. "But you're right, General. The *Yanquis* can never take Chapultapec, any more than they will be allowed to set one foot on the holy soil of Mexico City."

Despite Alfredo's brave words, Star couldn't help noticing, on their daily carriage promenades through the city, that more and more storefronts on the plaza were being boarded shut, and that many of the families they visited had already fled the city for the safety of their country estates. Still, the afternoon procession of carriages along the *paseo* continued, with the women in their rich gowns and the *caballeros* on their prancing horses following the carriages.

Several times Alfredo took Star on a carriage ride along the Viga, which was becoming an even more fashionable and popular place than the *paseo* for carriage promenades in the afternoons. The Viga was bordered by a wide, slowly meandering canal, covered by small boats and canoes expertly guided along by Indian men and women. In the mornings the boats were piled high with fruits, flowers, and vegetables being brought to market, and in the late afternoon the boats became floating flower gardens gliding by under a cloudless blue sky, while the Indians played their guitars and sang and danced lazily. If it were not for the filthy beggars who plied their trade everywhere, and the presence of marching soldiers, an unpleasant reminder of the war, Star thought she would never have witnessed a more peaceful, picturesque scene.

One Indian woman in a passing canoe caught her eye. The young woman wore a garland of scarlet poppies on her dark, proudly held head, her hair plaited down her back with a red ribbon. Her features looked as if they were shaped of terra cotta, her teeth flashing white in the crystal clear sunlight. Her hands and arms, moving in a graceful dance, were beautifully shaped.

"She's as beautiful as Malinche must have been," Star said, entranced. Then when Don Alfredo gave her a questioning glance, she smiled and asked, "Wasn't that the name of Cortez's Aztec mistress?"

"We call her Doña Marina," he said, and then, curiously, "How would you know of her?"

"You have an excellent library. I've been reading about Mexico's history, and how the Indian princess Malinche was given as a gift to Cortez when he first invaded Mexico."

Alfredo glanced at the young Indian woman dancing in the boat. "She could be a descendant of Doña Marina. There are Indians still around descended from those early Aztec tribes who never intermarried with the Spanish. They keep to their old ways no matter how the church has tried to root out their pagan rituals."

"Are they more pagan than the Spaniards who conquered a country and destroyed a whole civilization?" Star asked slowly.

Alfred laughed, surprised. "I had no idea you were such a romantic, Doña Estrella. I can assure you there's nothing romantic about the Indians. They're lazy, shiftless creatures, perfectly happy if they have their *pulque* to drink, a cigarillo to smoke, and a woman to sleep with."

"Yet you force them into the army, expect them to fight for Mexico?"

Her companion frowned. He was not accustomed to carrying on an intelligent conversation with a woman, much less having his logic questioned. But he hid his irritation as he replied blandly, "There's an old saying that an Indian will always fight for whoever gives him the biggest sombrero. As for an Indian's loyalty, if you have been wasting your time burying your pretty head in books, then you must know that Doña Marina betrayed her own people to serve her lover." The spiteful streak that lay always beneath the surface of Alfredo's nature abruptly surfaced as he gave Star a sly glance. "But then loyalty is never a woman's strongest virtue, is it, *señora?* Poor Cousin Miguel found out that truth, to his sorrow."

Star refused to rise to the bait, having already discovered that the best way to handle her host's unexpected malicious outbursts was to ignore them. She waved her fan before her face languidly for a moment before changing the subject by asking, "You've never told me, Don Alfredo, how you and my husband happened to meet."

"It was some years ago, when Charles first brought a caravan down the Santa Fe trail. He came to Mexico City to enjoy his profits. Unfortunately, he lost most of them at the monte tables, where we happened to meet one evening. He appeared to me to be an enterprising man with a happy lack of scruples, and we became partners in his various business enterprises. We lost touch for a while, then some months ago he returned to Mexico City with his Indian mistress and approached me with an idea for a new profitable business venture."

"You financed his gang of bandits and killers!" Star said, shocked.

Alfredo winced, giving her a pained smile. "Guerrillas, my dear Star. Patriots who fight for the cause of Mexico in their own way. If one makes a little profit on the side..." He shrugged practically. "I am sure there are many bankers and shopkeepers in your own St. Louis who are also making a fat profit from this war." He reached over and picked up her hand, holding it for a moment to his lips, as he murmured, "The fact that Charles's wife turned out to be fraudulently married to my Cousin Miguel was, I assure you, only a happy coincidence."

At the touch of his oddly leaf-dry lips against her skin, Star had an instinctive urge to pull her hand away, but reason overrode her distaste. She could not afford to offend Don Alfredo. At least he provided a roof over her head, and he was a wealthy, influential man. Perhaps if she handled the man diplomatically, she might, in time, be able to persuade Don Alfredo to secure passage for her to leave Mexico City before Charles returned.

That evening after dinner at the *casa*, though, she began to wonder if she could rely on Don Alfredo for assistance. He had been in one of his irritable moods all through dinner, snapping at the servants, complaining of the wine and the excellently cooked meal, and drinking, she noticed, more wine after the meal than he usually did.

When he poured still a third glass of wine for Star, and she demurred, he frowned, annoyed. "I insist, *mi bella*. It is boring to drink alone. And I have no intention of being bored, not tonight."

Reluctantly Star sipped at the wine, watching her companion covertly over the edge of the glass. Alfredo's usually sallow skin was flushed and one of the heavy-lidded eyes had a nervous tic. "Is there something special about this evening?" she asked idly.

Alfredo swallowed his wine in one gulp, then poured himself another glass, spilling some of the liquid on the mahogany table, where the drops sparkled in the candlelight. When he spoke, his voice sounded unnaturally shrill. "I will be reporting to General Gabriel Valencia's Army of the North at San Angel in the morning. It seems the *Yanqui* army have finally left Puebla and are marching toward Mexico City. I can no longer stand by. All must now rise to the defense of our sacred city." He lifted his glass in a wry salute. "As our esteemed Presidente Santa Anna has said, 'It is now war without pity unto death.'"

Star saw that the hand that held the glass trembled, and knew, with a sudden welling of pity, that Don Alfredo, for all his cynical smile, was terrified of being killed.

As if he sensed her sympathy, Alfredo leaned forward and grasped her hand, the black eyes searching her face hungrily. "There's something I want to show you. Come with me." He was pulling her to her feet, hurrying her down one of the long dark hallways where the wall sconces threw only pallid shadows over the walls and floor. At the end of the hall, he took a key from his waist pocket and unlocked the door. The room smelled of mildew, of disuse, although when Alfredo lit the lamps in the room, and the gold-framed paintings hanging on the wall seemed to leap to life, it was clear that the paintings, if nothing else, were regularly dusted.

Behind her she heard Don Alfredo laugh, a gleeful, lewd giggle that turned Star's stomach almost as much as the paintings themselves. Repelled, disgusted, yet fascinated, she could not for a moment turn her eyes away from the paintings that for all their obscene subject matter, the naked, twisted bodies of men and women in grotesque postures, were obviously beautifully and skillfully executed. The flesh tones of the bodies were so real she felt as if she could reach out and touch their warmth.

"My grandfather started the collection," Alfredo said, pleased, taking Star's stunned silence for appreciation. "There's none to match its quality in all of Mexico." Then, moving quietly over the deep-carpeted floor, he was beside Star, his arm around her waist tightening, turning her to face him. "That's why I wanted you to see them. I've always found particular enjoyment in taking my pleasure here in this room."

When Star, wrenched out of her shocked apathy by the touch of his hands on her body, began to struggle against him, Alfredo's grasp tightened, his voice, amused. "You needn't put on a show of maidenly modesty for me, *mi amor*. Any woman married to Charles Bradford has without a doubt been well tutored in the various, more interesting, methods of lovemaking. And surely you wouldn't deprive a soldier on the eve of battle."

Star was more embarrassed than frightened, until the arms around her forced her inexorably toward the deep-piled carpeting and Alfredo's mouth fastened on hers. The kiss was strangely passionless. Alfredo's mouth had a cool, almost rubbery, feeling on hers. All at once Star understood why she had been brought to this room—that Alfredo desperately needed the perverse excitement of the paintings to excite him and arouse his manhood.

She was startled at the strength in Alfredo's slight body, his slender, wiry arms, but her own body, for all its slimness, was not as weak or soft as it seemed. As she felt Alfredo's hand fumble at her skirt, she forced herself to remain perfectly still. Emboldened, thinking that her resistance had ended, he dropped his other hand to grope at her bodice. Then, with both hands on his chest, she shoved him backward as hard as she could. Caught off balance, he staggered, and with her legs now freed, she kicked him with her knee where she knew the blow would do the most damage. Alfredo gave a high-pitched scream and bent over clutching at himself, his eyes wild with pain and rage.

Star didn't wait to watch his reaction. Lifting her skirt in both hands, she flew from the room down the passageway to her bedroom, slamming and locking the door behind her. Then, since the lock didn't look particularly strong, she shoved a cabinet in front of the door, and a table for additional weight.

It was only then she sank down to the floor, her heart beating as if it would explode. She rubbed the back of her hand against her mouth, trying to remove the feel of Alfredo's mouth on hers.

It was fifteen minutes later that she heard footsteps in the hall, stopping outside the door of her room. For a few seconds the pounding of her heart was in her temples; her whole body shook. She knew that if Alfredo wanted, he could summon enough servants to break down the door, no matter how much furniture she piled in front of it. In despair, her eyes darted around the room. How stupid of her, she thought, not to have somehow secured a knife, some sort of weapon, these last weeks she had lived in the *casa*. There was not even a letter opener in the room.

Then, when she thought she could bear the waiting no longer, the footsteps moved on, away from the door. Exhausted, she climbed to her feet, falling into bed without bothering to undress.

She suspected it was pride that had stopped Alfredo from any further attempts to reach her, that he would not want the servants to see his humiliation in needing to break down the door to possess her. Perhaps he might even have been secretly relieved not to have to prove his manhood. In any case, Star thought, as she finally, unhappily fell asleep, she was sure Alfredo would never forgive her for having bested him, and she could forget any hope of securing help from him in starting a new life without Charles.

The next morning she awoke to the sound of bells. Although it wasn't unusual to hear church bells ringing in Mexico City— their clamor seldom ceased, morning and evening—there was a different sound to the bells this day, as if every church, convent, and cathedral in the city were pealing their bells in wild unison. Then, from the direction of the plaza, alarm guns thundered, shaking the *casa*.

Star rang for the maid. Remembering the barricaded door, she shoved aside the furniture and opened the door cautiously. The hall was empty. She had the feeling that she was completely alone in the house. Since it was impossible to remove her gown, which was hooked up the back, without assistance, she made her way to the kitchen. To her relief she found the sullen-faced Josefa, along with several other servants, huddled together, terrified.

"It's the signal, *señora*, the bells, the cannon," Josefa wailed. "The *Yanqui* army has been seen by the sentinels marching down into our valley. They are no more than half a day's journey away."

"Where is Don Alfredo?" Star asked, glancing around the kitchen, where it was obvious no breakfast had been prepared.

"The master left late last night," one of the older male servants replied. His face crumpled piteously. "He will be killed. Then what will happen to us? The barbarian soldiers will tear down our churches and take our women."

Somehow Star managed to convince the servants that Don Alfredo was certainly not yet dead and that the Americans would not interfere with their worship or molest their women. On this last subject, remembering her experience in Santa Fe, she was not quite as convincing, but she did manage to get Josefa to help her undress and the coachman to drive her to the plaza so that she could see for herself what was happening.

The great plaza was crowded with soldiers and citizens, and over the pealing of bells and military bands playing brassy music, Star could hear a mass of voices raised from thousands of throats in thunderous vivas. "*Libertad o muerte!*" It was impossible for the carriage to move across the plaza, and sitting, hidden in the shadow of the carriage interior, Star suddenly realized it might not even be safe for her, an American, to be present when emotions were running so high.

The next week she remained inside the casa. Occasionally she ventured up onto the *azotea* where, after the first noisy enthusiasm of the crowds, she watched the city grow ominously quiet as rumors raced through the populace. The Americans had been stopped at San Agustín, unable to cross the *pedregal*, a huge lava field, its jagged surface of black rock composed of deep chasms and bleak sharp inclines. Another rumor was that General Valencia had forced the retreat of the whole American army at Churubusco, and Santa Anna was furious when he received news of the victory because Valencia was his political enemy. The elation with which each report of victory was received, however, was overshadowed finally by the distant menacing thunder of cannons toward Padierna. The cannon's roar continued for hours, grumbling like a storm over the mountains.

Toward nightfall, it began to rain. The streets of the city immediately flooded as the rain fell in sheets. Lightning illuminated spires and rooftops, followed by the crash of thunder, louder even than the distant guns.

Withdrawing from the rooftop, Star had taken up a post at the window of the library looking out into the street, which at the moment resembled a small river streaming between the pavements. She had not bothered to light a fire, and she pulled her shawl tightly over her shoulders as she dozed in an armchair. Several times she awakened, peering out into the dark, stormy night, not sure whether it was thunder or cannon fire she heard beyond the city.

It was still raining, though less heavily, the next morning when she awoke and returned to her post at the window. The sound of gunfire could be heard from the direction of Contreras, and a gray pall hung over the city. Star could hear the clatter of hoofs as horses galloped, splashing, through the street, carrying adjutants on courier missions, or the cries of sentinels echoing from a nearby *garita: "Alerta! Alerta!"*

At dinnertime Josefa came and asked if Star wanted the meal served in the dining room, but Star shook her head. "Tell the cook not to bother. I'm not hungry."

There was a cold, hard knot of fear in her chest. All she could think about was Michael out there somewhere in the midst of the battle that she knew was raging around Churubusco. She shivered, remembering the premonition of disaster she had felt when she had seen Michael at the British Legation *baile*, as if she could sense the dark wings of death hovering over him. Panic shook her as if with a fever, and she began to pace back and forth in the library, her hands tugging at the ends of her shawl, pulling it closer. If Michael were dead, she thought, then she didn't want to live either.

The sound of the cannons lessened as dusk fell over the city, and by early evening Star was unable to remain quietly waiting in the house any longer. Some news of the battle must surely have reached the city by now.

Snatching up a black rebozo, she flung it over her hair and ventured out into the street, walking toward the *garita*. She was not alone in the street, she discovered. Men passed by her in the growing darkness, survivors of the battles that had taken place that day, their footsteps muffled, their uniforms torn and bloody. Most staggered by wearily; a few collapsed without a sound in the street, their blood mingling with the rainwater in the gutters. Star shrank back against a wall. One young soldier, surely not more than fifteen, his face covered by a bloody bandage, was being helped along by an older man. The young *soldado* cried in a childishly bewildered voice, over and over, *"Madre? Que pasa, madre?"*

A lancer, his beautiful uniform bloodstained and muddy, his black, highly polished boots coated with filth, rode slowly by. Star reached out a hand and caught at his arm. "Please, can you tell me what's happened?"

The man stared blankly down at her, as if he were not seeing her but looking inward at some indescribable horror. He spoke in spurts. "They overran Valencia... attacked him from the rear. God knows how they managed to cross the *pedregal*. That bastard Santa Anna refused to send reinforcements. He ordered Valencia to retreat. The general refused."

"General Perez? Was General Perez and his brigade there?" Star asked frantically, still clutching at the man's blood-stained sleeve.

The man shook his head. "Not at Padierna, *señora*. But there was another battle at the convent of San Mateo and the bridge across the Rio Churubusco." Awkwardly he lifted his wounded arm to his forehead in an attempt to salute, his face contorting with pain as he muttered, "You must excuse me, *señora*."

Desperately, Star approached other fleeing soldiers. Some looked at her blankly and kept moving. One, perhaps glimpsing her red hair, growled, *"Gringa,"* and shoved her aside. A carriage came dashing through the *garita*, splashing mud in its wake and onto the lancers surrounding it. The wounded soldiers on foot fell back to allow the coach passageway, their faces sullen, as they recognized the *presidente* insignia on the carriage. There were no "vivas" now for Santa Anna, for the man who had promised to fight to the death to save Mexico.

Star recognized one of the lancers riding behind the carriage, an aide-de-camp to General Santa Anna that she had danced with at the *baile* at the British Legation. Unlike the others, his uniform was pristine clean, untouched by blood or mud; only his face had a waxy look of shock. When Star called his name, he swung quickly down from his mount and came to join her, his voice alarmed. "You shouldn't be in the street, *señora*. It is not safe."

He remembered how beautiful this woman had been at the ball, with her hair the fiery crimson of the Aztec lily and those soft dove-gray eyes. Now her face was drawn as she stared at him imploringly. "Have you any word of General Perez's brigade."

"Only that he and his men were sent to guard the bridge across the Rio Churubusco. They held it for as long as they could, but the *Yanquis* kept attacking up the causeway. The artillery fire from the bridge cut them down, and still they came. When they ran out of ammunition at the bridge, they fought hand to hand. General Perez escaped, we know that, but the rest . . ." He shrugged helplessly.

"Señor Michael Kelly y Cordoba?" Star asked. "Do you know him? Michael Kelly? Did he escape?"

"I am sorry, *señora*. I do not know him." He frowned uncertainly. "He was not perhaps one of the San Patricios? I hear they fought like demons at the convent, tearing down the white flag when others tried to surrender. Unhappily, when the convent was finally captured, all the San Patricios were killed or taken prisoner."

"No," Star said, dejected. "He wasn't a San Patricio."

Then, as she started to turn away, the aide said, slowly, *"Señora*, you were with Don Alfredo at the *baile, verdad?"*

Star swung back, caught by the somber note in his voice. "Yes, I'm a guest at Don Alfredo's *casa*."

"He's dead, *señora*," the young man blurted out. "General Valencia sent him as a courier to our headquarters from Padierna, asking again for reinforcements after the *Yanquis* attacked. He delivered his message to Santa Anna in my presence. The general treated him badly, I'm afraid, screaming at him that 'Valencia should be shot on sight for his cowardice.' I remember how pale Don Alfredo looked, but he never said a word, just turned and left. I went after him, to offer him a brandy. He had already collapsed when I reached him. He had been shot in the chest, probably when he made his escape from Padierna. There was nothing that could be done for him. I am truly sorry."

Star nodded, tears mingling on her face with the rain that had once again begun to fall. "Did he say anything?"

"At the end, he was conscious. He looked . . . surprised, then he said, 'It is not so disagreeable, after all, this dying.' And he was gone."

The aide glanced around him, at the gray, sodden streets, at the line of exhausted soldiers streaming into the city, it seemed without end. "You should return home, *señora*. There is nothing you can learn here." His voice broke. "God help us. We have lost all, our honor and our country."

"Is the war over, then?"

The man shook his head wearily. "I think not. We still hold Chapultepec and the *garitas* into the city. For how long, who knows?"

"The wounded that are being brought into the city, where will they be taken?" Star asked.

"The hospital of San Andres of San Juan de Dios." And then, gazing down at her, startled, "You must not think of going there, *señora*."

Star, however, had already turned and left, returning to the *casa* only to change into one of the servant woman's clothes so that she would look less conspicuous, and once more covering her hair with the black rebozo.

She ordered the carriage brought around, and when the regular coachman refused, Georges, the burly husband of the cook, Martita, agreed to drive her to the hospital.

At first when she walked into the hospital of San Andres, she shrank back, unnerved at the scene that met her eyes. Dim wall sconces cast lurid shadows over blood-soaked bodies lying on pallets and litters in the corridors. The stench of putrid flesh, untended wounds, of blood and filth and gangrene, took her breath away. The moans and screams of the wounded echoed and reechoed against the thick gray walls. There was barely room to move between the pallets crowded side by side on the floor. But at least she was not the only woman there. Dark-clad nuns bent over the beds, doing what they could to tend the living and ease the dying; *soldaderas*, crying bitterly, some with children in their arms, went from bed to bed, seeking, like Star, the bodies of loved ones.

A coldness gathered inside of Star each time she bent over a wounded man, like the coldness she had felt at the *baile* when she had had the premonition that Michael would be killed in battle. Still, she had to keep on looking, forcing herself to stare down into faces twisted in agony or already composed in death, looking strangely peaceful in the midst of ravaged countenances, mutilated bodies.

She had reached the last corridor, had almost turned away, when she spied a man crouched on his haunches beside one of the pallets on the floor. There was something about the stoical Indian's face that made her hesitate, then rush to his side. "Manuel? Manuel, what are you—?"

Then she fell silent as she saw the man on the pallet at which Manual was keeping his patient, silent vigil. Michael lay as if he were asleep, his eyes closed, but his face was gray and covered with a cold sweat. The tunic of his uniform, one trouser leg, and his black hair were stiff with blood.

Chapter Twenty-two

*T*he day after the bloody battles at Padierna and Churubusco, at which Santa Anna lost ten thousand men, killed, wounded, or captured, an armistice was signed, a temporary cessation of hostilities so that the dead on both sides could be buried and peace negotiations begun. During the last week of August and the first days of September, the talks dragged on.

To Star, though, the possibility of peace no longer mattered. After finding Michael at San Andres, she and Manuel and Georges had quickly moved him to her bedroom at the Casa de Cordoba. Upon carefully cutting away the blood-soaked uniform and gently bathing the dirt and blood from Michael's body, she was relieved to discover that the leg wound, a saber cut by the look of it, was not deep enough to have severed the muscles in the leg. A blow to his head caused the concussion and the comalike sleep. But it was the bullet wound in Michael's shoulder, along with the loss of blood he must have suffered, that frightened Star the most.

From Manuel, who still had an aversion to talk, Star finally learned that the Indian had stayed with Michael when he left Chihuahua and joined the army. He had fought beside Michael at the bridge of the Rio Churubusco, and after Michael had been shot off his horse in the melee of the last futile defense of the bridge, it was Manuel who dug the bullet from the wound and somehow managed to bring the unconscious Don Miguel back to the city. Then, after helping Star undress Michael and get him into bed, he disappeared from the *casa* without another word.

Star cleaned the wound and wrapped wet cloths around

337

Michael's shoulder, but she had no medical knowledge of what more she should do. Despite her ministrations, the tissues around the ugly, gaping hole remained red and hot and swollen, while Michael's breathing and pulse grew steadily weaker. With the onslaught of sick and dying men into the city, there was no possibility of bringing a doctor to the *casa*. She found a medical book in the library, but it offered little advice and a great many warnings about the fatal result of a festering wound carrying poisons through the blood to the rest of the body.

She watched helplessly as Michael's body became burning hot one minute, then stiffened and turned freezing cold the next. He became delirious, crying out, shouting orders, flailing his arms wildly as he tried to climb out of bed. It took all of Star's strength to hold him in the bed. Most of the servants, at word of Don Alfredo's death, had left the house. The ones who remained crowded in the bedroom doorway, taking such gloomy relish in watching the drama of a man dying that, infuriated, Star slammed the door in their faces. She remembered what Cousin Sophia had done when, as a child, she had chills and fever. She kept Michael well covered with blankets and stone hot-water bottles tucked into the bed around him, but by the second day it was obvious that the chills and fever had grown worse.

In his delirium Michael fought over and over again the battle at the Churubusco bridge, urging his men to stand firm, raging at the ones who fell back. Then he was reliving the *jornada*, the terrible thirst, his mind drifting backward to the tortures he had suffered as a boy at the hands of the Comanches. Once he cried out, *"Querida, mi amor . . . donde esta?"*

Star reached for his hand and chafed it with her own, holding it to her breast as she whispered, "I'm here, *querido*. I'm here."

She was shocked at how cold his hand was in her own. He had tossed off his blankets again. Only a short time before he had been drenched in sweat. Now chills shook his body so that no matter how many blankets she piled on the bed, he seemed to draw no warmth from them. It was as if his life were being drained from his body with the terrible leaching chill.

Earlier, when he had once briefly come out of the coma, his eyes blazing up at her, but without recognizing her, she had forced a stimulant past his lips. Now she tried again, but he flung her hand away. Then Manuel was suddenly beside her, returning as quietly as he had left. With his strong arms he held Michael while Star managed to force some brandy down his throat. Once again Michael lapsed into a restless unconsciousness, his breathing shallow and slow.

Manuel reached into his leather pouch and brought out a dark, spongy material he handed to Star. "Keep wet, under bandages," he commanded.

Gingerly Star took the materials, which looked like nothing so much as damp pieces of bark and moss. How could she be sure it wouldn't make the wound worse, she wondered doubtfully. Then she remembered her father had told her once about a knife wound he had received on one of his first trips down the Santa Fe trail, and how an Indian woman's medicine had cured the cut when the white man's medicine had failed.

Manuel watched closely as she did as he directed, nodding approvingly when she had finished. Then he jerked his head toward the bed. "Rest."

Star protested, but it was like arguing with a stone. Manuel simply stared at her with his flat, opaque gaze and gestured again to the bed. Star was too tired to object further. She stretched out on the bed next to Michael, reaching for his hand, and telling herself hopefully that it felt a little warmer. She was sure she wouldn't sleep, but she had gone two days and two nights without rest nursing Michael, and exhaustion felled her like a sandbag. When she struggled again to wakefulness, she sat up, turning quickly to Michael. He appeared calmer, his breathing deeper and more regular, as if in a normal healthy sleep.

She removed the bandage at his shoulder. The flesh around the wound was still swollen, but it was not the violent red shade it had been earlier. As she redressed the wound, she studied the face of the man on the bed. Sleeping, Michael looked younger, more vulnerable, his lashes dark, curling against his cheeks, the flat-planed cheekbones more prominent in his thin face. The cold sweat was gone from his skin and he no longer issued delirious orders in the desperate lost battle.

Star pulled her chair up to the bed, hopeful that the last crisis had passed, even as her hand still held Michael's tightly. At last she turned to Manuel, a glow returning to her pale face.

She said gratefully, "There is no way I can thank you, Manuel."

The man shrugged, his face blank.

For the first time in days, Star was aware of sunlight from outside the bedroom window, the normalcy of street sounds, the *leperos* crying for coins, the vendors calling their wares, carriages clattering over the stone streets.

"Is there any news?" she asked eagerly. "Is the war over?"

Manuel shook his head. "I think there will be no peace, only talk. *Yanqui* soldiers were stoned in the Plaza, when they came buying supplies. Santa Anna is melting down church bells for cannon." He glided like a shadow to the door. "Tell Don Miguel I go join my family at Tacubaya."

"I didn't know you had a family, Manuel."

"Five sons," he said, and for the first time she saw a glint of amusement in the flat, dark eyes. "Now I am back, soon another on the way."

A murmured, almost coherent sound came from the bed, and Star turned quickly to Michael, but he was still sleeping. When she turned back, Manuel was gone.

It was another three days before Michael could take nourishment by himself, before his eyes didn't stare through Star but instead focused fully upon her, then traveled slowly around the bedroom. "How did I get here?" he asked warily.

"Manuel brought you to the San Andres hospital after the battle at Churubusco," Star said. "Don't you remember? You were wounded."

Michael frowned. "I remember, but not being hit. I remember the Americans rushed the guns at the bridge when the double-quick was sounded. We drove them off the causeway into the cornfields and ditches filled with six foot of water. Then we fired into the cornfields. One sergeant carrying the colors was hit, but he kept advancing against our fire until he fell and another man seized the colors, and he was shot, and then a third. Still they kept coming. They forded the ditches and stormed the bridge with their bayonets. I remember the screams of their wounded, the terrified horses and mules as they fell into the ditches."

Star listened, biting her lip against crying out at the scene of carnage that Michael described, somehow sensing that his reciting the horror aloud was as important to Michael's recovery as the bark that had stopped the spread of poison through his body.

When he tried to sit up, she forced him firmly back against the pillows. "You need to rest."

Now he did stare directly at her with that narrowed icy gaze she remembered so well. Then his face once more became guarded, closed to her. He gazed around him. "Where am I?"

So nothing had changed, Star thought, lowering her eyelids so Michael couldn't see the bleak despair there. "At the Casa de Cordoba," she said, adding quietly, "Don Alfredo was wounded at Padierno. He's dead."

"Poor bastard." Michael's voice was low, shaken. His mouth twisted in a bitter smile. "I hope he died on clean sheets. He would have hated dying in the mud." Then he closed his eyes and turned his face away from Star.

For the next several days as she tended to his needs, he hardly spoke to her at all, only to ask of any news of the peace negotiations. Star could tell him little. She never left the house, and the servants' tales were so garbled it was impossible to tell rumor from fact. Not that there were many servants left, just the cook, Martita, and her husband, Georges, and the old man who acted as the porter. The only reason Martita and Georges remained, Star knew, was because they and their families before them had been servants on the Cordoba *rancho*. After their marriage Alfredo had brought them to serve him in his home in Mexico City. Martita and Georges had always served the Cordoba family. Where else would they go?

To save extra work for Martita, Star ate her meals in the kitchen with the servants, then brought Michael a tray. Always she spent the night on a chair in the bedroom. Although Michael was stronger and had even taken a few steps, using a crutch that Georges had devised, she was still afraid his wound might open again. She had a recurring nightmare that he might bleed to death during the night if she slept down the hall.

There was another reason, too, why she bedded down in the large chair rather than occupying one of the many empty bedrooms in the *casa*. With the servants gone, the house seemed even more dark and forbidding, so that she hated to be alone in it. She could hear her footsteps echoing down the passageway in her trips from the bedroom to the kitchen. Often she would stop and whirl around, peering into the darkness, sure that someone was watching her, although there was never anyone in the shadowy corridor.

Each night she would wrap the blanket around her and spend half the night trying to find a comfortable position in the chair. One night as the chair creaked protestingly under her restless turnings, Michael snapped through the darkness, *"Nombre de Dios!* Get into bed and maybe we'll both get some sleep."

Reluctantly, she climbed into the far side of the bed, staying as removed from Michael as she could, her body tense, hardly breathing. After a few moments, by the sound of Michael's quiet breathing she knew he was asleep and she relaxed a little, stretching out her cramped limbs. Lying next to Michael, yet as apart as if they were in separate rooms, reminded her of those nights in the Dearborn when they had also slept so close together but far apart. Only then, she thought, her body hadn't been consumed with the yearnings that assulted her now at the thought of Michael's nearness.

Sighing to herself, she closed her eyes and told herself that she should be grateful that he was here beside her and not lying dead in some muddy ditch at Churubusco. Pray God, the war would be ended before he could be called back to fight again.

In the week that followed, though, the peace talks seemed to gather little headway. Martita, returning from mass, told how the priests spoke out against any peace with the "heretical Americans," and the Mexican newspapers, although ready to cede Texas and Upper California to the United States, were shocked at the idea of "selling" the loyal citizens of New Mexico to American masters.

Now that Michael was growing stronger, he insisted on reading the newspapers himself. His face grew dark with anger as he read of the captured members of the San Patricio battalion, who had either been hanged by the American Army or flogged and branded on the face with the letter D.

Although he still had difficulty using his right arm, and limped when he put weight upon his wounded leg, he had reached the stage of his convalescence where he was irritable at having to remain quietly in bed. And it only made him more waspish when Star ignored his bad temper and went serenely about her chores of nursing him, changing his dressing, bringing him his meals, even washing him, although he scowled fiercely and insisted he was quite able to wash himself.

He was well aware that his anger was not so much at Star as at himself. He couldn't seem to keep his eyes from following her as she moved gracefully around the room. She didn't take the time to arrange her hair in an elaborate hairdo these days, pulling it back loosely from her face and tying it with a narrow green ribbon at the nape of her neck, which only emphasized the beauty of her heart-shaped face, the delicately chiseled features. She had taken to wearing the Mexican woman's attire of a white cotton *camisa* tucked inside a colorful skirt, and when she leaned over her patient, adjusting his bandage gently, or ran the washcloth over his shoulders and chest, he was very conscious of the unbound soft flesh beneath the *camisa*. And since he had insisted that she spend some time each day away from the bedroom, taking the sun on the *azotea*, he couldn't help noticing that the skin at her throat and face had the faint pink-gold color of a ripe peach.

It was during the nights, though, when he pretended sleep and Star lay as far away from him as possible in the bed, that he was most disturbingly aware of her presence. He had been so sure that the deep, sweet passion he had felt for her had turned to bitter gall that he was chagrined to discover that just the thought of her lying so close could still have the power to arouse him.

It was unforgivable that he could still desire her, he thought angrily as he shifted his body in the bed to try and ease the pain in his shoulder and ignore the even more distracting ache lower in his body. She had not only run off and left him the moment her first husband appeared again on the scene, but had made a fool of him in the bargain, pretending to be held against her will to gull the ransom money out of him.

As he turned on his side to take the weight off his bad shoulder, he saw that the moon had risen high enough so that its rays, split by the wooden shutter, fell like silver bars across the sleeping woman beside him. She had tossed aside the coverlet and was curled up like a child in her prim, white cambric nightgown, a faint smile on her face as if her dreams pleased her. The gown had slipped away from one shoulder, and there was something particularly provocative about the all-covering decorous gown and the half-revealed pink-tipped breast.

A pain that had nothing to do with his wounds stabbed through Michael, and he groaned silently. Bracing himself on his good arm, he stared down at Star through narrowed, angry eyes. She had washed her hair that afternoon, drying it on the rooftop, and he could still catch the fragrance of the sun in her hair as it spread loosely over the pillow, looking almost black in the pale moonlight. He remembered the satiny feel of that hair, the shape of her skull beneath his hands, and the soft misty gray look in her eyes after they had made love. He remembered too much, he thought, how she had trembled like a wild, frightened creature in his arms when he had first held her, as if the touch of a man's hands terrified her, when all the while . . . His mouth twisted angrily. For how long, he wondered grimly, how many months had Charles been waiting in the wings? All Bradford had to do was snap his fingers and she had crept back to him like a bitch in heat.

In her sleep Star gave a soft murmur and stirred restlessly, moving closer to Michael, one leg kicking free of her gown as her hand flung out, palm curved inward, to rest against Michael's chest. He drew in his breath sharply. Damn it, he thought furiously, his gaze moving slowly over the lissome curves he could envision so clearly beneath the gown. He had paid well for that softly tempting body, hadn't he, for those sweetly curved lips that could smile adoringly and lie and cheat at the same time.

All at once the pain, the need twisting his guts became unendurable. In one swift motion, he flung his good leg over Star's body, pinioning her to the bed. Still half asleep, she felt the rough hands on her gown, at her breast, jerking her to consciousness. "Charles," she moaned softly. Always in some dark corner of her mind, there dwelled the lurking fear that he would return, that she hadn't escaped him after all, that she would never escape him.

"Wrong husband, my love," Michael said mockingly. Her eyes flew open, startled. His face was so close to hers she could see the savage fury glittering behind the slitted eyes, the cruel twist to his smile. He murmured tauntingly, "Is that why you came looking for me at the hospital? With Alfredo dead, and your husband . . . Where is dear Charles, by the way? Is he dead, too? I don't imagine a woman with your... peculiar appetite is happy too long without a man."

He saw her flinch, knew he had hit a nerve, and pressed on relentlessly. "And to think I even felt sorry for you, caught in the less than tender clutches of a man like Bradford. I remember hearing rumors about him in St. Louis, how he had left one of the girls in Madame Decamier's brothel half dead from a beating he gave her." He smiled coldly down at Star. "But then I understand there are women who enjoy that sort of thing. You should have told me, *mi querida*. You must have found my bedding you very dull in comparison."

"Shut up!" she whispered, her eyes brilliant with anger. "How dare you—"

"You forget," he interrupted her curtly. "It cost me fifty thousand dollars to insure your safe return. That's a high price for even the most expensive *puta* in the most luxurious bordello in Mexico. Even for those who perform... *special* services for their customers." His glance raked her body, his voice coldly insulting. "I'm not sure you're worth it, *querida*."

Staring into those dark green eyes, flat and expressionless, Star was suddenly reminded of a carving she had seen at a museum Alfredo had taken her to on one of their afternoon promenades. The carving had been of an Aztec priest, its stone face holding no trace of compassion or mercy. Fear began to mingle with her anger, remembering the cruelty in that bloodless, stone face. It would not be the way it had been with Charles, she sensed, with Michael savoring the pleasure of inflicting pain. With Michael, it would be vengeance, a retaliation for wrongs suffered, a savage sort of justice. Hadn't Michael warned her what sort of man he was when he told her of his boyhood in the Comanche camp, how Comanches mutilated, even killed, unfaithful wives. Panicstricken, she suddenly began to fight against Michael with all her strength as his body, like an inexorable weight, lowered, crushing the breath from her. Even as she struggled against him, though, there flashed beneath her fear a swift, ironic concern: he would tear his wound open again.

Then there was only the fear left as her gown was shoved up over her hips and his hands moved bruisingly over her body, before he forced her legs apart. She was still fighting against him, clawing and scratching, when he took her, thrusting deep inside her. She cried out in pain, or pleasure, she wasn't sure which. For the sudden, shocking awareness of his hardness moving within her, the fierce writhing movements of her own body against his as she still tried to escape him, awoke entirely different sensations within her than fear.

It was as if all the long-denied passion and aching frustration that her body had endured for so many long, lonely nights demanded release and swept aside all other emotions in this greater, stronger compulsion. A quick fire ran through her blood as she arched her body and reached mindlessly for the next plateau of pleasure to lift her, sweep her away. She no longer cared if it were love or hate Michael and she were sharing. It was only the feeling, finally, that mattered, like coming alive after months of being dead inside.

Michael was aware at once of the change in the woman he had taken so brutally; that her response had become in its own way as violent as his own attack upon her body. Her teeth bit into his flesh, her nails clawed his back, and the soft moans coming from her slender throat were not from pain but ecstasy. The silver-gray eyes behind the thick black lashes were shimmering with passion, not fear, and her mouth moving, open and seeking, against his, was not pleading for him to stop but seemed to be urging him fiercely on.

Half appalled, half furious—this was not how he had planned to repay her for cuckolding him, making a fool of him— Michael would have stopped, but it was impossible. His body, unfeeling of the red-hot stabbing pain from the wound in his shoulder, had become as treacherous as Star's. It was as if he had lost that last semblance of iron control he had always held over himself, even in the midst of the most consuming love-making. Insatiably, greedily, he was as uncaring as Star was of how he bruised and assaulted the soft body that clung to him with arms and legs entwined tightly, pulling him ever closer, so that it was more like a silent, frenzied battle than making love. And when it ended with unbelievable swiftness in a violent burst of sensation that left them both drained and exhausted, they continued to cling to each other with no victor, no vanquished.

It was Star who finally pulled free. Her nightgown was damp

with perspiration, and she let it drop to the floor as she went to the nightstand and, gathering cool water into the palms of her hands, laved her face and body. She noticed there was a smear of blood on her one shoulder, and she slipped into a gold velvet robe and came quickly back to the bed.

"Your wound is bleeding," she said anxiously to Michael, who had been lying quietly watching her. He said nothing as she quickly changed the dressing on his shoulder.

As she leaned over him, tightening the bandage, her robe slipped open and he saw the blue-black mark his hands had made on one pale white breast. Gently he touched the bruise, his voice sickened. "I never meant to..." Then he fell silent because he knew it wouldn't be true and there was no longer any need for lies between them. He had meant to strike out, to hurt her, to repay the debt Comanche fashion. And not just for her betrayal of him, he realized suddenly. He wanted to strike back at all those like her, with the same white skin and high-and-mighty arrogance. The soldiers who had marched into his country, who regarded the Mexican people, his people, as somehow lower creatures, as beneath their Anglo-Saxon superiority, so that they had a God-given right to steal and plunder the Mexicans' land.

Feeling ill at ease beneath that bleak stare, Star pulled the robe shut and started to turn away. "It doesn't matter," she said.

Michael caught her hand so she was forced to turn around and face his probing glance. "I have to know," he asked quietly. "Why did you stay with Charles?"

She frowned, faintly, her voice uncertain. "I told myself it was because he was my husband. Even if you would take me back, even if I somehow got a divorce, we could never marry. Your ... *my* religion now, would never permit it. And there was Rosita. He threatened to kill her if I didn't write the ransom notes, make her believe I wanted to stay with him of my own free will." She shook her head, her face suddenly desolate as she remembered her wanton behavior in Michael's arms only a few moments before. "Perhaps those were only excuses I made to myself. I'm not sure anymore. Everyone I love seems to end up hurting me, hating me. My father, Charles, and now you."

Michael pulled her gently down on the bed beside him. "I don't hate you, *querida*," he said quietly, then shrugged ruefully. "Perhaps we both went a little *loco*." As crazy, he thought, as his blaming Star for what had happened to his country, forgetting there were many Americans who were outraged by their country's militaristic takeover of Mexico. The Mexican newspapers had even quoted a Congressman, Abraham Lincoln, who had stood up in Congress and declared that President Polk had begun the war "unnecessarily and unconstitutionally."

His arm encircled Star, pulling her closer, then he winced as his newly dressed wound protested, sending rivulets of pain down his arm.

Star was instantly alarmed. "You mustn't! I may not be able to stop the bleeding a second time."

"You worry too much, *querida*," Michael grinned, effectively stopping any further objections as his lips covered hers. He felt her mouth part, soft and warm, beneath his. He heard her sharp indrawn breath as his lips moved from her mouth slowly to the dark, soft hollow in her throat, to the deep valley between her breasts, wooing her all over again as he had that night in Chihuahua, stroking her body with long, gentle caresses as if he had all the time in the world, as if the pleasure could be prolonged indefinitely.

Only this time when he felt her velvet soft tongue caressing the spot where her teeth had bitten before, there was no driving need to hurt in the slowly rising passion that possessed the both of them, only a wild, delicious sweetness, a desire to give pleasure to the other. Until finally neither wanted to wait any longer. Michael moved to cover her body with his own, but Star would not let him. "Your wound," she murmured. "You mustn't."

Then, a faint pink of embarrassment for a moment coloring her face, she whispered, "Let me," and slid her own body over his. The moment she touched him, though, the embarrassment disappeared, and there was only the delirious joy and wonder spreading through her body in ever widening circles. All lingering feelings of guilt and fear were banished forever as she gave herself completely to Michael, her body moving at first hesitantly, then proudly, exultantly, in one long silken caress against his hard, muscular body, again and again, until a groan broke from his lips and she felt herself become a part of him as he became part of her.

Later, as she lay quietly encircled by his good arm, her head resting on his chest, listening to the sound of his steady breathing, she told herself that she mustn't expect it to last. She was still married to Charles. And no matter if she would happily become Michael's mistress, in time he would want more, deserve more than that. He would want a wife like Elena, children to carry on the Cordoba name, who would someday inherit the Cordoba estates now that Alfredo was dead.

But for the moment she snuggled closer to Michael, curving her body to fit against his as she drifted off to sleep. For the moment, this was enough.

Chapter Twenty-three

Star awoke early the next morning and slid carefully out of Michael's arms, dressing quietly so as not to awaken him. As she left the room, she heard a distant rumbling sound like thunder. She glanced quickly back at the bed to see if the noise had awakened Michael, but he was still sleeping heavily.

In the kitchen, she found Martita and Georges sitting at the table, talking softly. She could hear the booming sound, louder now, a storm to the southwest of the city, she decided. Only as she glanced out into the small, overgrown patio, she could see it was a bright, sunny morning.

"It is thunder, isn't it?" she asked Georges uneasily.

"Not thunder," he replied gravely, his black eyes unblinking in a wrinkled face. "It is the *Yanqui* guns, shelling Chapultapec."

So the peace negotiations had ended, Star thought unhappily. It would start all over again, the terrible battles, the final carnage as men died this time to take Mexico City itself.

Star remembered her visit to the walled and fortified castle perched high on the jagged rocks of Chapultapec. "They can't possibly take the castle, can they?" she asked. "The cliffs go straight up."

Georges shrugged. *"Quien sabe, señora?* From the north, no, but perhaps along the west slope through the cypress groves of Montezuma. If the *Yanqui* devils can get past General Bravo's guns pointing down their throats."

"Pobre ninos," Martita said sadly.

Star recalled the young cadets she had met at the military school. "Surely they won't be expected to fight?" she asked, heartsick at the thought. "They're not much more than children."

"They are *soldados*," Georges said, gazing impassively at Star.

Star shivered. And if Chapultapec fell, what next? She remembered the horror stories that had followed the fall of Monterrey, the killing and looting as General Taylor's soldiers had smashed their way through walls from one house to the next, more like a rampaging mob than disciplined troops, with the blood of soldiers and civilians alike being shed in the battle. But those had been volunteers fighting at Monterrey, she reminded herself quickly, and the men with General Scott were mostly regulars, while General Scott himself was a professional soldier.

At first the thudding noise of the shelling in the distance drowned out the knocking at the front gate of the *casa*. A look of surprise flitted across Martita's face. It was unusual for the Casa de Cordoba to have visitors, much less so early in the morning.

She hurried out of the room, with her husband moving more slowly behind her. When Martita returned ten minutes later, alone, her face held a look of awed excitement, her black eyes sparkling. "You must come at once, *señora*," she said. "Doña Isobel is waiting to speak with you in the *sala*."

"Doña Isobel?" Star asked, puzzled.

"Señora Isobel Diaz de Cordoba," Martita said, shocked at Star's ignorance. "Don Miguel's grandmother, the old one herself. It is a great honor that Her Grace should visit you. You must not keep her waiting."

Star dropped her shawl onto a chair and walked slowly back down the hall to the small room off the grand *sala* that Alfredo had used to entertain his closest friends. Martita had opened the shutters, she saw at once as she entered, and, unhappily, the fact that the room had not been recently cleaned was immediately apparent. A thin coating of dust covered the table and chairs. Her visitor was not seated, but standing in the middle of the room. She turned at once when Star entered. Doña Isobel was dressed completely in somber black, with an exquisitely embroidered mantilla covering hair that was still glossy black, without a touch of gray. The face turned to Star was unlined, but the skin had the pale yellow color of parchment, brittle and luminous. If one looked closely one could still glimpse the beauty that must have been the woman's in her youth. For all that Doña Isobel was not five feet tall, she seemed to dominate the room, and something about her face, the way the dark intense eyes narrowed as they studied Star, the black brows slanted over deep-set eyes, reminded Star at once of Michael.

Doña Isobel spoke at once with deliberate cutting arrogance. "You are Señora Bradford, my grandson's mistress?"

Star took a deep breath to still the anger that leaped inside of her. "I was, or thought I was, Don Miguel's wife," she said quietly.

The woman shrugged impatiently. "Alfredo told me of the . . . misalliance, that legally you have no hold on Don Miguel." And then abruptly, "How is my grandson?"

Star caught the catch of anxiety beneath the sharpness and said quickly, "His wound is healing. The shoulder was the worst." She realized how frantic with worry Doña Isobel must have been, wondering if her grandson had survived Churubusco, and apologized. "I didn't know where you were staying, or I would have sent word to you." It occurred to her to wonder how Doña Isobel had known that Michael was here with her and then thought, Martita, of course. Martita, who had worked on the Cordoba *rancho* as a girl, who must have learned where Doña Isobel was staying and, knowing how worried her former mistress would be about her grandson, had sent her word.

Those dark expressive eyes were still studying her face with that same pitiless, probing stare that she recognized from Michael. "Elena is right," the woman said, grudgingly. "You are very beautiful. It is no wonder Miguel has lost his wits over you." And then, with studied cruelty, "Still, my grandson always has had his way with women. You've perhaps already discovered that, *señora.*"

A pulse had begun to pound in Star's temple. Her voice rose coldly. "What is it you wanted, Doña Isobel?"

One black eyebrow arched, surprised. "To take my grandson home, of course, to his *rancho* and the tender loving care of his betrothed."

"Betrothed?" Star echoed, dumbstruck.

"His brother's widow, Doña Elena. They are to be married as soon as Michael has sufficiently recovered from his wounds. It was arranged between Michael and Elena before he left for the army."

"I . . . I didn't know," Star said faintly. Vaguely she was aware of the shelling in the distance, echoing the pounding of her own heart in her ears. Dust motes drifted lazily in a stream of sunlight and the floor seemed to dip beneath her feet, so that she sat down abruptly.

It was several seconds before she heard Doña Isobel's voice clearly again. "I'm sorry, señora. I have no wish to hurt or harm you. But with Esteban and Alfredo both dead, it is necessary that Michael marry and that his wife bear children to carry on the Cordoba name. That is how it must be, you understand." When Star said nothing, she continued ruthlessly. "I have been told you already have a husband, señora."

Star nodded and then cried, her voice miserable. "I can't. I won't give him up." It was one thing to accept Michael's leaving her on some distant day when she was lying sheltered in his arms, as she had been the evening before. It was another to face the reality in the cold, hard light of day.

Doña Isobel said softly, "I think you will, señora. I think you have no choice. What can Miguel offer you but to be his mistress and bear his illegitimate children?" She must have seen the young woman flinch, but she could not have known the pain that twisted through Star then. I can't even do that, Star thought, give Michael a child. Doña Isobel's shrewd black eyes rested on Star's stricken face. "I do not believe you are a woman who would settle for such a life, no matter how deep your feelings run for Miguel."

Star grasped her hands together in her lap to still their trembling. She spoke with difficulty. "What makes you think Michael will leave me, that he'll let me go?"

"He won't," his grandmother said flatly. "You must leave him. There is no other way. I know my grandson. He is stubborn, like his grandfather. You must go today, at once, without seeing him again. I will tell Miguel that you have gone to stay with friends and to wait for the return of your husband. He will be angry, but there is nothing he can do. He is not well enough to search for you, and in time, he will see the wisdom of your decision."

Star shook her head, wearily. "I have no friends in Mexico City."

Doña Isobel frowned, as if this were a difficulty she hadn't envisioned. She glanced around the room, eyeing the dust with distaste. "You could stay here, I suppose. It is the last place Miguel would think to look for you, although it would be better if you left the city." She cocked her small head toward the sound of the guns. "If Chapultepec is crushed, it will not be safe for you to remain." Then she broke off, her voice bitter, "I forget, *señora*. The barbarians at our gates are your people. You should be safe with them." She reached into a beaded bag she wore at her waist. "You will be paid, of course, for your inconvenience. I'm sure Miguel would insist."

"No!" Star jerked to her feet, her face flushed, anger making her forget the anguish licking at her nerves. "I don't want your money." After the Legation *baile*, Alfredo had pressed upon her a simple diamond necklace, insisting, over her objections, that she keep it as a memento. The sale of the necklace should tide her over until she could make some sort of permanent plans. And Doña Isobel was right, she thought. She would have to leave at once, without seeing Michael again, or she would never find the courage to leave at all. She could ride around in the carriage for a few hours until she was sure that Michael had left the house with his grandmother. And then return. She did not think any further than that. It was difficult enough looking ahead a few minutes, much less an hour, as if staring into a dark abyss.

Martita appeared in the doorway with a rebozo, which Star adjusted over her head with fingers that felt oddly numb. Just as suddenly, the carriage was at the front gate, Georges waiting to assist her inside before climbing on the coachbox. Star couldn't help thinking wryly how sure Doña Isobel had been that she would win. She must have arranged for Star's leavetaking even before Star had agreed to the terms the woman had laid down.

At the last moment the older woman reached out a hand and touched Star's face lightly. She was moved in spite of herself by the frozen misery she saw in the young woman's face, the enormous gray eyes bleak as a gray winter's sky. "I am sorry we met this way, *señora*." Her voice dropped softly, reminiscently. "When I married my husband, there was another young *caballero* I loved desperately, but it was not permitted that we marry. I was very young and foolish. I thought I would die with the pain. Of course I didn't. Instead, I learned in time to love my husband. I will pray for the same good fortune for you, *señora . . .*"

The blessedly numb feeling spread through Star's body, staying with her as the carriage drove slowly by the lushly green Alameda, then down into the Grand Plaza. Star was dimly aware of shopkeepers boarding up their windows, of carriages drawn by mules, packed with family possessions hurrying toward the Guadalupe gate, leading out of the city to the safety of the countryside. The poor hurried by on foot, carrying mattresses, children, baskets of food, birds in cages, or pulling carts loaded with chairs and tables. Military couriers on horseback dashed through the streets, scattering groups of *leperos* in their dirty rags. Once the carriage had to pull to one side as a troop of soldiers marched by, reinforcements sent by Santa Anna that were never to reach Chapultepec. In between bouts of mortar fire and answering cannon fire, a quiet hung over the city, like the ominous calm before a storm.

At a small church off the *paseo*, Star had the carriage stop. Pulling the rebozo low over her head, she went into the church and knelt in the rear, not to pray but to weep. The tears she had been too proud to shed before Doña Isobel welled up inside of her now. Her kneeling body was racked with sobs. She buried her face in her rebozo and wept for the lonely years ahead, for the love she and Michael could have shared that was lost forever, for the child she had lost in Santa Fe, and the children of Michael's that she would never carry.

No one noticed her tears. Other women in the crowded church, some dressed in satins and richly embroidered silks, others in simple *camisas* and skirts, were weeping, too. They knelt and listened to the priest exhort them to "pray for deliverance from the heretics threatening to invade our city and despoil our homes and churches, to deliver Mexico from the hands of her enemy."

Finally there were no more tears left to be shed, only a vast emptiness inside of her. She rose stiffly to her feet, and walked out of the church to where Georges was waiting for her nervously. "We should return to the *casa, señora,*" he muttered. "There is much hatred for the *gringos,* you understand, and if you are seen..."

They drove back to the *casa.* The moment Star stepped into the house, she knew that Michael was gone. If the house had seemed cold and unfriendly before, now it was like a great empty shell. Martita met her at the door, urged her to drink the hot chocolate and eat the sweetmeats and honey cakes she had prepared, but Star had no appetite.

Instead she went into the library and found a pair of field glasses she remembered seeing there earlier, and climbed the narrow stairs to the *azotea.* On the rooftop, she seated herself on the parapet, behind the oleanders and orange trees in tubs, and trained her glasses on Chapultapec. With the glasses she was able to see shells screaming over the cypress groves bursting against the gray stone castle walls and roofs, and the batteries of Mexican artillery returning the salvos. The blue-gray smoke from the explosions drifted upward toward the Mexican colors waving high above the observatory of the castle. The duel continued until nightfall, when the guns fell silent. Despite the terrible damage the men and walls of the fortress must have endured, the Mexican flag still flew.

It was a warm night, and rather than return to her bedchamber and the empty bed that could only remind her much too painfully of Michael, Star wrapped herself in a blanket and slept in a chair on the *azotea.* It was a brilliant clear night. Bright gold stars were caught in a milky dark blue sky, blue even in the moonlight. From the walled gardens below Star caught the scent of night-blooming jasmine, the only sounds the splashing of a fountain, the clatter of a horse's hooves on the street. The hushed beauty of the night was like a soothing balm on Star's nerves, rubbed raw by the events of the day.

At six o'clock in the morning, when the velvet darkness of the night was scarcely tinged with the gray of dawn, the frightful cannonade began again. One gun roared, then another, bright flashes in the early morning grayness. Star got to her feet and tried not to think about General Bravo, his men, and the young cadets still trapped in the fortress. How could they

possibly hold out against such a murderous bombardment? she
wondered. How many young men were already dead or dying,
blasted to pieces by the shells that crashed through the walls
and roof of the school.

Martita and her husband joined Star on the rooftop. She saw
that on all the rooftops of Mexico City, in the church towers,
wherever she looked, people had quietly gathered to watch the
battle of Chapultapec. At eight o'clock the guns fell silent, the
signal for the assaulting troops to make their charge against
the castle. Star could only guess at the action now, the battle
raging on the western slope as men fired from behind the huge
cypress trees, then sprinted forward to the protection of the
next huge trunks. With her glasses she could glimpse the scaling
ladders flung up along the wall of the castle, then hurled back
by the defenders, with their load of climbing men still clinging
helplessly to the ladders. More ladders were dragged forward;
more men climbed upward along the wall, to fall like rag dolls
to the rocks below. Gradually, though, a few, and then a few
more, reached firm footing on the fortress parapet, tiny figures
attacking with bayonets and swords, rifles used as clubs, against
the surviving defenders of Chapultapec.

By nine thirty it was over, the Mexican red, white, and
green tricolor lowered, the Stars and Stripes flying in its place.
Long before then Star had stopped watching the battle and
retreated to the comparative calm of the library. By late afternoon, though, as the American troops fought their way down
the causeways, running a gauntlet of lead and iron from enemy
fire, the noise of the artillery and mortar fire began to penetrate
even the thick walls of the library.

An explosion rocked the room, and the book fell from Star's
suddenly nerveless hands. A fine lime dust drifted down from
the ceiling. She sprang to her feet as a picture fell from the
wall behind her and crashed to the floor. The sound of her own
heart thudding loudly in her chest could not be heard over the
deafening booming cannonade from the Citadel. Star flung her
hands to her ears as the world seemed to explode to pieces
around her.

Glass shattered in the windows and the crystal chandelier
overhead jangled and swung crazily as the house shuddered
under the concussion. A shell, missing its target, landed several

houses away, making the walls of the house tremble around Star. She was too paralyzed with fear to move. She could not believe this was happening.

It was Martita who found her and dragged her into the hall. "The wine cellars, *señora*. We'll be safe there. Come with me."

Then she was stumbling down a dark stone staircase behind Martita and Georges into a series of dank-smelling tunnels. Martita had brought along candles and blankets, but the dampness of the earth worked its way upward through the pallets Martita arranged on the floor, making Star shiver from both the cold and her reaction to the terror of the bombardment.

Martita passed Star a bottle of *mesquel* and Star drank from it quickly. The liquor scalded her throat like fire, making her cough. The second swallow, though, was easier, sending a cozy warmth through her body. If she didn't sleep, at least she managed to doze off.

Georges was gone when she awoke, and Star and Martita returned to the first floor of the house to survey the damage done by the shelling. Aside from the litter of shattered glass, fallen plaster, pictures and clocks tumbled to the floor, Star was relieved to see that the house had not suffered any direct hits.

"It is over," Georges said sadly, returning an hour later. The Mexican army had marched out of the city shortly after midnight. What was left of the Mexican government—Santa Anna had disappeared with the troops—had surrendered Mexico City to the American army a few hours later.

Star climbed up to the *azotea* and, for the last time, watched a victorious American army march into a Mexican city. As in Chihuahua, the conquering soldiers were a sorry, bedraggled lot. But following them came the music and roll of kettle drums, and a mounted band of nattily dressed dragoons, riding with drawn swords. The tall, magnificent figure of General Winfield Scott in full dress uniform, white-plumed chapeau and gold epaulettes, riding a bay charger, led the victory march down the Street of the Silversmiths and into the Grand Plaza.

Star saw the faces of the people watching from the rooftops, like herself, or at the windows of *casas* and churches. Others stood along the streets, some sullen-faced, some shocked and quietly weeping, a few waving happily at the passing soldiers.

She felt no elation as the victorious dragoons rode by, the sunlight flashing on their drawn swords but casting a long, dark shadow like a stain on the rose-gray walls. The American army had not really conquered Mexico, Star thought. Oh, they had seized Mexican territory and planted the American flag over Mexico's capital, but the country itself, the ancient, cruelly beautiful land, the proudly passionate Mexican people, would forever mystify and elude the victors.

Unhappily, she turned her gaze away from the swaggering, triumphant army. At least the war, just or unjust, was finally over, and Michael would be safe. Michael. In the excitement of the last twenty-four hours she had managed to barricade her mind against memories of him but now, in an inexorable tide, the memories rushed back. She saw Martita watching her curiously, as if the pain she felt showed in her face, and she retreated hastily to the privacy of her bedroom. She walked back and forth between the window and the bed until the pain mercifully passed, leaving again the blessed numbness as she once more carefully, painstakingly restored the barricade in her mind.

At last she stopped the frantic pacing and dropped wearily into a chair. She must make plans, she thought. She couldn't stay here at the *casa* indefinitely. Even if Michael didn't, in time, find her, there was always the alarming possibility of Charles returning.

She found the diamond necklace Alfredo had given her. There were *tiendas* along the arcade in the Plaza, she remembered, where jewelry was bought and sold. The necklace should bring her enough for passage to Acapulco, and the boat trip to Mazatlán. She didn't think beyond that point. She remembered that she had felt almost happy in that sleepy, sunny port city. Perhaps there was a wealthy Mexican family who would need an English-speaking governess, or, thanks to the nuns at the convent school, she could sew a fine seam.

She wanted to take the carriage immediately to the *tiendas*, but Martita and Georges, shocked, would not hear of her leaving the casa. "It isn't safe on the streets, *señora*," Georges protested. "There are mobs of *leperos*, released convicts, and disbanded Mexican soldiers roaming the city, fighting the occupying American troops from rooftops and street corners. Haven't you heard the musket fire?"

The last-ditch battle in the streets of Mexico City continued all day and into the night, as Star tried in vain to sleep. Finally, deciding a cup of warm milk might help, she pulled a robe over her nightgown and started down the hall, candle in hand, toward the kitchen. She had reached the side hall when she felt a draft of cool air around her ankles. The candle flame flickered and went out. The hall plunged into darkness around her at the same moment she felt a hard arm circle her waist, a hand fasten tightly over her mouth.

"Don't scream, *querida,*" a familiar voice whispered in her ear.

"Michael!" She turned happily in his arms, burrowing herself against him. "How did you—" His hand once more covered her mouth.

"Keep your voice down," he warned quietly. "It seems I'm not the only one to break into the *casa* tonight."

She saw then what she hadn't noticed before, a pale light slanting from beneath the door to Alfredo's bedroom.

"Looters," Michael said grimly. "They're all over the city, like vermin. They've already ransacked the National Palace and the shops along the plaza. They probably thought this *casa* was deserted." He gave her a gentle shove. "If there are any servants left, fetch them. I'll see if I can't surprise our visitors."

She saw him take a pistol from his belt as she fled silently into the kitchen. Martita and Georges had a room above the stables, and she was halfway across the courtyard when she heard the shot. Without thinking, her heart pounding in her throat with fear for Michael's safety, she turned and ran back into the *casa*.

The door to Alfredo's bedroom was flung open. Standing, poised and wary in the lamplight, facing each other like figures in a tableux, were Michael and Charles. An acrid smell of powder still hung in the air between the two men. A pistol was in Michael's hand, another pistol lay on the table before Charles, along with a pile of diamond jewelry. Drops of blood fell from Charles's hand to lie like rubies among the dazzling diamonds.

"Charles, what are you—" Star fell silent because it was obvious what Charles was doing as she glanced from the cleverly hidden opening behind a wall panel to the Cordoba jewels before Charles. "Isn't it enough that Alfredo is dead?" she asked, outraged. "Do you have to steal from him, too?"

"Let's call it dissolving a partnership, my sweet," Charles said nonchalantly. "Alfredo has no more use for the diamonds. I do. They'll bring me a fortune in New York." He smiled thinly. "I find I've grown weary of Mexico."

"How did you know where they were hidden?" Michael asked. Star saw that the muscles around his mouth were pulled taut and wondered, worried, if his shoulder wound was bothering him, although his hand held the gun steadily pointed at Charles.

A sneer twisted Charles's mouth. "Your cousin got drunk one night. He brought me here to his bedroom. Before I managed to convince him I wasn't interested in his manly charms, he had shown me how to open the panel in the wall." His glance flicked from Michael to Star as he murmured, "I've often wondered if Alfredo's fondness for young men was a family trait."

Then the malice in his face faded and became for a moment contorted with fear as he gazed into the barrel of the gun, as black and murderous-looking as Michael's narrowed eyes.

In the sudden stillness, Star could hear her heart thudding. She flung out a hand to Michael. "Michael, please," she whispered.

"You have two choices, Bradford," Michael said coldly. "I can shoot you here as a looter, or I can turn you over to the American authorities who will, no doubt, be happy to get their hands on El Güero, and you'll be promptly hung."

Charles glanced at Star. "How embarrassing that would be for you, my sweet, to have a husband proven a traitor twice." Then, his voice hardening, "Fortunately, I have no intention of dying at all."

Star saw the triumphant gleam in Charles's amber eyes, and a warning sensation made her cry out, "Michael, look out!"

It wasn't Michael who was in danger, though. It was herself. She sensed rather than heard the stealthy movement behind her, felt something cold and hard pressed against the back of her head. A hand grasped her right arm and, twisting it viciously behind her, thrust Star forward into the room.

Michael half turned, but it was too late and he knew it, even before Charles said, "I wouldn't try it if I were you, Kelly. Theresa would take great pleasure in blowing off the back of my wife's head. She's a bloodthirsty little creature. Now if you'll just hand me your gun, slowly."

Michael hesitated. "Michael, don't!" Star cried desperately. "They'll only kill you, too."

The hand on her wrist tightened, twisted harder, and a gasp of pain broke from Star's lips.

Michael stepped forward and without a word placed his gun on the table. Charles smiled smugly. "You should have known as a military man, Kelly, that I'd keep my flank covered." Then, as he saw Star's body growing limp, as if she were about to pass out from the pain, he said sharply, "That's enough, Theresa. She's no good to me unconscious."

Star felt the crushing grip on her wrist fall away, but she could feel the gun still at the back of her head.

Michael leaned against the wall, his glance meeting Star's for one swift moment before he turned to Charles, his voice as impassive as his face. "I don't suppose it would do any good to ask you to take me and let Star go. What harm can she do you?"

"A good deal, I'm afraid," Charles answered. "I plan to start a new life in New York with a new, respectable name. A wife, particularly one who knows my shortcomings so well, would be a stupid, if not fatal mistake. No, I'm afraid my solution is more practical. No one will be too surprised to find you both dead, shot by looters who have ransacked the house. Especially when the servants are found, too."

"Martita and Georges," Star whispered, horrified. "You've killed them!"

Charles frowned. "Of course not, but they're both bound securely in their room. If they were dead, they wouldn't be able to swear to the fact of looters breaking into the house, now could they?"

"Someone will recognize you," Star said, suddenly too angry to be afraid. "Even in New York, you'll be found out."

"I doubt it," Charles said. "People have a way of not questioning too closely the reputation of a man with a great deal of money." He ran his hand lovingly through the diamond jewelry, then picked out a diamond pendant hanging on a chain of tiny, gold-circled diamonds.

He walked over to Star, and she forced herself not to flinch away from him as he fastened the pendant around her neck. Then he stepped back, studying her through half-closed eyes. Her struggle with Theresa had torn open her robe, and she could feel the diamond pendant, icy cold and heavy, hanging between the deep valley of her breasts.

Charles ran his tongue over suddenly dry lips. Star saw the gleam in the golden amber eyes, and remembered that predatory look from the past, the familiar flush rising in Charles's face, she could feel the fear building up inside her even as she held herself perfectly still.

"What a shame you can't accompany me to New York, my pet," Charles said, his voice thickening as he reached out and cupped a silken breast in his hand. "I keep forgetting how incredibly lovely you are. You put even that diamond necklace to shame."

Pleased, he watched the fear leap into her eyes, felt the trembling of her flesh at his touch, and an answering urgent need in himself, long frustrated these past weeks. He had been too busy fighting and running. The Americans had brought the Texas Rangers down to Vera Cruz to rid the road between the port and Mexico City of the guerrillas who terrorized travelers, and El Güero had barely escaped their vengeance. There was Theresa, of course, but he had long since tired of her body, too eager to please him, and the smell of her skin, rancid, roughened by the outdoor life they had led. Star's skin, he remembered, had the texture of fine silk, sweetly scented. And the fact that he knew she despised him only added to the sense of anticipation he could feel growing inside of him.

"It occurs to me there's no need for you to die, my sweet, not immediately," he said, smiling. It was a parody of the boyishly charming smile that he had always used as a weapon against women, but it was now grotesque on a face whose jowls had grown heavy, deep lines cutting from his nose to his mouth. "Perhaps if you're very . . . accommodating, I might even change my mind and let you live."

He heard a movement to the side of him and, turning, saw that Michael's face had gone completely blank, only his green-black Indian's eyes were deadly, his body tensed.

"Don't try it, Kelly," Charles said, laughing softly. "Theresa can pull that trigger faster than you could reach me." He smirked at Michael, the transparent brightness of the amber eyes like windowpanes behind which nothing human lived. "It might be amusing, having you watch. Her screams will be the last thing you'll hear before Theresa puts a bullet into you."

His arm slipped around Star's waist, yanked her toward him, toward the bed.

"No!"

Charles stopped, staring baffled at Theresa, who said again, "No." Her face was venomous as she kept the gun pointed at Star. "There isn't time."

Charles scowled. "There's time if I say so."

Jealousy struggled with loyalty in Theresa's flat black eyes, her throat working convulsively. "Why do you need her? You said you were going to kill them both."

Star pulled herself free of Charles's grasp, and turned to face Theresa. A faint hope burned fitfully as a candle's flame inside of her. "You always did forget your place, Theresa," she said, her voice patronizing. "*I'm* Charles's wife, not you."

"You're not his wife," Theresa spat angrily. "He told me one night how he paid that man in Independence to pose as a preacher and marry you."

Charles's face hardened as he eyed the Indian woman, then, recovering his composure, he shrugged, smiling at Star. "Well, I suppose our lack of marriage lines can hardly make any difference now."

"All along, your acting so uppity," Theresa snarled. "And you had no more right to wear that wedding ring than I did. He belongs to me. He has from the first moment I saw him. He never belonged to you, never!"

Star heard the raging jealousy in the woman's voice, the pain behind that jealousy, and wondered, did Theresa already suspect that she no longer mattered to Charles, that no woman ever would matter?

She made her voice deliberately taunting. "And you, Theresa? What do you think will happen to you when Charles leaves Mexico? You don't suppose he'll take you with him to New York, an illiterate, dirty, half-caste whore. They'd laugh him out of society. Oh, no, if I want him, he's mine. And there's nothing you can do about it."

Behind her, Charles scowled, sensing that matters were getting out of hand. He knew Theresa's hair-trigger temper. "Shut up, Star," he ordered.

But the two women, caught up in their own private deadly vendetta, did not hear him. Star smiled mockingly as she watched the uncontrollable fury flame in Theresa's eyes. She ran her hands lightly, caressingly over her young, proud taut breasts, flaunting their gleaming whiteness, her voice cruelly goading. "I'm the one he desires, Theresa, not you. It's my body he wants, not some black, ugly half breed. Don't you know that by now?"

Then was appalled herself at the twisting anguish that ravaged Theresa's face, and felt her own body grow leaden. She could not go through with it, she thought helplessly. She couldn't exact such a terrible price from another woman, not even Theresa.

As if from a great distance, she heard Michael's cry, "Get down, Star!" At the same time, everything seemed to happen at once. Her body was knocked to the floor, an explosion shook the room, and a long, drawn-out horrible scream that seemed to go on and on. Charles's voice, Charles screaming.

She scrambled to her knees, gasping, trying to suck breath into lungs that had all the air knocked out of them. She watched as Charles slowly doubled over, his hands clawing at his white shirtfront, slowly growing red where Theresa's pistol shot had caught him full force in the chest. She saw the blood run between his fingers. He was still screaming as he slid to the floor, the high-pitched, furious scream of a wild animal caught in a death trap.

Theresa flung herself down beside him, cradling his head on her lap, moaning frantically, "No. Not you, her. It was meant for her."

The terrible ululating screams stopped. Charles's sensuous mouth grew lax, the amber eyes slowly lost their sheen, and the once handsome boyish features seemed to blur, then became smoothly blank.

Theresa rocked the dead man in her arms, keening, an Indian squaw's ritualistic wail. Then in one swift movement she turned upon Star, her voice wild. "It was you. You killed him, *gringa* devil!" She clutched the revolver, lifted it, and pointed it at Star's face.

But Michael had reached the table and picked up his gun. The second explosion sent Theresa's revolver spinning from her hand out of her reach. She turned to stare at Michael. Not a muscle in her face moved as she waited, uncringing, for the next bullet to find its target in her body.

"It's finished," Michael said, his voice flat. He gestured toward the door. "*Vaya!* If I ever see you again, you won't be so lucky."

For a moment the woman hesitated, then, like a shadow, one minute she was there, the next she was gone.

Star was still crouched on the floor, and he gripped her shoulders, pulling her to her feet. "Damn it, what do you think you were doing?" he demanded furiously. "You could have been killed."

Then he saw that the wide gray eyes were uncomprehending, dazed with horror. Her slender body shook helplessly as her hands tried to unclasp the diamond necklace. With a low curse, he tore the necklace from her and flung it to the floor. He could still feel the convulsive trembling through her body as he carried her to the bedroom.

He sat on the bed, cradling her in his arms, stroking the tangled auburn hair and murmuring over and over again, "It's over, *querida mia*. It's ended," until at last the gray eyes were once more clear, unclouded with horror, and her breathing grew quiet. He settled her on the bed and pulled the coverlet over her. But when he tried to leave, she gripped his hand.

"I'll be back," he said. "I have to see to the servants."

When he returned, he brought with him a glass of brandy and insisted that she swallow the contents. Her face was streaked with tears. "Martita, Georges: are they all right?"

"Georges has a bump on his head, otherwise they're fine," he assured her.

"The authorities will have to be notified, won't they, about Charles and Theresa," she said.

"With the chaos in the city, one or two dead looters could easily disappear without a trace," Michael said grimly. "Only I want to make sure that this time Charles Bradford stays dead.

Georges is taking the body to the American military authorities at the Palace."

"They'll question me then, won't they?" Star asked, trying to keep the dismay from her voice at the thought of answering a stranger's questions, reliving those moments of horror in Alfredo's bedroom. "They'll find out Charles was my husband."

"According to Theresa, he wasn't your husband," Michael reminded her. "And I see no need for you to be questioned. The Americans put a price on El Güero's head some time ago. It won't be difficult to prove that Bradford and the outlaw are the same man. As for how he died . . ." He shrugged. "Georges will only be too happy to swear that he shot El Güero when he caught him robbing the safe in the *casa*. Georges can use the reward money."

Star lifted her tear stained face to Michael. "But I did kill Charles," she said softly. "I goaded Theresa into firing at me, hoping that I could drop to the floor and the bullet would hit Charles instead. But at the last moment, I couldn't . . . I couldn't go through with it."

"I know," Michael said quietly. "I saw it in your face." He could still feel the wrench of terror that had gripped him then. If either Charles or Theresa had noticed how he had been edging closer while Star had been taunting Theresa, if he'd been a second later in flinging his body against Star's, it would be Star lying sprawled dead, now, on the floor of Alfredo's bedroom.

He walked away from the bed, then turned to face Star, baffled. "Why? Why did you change your mind?"

"It was Theresa. She loved Charles. He was all she had. Suddenly I . . . I just couldn't trick her into killing him." She shook her head and laid back against the pillows, her voice weary. "Oh, I'm not sure now what I thought, how I felt. I just . . . froze. What does it matter anyway? As you said, it's over now."

Michael all at once understood. "I suppose my grandmother told you about Elena."

Star nodded. "The morning she came to see me. Doña Isobel said the marriage was all arranged."

"Arranged by my grandmother," Michael said, smiling thinly. "Not by me, and not by Elena. How do you think I knew you were still here at the *casa?* Elena told me. Not right away. It took me a day to get the truth out of her, but this evening she broke down and told me that you had never left the *casa.*"

"Why should she help you find me?"

"After Esteban's death at Monterrey, my sister-in-law planned to enter the Convent of the Encarnación," Michael said. "It was what she wanted, but my grandmother insisted that it was Elena's duty to marry me. And Elena didn't have the nerve to stand up against Doña Isobel." Michael grinned ruefully. "I don't blame Elena. There aren't many that have the courage to go against my grandmother's wishes. She has a habit of riding roughshod over anyone who stands in her way."

He stalked back to the bed and glared at Star. "What I don't understand," he said coldly, "is how you could think so little of me that you'd believe my grandmother's outrageous lies." His eyes darkened angrily. "I warned you, *querida*, that night in Chihuahua, that I'd never let you go. You could never have run far enough. I would have torn Mexico apart looking for you, and killed any man I found you with," he added, almost indifferently.

It was, Star knew, his grandmother's inheritance in Michael speaking, the passionate Spanish side of his nature. How very much like his grandmother he was, she thought suddenly, hiding a smile and knowing he would deny it vehemently. She suspected, that like his grandmother, he would be at times overly possessive, arrogant, even overbearing, but she remembered, too, how gentle, how patient he could be. He would be a devoted father.

She caught her breath sharply. That was part of Michael's inheritance, too, she remembered, the *machismo* of fathering sons.

She got out of bed and, reaching for her robe, pulled it around her as she moved across the room, away from Michael. "There is something I should have told you before," she said, speaking slowly, painfully. "After what happened in Santa Fe, the army doctor said . . . he told me there's a possibility I'll never be able to bear children."

For a moment the silence in the room was so deep she could hear the ticking of the clock on her dressing table, the distant sounds of the street vendors calling their wares as the sun rose over a Mexico City that was once more stirring to life after its night of warfare.

She felt Michael's arms around her, turning her so that she had to look at him, at the dark eyes that were filled with love and pain.

"Did you think it would matter, *amor mia?*" he asked softly. "*Querida . . . mi alma . . .*" He gathered her tightly in his arms as if he were trying to take her hurt into his own body. His voice was fierce. "And whether or not we are blessed with children is *en la mano de Dios,* not some army doctor."

Then his mouth found hers hungrily until, breathless, she drew away, her lips still parted. He could see a rosy flush running down between her breasts.

Laughing, he traced the path of that blush with his fingers, murmuring, "Maidenly blushes, still? After all, we are married." Then cocked a thoughtful eyebrow. "At least I think we are. Just to make sure, we'll be married again here in Mexico City before we leave for the ranch."

"We'll be living at the ranch?" Star asked, hesitantly.

"Where else?" Michael demanded.

"Your grandmother . . . she'll be furious."

"No doubt," Michael said. Then, glancing at Star's uncertain frown, he added firmly, "The ranch is Doña Isobel's home. I can't ask her to leave, nor would I want to, not even for you, *querida.*" He grinned teasingly, "Don't tell me that you're afraid to share the *rancho* with my grandmother, Star?"

No, Star thought, looking into her beloved's face. She would never be afraid of anything, not with Michael beside her. In any case, she wasn't Elena. Her chin lifted haughtily, but her voice was demure enough as she murmured, "I'm sure your grandmother and I will get along very well."

Michael recognized that arrogant tilt to Star's chin and the stubborn glint in those wide gray eyes. He had seen that look on her face often enough before, at Bent's Fort, on the trail to Santa Fe, crossing the terrible *jornadas* to Chihuahua.

And as he once more gathered Star into his arms, disposing

of the torn gown in one swift motion as he carried her back to the bed, he decided, with a wry amusement, that this time in one slim, red-headed girl with a will of iron beneath a velvet soft body, Doña Isobel had finally met her match.